He knew perfection when

Moving toward Angela, tilt her face up. She didn't flinch or turn away, even though he knew she'd been trying hard to keep her distance. But beneath her cool exterior, he sensed the physical attraction he felt for her was mutual. "I see who you are, Angel, even if you don't."

She blinked up at him, swallowed, and then slowly licked her lips. The unconscious act was so sensual his body instantly reacted. "Who do you see when you look at the sculpture?" she asked as if his answer was the most important thing in the world to her.

He looked deep into her eyes, stroking his thumbs across her cheeks just as he had earlier with the sculpture, only this time reveling in the feel of very warm skin. What he saw in her that moment was the same thing he'd seen in her likeness as he'd worked the figure—the same qualities he'd experienced in his dream. He saw a woman of inner-strength unlike anyone he'd ever met before. He saw innocence coupled with a natural and innate sensuality. He saw keen intelligence, which somehow managed to co-exist with a trusting heart. But he also sensed pain, making him wonder what in her life could have possibly hurt so much it had left emotional scars. Using more willpower than he thought himself capable of, he gently lowered his lips to hers for the merest whisper of a kiss.

But the moment he felt her soft lips beneath his, felt the same heated response from her he remembered from his dream, his good intentions flew out the window. He took her in his arms, pressing her slim, curvaceous body to his, igniting passion.

This book is dedicated to the memory
of baby Wyatt, whose gentle spirit and
ready giggles enriched so many lives.

Other Books by Rebecca Anderson

Glass-Slipper-dot.com

Acknowledgements

I want to thank my wonderful editor, Linda Kichline, who believed in me once again, and who has let me tell my stories my way. Thank you Pam Scheibe for your friendship as well as your expertise and insight into the world of Astrology. Thanks also to my wonderful Orange County and Inland Valley Chapters of Romance Writers for their support, knowledge, and laughter. Thanks goes to Patricia Wright, Linda McLaughlin, Helen Haddad, Linda Prine, Jackie Radoumis, Barbara Clark, Janet Cornelow and Ann Farrell of my Plot Group for having unbelievably creative minds and giving natures. Thank you Tamara Thorne for your friendship and for showing me that the horror and romance genres aren't all that far apart. And thank you, my book group sisterhood: Vicky Martin, Wilma Young, Linda Wray, Linda Carroll-Bradd, and Patt Sweet, for the great dinners, hours of laughter, and lively discussions of family, friends … and, of course, books. As always, thanks to my children for being the magic in my life, my grandchildren for helping me see the world through their eyes, and for my Prince Charming of thirty years, Fred, for his emotional, financial and spiritual support of my writing.

Wizard's Moon

***

Rebecca Anderson

ImaJinn Books

WIZARD'S MOON
Published by ImaJinn Books, a division of ImaJinn

Copyright ©2002 by Rebecca Anderson

ISBN: 1-893896-62-5

10 9 8 7 6 5 4 3 2 1

PUBLISHER'S NOTE:
This book is a work of fiction. Names, characters, places and incidents are products of the author's imagination or are used fictitiously. Any resemblance to actual events or locales or persons, living or dead, is entirely coincidental.

Books are available at quantity discounts when used to promote products or services. For information please write to: Marketing Division, ImaJinn Books, P.O. Box 162, Hickory Corners, MI 49060-0162, or call toll free 1-877-625-3592.

Cover design by Rickey Mallory

ImaJinn Books, a division of ImaJinn
P.O. Box 162, Hickory Corners, MI 49060-0162
Toll Free: 1-877-625-3592
http://www.imajinnbooks.com

ONE

JACHIN: (jA´-ken): One of the pillars of Solomon's temple. In Tarot: Stability and mercy.

Mercury: One who can communicate with the universe. A channel for the gods.

With a violent start, Jachin Morgan awoke from a vivid dream. His heart raced at the feeling of imminent danger, and the air crackled with electric energy as his repressed dark powers hummed to life. From deep within came an instinctive force so great that his every muscle went rigid — ready to do battle. Ready to protect. Ready to kill.

He threw back the sheet and bolted out of bed into an attack stance, his eyes searching the room for his enemy. But the only movement came from the peacefully billowing drapes flanking the French doors. While consciously calming his breathing, he willed his heart rate to slow. The danger had been in the dream, not here. After a few seconds, the unwelcome dark force emerging from within himself began to retreat, leaving him wondering just who the hell the woman was he had been ready to protect. And who—or what—had he been ready to call on the darkness to kill? He'd never killed anyone. So why had the urge felt so natural? And why, as he emerged from the dream, had the urge to kill come upon him as easily as breathing?

Blinking and looking around the bedroom, he realized everything appeared muted and dull in comparison to his dream world. For a moment he wondered if *this* might be the dream world.

Was his true existence in the mystical world of ancient forests and lurking shadows he'd only moments ago left behind? Or was his reality to be found in this modern room with the ocean breeze from Laguna Beach blowing in with the dawn?

He strode to the open doors, a lingering uncertainty following him. Stepping onto the deck to take deep, salty breaths, he ran his fingers through his hair. Its shoulder-length thickness and coarse texture gave him a sense of tactile reality. The scrape of rough stubble on his face felt real, too.

But the dream had seemed even more vivid. He knew that it was nothing more than a trick of the mind—an illusion born of suppressed longings and unmet needs.

Over the past two weeks, he'd had the same dream, and that in itself was strange since he had never before dreamed, not even as a child.

But this morning's dream had been different from the others. This time, aside from the feeling of danger, the dream had been so raw in every detail that he'd come away with a tactile knowledge of the place in his vision.

As always, the dream had begun with him moving through lush forests inhabited by gentle people who harmoniously coexisted with all manner of mythical beasts.

But in this morning's dream he had been in pursuit of an evil entity, an obscure being who managed to roam just out of sight and beyond his reach. He'd been able to sense the nearness of the threatening *thing* and had been acutely aware of the predatory darkness of its soul.

Jachin stared into the morning fog, remembering. In the dream his perception had operated at such a heightened state that even the forest surrounding him had pulsed with life, seeming to regard him on his quest. It had seemed so real.

And another thing had felt real. The memory of whom he'd been protecting came back in a rush. He'd been protecting a woman. The notion was bizarre at best. The only defensive inclinations he possessed were for self-preservation.

Closing his eyes, he recaptured the woman's image. Short layers of blonde hair framed an oval face and laughing aquamarine eyes.

As her image jelled in his mind, he suddenly realized whom he'd been dreaming about, and he snorted in self-derision. He'd been dreaming about one of the women in his latest sculpture— *The Dance*—a life-size bronze of three women. In true Freudian *élan* he had created the perfect fantasy woman in bronze and then used his dream to transform her into a make-believe flesh and blood woman capable of fulfilling his deepest desires.

As foolish as the realization made him feel, he didn't hesitate to recall the overpoweringly sensual feeling of slowly brushing his fingertips over the satin curve of the woman's hip. Or the scorching heat of her flesh pressed intimately against his own. After one dream-night with her, he knew in exquisite detail every inch of her lovely body, from the clover-shaped birthmark on her left hip to the delicately sensitive spot on the inside of her thigh that drove her wild when kissed.

Even now he wondered at the way she'd lovingly given herself to him without reserve as he'd pulled her naked body to his in passion so intense that it still left him breathless and fully aroused. He slowly rubbed his tingling hands together in an effort to recapture the tactile memory. But it wasn't a true memory. It was only an illusion his subconscious had conjured to compensate for a life of cutting his feelings off from humanity.

"*This* is real," he said aloud as he gripped the deck railing, and the cold, hard wood jabbed into his palms. He closed his eyes, only to once again see the woman's face. This time he saw terror reflected in the depths of her eyes, and the name *Angel* came to mind as his heart reacted with a jolt. He somehow knew he had been the cause of her terror. Was he, even in his dreams, damned to cause pain to those he loved?

Love? Ridiculous thought. And dangerous. He hadn't allowed himself that emotion for a long time, and he didn't want anyone to feel it for him. Even in his dreams.

"And she *was* only a dream," he reminded himself as the screech of gulls rose over the surf's boom, and the fog's mist prickled his feverish, naked skin. His hand went to the lightning-bolt shaped pendant around his neck, and he opened his eyes to dispel the woman's disturbing image. Why did he feel that he'd somehow deserted her by awakening?

He looked at the mist-shrouded beach. His bedroom. The deck. How was it he had never before noticed they were as bland as a piece of sun-bleached driftwood? Once again he got the feeling he didn't belong to this world. It was a feeling he'd had many times in his life, but never more intensely than at that moment. Only the strange world of darkness and beauty in his dream felt substantial. He had seemed at home walking the loamy floor of the verdant dream forest, and even before inhaling he had known he would smell the sweet scent of damp leaves.

Making love to the woman had felt right, too. Their bodies, minds and souls had been perfectly attuned, and walking through the dewy forest with her at his side had been the only time in his life he ever remembered feeling truly at peace. And truly whole. Jachin knew it was a feeling that he'd never experience in the real world. Only in his sleeping hours with his sculptured fantasy woman could he find that feeling of completeness, which others took for granted. His dangerous powers prevented him from the unguarded luxury of loving or being loved. He must at all times maintain tight control over his dark side. One slip—one unguarded moment of weakness—and it would consume him as well as anyone who thought they *loved* him.

He forced his gaze toward his feet to further reassure himself that he hadn't actually walked across a damp forest floor. His dry feet helped to support the truth that he was awake and that he had just had an unusually vivid dream.

Although his sense of reality was slow in returning, one essence of the dream held fast—the feeling that the danger in the dream had followed him into the real world.

With a disgruntled sigh, Jachin sat in a canvas deck chair to gaze toward the encroaching fogbank. The breeze-spun haze only hinted at what it might conceal. He could almost believe that if he walked down the deck's access stairs, across the sand and into the surf, he would be able to pass through the fog and once again enter the strange dreamland. And embrace the woman.

At the thought of her, he stood and paced the length of the deck, the wood planking beneath his feet vibrating with the force of each step. His mind kept repeating the word *protect*. He shook off the unwelcome feelings and strode determinedly into the house.

Even in a dream, Jachin Morgan was no one's hero. And his instincts said that a hero is exactly what the woman needed.

***

"It's going to be just fine, Boaz." Angela Dawn steered the rental car onto the access road toward Half Moon Bay's coastline. All during their trip from their home in Sedona, Arizona to the little California seaside community, Angela had reassured her roommate, Boaz Hamilton, that coming to see her biological aunt was a good thing. But Boaz was so withdrawn that Angela felt like she was on the quest alone. Her friend's pensive mood had started when Boaz had received a strange letter from a woman claiming to be her aunt, and Angela knew Boaz had conflicting emotions. Who could blame her? In nearly thirty years, it was the first contact Boaz had had from anyone in her birth family.

Although the woman had urgently requested Boaz come immediately to see her, Boaz had been reluctant. But from the moment she had shown Angela the letter and the half-dollar-sized green stone accompanying it, Angela had felt compelled to do as the aunt asked. Just touching the strange stone that looked like a rounded emerald gave Angela an anxious sensation in the pit of her stomach that urged her to respond to the woman's request.

Lost in her thoughts, Angela started when Boaz said, "I've got a bad feeling about this. It's a premonition of doom."

Boaz brought her feet up to sit cross-legged on the car's seat and twisted her long red curls onto the top of her head. She secured the mass with a large, claw-type hair clip. Dressed in denim bell-bottoms, a halter-top and small, round sunglasses, Boaz looked like she belonged in the 1960s instead of the twenty-first century. The only thing that brought her into the present was the tattoo on her right hand. The dotted pattern formed a swirl—a design Boaz had created herself and which spread across the top of her hand like a celestial galaxy. She'd gotten the tattoo the day she turned eighteen, much to her parents' horror.

Angela said, "You know it's possible you're just having the normal adoptee-going-to-meet-birth-relatives kind of nerves. Not every anxious feeling is a premonition." As if to contradict her words, the tingling in Angela's stomach returned, but she ignored it. "Those of us who aren't gifted intuits do have feelings of foreboding, too, you know. Only we call them jitters, not premonitions. You could be having a normal reaction to a stressful situation."

Boaz looked at her and smiled. "Yeah, you're right. Maybe I'm just over-tired and anxious about the meeting. And I haven't been sleeping very well. Every time I fall asleep, I have that same dream I told you about. Only it gets more detailed and more bizarre each night."

"Well, if it will make you feel any better, your descriptions were so vivid that last night I dreamed about that forest of yours."

Boaz sat up straight, putting her feet on the floor and staring out the window as if seeing the dream again. "Did yours have a dragon? Mine did. Sort of anyway. It wasn't your typical fairy-tale, ten-story-tall dragon...more like a huge, fire-breathing alligator. Or an overly large Komodo dragon. No, it was more like those big lizards in Jurassic Park, you know the ones that spit acid?"

Instantly Angela remembered the sensation of heat and of a great beast chasing her. "Well, I didn't actually see a dragon, but at one point I felt certain something horrible was chasing me. But then, when I turned around, instead of the expected fangs and fiery breath, I saw, well ...," She put one hand to her suddenly flushed face as sensual images flooded her mind. "Okay, you're going to think I'm crazy, but I saw Jachin Morgan...You know, that famous sculptor. And he was naked." Her face grew warmer. "We both were." She fanned her flushed cheeks, chuckling. "And if what we did counts, I don't think I'm a virgin anymore."

What she didn't elaborate on was that after her dream, Angela was sure no living man, not even super-icon Jachin Morgan himself, could live up to the virile power of her dream lover. Her lack of true experience had evidently let her mind have free rein.

Boaz slapped her leg as she hooted with laughter. "No fair! I get dragons, and you get sex. Oh, I definitely like your version better. Except I'll take Brad Pitt if you don't mind." She gave Angela a sideways glance, still smiling. "You know, you're never going to get laid if you don't start living in the real world."

Angela cringed. "Getting laid sounds so crass. I'd rather .make love." Her thoughts took her back to the dream, and her skin tingled.

Boaz laughed again and said, "Don't knock it until you try it." She looked thoughtful. "You know, our philosophies about sex aren't all that different. I'm all for 'making love,' too, but I have a strong feeling that once I give myself like that to a man— you know, heart and soul—I'd be committed for life. And I'm not willing to wait around to find that one guy. What if love never happens? You, on the other hand, seem to think you're committing some kind of sin if you fool around a little."

Angela knew her views on casual sex—views that had kept her a virgin at twenty-six—weren't in vogue, but she didn't care. She just didn't want to share that kind of intimacy with a man she didn't care deeply about. So, she remained determined to fall in love first, get married, then give herself mind, body and soul to the man she would spend the rest of her life with.

The smile on Boaz's face died as they turned down the street they were looking for and headed straight into a thick bank of fog.

"Where'd this fog come from?" Angela asked, barely able to see three feet in front of the car's bumper. She slowed to a crawl and rolled down her window to stick her head out for a better view. Cool mist brushed her cheeks, and she shivered. "It was perfectly clear just a block back."

"It's kind of nice," Boaz said, seeming to relax as she peered out the car window. "Hey, there's a house. Yes, it's the number Marrion Chadwick gave in her letter."

Angela pulled up to the curb, astonished to see that while the yard seemed to be a neglected mess, the small blue Victorian house was so pristine she expected she would be able to smell fresh paint when they walked up the steps.

"Wow," Boaz said then looked away from the house. She took a deep breath. "What if this aunt thinks I'm strange because...well, because I am." She grabbed the half-sun pendant hanging from a gold chain at her neck, a gesture Angela recognized as a sign of stress.

"You're not strange, Boaz, you're gifted. And your powers are only one of many things that make you special."

Boaz put her hand on the door handle, but didn't open it. "I can see it now. I sit down, trying to put my best foot forward with this woman, and calmly ask, 'Ahem, excuse me, but am I the only one in the clan with *peculiar* powers?'" She raised her voice, obviously agitated. "'Or am I the only freak to fall off the family tree?' I guess now that it comes right down to it, I don't feel overly anxious to have my birth family find out I'm weird. What if it's why they gave me away in the first place? I'm really not into the whole set-yourself-up-for-rejection thing."

"Boaz, do you really think your powers were evident at your birth? That you levitated the doctor in the delivery room or something? I'm sure your mother was doing what she thought best for you when she gave you up. I just know she had a really good reason. The sooner you see this aunt, the sooner you can have your questions answered. She sounded really nice in her letter." *Strange*, Angela thought to herself, *but nice.*

When Boaz didn't respond, Angela said, "What happened to my fearless roommate? You know, the adrenaline junkie who dragged me to every roller coaster ride in the US? Just think of this visit as an amusement park ride. Scary, but worth it for the adrenaline rush alone."

Angela couldn't tell if her pep talk was working. You pretty much knew what to expect with a roller coaster. Controlled terror. You might be thrilled and end up out of breath, but your safety was never in doubt. Marrion Chadwick was an entirely different matter. Who knew what the outcome of this ride would be? Judging by what Angela could tell from the woman's letter, she wasn't Aunt Bea from *Andy Griffith*. This ride could very well have no safety controls. As odd and diverse as her own family was, Angela just couldn't see any of her relatives throwing out words like *divine destiny* and *ancient prophecy* when they talked about their heritage.

Well, that wasn't exactly true. There was slightly senile Uncle Harold MacAlpin, her uncle on her mother's side, who was intensely proud of their Scottish roots and insisted those roots grew through mystical connections. No one took seriously his claims of an ancient curse on the family, mostly, she supposed, because he could never explain exactly what that curse was. All Angela remembered him saying was that it had to do with treason and redemption. Evidently someone along the way had redeemed the family, because, other than a set of parents who traveled for a living, she saw no evidence of a curse in her slightly dysfunctional, all-American family.

If Boaz's aunt Marrion Chadwick was any indication, there must be many families out there with "Uncle Harolds."

Angela made the first move and opened the car door, suddenly extremely anxious to meet Boaz's aunt.

Two

Jupiter: Rules high magick, higher mysteries, favors start of new undertakings.

Marrion had closed the well-worn copy of *Advanced Alchemy* the moment she heard the automobile stop outside. With a snap of her fingers the book disappeared. She rose nervously from her armchair, unable to remain still. Boaz was near. Any moment now her niece would ring her doorbell, and no amount of meditation could quell the knot of anxiety that had been in Marrion's chest for the past two days.

In a few minutes she would be face-to-face with only one of the triplets, when she had hoped all three would be here. But last night Kadien, the most powerful of all dark wizards, had kidnapped Lilith. He now held her captive in his stronghold on the magic isle of wizards, Sena, and he had used the troll Gaban to ensure that Jachin wouldn't be at today's reunion. Thankfully, he hadn't been able to interfere with Boaz, and she'd have to convince the young woman to help her reach Jachin. Once reunited, brother and sister would then have to rescue Lilith.

Marrion hadn't seen any of her sister's children since their momentous birth at the last *Saturn Return*—the Time of Cosmic Reckoning. Now a jumble of concerns flitted through her mind. Were the events unfolding as they should? Or had her sister Vivian threatened the prophecy's final outcome by hiding the children away from the world of magic during their growing years? Had Kadien's interference changed the prophecy's course?

Knowing there were no answers, Marrion accepted that she would just have to have faith and do as her heart directed. Since Vivian had disappeared almost immediately after the children's birth, it now fell upon Marrion to enlighten the triplets to their destiny and prepare them for the confrontation ahead.

Marrion wondered how far the children's unenlightened human caretakers had let their magic find freedom. Had their abilities progressed enough that they could fulfill the prophecy, or was all of mankind—both on Earth and Sena—doomed.

Picking up her large tabby cat, Emmeline, Marrion nervously fiddled with the cat's multi-color stone-encrusted collar. She held Emmeline up to look into her pale green eyes, and the cat returned an unflinching stare. "You know this is the beginning, don't you?" The cat blinked an affirmative response.

She put Emmy on the polished mahogany end table then waved aside the snow-white lace curtains to peer out at the automobile on the street, mumbling, "The poor dear doesn't have a clue as to how drastically her life is about to change. Neither do the others. Not that they would have a choice if they did know. Their part in this drama was set eons ago."

Why hadn't Vivian let her raise The Three in the world of magic? Marrion was a powerful wizard in her own right, and she would have protected the children from those who might want to stop them from fulfilling the prophecy decreed so long ago by the wise ones. After all these years Marrion was no closer to figuring out what could be horrible enough to compel her sister to abandon her children to the Lutes and, in doing so, jeopardize the forces of light.

She looked out at the fog she'd conjured. Manipulating water and light to create the mirage was absolutely necessary to help Marrion create the temporary illusion of a perfectly maintained turn-of-the-century house. Normally the abandoned and dilapidated house Sena's inhabitants used when they teleported into the mortal world went unnoticed by the Lutes. The fog was necessary to obscure the enchantment Marrion had put on the old house. The enchantment made it appear, down to the last stick of furniture, as fresh and flawless as the day the original owners had moved in, and it wouldn't do to have one of the locals take notice.

As Marrion watched Boaz and her companion leave the automobile, she sighed deeply. "This is it, Emmy. May the Ancient Ones save us all."

***

"I'm a triplet?"

Angela listened as Boaz responded in awe to what her aunt had just told her. Marrion Chadwick had met them at the door and, without giving Boaz so much as a welcoming hug, led them into the lilac-scented Victorian living room. They'd barely sat down on the mint-condition antique chairs when the woman, without preamble, announced that Boaz was a triplet.

As Angela looked at the two women, she had to admit they were eerily similar. Although Marrion Chadwick was middle-aged and had a thick braid of silver hair, she was, like Boaz, around six feet tall. And she carried herself with Boaz's characteristic grace and confidence. Were all the women in Boaz's birth family Amazons? But the most startling part of the woman's appearance was that she had a smaller version of Boaz's tattoo on her right cheekbone. Angela had thought the design was unique, and to see that the older woman had a tattoo on her face was bizarre enough. But to see that it was the same as Boaz's, was, in Angela's mind, downright unsettling.

Boaz rubbed her temples, the tattoo on her hand undulating with the movement, as she asked, "So where are my siblings? A brother and a sister, you said?"

Marrion quickly looked away, and Angela thought, *That's a look of avoidance if I ever saw one.*

The woman said, "In time, dear, in time. Since you received my letter things have become quite complicated...and urgent." She turned to Angela. "Before we go on, though, I must ask if I might talk to Boaz alone. What I'm about to tell her is, well...privileged." She smoothed the folds of her floor-length caftan.

Marrion's voice held a strange, far-off quality, but Angela couldn't pinpoint anything particular. Maybe it had something to do with the slight ringing in her ears that she had been experiencing since walking through the door.

Angela looked for Boaz's response to Marrion's request.

Boaz quickly shook her head as she took hold of the pendent around her neck. Boaz's other hand reached out to grab Angela's. "I want Angela to stay."

Marrion took a deep breath, and scrutinized Angela. "I sense that you are truthful and honest. Will you give me your word not to divulge this information to anyone?"

Why would she talk to anyone about Boaz's adoption? Angela took a secure hold of Boaz's hand to give her the support she needed. She shrugged. "Sure, you have my word."

The woman turned back to Boaz. "It will rest upon your shoulders if this outsider can't be trusted." Her glance flickered to the pendant at Boaz's neck.

Angela felt a prickle of unease with Marrion's warning. She'd never before felt like an "outsider" in Boaz's life.

With a resolute tilt of her chin, Boaz said, "I'd trust Angela with my life."

Angela could tell by Boaz's words and stiff posture that she wasn't quite ready to accept this woman. Or maybe her defensiveness came from a need to prepare herself for the possibility of not being accepted by her family. After their years of friendship, Boaz knew Angela completely and unconditionally accepted her, but Angela still felt pleased by her friend's declaration.

"Let's hope it doesn't come to that," Marrion said, the warning in her voice causing the hair on Angela's neck to bristle and a chill to shiver up her spine.

At a sudden, silent movement, both Angela and Boaz started. But it was only the large tabby cat jumping into Marrion's lap. Marrion settled back in her chair as she lightly stroked the animal. "So be it. I need to begin by asking you a few questions, Boaz." Again her gaze went to the pendant.

Boaz took a deep breath, seeming to steel herself. "What do you want to know?"

Marrion stated, "I'm aware you have certain magical abilities, as do all our kind. And since I didn't discover your whereabouts until three days ago, I haven't been able to ascertain how far your skills have developed in the unenlightened world. I'd like to know the extent of your powers."

Angela saw the tension slowly drain from her friend's shoulders as Boaz asked, "You have...powers, too?"

Marrion reached across the table separating them, not quite touching Boaz's hand. "All wizards do, my dear, although their level of skill and abilities vary."

Boaz jumped up, squeaking out an incredulous, "Wizards?"

Angela wanted to groan. She'd practically forced Boaz to come and meet this aunt, only to have the woman turn out to be a nut case. Sure they might share powers. But *wizards*? Living in Sedona, Arizona, a town known for its spiritual centers, had inevitably made Angela aware of certain spiritual groups, like Wiccans, or White Witches. But the word *wizard* conjured up visions of Arthurian legends, of Merlin, and of the malevolent Morgan Le Fey. It made her curious, as well, about what other 'abilities' Marrion might be referring to.

Marrion said, "Sit down, my dear. I have many things to tell you, and much will, like as not, sound unbelievable. You'll wear yourself out if you continue leaping up and down." Once Boaz was seated, Marrion continued. "You come from a royal house of wizards. Your mother, Vivian—my dear sister—was a wizard of the highest power."

Boaz stiffened. "Was?"

"Your mother has made neither physical or psychic contact with anyone on Sena—that's our island home and spiritual oasis from the unenlightened world, your true home—since your birth nearly thirty years ago. I'm assuming Vivian has passed over to the spirit world." Marrion's hands fidgeted. "The night she left with all of you, she did entrust me with her Book of Light. I knew then that something was terribly wrong, or she would never have relinquished the book. From generation to generation it has been passed down to the firstborn female in our family, and it could be used for evil if allowed to fall into the wrong hands. When you return to Sena, it will be entrusted to you and your sister, Lilith. It will be up to you both to protect it with your lives. The information contained within it is the most powerful in all wizardom." She sighed as she looked back to Boaz. "Try as I did, I could not convince Vivian to tell me the cause of her distress that night."

Forget the book, Angela thought. Marrion's treasured sister left her children. They were more significant than some musty old book. Suddenly, Angela sneezed violently, as if her allergy to dust had been triggered.

"Excuse me," she said as she retrieved a tissue from her pocket. Looking around she couldn't imagine how a speck of dust would survive in Marrion's immaculate house. Her nose began to tingle, and she found herself gripped in a frustrating struggle with a pending sneeze.

"Bless you," Boaz said, then returned to her conversation with her aunt. "What about my birth father? Is he still alive?"

Marrion shrugged and glanced away, looking sad. "Your mother wouldn't reveal his identity. I only know that when she realized she was pregnant, she became distraught and closed her thoughts off from me. Then, when you three were born, she seemed both overjoyed and heartbroken at the same time. Poor dear," she said as if speaking to herself. "Maybe she feared the prophecy." Then she returned her attention at Boaz. "She gave me The Book of Light for safekeeping, and then she left with the three of you. She insisted she had to hide her babies to protect them, and before I could stop her, she was gone. I haven't seen her, heard from her, or sensed her presence since that day."

Boaz looked confused. "Hide us from what?"

Marrion shrugged again. "I don't know from whom or what she was hiding you. She was strong enough to stand up to any wizard's magic, even the great Kadien. I guess she had her reasons, but we may never know what they were. I still can't understand why she'd leave you with the Lutes, of all people."

"What are Lutes?" Boaz asked.

"Lutes are those humans not of our race—the unenlightened race of non-magical people you were raised with."

"I guess I'm a Lute," Angela stated in a dry tone. Although the word sounded lyrical enough, Marrion's reference was obviously less than flattering.

Marrion chuckled, putting her fingers over her lips. "Oh, I'm sorry dear. For a moment I'd forgotten you weren't one of us. You're so nice and tall, unlike most Lute women." She rearranged the cat in her lap. "I'm afraid this is going to sound rude, but we've come to refer to your race as Lutes, which was derived from the word pollute, because they are the great polluters of the universe."

Angela opened her mouth, ready to protest, but closed it, unable to deny the charges. The planet was a mess, and humans were to blame.

Boaz stared thoughtfully at her aunt, looking as if she was quietly assimilating everything. One of the things that struck Angela as strange was that Boaz seemed to be accepting without question the woman's claims of being a wizard. Angela, on the other hand, had a hundred questions she was dying to ask, but she didn't want to interrupt.

Boaz said, "It's been thirty years since my mother left us here. Why have you suddenly decided to reunite my sister, my brother and me?"

Marrion sighed heavily and absently rubbed at the tattoo on her check. "I've only recently located you. With the time of prophecy at hand, the planets are in an alignment, and your powers enhanced. I was at long-last able to form a psychic connection to you as well as your brother and sister." She looked uneasy. "The only problem is, if I could form that bond and find you, so could...others."

"Who are these others? Are they the reason my mother was concerned for our safety?" Boaz asked.

Marrion drew the cat to her. "I'm not sure what your mother's concerns were, but I'm talking about Kadien, who is lord of the dark wizards. If I had been your caretaker, I wouldn't have let him get close to you. Nor would your mother, if she had stayed in Sena. Her powers were equal to his. And I cannot see Kadien challenging the Power of the Triad, even when you were children."

The woman looked away quickly as she continued. "No matter what the danger, it is the foretold time of prophecy. Time for Jachin, Lilith and you to band together and fulfill your destinies. The entire wizard community and most of Sena's inhabitants will help you."

Angela found she could no longer hold her tongue. "What kind of prophecy? What's supposed to happen? And just what is Boaz supposed to do about it?" Surely the woman wasn't seriously talking a Nostradamus-type-doomsday? *And me without my apocalypse-survival kit.*

Marrion closed her eyes as if looking inward. Then, without opening her eyes, she began telling a story in a tone of great reverence.

"Long ago the religions divided, breaking away from The Great Circle. A celestial tremor unsettled the balance of light and dark. As the worlds of magic and mortal turned their backs on one another, all were held in great peril as The Dark Powers reigned, preying on this fragmentation.

"But the ancient ones were given hope for the future. The stars foretold of coming events. It was shown to our people that, during the sunset of Pisces, a momentous birth would take place. Triplets shadowed by the eclipse would be born into the world of magic. The children of the fire, air and water would grow strong in the ways of magic until the time of reckoning.

With Saturn's Return—the time of cosmic reckoning—the trinity would confront the reigning Lord of Darkness. Great battles of spirit would rage, and the veil between the magic and mortal worlds would shift. The mortal magic of She Who Holds the Scorpion would compromise the Heart of Darkness and determine the victory of The Power of The Triad."

Suddenly, her eyes snapped open and gave Angela a sharp look. "What is your surname and what astrological sign were you born under?"

"My last name is Dawn. I was born in December...I'm a Capricorn."

Marrion looked disappointed. "Oh, not a Scorpio, so obviously not the one the prophecy foretold."

Angela was surprised to feel a deep disappointment. She had to admit that being part of some ancient prophecy would be exciting.

Boaz looked thoughtful. "Marrion, I've studied a little astrology. I know some people believe the Age of Pisces is roughly until the year two thousand and sixty," she said, referring to her aunt's reference to the prophecy. "And that the *Saturn Return* happens every twenty-nine years. Is that right?"

Marrion nodded, looking excited.

"What do those events have to do with me?" Boaz asked, sounding as confused as Angela felt.

Marrion's smile was broad. "I'm so glad you've studied the arts. Well, to explain...our people seldom have more than single births. Twins are an event. Triplets are unheard of." She paused and gazed directly at Boaz. "Until you three. Your birth is a part of The Great Prophesy. You are the ones ordained to confront The Darkness."

Angela felt dizzy trying to assimilate everything Marrion was saying. Confront what 'Darkness?' And confront it with what? The Tae Bo classes she and Boaz had taken didn't cover defending oneself from *The Darkness.*

By the look of intense concentration on Boaz's face, Angela could tell she was taking her aunt seriously.

Boaz said, "And what if one of us doesn't want to—or can't—face this supposed challenge?"

Marrion's smile faded. "You must come to terms with your destiny. You are all equal to the task. We need to reunite you with your brother and sister, so you can combine your powers, but we have a problem. I'm afraid Lilith has been abducted by the very entity you are to challenge. Kadien."

"Abducted?" Boaz said in alarm. "What do you mean abducted?"

"In Lute terms, Kadien has kidnapped Lilith. By use of his

dark powers, he has transported her to Sena," Marrion said.

Angela's eyes flew open as she recognized the name of the mythical Otherworld. "You mean Avalon?"

"Yes, Sena has been referred to as Avalon, " Marrion said.

"Lilith was kidnapped and taken to Avalon?" Boaz asked.

Marrion nodded. "Yes, by the Dark Lord himself, Kadien. But he has not harmed her." She sighed heavily and shook her head. "This wouldn't have happened if you three had remained on Sena. The Dark One could never have taken you if you had remained together."

"Why would he kidnap her?" Boaz looked as frightened as Angela felt. Would this Kadien also come after Boaz?

"The counsel of elders met just this morning to discuss the matter. We believe The Dark One took Lilith to make sure the three of you were kept apart. The Power of The Triad is incomparable, and Kadien knows this. If he keeps you apart, the threat is not so great." As an aside, she said, "Your sister Lilith's powers are in the healing arts. She is a medical intuit and has chosen to become a pediatric surgeon in the Lute world. Your brother's powers are with the metals and fire. He has chosen art as his medium."

"How do you know Lilith is okay?" Angela asked. She wasn't even convinced there was a Lilith, let alone a Lilith who was being held captive by some...what had Marrion said? 'Dark Lord?'

"We can observe her, " Marrion answered, "and we have seen that, for the time being at least, she is being treated well." She turned her attention back to Boaz. "The entire Light Wizard community is praying for Lilith's safety. You and your brother must find a way to reach her so that your powers can combine, and you can fulfill the prophecy."

"To hell with the prophecy," Boaz said, leaping to her feet. "My sister has been kidnapped. We need to call the police!"

"The Lute police can't help your sister," Marrion said. "And I assure you that for the time being she is in no danger. Come. To ease your mind I will show you how your sister is doing."

Angela stood along with Marrion and Boaz, wondering where in hell Marrion was going to take them to show them Lilith. Hadn't the woman just said Lilith was in some Otherworld called Sena? She shot Boaz a concerned look, but Boaz just shrugged her shoulders as she anxiously chewed on her lip.

As they followed Marrion into the next room, Angela noticed loud creaking from the hardwood floor. She looked down and frowned. The highly polished boards were flawless, but with almost every step she heard a creak, and she could feel a slight give when her foot pressed down. *Strange,* she thought as they entered another room.

They walked into a beautiful old-fashioned parlor complete with tasseled red velvet drapes, brocade settees, and a round table with a large, opaque white bowl in its center. The room felt light and airy even though the furnishings were dark. Marrion motioned them over to the table to peer into the bowl. Although Boaz gamely leaned forward to gaze into it, Angela stood at the table's edge. This visit was getting stranger by the minute, and she was beginning to regret convincing Boaz to come.

Marrion picked up what looked like a small tree branch dotted with multi-colored stones and waved it over the bowl. She chanted a string of words Angela couldn't understand.

When Marrion stopped chanting, she said, "Although I could not rescue Lilith, I've put her into a deep sleep with a lovely spell that will allow her to dream about her future husband. Take a look."

Angela wondered if Marrion had a spell to ease the knot of apprehension in her stomach. Both women were peering so intently into the bowl, Angela couldn't resist leaning forward and peeking in. What she saw caused her to blink several times. She simply couldn't be seeing what she was seeing. It had to be a trick. Looking at the ceiling, she searched for evidence of a hidden camera or some other projection device. But she saw only smooth, white plaster. She returned her gaze to the bowl. Could there being something inside it or under it?

The vessel held a clear liquid, and the strong scent of cedar and citrus rose up to tease Angela's nose. The liquid's surface was smooth as glass. But instead of seeing her own reflection, Angela saw the image of a woman lying on an enormous four-poster bed, her long white-blonde hair splayed across the pillow. While the beautiful young woman looked modern enough in her slacks and a soft blue cardigan, the room looked like something from a medieval castle. A trunk sat at the foot of the bed, and a heavy wood table and chair sat by a long, narrow window with leaded glass panes. The walls of the room looked like they were made of stone.

Boaz broke the silence by asking, "Where is she?"

"She's in Kadien's fortress on Sena." Marrion spoke in a hush, as though she didn't want to wake the sleeping woman. "You and your brother must go there and release her."

Angela had to wonder how one 'released' a person from the fortress of a reportedly powerful dark-lord-wizard-guy. She was pretty sure a polite knock on his door and a "pretty please" wasn't going to do it. "Trick or treat" was more like it.

The liquid in the bowl grew cloudy then went dark. Marrion turned away, and they followed her back into the living room. Evidently there was a time limit on the bowl's reception. Angela had to admit, if it was a trick, Marrion had done a good job with the whole image-in-the-bowl thing, but what would Marrion have to gain by deceiving Boaz? Her friend didn't have any money or anything else that would warrant such an involved scam. But if it wasn't a scam, it would mean that Marrion was on the level. Could that be possible? Angela's common sense said no, but there was something inside her saying that common sense didn't apply to this situation.

Marrion gave Angela an appraising look as they sat down. "It is not possible for you to go to Sena. Out of necessity...and choice...we have shunned all modern technology and adhere to the old ways. And Lutes are no longer allowed. Although I sense you know much about our world, it is forbidden for you to cross over. "

Angela realized she'd been feeling a thrill of anticipation at the prospect of going. Now she felt keen disappointment.

Marrion turned toward Boaz. "I need to know the extent to which your powers have been developed. Did you get any unusual vibrations from the letter and stone I sent?"

Boaz looked confused. "No, should I have? I'm usually very perceptive."

"I did." Angela found herself blurting.

Both women looked at her. While Boaz's expression asked why Angela hadn't told her, Marrion's face registered puzzlement.

Angela took the letter and the stone from her jacket pocket. Since Boaz had shown little interest in bringing them along, Angela had figured it wouldn't hurt to keep them with her. Holding up the green stone, she said, "I felt drawn to you from the first time I touched this."

Marrion looked shocked and confused. She put her hand to her cheek. "Surely that isn't the summoning stone enclosed with my letter."

Boaz took the stone from Angela, examined it then handed it to Marrion. "Yes, I'm sure it is."

Marrion shook her head as she contemplated the stone. "A mistake has been made. I distinctly remember instructing that a yellow *air stone* be sent to summon Boaz because she is The West. A green *earth* summoning crystal clearly represents The South."

Oh, clearly, Angela thought to herself. Earth, Air, South, North, green, yellow? It all made perfect sense. Not! Boaz might be into the whole crystal, metaphysical thing, but Angela had no idea what Marrion was talking about.

Marrion gave Angela a strange look. "You say you felt something from the stone?"

Had it been her overactive imagination? No, she was sure she felt, as Marrion had said, "summoned." "Yes, I felt something. And it feels like the stone heats up when I hold it. Is that supposed to happen?"

The woman seemed even more confused, giving Angela an appraising look. "Strange. I'm not sensing magical powers from you, but then my senses are …" She looked hesitant. "Well, they are diffused at the moment. The spell I cast should only have worked on one of our people." She shrugged and shook her head as if to clear it. "But then, if an earth stone was inadvertently sent to an air sign, it shouldn't have worked at all."

"Maybe it was just wishful thinking on my part." Angela said, deciding it was time to get out of the conversation altogether. "Boaz is the one with the powers."

Marion said, "Would you please open your mind to me, Boaz, and allow me to intuit your strength?"

Boaz shrugged. "Okay." She looked at Marrion and relaxed.

Marrion closed her eyes while lightly rocking back and forth. When she opened them, she said in a voice filled with awe, "The extent of your latent powers is incredible. Unlike any I've ever known. That only confirms your place in the prophecy. But your magic is nearly dormant through lack of use. Once you reach Sena, we'll need to prepare you to face Kadien."

Dormant? Angela had seen Boaz move objects, for heaven sake! And light candles with no more than a breath. That didn't sound dormant to her. What else was she supposed to be able to do? Spin straw into gold?

"What do I do when and if I find this Kadien?" Boaz asked. Marrion's answer was as obscure as the letter she'd sent Boaz. "All will be revealed on your journey. There will be...*guides* along the way. And The Book of Light will answer many questions."

Angela had a boatload of questions that she didn't think some dusty old book could answer. Boaz, on the other hand, seemed to be accepting Marrion's response without a qualm. She wanted to tell her friend not to be gullible, that this was an insane situation. Yet something inside her said this wasn't insane, and that scared the daylights out of her.

"I'm afraid," Marrion said, "it will be up to you to approach your brother for help. He has not responded to my summons, and I have been cut off from telepathically connecting with him. Although I cannot travel with you at present, when you reach your brother, Jachin Morgan, and it is time to cross over to Sena, I will once again be in contact to show you the way. Boaz, you will have to say good-bye to your friend Angela at that time."

Angela experienced a knot of disappointment at not being included on this Mission Impossible team even though the thought of being included scared her to death. The only Avalon she'd be visiting in this lifetime was on Santa Catalina Island. If Marrion was to be believed, the other Avalon—the nebulous, mythical one—was Boaz's destiny, not hers.

Marrion went on, addressing Boaz. "Your journey to Sena must be made during the Wizard's Moon of Oestarra—the full moon of spring. A portal between our worlds will open briefly. That event occurs in two days' time. You must reach your brother and persuade him to accompany you. I sense he will be reluctant. His soul is conflicted. We also have another problem." She went on to tell them about a troll named Gaban, who was covertly inhabiting an acquaintance of Jachin's.

As Angela tried to grasp the notion that trolls existed and that one was "inhabiting" a human, something else Marrion said suddenly registered with her. She felt a thrill of excitement. The woman had said the name *Jachin Morgan*. "Marrion, are you talking about *the* Jachin Morgan ...the famous sculptor?"

Marrion nodded. "Yes. You've heard of him?"

Boaz chuckled as she shot Angela a knowing look. "Well, we've never seen him in person, but we know who he is. Angela loves his…" She paused long enough for Angela to feel heat creep up her neck. "…*work.* You're a big fan, right, Angela?" Her smile was definitely of the Cheshire cat variety.

Angela cleared her suddenly gravelly throat and vowed to never share another sexy dream with her friend again. "I think he is very talented." She ignored Boaz's impish grin.

"I understand he is considered quite accomplished among the Lutes," Marrion said. She opened a small drawer in the end table, took out a brochure, and set it on the coffee table in front of Boaz. "I obtained this for you, Boaz, since I didn't know if you were already familiar with Jachin's work. I'll just give you a few moments to look it over." With that she rose from her chair and practically floated from the room, her cat trailing silently behind.

Angela waited until she saw the swinging kitchen door close before she blurted, "Jachin Morgan is your *brother*? Get outta here!"

Boaz studied the brochure. "Can you believe it? I have a famous brother." After a few moments Boaz handed the tri-fold paper to Angela. "We certainly don't look anything alike."

Angela studied Jachin's picture in the brochure, comparing the three siblings. "Well, I'd say all three of you are about as different as you can get and still have shared a womb, although you're all giants. Even though Lilith was in a…well, bowl, I got the impression she's tall, too."

Boaz nodded.

Angela looked at the unsmiling face of the outrageously handsome man she recognized all too well from her x-rated dream.

Her thoughts must have shown on her face, because Boaz laughed and said, "Hunka, hunka burn'n…dream, huh?"

She just wasn't going to let up on Angela's sex dream confession. Angela nodded, deciding not to let Boaz get to her, especially while she was trying to block the sensual images that were flashing through her mind and doing crazy things to her insides.

As she continued to stare at the man on the brochure, she said, "No doubt about it, you both carry the same superstar-gorgeous genes." While Boaz was a fiery redhead, full of love for everyone and everything, and Lilith had pale blonde hair, and porcelain skin, Jachin had coal-black hair and displayed a look of unapproachable aloofness.

Boaz chuckled wickedly. "Maybe I could fix you up now that I have connections."

"Sure Boaz, you do that. You fix up Mister-worldly-and-talented-Adonis with your gauche, inexperienced, plain-Jane history teacher roommate. I think every girl dreams of being *the prom date from hell.* I'm sure he'd be thrilled."

Boaz shook her head. "You really don't see yourself, do you?" She got up, pulling Angela with her to stand in front of the gilt-framed mirror over the sofa. "Uh-huh, pretty damn ugly...if you hate that Gwenneth Paltrow look. Tall, elegant, slim and beautiful. I'm gonna throw up if I go on." Boaz chuckled as she returned to her seat to study the brochure on Jachin's artwork.

Angela stared at her reflection. She saw an average face with average blue eyes perhaps a bit too big for her face, an unremarkable nose, and an average mouth that tended to turn up at the corners. The only really great thing she saw was her hair, but the color wasn't truly her own. Just two days ago it had been average, straight, and hovered somewhere in the medium blonde range. Then Boaz had talked her into an outrageously short and sassy cut and highlights. It looked great, but underneath she was still...average. That was Angela Catherine Dawn, from her size eight shoes to her thirty-four "C" bra. Average. No sense in Boaz trying to convince her otherwise. There was simply no way anyone like Jachin Morgan would ever give her a second glance. From the magazine articles she'd read, he had his choice of flawless women and took full advantage of that fact.

She decided to change the subject. "And you were worried about your aunt thinking you were weird. So, what do you think of everything your aunt said?" Angela thought it was beyond the Twilight Zone, yet she had seen Boaz do some incredible, unexplainable things in the past. And there was that bizarre miniature-Lilith-in-the-bowl thing. Could that have been some elaborate trick? But if it was, what would be the point?

Boaz looked up. "I feel in my heart that what Marrion says is true. It all adds up to visions and memories I've experienced for a lifetime." She went back to looking through the brochure. "What about you? What do you think?"

Angela considered all she'd heard and seen since she'd known Boaz. "I have to admit, I'm more open to it than I would have been before I met you, but you have to admit that Marrion's claims sound ludicrous." She lowered her voice. "Even delusional. And yet, the whole wizard-world thing seems to ring true to me on some elemental level. Especially when I apply it to you."

Could the magical Arthurian tales of Merlin be based in truth? Was there actually a race of wizards? If so, where did they originate? And was Boaz really one of them? As far as Angela was concerned, the jury was still out. Sure, Boaz had unusual powers, and all her relatives might have powers. But did that make them wizards?

She thought about Jachin Morgan. Now there was a man who the word *wizard* fit like a kidskin loincloth. For many years the mythical, otherworldly figures of his sensual work had held Angela spellbound. Was he as sexy and perceptive as his work—and her dream—indicated? Or was he as dark and unapproachable as he looked on his brochure?

Soon, she'd know the answer. The question was, did she really want to?

THREE

Venus, the Goddess planet: Sensual Maiden. One whose psychic and magickal powers are dependent on others.

As anxious as Jachin was to get to his workshop before the tourists began to stir, he found himself stopping in his tiled entry. He stared at the stack of unopened mail, most of which had been sitting on the entry's heavy wooden credenza for two days. But only one piece of mail held his attention.

His hands itched to pick up a small manila envelope, just as they had each time he'd passed the damn thing during the last two days. Why were his powers responding to it? It was just an inanimate object, albeit an object sent by someone of flesh and blood. Although he didn't want to acknowledge either the ramifications or the importance of someone being able to trigger his powers, he knew he would eventually have to open the envelope. His senses told him that something within the package— something with deliberate intent and purpose—was beckoning him. The pull he felt was almost hypnotic.

Instead of giving in to the force and reaching for the envelope, he diverted his hands to the rich curves of the furniture's carved edge, finding pleasure and comfort in the energy and texture of the wood. A long, sinewy Chinese dragon wrapped itself around the credenza. It was lifelike enough to give the impression that it was merely caressing the wood, not a part of it. Like a pet craving the stroke of its master's hand, the dragon's scales seemed to ripple with pleasure at his touch.

"Enough avoidance," Jachin said to the carving, fancying that the eyes glowed in response. He could no longer put off facing the urgent message his senses told him the envelope contained.

The moment he touched the envelope he responded to the energy emanating from within. Tearing it open, he cautiously poured the contents into his hand. A lavender scent wafted through the air as he looked at the letter and the blood-red stone. Then a rush of images assaulted him with a force so great he had to fight to breathe. The dream of last night came back in vivid detail.

Images of stone walls, dark caves and the smiling face of his dream woman flashed through his mind, giving him the absurd notion that the dream was somehow connected to the stone. The smooth surface immediately grew warm against his skin.

Closing his mind to the images, he focused his gaze on the letter. He snorted derisively as he read it. After thirty years a woman claiming to be his biological aunt insisted he come see her immediately. He wasn't about to go rushing off to meet her. Nothing she could say would change the fact he hadn't been wanted, that he'd been given away at birth.

He tossed the letter and stone on the tabletop, the bitter resentment of a lifetime causing his chest to ache. "You're thirty years too late, old woman."

The dark force he'd felt surface upon awakening that morning tried to resurface. Like a cloud passing over his soul and chilling his emotions, the rage he'd fought a lifetime to subdue began to take hold. He fought against it with every ounce of his considerable will, but the force was strong. He couldn't give in to it. Even acknowledging the darkness gave it life, triggering his greatest fear—that it would one day win. That it would possess him completely. That one day he would lose the battle.

But fighting against the force only seemed to give it more power. He attempted to focus, to calm his breathing. But the darkness gathered strength despite his efforts. Around him the room began to shudder.

"I don't care about my past," he ground out between clenched teeth. But the force couldn't be fooled. It grew stronger. "I will not give in to the darkness."

A swirling vortex of energy emerged from him, moving across the room like a small, violent tornado. Images blurred as the energy moved around the room. It hit the thick wooden front doors with the force of a sledgehammer, splintering the wood as though it were paper.

Then, like a candle blown out in the wind, the darkness within him vanished, and the room fell eerily silent. Within seconds his heart rate and breathing had returned to normal.

"Damn!" Jachin shook his head. He'd learned to control the creative side of his powers, the side that allowed him to render his bronze sculptures. But the destructive side had a mind of its own. He was certain that one day that side would conquer him.

He raised his hand, pointing his fingers at the door, and silently commanded the elements in the wood to gather and once again take their previous form. It was a simple enough task since the elements were already at hand. With a burst of electric energy, the door was restored as if nothing had happened. A sinking feeling remained that one day he would destroy something that was beyond his powers to restore.

The early morning fog beckoned him with its freshness, and he walked through the repaired open door and into the early morning. The door closed softly behind him.

Consciously shutting himself off from the dream and the letter, Jachin walked through town, the morning blessedly peaceful.

Welcoming the chilling breath of fog, he walked in his shirtsleeves and light-weight cotton pants the half-mile from his cliffside home to his studio-gallery. He tended to run hot, and the cold air had a calming effect.

He figured he had another hour before Southern California's marine layer would burn off. Then the sun would bring with it hoards of Spring Break vacationers to crowd Laguna Beach's halcyon streets and sandy shore. By then he would be in his workshop, oblivious to the noise of giggling teens and carefree families living run-of-the-mill, so-called *normal* lives.

While Jachin walked he reflected. It wasn't that the tourists actually bothered him. In fact, as long as he kept them in his periphery, kept the specter of their *Brady Bunch* lives at bay, he could observe their presence with philosophic detachment. He would never fit into their world. So why should he try?

He roused himself from the reflective mood. Today he would bury himself in his work. For a few blissful hours at least, he could put from his mind both the illusive real world, of which he could never truly be a part, and the dream world that seemed all too real and seduced him with open arms.

At least those were his intentions.

He couldn't help musing about his latest sculpture, *The Dance*, and his newfound "relationship" as dream lover with one of the sculpture's three women. Just the thought of her and how she'd responded to him in his dream set up an uneasy yearning in his chest.

The sculpture's other two subjects had him puzzled, too. For the first time in his life he'd done a piece without live models.

He'd been driven by some unknown force to begin the work. Then the three women just seemed to *happen* as he sculpted. It was as if they already existed in the clay and only needed uncovering.

As he stopped by his usual sidewalk newsstand to pick up coffee, he said to the newsstand owner, "The usual, Carl. One black, one with extra sugar." He leaned against the counter, looking into the retreating fog and focusing inward to visualize the sculpture.

Carl's nervous, "Sure, Jachin," jerked him away from his thoughts and put him on alert. He quickly took in his surroundings. Quiet streets. Shops and galleries still closed. A lone jogger in the distance almost obscured by the mist. Jachin looked at Carl, but the man avoided eye contact.

Then Jachin saw why. A tabloid's glaring headlines hit Jachin with a solid right jab to his solar plexus. His heart bolted into overdrive. Grabbing the newspaper he read:

Jachin Morgan, in league with the Devil!

If you've been wondering, along with the rest of us, how the work of famous sculptor, Jachin Morgan, is so uncannily lifelike, wonder no more. His abundant wealth, charismatic good looks, and unearthly talent have the most sinister of benefactors.

This reporter's interview with a former lover of Jachin Morgan reveals the source of not only his talent, but reveals the fact that the wealthy, enigmatic man has evil powers.

Morgan's former mistress, Tilly Angstrom, is quoted as saying, "He told me himself he was in league with the Devil. He really did. And whenever he got angry—which was often—weird things happened. You know, like light bulbs bursting, car alarms going off. And, oh, one time, I swear, he made a lightning bolt hit some guy's car, just because the guy wouldn't get out of what Jachin considered his personal parking space! I asked him how he got so mean, and he said he'd sold his soul to Satan! I swear, he really did."

Tilly! Jachin had pushed the painful, long-ago memory of Tilly Angstrom so far into the recesses of his memory he hadn't even considered her when several recent questionable articles about him had surfaced. And now all the condemnation and pain he'd felt so long ago resurfaced. Tilly had been his one attempt at what he then considered a *normal* relationship. It had failed miserably.

He looked back at the paper. The article's reference to Tilly as his mistress was ludicrous. At eighteen, she'd been no more than a free-spirited young woman with an adolescent's propensity for sexual experimentation, and he had only been twenty-one at the time. Too late, he'd discovered Tilly Angstrom to be a beautiful, self-serving idiot. When she first discovered his powers, she'd freaked. Then she'd quickly grown accustomed to the manifestations of his emotional energy and began to treat him as if he were some kind of freakish pet. It was at that point he ended their relationship.

He read on.

> *Ask yourself if the dark and brooding image of icon Jachin Morgan is mere promotional hype or a true look into a demented soul. Our source reveals that Jachin Morgan's work, accomplished with the help of black magic, must be done outside the public eye, and in the utmost secrecy. It is said the complicated foundry process to transfer a clay image into bronze is not needed by Mr. Morgan, who, instead, uses the sinister art of alchemy.*
>
> *This reporter has delved deep for the truth, going to a respected white witch for inside information. She states that in Morgan's most recent bronze, entitled, "The Dance," he has assuredly used the powers of darkness to capture these women's very souls!*

"Damn them," Jachin ground out between clenched teeth. And damn Tilly. Why had she decided to speak up now, after eight years of silence? Of course, he was sure one of the tabloid reporters had tracked her down and convinced her to sell him out. He couldn't believe her betrayal could hurt after all this time, but it did. But the fact remained that even Tilly didn't know how he turned his sculptures into bronze. The reporter had to be guessing on that particular point, and the reporter's words, *powers of darkness*, echoed through his mind.

He fingered the lightning bolt-shaped pendant resting at the front of his shirt. The newspapers and magazines next to him began to flutter as if lifted by a sudden wind. But the morning was dead calm.

Jachin forced himself to stop reading and compose himself. He already knew what nonsense the tabloid spouted. What was more difficult to shake off was that it would be believed by far too many people. Soon other newspapers would send reporters, who would put their own sensational slants on the story. Fuel would be added to his growing reputation as an evil entity. Why couldn't people just leave him in peace? He hadn't asked for the fame, and *infamy*, he'd been saddled with.

With a concerted effort, he restrained the impulse to throw down the payment for his coffee. The tabloid article wasn't Carl's fault. As Jachin took the two insulated cups and stormed off toward his studio, the hold he had on his anger began to slip. Several car alarms went off as he passed, shattering the early morning silence. Dogs could be heard barking in the distance.

If the public only knew the real Jachin, he thought, they would laugh at the outrageous accusations.

Or would they?

Jachin wasn't sure who he was. Or, for that matter, *what* he was. Only one thing he knew with certainty. He wasn't like other people. And the only meaningless clue he had to his true identity was the pendant his mother said came with his adoption papers. He wasn't sure why he'd begun wearing it when he'd left home at seventeen, but for some reason it gave him comfort.

He took a deep breath, willing himself to unwind the ball of anger deep in his chest, not relishing a repeat of the morning's earlier disaster with the door. The tension eased, and a steady calm descended over him. He neatly locked his emotions away in his inner vault.

"Hey, ho! Jachin Morgan, my man."

As Jachin crossed the street, he looked for the source of the greeting. Sean Scot, the quirky old geezer who owned the used book shop next to Jachin's studio-gallery stood at the curb. The man momentarily diverted his attention from Jachin to face the road and wave at the occupants in a passing car. Jachin had grown accustomed to the startled looks and the question in people's eyes at the stranger's wave.

Once the car was out of sight, Sean turned back to Jachin. Something was different about Sean this morning, but Jachin didn't want to put the energy into figuring it out.

He acknowledged the man with a brief nod. "Sean."

He made it a practice to speak as little as possible to the man, not wanting to encourage conversation. The Laguna Beach locals knew Sean as *The Greeter* because he spent most of his days standing curbside, greeting passersby. And as far as Jachin could tell, the man left his shop of dusty used books unattended a majority of the time.

Jachin's efforts to avoid Sean rarely paid off, though. The old guy seemed to have made it his mission in life to ensure Jachin didn't go through a single day in peaceful isolation. Noticing his gallery manager, Mildred Holmes, already sitting at her desk, Jachin pushed open the gallery's wide glass doors and went in. Sean followed.

Looking at Mildred, Jachin silently pleaded with her to somehow get rid of the old guy.

She simply looked back to her slim computer screen. "Good morning, Jachin. Sean, you're looking exceptionally dapper this early morning."

For some reason, Sean looked uncomfortable with her compliment and shifted uneasily, quickly donning a smile. "Why thank you, Mrs. Holmes."

Mrs. Holmes? Jachin saw Mildred quickly hide her perplexed smile by turning back to the computer. Since when did Sean refer to Mildred as "Mrs. Holmes?" Jachin scrutinized Sean more closely, but other than the man being better groomed than usual, he saw nothing out of the ordinary in the slightly stoop-shouldered man. Was Sean trying to impress Mildred? He chuckled to himself. Now there was a thought. June Cleaver and Colombo? *Poor old guy*, Jachin thought, *it's never going to happen*. Jachin and Sean belonged to the same association of misfits and social outcasts, while Jachin was pretty sure he'd find Mildred listed in the dictionary under the word *normal*.

Jachin noticed a strong odor of mothballs or some kind of cleaning fluid, although he couldn't pinpoint what it was. "What

is that smell, Mildred? Did the cleaning staff come in last night?"
He had a standing order for them never to use strong-smelling or
caustic cleaners in his gallery. And they were never supposed to
come in without making specific arrangements with Mildred in
case Jachin was working, which he did at all hours.

Mildred sniffed, her expression turning to one of concern.
"No, the cleaning service isn't due until tomorrow, but I know
what you mean. It's really strong, isn't it? Don't worry, I'll track
it down and get rid of it." She became distracted by something
she saw on her computer screen.

Mildred smiled up from her glass desk, obviously delighted
by something she was reading. The glow from the screen gave
her short silver hair a soft, blue cast. "Jachin, we sold another
five pieces at the Seattle gallery!"

Jachin shrugged as he set the sugared coffee on her desk. He
no longer cared about sales. Over the past ten years he'd
accumulated more money than he could spend in a lifetime. He
only cared that in his sculpting he'd found an outlet for the odd,
otherwise uncontrolled powers that had plagued him his entire
life. Only by putting his energies into sculpting and then
transforming clay into bronze could he diffuse the energy and
maintain any kind of control over his ability to affect magnetic
fields and electricity. Without the sculpting, he knew that the
uncontrolled *event* of earlier that morning would have become
routine.

Sean interrupted Jachin's introspection. "No doubt about it,
Jachin, you touch people with your work." He seemed to be
studying him. What was with the guy today? His normal look of
relaxed distraction had been replaced with edginess.

Jachin dismissed Sean's odd behavior and walked to the door
at the back of the building that led to his studio. As thoughts of
the tabloid and Tilly resurfaced he felt compelled to turn back to
Sean. "The last thing on Earth I want, Sean, is to *touch* people."
Ever again, he thought. Suddenly the studio smelled like vanilla.
Weird.

Sean, usually easier to dismiss, chuckled as he gave Jachin a
long, speculative look. "You may act like you detest humanity,
but your work is a study in human nature. It would be impossible
to not understand human emotion and still create what you do.
And you do touch people, as deeply as if you went inside their

heads, took a look at their dreams, desires, and wishes and then turned them to bronze. What they see and feel in your work is as close to magic as mortals can come."

It suddenly hit him. Sean must have read the article. And his reference to magic and that Jachin might not be mortal hit irritatingly close to home. Well, if Sean was looking for confirmation that Jachin had some special powers given to him by the devil, he was going to be sorely disappointed. Jachin's laugh was mirthless. "If I were truly magic, I'd turn the *people* into bronze, not their dreams." Tilly came to mind, and a list of others who'd betrayed him began to form. He put a stop to the destructive thoughts. He didn't need to encourage his dark side.

"I don't want to be disturbed, Mildred. No calls—"

Raising her hand and closing her eyes as if to shut him out, she said, "I know, I know. I've worked for you seven years." She made a brushing motion with her hand. "You just go in there and work your magic, Jachin, and I'll make sure, just as I always do, that you aren't disturbed." She turned back to her desk, shaking her head and smiling at Sean, who still stood there.

Jachin would never admit it, but he got a kick out of the way Mildred never took guff off him. She was one of the few people in his life who was neither intimidated nor impressed by him. It was probably why they'd been together so long. The woman had spirit, a keen business sense, and, for reasons Jachin couldn't fathom, was dedicated to promoting his career. But the thing he liked most about her was she never made him feel different, or even special. She pointedly ignored his dark moods and consistently blamed the power company and the city's old wiring for the occasional strange happenings when Jachin's powers got out of hand.

He closed the door behind him, entering the cool workroom. Immediately silence enveloped him, and he took a deep breath, truly relaxing for the first time that morning. Illumination from the vast skylights flooded the entire workspace, giving the room a cavernous, otherworldly feel. And to him this was another world. Completely shut off from the outside, this was his sanctuary. A place where he could let down his barriers and truly *be*. His sculptures offered no censure. It was the only place he let his emotions have free rein, then quickly put them into whatever piece he was working on at the time.

He'd made a point of eliminating any kind of modern technology in the workroom, comfortable in the uncluttered freedom. When he worked at night he used kerosene lamps and candles, which gave off sufficient light since most of the time he worked using his tactile rather than his visual senses. For some reason he felt more aware of all of his senses in the dim lighting.

Returning to his concern over the strong smell when he'd entered the gallery, he checked the oil lamps to make sure none had somehow tipped over and spilled. All of them rested on the tables, just as he'd left them the night before. He wondered again what could have caused the awful smell in the outer office. Probably some kind of spill in the alleyway behind the gallery had sent the noxious fumes into the building. Then he realized Sean had been in the room. The old guy was probably wearing a coat that hadn't been out of mothballs for years. And the strong vanilla scent was probably from Mildred.

Taking a swig of coffee, he set the cup on a worktable then went to the center of the room to whisk the drape off *The Dance*. A pedestal raised the sculpture two feet off the floor.

Three bronze women stared back at him, and he fancied he could hear their mingled laughter. A premonitory thrill went through his entire being, just as it did every time he looked at the piece. He knew without a doubt this was his masterpiece. Although each of his sculptures was one-of-a-kind, this went beyond being merely unique. If ever one of his pieces was divinely inspired, it was *The Dance*. Although Mildred had already listed it as available and several offers had been made, Jachin couldn't bring himself to either sell it or to put it in one of his galleries where just anyone off the street could view it.

The trio in the piece, dressed in what appeared to be free-flowing, gossamer material, danced in abandon through a meadow, each holding onto the other, as if they might almost be physically joined. No, *spiritually joined,* he suddenly thought. Maybe he should have called the statue *The Sisters*. And now, just as they had from the moment he'd given life to their faces, they seemed to be begging him to join them in the carefree dance.

He snorted. The word *carefree* wasn't one that often came to mind. At all times he remained aware that his strange abilities made it imperative he keep his guard. Unguarded, frivolous moments could mean disaster.

He studied the piece. In college he'd dabbled enough in psychology to make him aware that the three women quite possibly represented something lacking in his life. It was obvious what the woman who had found her way into his dream represented. But he couldn't pinpoint the other two. Maybe the sculpture embodied the freedom of spirit he'd always hungered for, but endeavoring to figure out the piece's message could only lead to uncovering emotions he was better off leaving buried.

He walked slowly around the figures, taking in their every feature, almost as if he hadn't created them. One woman had long spiral curls—red, he imagined—and a maverick look in her eyes. Another appeared to be soft and benevolent, yet radiated an inner strength.

But it was the center figure he found most enchanting. This exquisite woman he knew intimately. With short hair swept away from her face by an imaginary wind, she now seemed to regard him as though she could read his thoughts and understood the turmoil raging inside. One slender, outstretched arm beckoned him.

"Who are you?" His voice rumbled through the quiet of the hanger-like studio. He reached out, intending to touch the fingers he knew as well as his own. He had the odd feeling that if he touched her, he would know who she was. But before his heated flesh touched the cool bronze, he pulled back.

He didn't want to know.

***

Gaban, growing more accustomed to the human he inhabited, smiled at Mrs. Holmes. It never hurt to make allies. One never knew when they could be of use. Although he'd just had one of his frequent dizzy spells, which left him wondering where he'd been, he had quickly recovered. Neither Jachin nor the woman had seemed to notice anything out of the ordinary, so he must not have given himself away. He had gone on to spend several minutes in inane conversation with the woman, which to all outward appearances seemed to please her.

Her smile was gracious and kind, making Gaban wonder what her true thoughts were regarding this Lute human he'd borrowed. He quickly read her thoughts and found to his surprise that she harbored true affection for the inconsequential old man called Sean Scot. Humans. Their motivations were intriguing. What did this human Sean Scot have to offer her?

She said, "Did Jachin seem unusually upset this morning?"

Gaban had felt Jachin's anger as a powerful energy, and he'd been tempted to bait him into directing some of it at him so he could absorb it as his own. But the contact would have given him away, and Gaban was forbidden to make himself known. "He must've awakened on the wrong side of the bed."

She chewed her lip. "I get the feeling something is wrong."

Gaban had to wonder if this Lute woman's *feeling* was a primitive level of the highly developed sixth sense of the wizards of his world. He surprised himself by saying, "The boy is fighting demons within." Now where had that come from? The dizziness returned, and he had to concentrate to subdue his human host. From what he'd been told when he'd been given instructions and powers from Lord Kadien, Lutes were unable to resurface on their own when inhabited. Maybe this was a stronger Lute than Lord Kadien thought. Gaban had experienced several blackouts, and he had to wonder if Sean Scot had caused them. He brushed his concerns aside as he felt a resurgence of his temporarily bestowed powers.

The woman looked amused as she exclaimed, "Demons? Sean, you should know Jachin better than that by now. He may come across as dark and moody to the world, but it's all an act. I happen to know just how kind he is." She glanced toward the door to Jachin's studio before she went on. "He would kill me if he knew I was telling you this ..."

Instantly alerted to possible usable information, Gaban leaned closer.

She continued, "But Jachin has given millions to charity. And all anonymously I might add."

Well, Gaban thought, *that information is of no use to me.* Still, he feigned curiosity.

The woman seemed to reject Gaban's previous *demon* comment with the wave of her hand. "Why, Sean, his moods are only a defense mechanism. There are no demons in Jachin."

Gaban kept his Lute smile pleasant as if concurring with her appraisal of Jachin, all the while thinking, *Oh, my lady, if you only knew.*

*** * ***

The day after the tabloid article, Jachin, clad only in shorts, sat on his balcony and watched seagulls swoop and dip with the light wind. The cooling breeze was welcomed by his perpetually fevered skin.

He ignored the ringing phone, a constant since the article. Out of some perverse sense of keeping in touch with reality, he refused to turn off the ringer. Not only had the phone become his enemy, he couldn't even go out of his house without being accosted by reporters vying for exclusives. Or worse, by nutcases who had taken the article seriously and wanted to become his disciples! He watched the ocean surge toward the shore, the strand of beach disappearing an inch at a time with the encroaching high tide.

"Hey ho! Jachin, my man." The unwelcome voice came from behind him.

He didn't jump at the unexpected intrusion. He didn't flinch. He didn't even bother to turn to face the man. Before he'd even heard Sean, his senses had alerted him to his presence.

"How the hell did you get in?" Jachin kept his voice calm, although he felt anger begin to simmer inside him. So much for his state-of-the-art security system. And he'd have to do something about it, because if Sean could walk into the house without setting off the alarms, the press or some nutcase could also get inside.

Sean seemed unfazed by the question as he came out onto the deck and seated himself comfortably in one of the canvas-covered chairs. "Jachin Morgan, we need to talk."

The only reason Jachin could come up with for Sean's uncharacteristically bold visit was that the man was connected with the tabloid article and wanted more inside information. Well, he would leave disappointed. In fact, it was all Jachin could do to restrain himself from jumping up and physically ejecting Sean from the house. Although the old man was only a couple of inches shorter than Jachin, he was bent with age.

Jachin had, in many ways, trusted Sean Scot. He'd even gone as far as to consider him a friend. The betrayal simmered deep in is chest.

"Jachin?" Sean's voice held a hard edge Jachin had never heard before. It caused him to listen more attentively as Sean said, "I repeat, we need to talk." The aroma of vanilla wafted from Sean. It was the same scent he'd smelled in the gallery yesterday. If Sean smelled like vanilla, then the scent of mothballs must have had another source.

He continued watching the gulls, which suddenly seemed disoriented in their flight. They veered awkwardly, as if caught by a sudden gust, although the breeze was mild. He calmed himself. No need to cause the birds' internal balance to go haywire.

"No," he finally said, "we don't *need* to talk. You *need* to leave me in peace."

Jachin continued to wonder at this sudden change in Sean. His usual silly demeanor had been dropped, and his voice held a warning as he said, "Only one road leads to the peace you are seeking, Jachin. But that road is lined with danger."

At that Jachin did turn to look at his unwanted guest. He was well aware of the threat to his peace of mind from the tabloid article. But what Sean didn't know was that Jachin's emotional fallout from the article also posed a threat. "I strongly suggest you leave now, Sean. You may not realize it, but you're the one in danger." Without the outlet of Jachin's work, which media hounds and would-be followers had temporarily forced him to abandon, the excess energy from his powers could slip without warning.

Sean sighed heavily. "I'm not afraid of you, Jachin. In fact, I've come to help you." Again, the aroma of vanilla.

What could ineffectual Sean Scot possibly do to help him out of this media nightmare? He couldn't help the snort. "How are you going to help me?"

"I'm going to tell you who you are."

"Now you're a shrink?" he drawled, deciding Sean had finally lost it completely

"I'm not talking about who you are emotionally, Jachin. You'll come to terms with that soon enough. I'm talking about your heritage. You must be told in order to protect yourself against those from your past who would use you."

Jachin smiled. Like the old man could have any idea who Jachin was. He'd been abandoned at birth, and any traces of his past were presumably in sealed files. He fingered the pendant, the only link with his past. "You've got my attention," he said derisively. "Who am I, Sean?"

The man's gaze was direct. "You're a powerful wizard."

Jachin roared with laughter. It was the first time he'd laughed in a long, long time.. Maybe the old man's visit wasn't such a bad thing after all. Jachin was in need of a jester, and Sean was perfect.

Wizard did sound slightly better than *devil.* "Don't believe everything you read."

"I don't have to read anything, Jachin. I know who your parents are...or were."

Sean's attempt at seriousness gave even more levity to the claims. Jachin stared at him. "Oh yeah? Did you look in your crystal ball?" How in the hell could Sean Scot, who spent his days waving to tourists, know anything about Jachin's true past?

The man again looked straight into Jachin's eyes, and something Jachin saw there caused his laughter to die. He swallowed hard. Why was he even taking this seriously? Wizards? It was out of the question.

"My boy, you were born in a far away land nearly thirty years ago to a white wizard by the name of Vivian."

He looked like he was waiting for acknowledgement. But Jachin was busy trying to figure out the real purpose of Sean's visit.

"You don't believe me," Sean finally said.

Jachin feigned a look of shock, then he got up and took Sean by the arm, urging him from his chair. "No, I don't believe you, and you can leave the same way you came in. You'll have to excuse my bad manners, but I'm not in the mood for visitors. And I suggest you take a nice long vacation. You're beginning to lose it, my friend."

"When you're ready to talk," Sean said as Jachin ushered him through the deck's doorway and into the living room, "you know where to find me. But be warned. Time is short."

Jachin had nothing more to say, so he let go of Sean's arm and went back to the deck, shaking his head as he slid the door closed. He had to wonder if the entire world was off kilter. First the dreams, then the letter from Marrion Chadwick claiming to be his aunt, followed by the article, and now this bizarre change in Sean. He eased himself into the deck chair. Watching the ebb and flow of the sea seemed to be the only thing to truly calm him. After several minutes he realized he shouldn't have been so abrupt with Sean. Maybe the old geezer was having a stroke or something. He'd call Mildred and have her go over to the bookshop to check on him.

An hour later Jachin walked into his house, intending to re-set the malfunctioning alarm. He was certain he'd set the outside senso. s. But when he got to the panel by the front door, to his astonishment he found everything set as if untouched. He tried the front doors. Both were still bolted. From the inside.

"Strange," he mumbled. How in hell had Sean gotten in? Or out? Unsettled, he walked over to unplug the still ringing phone, and the house instantly quieted. If only it were that easy to calm the turmoil simmering inside him. His gut told him that somehow the dreams, the letter and Sean's strange behavior were all connected, and with that thought came a feeling of impending doom.

***

Angela stood with Boaz before two enormous wooden doors carved with exquisite griffins. She and Boaz had driven directly from Half Moon Bay to Laguna Beach in order to find the man Marrion said was Boaz's brother. Jachin Morgan.

"Boaz, I can't believe we're standing at Jachin Morgan's door. I feel like Dorothy confronting the Wizard of Oz."

"If what Marrion said is true, you're not far off the mark. Let's just hope the Wicked Witch of the West isn't lurking somewhere close by." Boaz glanced behind her.

Angela was so filled with nervous excitement she could hardly stand still. She looked around at the security-gated front drive that Boaz had magically opened with a concentration of her powers. The immaculately landscaped, cliffside home had to be worth millions. Angela knew her voice held awe. "Jachin Morgan, the sculptor, is your brother. Who'd have thunk it?"

Boaz began to fidget with her pendant. "What if he's not here?" She closed her eyes as if to focus inward, but quickly opened them again. "I can't read anything. I'm so nervous I can't concentrate!"

Angela gave her friend a quick hug. "He'll be here. And if he isn't, we'll just camp out on his doorstep and wait." Her laugh was self-deprecating. "God, I sound like a groupie. I told you I was gauche."

Boaz smiled. "I'm as nervous as you are." She looked around in wonder. "Do you think a housekeeper or someone will answer the door? He looks super loaded."

But when the door suddenly flew open, it was no mild-mannered housekeeper they came face-to-face with. Jachin Morgan himself towered above them in glorious, practically naked splendor, looking like an angry god. Angela couldn't help taking note that his publicity photos didn't do him justice.

Longish black hair, tied back, flowed away from a regal forehead. And how could a camera hope to capture those magnificent shoulders? Angela was astonished to see that he had a large tattoo on his upper arm, the dotted design vaguely similar to Boaz and Marrion's. Scowl aside, Angela had to admit, Jachin Morgan was just about as perfect as they come. And every bit as sexy as he'd been in her dream. Her stomach fluttered.

"How did you get past my security gate!" His voice, as deep and smooth as Sean Connery's, rumbled like distant thunder. Or was the thunder real?

Boaz dove right in, her tone a determined match for her brother's. "I know you don't know me, but I'm your sister, Boaz Hamilton. I need your help. You got a letter from our birth aunt, Marrion, right? She told me our sister Lilith has been kidnapped." Then Boaz startled Angela by flinging herself into Jachin's arms with a muffled, "I can't believe I have a brother!"

Much to Angela's relief, Jachin didn't push Boaz away. Instead he stared at Angela. His startled expression seemed to be pleading for help with a woman he obviously thought was deranged.

Then his expression changed from surprise to utter shock, and he stared at Angela as though she was a ghost. His head-to-toe scrutiny of her, although lightning-quick, was thorough enough to cause her face to flush with heat. She had the unsettling feeling she'd forgotten to put clothes on that morning, and she found herself pressing her hand to her chest to make sure it was indeed covered.

Then his eyes searched hers. For what she couldn't imagine. Angela found herself held as if by a magnet to those eyes. Dark brown, his eyes held shards of burgundy in their crystal depths. How unusual, she thought to herself as she continued to stare. And stare. He must think she was an idiot. And that's exactly what she felt like, a hotly flushed, dumbstruck idiot.

***

As Jachin studied the embodiment of the woman in his sculpture and his dream, his body and mind reacted with sensual awareness. He gently tried to detach the other woman's hold, which felt like an octopus' tentacles. Finally he managed to break away from the woman who claimed, incredibly enough, to be his sister. He secured her at arm's length. When he looked at the redhead's face he realized that she, too, was one of the women in his sculpture.

At the very moment he heard himself mutter, "I don't have a sister," his mind reeled with the innate certainty that she was telling the truth.

But reason kicked in, making him wonder if this could somehow be a trick. Had one of the tabloids hired the two women, knowing they were identical to the women in his sculpture? That seemed unlikely, since he alone knew the piece didn't have actual models.

As he looked at the tall redhead he had a dizzying feeling of *déjà vu*. It was as if he'd known her his entire life. A score of emotions washed over him, and for an uncertain moment, he felt as though he were drowning. Excitement. Fear. Validation. Happiness. Sadness.

Anger.

In an effort to stop the unwanted feelings Jachin grabbed hold of the one emotion he'd had so much experience in controlling—the anger—then swiftly, mercilessly smothered the others until they no longer posed a threat to his composure. Within seconds he'd gained some measure of control.

Rubbing his temples in frustration, he silently motioned the two into his living room. He chose to remain standing, since the unreasonable need to bolt for the door suffused his muscles with enough adrenaline to run a marathon.

He warily studied the two women. If the redhead was his sister, then what was the blonde's connection? That presented him with a disturbing thought. The hot and primal spontaneous attraction he'd felt toward her was anything but brotherly, and he fervently hoped that she wasn't going to announce they were related.

The blonde walked to a chair but continued to warily regard him. As his mind went over the redhead's previous statement about someone being kidnapped, he found himself rubbing a hand over his chest. He noted with satisfaction that the blonde's eyes followed the movement. The woman in his dream possessed an open, easy sensuality. Did this woman? Placing his hands on his hips, he again watched for her reaction. Would she respond to his challenge?

Her eyes slanted as she met his gaze, and the corner of her mouth turned up in an amused smirk that said she was on to his game and was refusing to play.

He turned to the redhead, and as he gazed at her, he felt overwhelmed. He noticed the tattoo on her hand, but quickly pushed away the notion it somehow connected them just because it was similar to his. "Boaz Hamilton, you said?"

She nodded, smiling. "And this is my best friend and roommate, Angela Catherine Dawn."

Immense relief washed through him upon hearing he wasn't related to the woman. Angela Dawn. The name Angel in his dream was close enough to give him a premonitory thrill. The name Angel suited her, and an immediate image of an angel soaring toward the dawn flashed through his mind. He knew he would one day turn that image into bronze. He said to Boaz, "Did you say something about a letter?"

Looking bewildered the redhead took a seat on the sofa. "Jachin, you act like you don't know what I'm talking about. Didn't you get Aunt Marrion's envelope with the letter and the stone?"

He chose not to divulge how much the letter had disturbed him. "I get all kinds of weird letters. I just thought she was another nutcase. Besides I have a...situation to deal with." Dealing with a past that was best forgotten could wait until the media frenzy calmed down.

"I can't believe you didn't feel compelled to respond to Marrion's letter." She frowned then sighed heavily. "When I got mine, Angela and I immediately went to see her."

He shrugged. "As I said, I've got better things to do. Besides, what's the rush? Someone need a kidney?" Although it was said facetiously, he began to wonder if he might be close to the truth. These people obviously wanted something from him.

Boaz cocked her head. "Would you refuse?" Before he could respond, she said, "Did you know that you are a triplet?"

The notion he might have one sibling was enough to absorb for one day. Now she was telling him there was another? Triplets? Curiosity, along with a strange sense that she was telling the truth, made him ask, "Are you one of these triplets? Or are you just another sibling?"

"Yes, I'm one of the triplets, and as far as I know there are only the three of us. You, me, and a sister named Lilith." Then her chin dimpled in obvious distress. "She's been kidnapped."

He forced himself to remain calm. Although a sense of urgency came with the word kidnapped, he pushed it aside. What did she expect *him* to do about it?

"When was she kidnapped?"

"From what Marrion told us, Lilith was taken yesterday," Boaz replied.

"What are the police doing about it?" He looked from one woman to the other, the avoidance he saw in their eyes causing a sinking feeling. Surely they had called the police!

"The police can't help her," Boaz said, confirming his worst fear. "We're the only ones who can reach her."

Did they really expect to rescue a kidnap victim without police help? He knew his expression was incredulous. Who did these two think they were, Charlie's Angels?

"'We', as in …?"

The blonde spoke. "You and Boaz. The police won't be able to find her."

It took Jachin a moment to tear his gaze from Angela's as he remembered what her skin felt like. Hot satin. And now here she was no more than three feet away. The urge to breach the distance was overwhelming. He swallowed, his throat suddenly dry.

Now was not the time to concentrate on sexual fantasies. His supposed sister had been kidnapped, and his other supposed sister hadn't called the police but expected to handle the situation herself. Hadn't she watched television and the movies? Everyone knew the police were better equipped to handle kidnappings than amateurs.

Forcing his thoughts and gaze to Boaz, he suddenly realized that somewhere deep in his gut he recognized the truth that he was in some way connected to her. But, although they were both tall, that's where the physical resemblance ended. She was a fiery redhead with flashing blue, almost violet, eyes, while he was dark and with brown eyes. As full of light and life as she seemed, she was the complete antithesis of the darkness he knew resided in his soul. They couldn't possibly be related, let alone be triplets. Still, the psychic connection he felt with her was undeniable.

She *was* his sister. He knew that as well as he knew his own name.

After all the years of feeling alone in the world, it felt strange to realize that all along he'd had a sister—no, *two* sisters—in the world. Unexpectedly, his throat closed with emotion, but he quickly swallowed back the unwanted feelings as he felt a jolt of static electricity, the usual precursor to a spontaneous burst of power. Taking a deep breath, he forced himself to push away the feelings, all the while wondering if his sisters shared this particular curse. No matter what, both Boaz and Lilith would be better off without him and the danger he posed.

"Boaz, if it's ransom money you're after—"

"No!" Boaz broke in. "We don't need your money. We just need you."

"You need to call the police." Even as he said it, he knew that the police couldn't help. His instincts said that only his powers could help. But if his dark side surfaced, he could very well hurt the wrong people. He was tempted to ask Boaz if she had powers, too, but thought better of it. If she didn't, she might be even more insistent he help her, and he just couldn't risk it.

Boaz sat wringing her hands, visibly agitated. "There's so much to explain." Then she quickly got up and fled toward the balcony, saying as she went, "Angela, please tell him what's going on. I've got to get some air."

As Boaz disappeared out the sliding glass door, he crossed his arms, looking at Angela. Again, he remembered the feeling of her skin and recalled the way she'd moved beneath him in his dream. He wanted to go to her and sweep her into his arms and....

He cut off the thought and said, "Maybe I'd better sit down." He sat across from her where he could watch her lovely face as she spoke, but where he wouldn't be quite so tempted to touch her.

She shrugged as she looked toward the deck where Boaz stood. "Sometimes emotional energy builds up in Boaz and overwhelms her." She smiled. "She calls it EOD...Energy Overabundance Disorder. She'll be back in after she has a few minutes to meditate and calm herself."

That answered one question. Excess energy ran in the family. "What did she want you to tell me?"

She cleared her throat. "Well, it's like this ..." Her voice trailed off, and she bit her lip.

Jachin raised his eyebrows. Why didn't she just come out with it?

She started again, this time looking directly at him. "Jachin, do you have...well, special abilities?" She quickly added, "More than the obvious artistic ones, I mean."

He went on instant alert. He'd spent half his life guarding his secret, and he wasn't about to spill his guts to a stranger. After all, what did he really know about her? Nothing, except the fact she had the most disarming way of chewing her beautiful lower lip. With any other woman he might have found the movement calculated and an instant turn-off. But when *Angel* did it, it was provocative as hell.

He repeated her words. "Special...*abilities*?" Only he drew them out slowly, smiling as he let his gaze rake over her. "What did you have in mind?"

She blushed, her fresh, smooth skin taking on a sun-kissed appearance. It was charming, and he made a mental note to try to make her blush whenever possible. She ignored his innuendo, and sitting up a little straighter, she said, "Boaz has special gifts. Do you know anything about telepathy and telekinesis?"

Jachin felt his heart jump, but he maintained his posture of indifference. Was she saying Boaz had powers? He looked to the deck where Boaz stood looking out to sea, the wind buffeting her hair and her summer dress. She looked as at home in the elements as he'd always felt. "Yes, I know what they are." He decided not to jump to conclusions, to just let Angela finish.

"Well, um, do you have them?"

Sean's words from earlier in the day came back to him. He'd said Jachin was a wizard. Preposterous. The last thing Jachin wanted was that particular brand, especially now. It would only confirm the tabloid article.

"No, I don't," he said, deciding that was truthful enough. His powers were related to electricity and metals. He'd never read anyone's mind, nor psychically moved an object.

She looked crestfallen, and he was tempted to recant his denial. He softened his tone. "Why do you ask if I know about those psychic talents?"

Angela glanced toward the deck, then back to him, staring as if to study his reaction as she announced, "Boaz has those powers."

He fought to maintain his composure. Did this mean his other sister, Lilith, also had powers? Maybe his powers weren't anomalous after all. Maybe he wasn't really a freak of nature. He kept his voice emotionless, even though his heart raced. "Can she prove she has these...powers?"

The look Angela shot him was both censuring and filled with disappointment, but she got up and went to the door, asking Boaz to come in. Jachin watched her, enjoying the view of Angela's shapely bottom and the casual yet enticing way her hips swayed as she walked. She wore shorts and a tank top, leaving a fair amount of skin exposed, yet there was nothing overtly provocative in her attire or her movements. In fact, she seemed totally unaware of how sexy she was.

When Boaz came inside, he said, "I hear you have certain...abilities. Would you mind showing me what they are?" He wasn't about to reveal the fact that he had powers until he knew if Boaz was on the level. Even then he wasn't sure he would divulge the extent of his own talents.

Giving him a nervous glance she walked to a grouping of candles sitting on an end table. She leaned over the candles and gently blew. All six candles lit with a *poof.* Then she moved her hand in a circle over them and they began to rise off the table. They remained suspended in air for several moments. When she lowered her hand, the candles settled once again on the table.

Jachin was itching to find out if he could match her skill. It had never even occurred to him to try and make fire appear, or to move objects. He had focused all of his energy on turning clay to bronze. Could Boaz change metals, too? Keeping his tone flat he asked, "What else can you do?"

As he waited for her response he looked at Angela, who stood watching Boaz with rapt attention. She was biting her lip again, and he had a sudden urge to cross the room and stop the action by pressing his lips to hers. He wanted to discover if the feel and taste of her mouth would match those of his dream Angel.

Boaz's chuckle brought his attention back to her. She said, "You want to know what else I can do? I can read your mind. I know you wish you could...," she paused and looked at Angela, "...stop Angela from biting her lip." She crossed her arms and smiled knowingly.

She'd read his mind! He not only felt violated, but fear snaked through him. Could she see who—or *what*—he really was? The thought that she might be able to unsettled him in a way nothing else ever had. If she was able to see the darkness within him, she would have no other option but to reject him. He didn't think he could handle that.

"You have no problem intruding on people's private thoughts?" he asked, his voice cold and resentful.

"I only did it because you asked what else I could do," she replied, her tone defensive. "I'm not into voyeurism...of any kind, and I don't don't go around reading people's thoughts. I'm sorry if I offended you."

He shrugged away her apology. "What else can you do?"

Boaz's shoulders stiffened, and her chin went up a belligerent notch. "Brother or not, Jachin, I'm not here to entertain you. I'm not a carnival act." She took a deep breath and said,   "My turn. Can you read minds and move objects?"

"No."

She shoulders sagged in defeat. "Then you don't have any special powers?"

He sighed, exasperated. Whatever bond they shared, it was powerful enough to make him care about upsetting her, because he felt compelled to confess,   "Yes, I do. They just aren't the same as yours."

Her face brightened, and she walked across the room to take hold of his arm in a gesture of appeal. "Please, Jachin, this is really important to me. Tell me what you can do."

He glanced at Angela, whose eyes were wide in anticipation. But he was still having trouble disarming the defense mechanisms he'd so carefully put in place. However, the pleading look in Boaz's eyes and the warm feeling of connection that came from her hand resting on his arm stirred something inside him. His self-protective armor began to chafe with confinement, and he realized he wanted to believe his secret was safe with his sister and the beautiful *Angel*.

Still, he hesitated before he finally admitted, "I can control electricity, and I can change metals."

He'd finally said it aloud. He'd never before said the actual words, not even to his parents, who'd made it clear they didn't want to know. And after so many years of silence, it felt oddly liberating to have it out in the open. The silly notion that he was "outed" made him want to laugh, but he restrained himself.

Tears sprang to his sister's eyes, and Jachin instinctively put his hand over hers. She instantly stepped away, quickly brushing away the moisture on her cheeks

"What's wrong?" he asked, wondering at her sudden distress.

Boaz glanced nervously at Angela, then back to Jachin. "It's just that my tears...well, they can sometimes—"

"Your tears have the ability to burn skin. Certain people's skin anyway," he finished for her. One more thing they had in common, and one more thing about himself that suddenly wasn't so weird.

Boaz nodded. "You, too?"

Although Jachin hadn't cried since he was a child, he remembered well how his tears had once burned his father's skin. The incident had been life changing. At that moment Jachin had known for certain what, until then, he'd only suspected. His father didn't like him. Much to his mother's chagrin, she'd discovered early on that his tears had the ability to burn some people's skin. It was several years later, however, that he'd realized they only burned those people who didn't like him or were inherently bad. He knew his father wasn't a bad person, so when his tears had burned him, he'd understood that his father simply didn't like him. Much later Jachin had learned that his mother had coerced her husband into adopting. And though he made every effort to be a good father, he was never truly able to accept Jachin and his strange ways.

He looked at his sister. "Did you think your tears would burn me?"

She looked startled. "Do your tears burn people?"

"Only some people," he confessed. "So, did you think your tears would burn me?"

"No, it was just a reflex. They only burn people who don't like me or who are inherently bad souls. You're my brother—my triplet—so I know you don't fall into either category."

Jachin knew she might be wrong and her tears might very well burn him, but he wasn't about to put his theory to the test. The darkness within him needed no confirmation. He knew it was real.

Boaz stepped toward him, again putting her hand on his arm. "Jachin, you must help me rescue Lilith."

He sighed. "I'm afraid you've come to the wrong place for help, Boaz. The tabloids have declared me the freak of the hour. I can't leave my house without being mobbed. But I will call the police and make sure everything possible is done to find her."

She glanced at Angela before she said, "You may change your mind after you hear what I have to say. Maybe you should sit down."

He heard the uncomfortable echo of Sean's earlier words, and he was sure he wasn't going to like what she was had to say.

They all sat down again.

Twenty minutes later, all Jachin could do was shake his head in denial. Boaz's outrageous explanation about the *Otherworld* and their heritage was unbelievable. "You can't be serious. You can't possibly believe we're wizards." He ran his hand through his hair, taking out the band at the back of his neck, freeing his hair. "Boaz, listen to me. We may have unusual abilities that set us apart from most of the world, but that doesn't mean we come from a race of wizards. No alternative universe, or whatever you want to call it, exists. It's a myth. Surely you must realize that. And a divine prophecy? That's pure cult propaganda."

But even as he spoke, he could see by her expression that she did believe everything she'd told him.

"Think about it Jachin," she said. "Marrion told me she connected with all of us through our dreams, so I know you've been having them, too. Marrion said they're called 'glimmer dreams,' and they're more like memories. Sometimes they're even premonitions. Think about it, Jachin. The place you're dreaming about —that I'm sure all three of us have been dreaming about— is real. We have to go there to find Lilith. Then, together, we can face the dark force Marrion told me about."

Jachin studied her, feeling frustrated. Didn't she know how foolish she sounded? But what if she was right? He looked toward Angela. What if he and she really were destined to become lovers? He rejected the thought that his dream of Angela might be a premonition of their future.

"I say we phone the police and give them all the information you have about Lilith's disappearance and let them handle it. They're trained to handle this kind of thing."

"And what do you think you should tell them?" Angela asked, sparks of defiance in her eyes. "That some dark lord of the

Otherworld kidnapped your sister, and they'll need to go to Sena to find her?"

Jachin's temper surfaced. What did these women expect from him? Even if he did believe in this Otherworld, he couldn't just disappear and leave the whole media mess for Mildred to handle. He felt his frustration and anger beginning to take hold, and the last thing he wanted was for Boaz and Angela to see the result of his uncontrolled powers.

Taking a deep breath, he said, "Listen, Boaz, I want to help, but I'm not Rambo. If you're not willing to call the police, I don't see what I can do." He stood up. "Why don't you come back tomorrow? Let me think about this tonight and see if I can come up with something that will satisfy us both." By tomorrow he would have a chance to work off some of his rogue energy.

He would need to sneak into his studio tonight to get some supplies in order to set up a temporary studio here at home since he couldn't chance going to the studio during daylight hours until the media gave up. Although Mildred would be happy to bring him supplies, he also wanted to take another look at *The Dance* now that he'd seen two of the subjects in the flesh.

Boaz again swiped at tears. "How can I make you understand how important—and urgent—this is?"

He walked them to the door, repressing the thought of the unknown Lilith being held against her will by some unknown entity. "I'm sorry, Boaz. When you're ready to let the authorities handle this, I'll do whatever I can."

Boaz looked frustrated, but she placed a kiss on his cheek before she walked through the door, saying, "I'll see you tomorrow, and I know that by then you'll see the light."

Angela shook her head as she stood at the door and frowned at him. "You're making a mistake, Jachin. You know in your heart she's telling you the truth. I can see it in your eyes."

His breath stilled in his chest. At that moment Angela wore the exact expression as she wore in *The Dance*. It was a look that said she knew and understood that he waged an inner battle, yet she begged him to trust her.

"Good night, Angela," he said, refusing to let himself give in to her. *The Dance* was just a sculpture, a figment of his imagination. If this woman knew the real truth about him, she'd run out of here so fast she'd be no more than a blur.

With one last penetrating look, she turned and followed Boaz without saying another word.

Goodnight, *Angel,* Jachin silently said to her retreating back, and then he shut the heavy wooden door and shot the bolt home.

Striding to his CD player, he punched the button, cranking up the volume loud enough to allow the thrumming, metallic sound of rock and roll to drown out his conflicting thoughts. If what his sister said was true and he *was* some kind of wizard, it would only confirm what he dreaded most. Dark, destructive forces were at work within him.

If Boaz and Angela were looking for a hero to help them save the day, they'd come to the wrong man. There was no way he could help them, because he'd end up destroying them all.

FOUR

Saturn: The teacher. Testing one's fears and limitations.

Jachin waited until two in the morning to chance walking to his workshop. The galleries and stores along the way would be closed, and all but a few tourists ensconced in their motels. The reporters and misdirected devotees would have given up for the night and slithered away. Even snakes needed rest.

A light fog made him feel more like a shadow than a person. Still, he took unlit side streets, avoiding the town's main street.

As he let himself into his darkened gallery, beams from a passing car arched bands of light across the walls. The numerous bronze figures seemed to dance around the room as shadows and light changed places. The illusion evaporated as the car passed, the statues resuming their frozen poses.

Afraid that some diehard reporter or paparazzo might still be around, Jachin didn't chance turning on the gallery's subdued recessed lighting. Instead he waited until he was behind the closed doors of his windowless workshop to strike a match to one of the lanterns. Taking off his coat, he rolled up his sleeves, anxious to get to work to relieve the repressed energy.

But first he wanted to check something. He slid the covering off *The Dance* to study the faces of the women, comparing them to Angela and Boaz.

A far-away scent of vanilla brushed past Jachin, reminding of his last meeting with Sean.

And just as that thought formed in his mind, a voice said from behind him, "You've captured their souls, have you not, Jachin?"

This time Sean's abrupt appearance did startle Jachin, causing his pent-up energy to leap out of control. The alarm in a nearby building went off.

He spun around to face his intruder. "What the hell are you doing here? And how did you get in?"

Sean sat on a worktable, studying Jachin. "Almost magical, isn't it?" He ignored Jachin's question and nodded toward *The*

Dance.

Jachin felt tension build. He'd had his privacy invaded once too often in the past twenty-four hours. "You need to leave before—"

"Before what?" Sean interrupted. "Before you accidentally hurt me? You can't, you know. Accidentally anyway. I have certain powers, too, and I've learned how to deflect rogue energy."

Jachin stared in confusion at the man. Until now, no one in his life had had unusual powers, and now it had suddenly become the norm. What next? Would Mildred announce she could fly?

"You don't believe me?" Sean blithely pointed to the drape Jachin had just removed from *The Dance*, and the piece of cloth neatly rose in the air, folded itself into a rectangle and then settled on the table next to Jachin.

"Jachin," Sean said, "quit trying to rationalize away what's happening. It won't work. Why do you insist on believing you're the only one in existence with powers? There are many of us."

Jachin ran his hand through his hair, not sure he wanted to believe what he'd just seen yet knowing it had to be real. If Sean had known all along about Jachin's powers, why had he hidden his own powers from Jachin until now? "So, who are you...no, *what* are you? And what do you want from me?"

Sean got up and walked slowly around the studio. Jachin was amazed to see Sean begin to shrink. When he metamorphosed into an old woman, Jachin gasped in shock.

"My dear boy," the grandmotherly woman said, "just like you, I am a white wizard. All wizards have magical powers. The magic differs from wizard to wizard. Each individual possesses specialties, but we all have the power of the eternal force. Why is it so difficult to believe, given your own abilities?"

Then the woman morphed into a man in overalls, his face lined and weathered. "I have been waiting for you to reach the age of wizard maturity. Now is the time, my boy, to embrace your powers...to sharpen them. Your sister Lilith needs you. All of white wizardom is expecting you to take your rightful place."

Jachin found his tongue, the calm strength of his voice surprising him. "*White* wizardom? As opposed to—?"

The man put his hand in the pocket of his overalls, rocking back and forth on the heels of his work boots. "Dark wizardom, of course. Those who have chosen to draw their power from the dark forces of the universe. They use their magic to dominate through chaos, and in doing so seize the powers of those they have conquered. Whereas white wizards use their powers synergistically, to maintain balance in the universe."

So where did that leave Jachin? He certainly didn't consider his power to create bronze sculpture to be synergistic. Had the tabloid been closer to the truth than he'd thought? Did he draw his power from the dark forces? Was he, as the reporter had said, "in league with the devil?" Or, more appropriately, with Sean's dark wizards? He could remember several instances when he was young and had drawn upon his anger for the power. The experience had been both terrifying and thrilling.

When Sean shifted back to his normal appearance—or at least into the familiar body that Jachin recognized—Jachin felt a calm acceptance. It was as if some instinctual knowledge assured him that everything Sean told him was true. He, Jachin Morgan, belonged to a race of wizards .

Sean broke into his thoughts, saying, "Jachin, we have work to do. You have much to learn, and time is of the essence. You must find Lilith and accept the larger quest. The Dark One must be faced."

"The Dark One? Who the hell is 'The Dark One?'"

"The leader and most powerful of the dark wizards, Kadien. You must face him and fulfill the prophecy. You must defeat The Dark One and save us all."

"What if I don't want to?" The real question was, *what if he couldn't?* As far as wizards went, Sean had just given him plenty of evidence to show he wasn't all that gifted. How was he supposed to stand up to a powerful wizard who'd had a lifetime to hone his skills?

"If you don't go to Sena, our island home, then Kadien will come into your world to challenge you."

"Let him."

"Jachin." Sean walked toward him. "The Dark Lord already works from our world in Sena to control the will of this world's weaker beings. This is evidenced by the growing chaos...the wars, the divided peoples. If Kadien were to actually come into your world, many more would succumb to this evil. And if that isn't enough to make you see reason, then consider this. Kadien will focus his powers against those you love. He will use them to control you."

Love? Jachin almost laughed, but he knew it would be a bitter laugh. If Kadien had to have someone Jachin loved to control him, then both he and the world were safe. The steady stream of women Jachin let share his bed, he never allowed close enough to entertain the possibility of love. His adoptive mother, the only person he'd ever truly loved, had died a long time ago. And with her went the last person on Earth who cared one ounce about what happened to him.

"How do you know my powers aren't those of a dark wizard?" he asked. He shut his mind to the image of his father's accusing eyes and the hint of fear he had sensed in the man whose approval had once meant so much.

When Sean didn't answer, he said, "What if I can't control my powers? What if I do go on this...quest, or whatever you want to call it, and I can't control my own dark side." Strangely enough it felt good to voice the question he wrestled with on a daily basis. Could Sean assure him that, once released, Jachin's dark side wouldn't consume him?

"Only you can answer those questions, Jachin, but I know that your mother was goodness personified, and her blood runs in your veins."

Anger and frustration surfaced with Sean's reference to his birth mother. And the feelings weren't associated with goodness. Maybe the blood running through his veins wasn't that good. Did a woman who was 'goodness personified' abandon her children?

Maybe he and his mother had more in common than Sean realized. Maybe she had fought the same demons as Jachin and, like him, had only managed to fool those around her. And if his heritage was that of darkness, he didn't have a hope in hell of ever conquering his dark side. He was born to it.

Was that the conclusion his mother had come to so many years ago? He felt the first stirrings of compassion for the woman he had hated all these years. Maybe she had given up her children to save them from her own dark side.

"You've got the wrong wizard, Sean. Do it yourself. You obviously have greater powers."

"No, I don't," Sean said. "The force deep within you has been untapped in this world of the unenlightened. Once you reach

Sena, all will be revealed to you, and you will gain the full measure of your power."

Jachin opened his mouth to object, but Sean said, "You must fulfill your destiny. The future of mankind rests in your hands."

He said, "Isn't that a little dramatic? I'm no messiah."

Sean's smile was enigmatic. "We all have our parts to play in the balance between light and dark. Your part was ordained before you were born."

"Are you saying I don't have a choice?" The man couldn't be serious.

"You have a choice," Sean said. "Wizardom, white and dark alike, are based on free will."

FIVE

Oestarra: Spring. Plans are put into effect. Perseverance over obstacles.

Jachin stood in his small home-workshop and worked the clay, the face before him quickly taking form. All afternoon he'd been experiencing an unexplained feeling of loss so great that the only way to assuage the pain was to work. He had no idea what had caused the strange feeling. All he knew was that a gnawing emptiness had tunneled deep into his gut. He wondered if it could be a strong prophetic warning that something had happened to Boaz or Lilith. But since he hadn't bothered to find out where Boaz and Angela were staying, and his attempts to telepathically connect with Boaz had failed, he had no way to contact her.

As he held the clay face in his hands and stroked his thumbs across the ridges of the woman's high cheeks, he could almost feel a bone structure beneath, almost feel the taught resilience of live skin. It made him feel as if when he completed the finishing touches, the woman—Angela—would open her eyes and look at him.

Concentrating on Angela's face somehow mellowed the tightness in his chest.

An hour later he completed the sculpting part of the work. It was an intricate piece that would normally have taken hours to form, but it had practically emerged from the clay of its own free will. Now he could spend some of the pent-up energy he'd been harboring for the last two days.

He stood away from the form, raised his arms upward and closed his eyes, focusing to gather the power. A vibrating hum surrounded him as he concentrated on visualizing the sculpture in bronze, asking the elements to come together to transform the clay. When small electric jolts raced through his arms and he felt the energy begin to swirl within him, he knew it was almost time. A high-pitched whine blocked out all other sound as the force gathered. His senses heightened to the point of pain, but still he concentrated on gathering energy to his core.

With great effort he opened his eyes and slowly walked toward the sculpture, taking with him the swirling red ball of concentrated energy. Then he focused on moving the circle of light from his body into the image on the table, holding his hands over it to contain the power. The resulting electric arcs snapped and hummed wildly. Each Jacob's ladder of lightning that emanated from his fingertips struck the sculpture and was then absorbed into it.

The clay began to transform, the malleable surface hardening as the force within him extracted the needed elements from the surrounding atmosphere. As the hum slowed and the crackling became more infrequent, the sculpture finished its transformation, turning from clay to burnished bronze.

Jachin felt the last of the energy leave his fingertips, and he stumbled back, physically drained yet spiritually exhilarated. Soaked with sweat, he leaned heavily on the desk at the side of the room and fought to catch his breath while he studied his handiwork. It was perfection. But then, so was his subject. He knew that this, at least, had been created with the purest of positive energy. And that thought gave him hope that his soul couldn't be all darkness.

The sound of the doorbell made him swear, and he quickly grabbed a nearby towel and wiped his sweat-drenched face and clay-stained hands. He breathed deeply, trying to regain his composure as he made his way to the door. Stripping off his soaking shirt and tossing it across a chair, he slung the towel around his neck. Who could have breached his security gates?

A quick glance at his security camera's screen showed Boaz and Angela standing at his door. Relieved they were both safe and that his feeling of doom had nothing to do with them, he opened the door.

By the look on the two women's faces he knew he must look dreadful. That was confirmed when Boaz asked, "Are you okay?"

A normal energy level was returning, but he could feel the muscles in his arms twitch with exhaustion. "I'm fine. Come in," he reluctantly added. He didn't mean to sound inhospitable, but after using his energies to create, he always felt vulnerable and weak until his strength returned. And until it did, he didn't want to be around anyone, let alone Angela or Boaz, both of whom triggered unwanted emotions and reactions he wasn't sure he could control while his defenses were down.

Jachin noticed that Angela's gaze was focused on his chest, and he felt desire spark within him. He smiled inwardly at the acknowledgement that not *all* of his energy had been depleted. The small dimple that came with Angela's repressed smile was a thousand times more enticing than the one he'd carefully placed on her likeness. Although both the bronze representations of her were lifelike, they had no hope of ever doing her justice. The real *Angel* was flesh and blood, with lips that could respond with passion to his kisses, and hands that could roam over his body, driving him wild with anticipation. More than that, the real woman had the eyes of his dream woman. But could the flesh and blood woman look into his soul like her dream counterpart and accept what she saw there?

He reined in the wayward thoughts, knowing that he would have to placate himself with her image because any kind of emotional relationship was out of the question. He'd committed emotional suicide with Tilly. He wasn't about to make the same mistake twice. And where he'd felt no remorse at allowing himself to surrender to Tilly's morally unprincipled charms or saddling her with his demons, he instinctively knew his dark side could destroy a sensitive woman like Angela. She moved with strength and self-confidence. Yet how could she possibly be a match for his dark side?

Once they were seated in his living room, Boaz said, "Jachin, please reconsider. We need you to go with us to Sena."

He folded his arms across his chest. "I don't believe there is a *Sena*, or any other kind of wizard world. So I think you're both going to be disappointed."

Angela said, "We met Sean Scot this morning. He confirmed everything your aunt told us."

Jachin arched an eyebrow. "And how do you know they're not from the same loony bin?"

Boaz kicked off her sandals and crossed her legs beneath her on the leather sofa. "I don't get it. Why are you so reluctant to believe in where we come from? I feel in my heart...no, not just my heart. I believe with every ounce of my being that what Marrion and Sean told me about our heritage is true. The dreams I've had are of my home...our home, Jachin." Her eyes took on a challenging glare. "I dare you to look at me and tell me you don't feel it."

Her childish dare was so sibling-like, Jachin almost laughed. He stood and walked over to where she sat. He leaned down, braced his arms against the sofa and looked her straight in the eye. It was easy enough to tap into his dark side for the lie. "I don't feel it."

A slow smile brightened her face. "You forget, I can read minds." She smiled in triumph. "And I don't believe you."

He had to hand it to her. She was determined. And part of him was curious. Just how did they hope to get to this supposed parallel universe? He straightened, folding his arms across his chest to look at both women. "I'll make a deal."

"What kind of deal?" they said unison, and a pleased look passed between them.

"I'll go with you when you *attempt* your journey. But only if you agree to call the police about Lilith's disappearance once you discover there is no *Otherworld*." He was ninety-nine percent sure he would be proven right.

The moment Boaz jumped from the sofa he knew he was going to be attacked with another embrace. She flung her arms around him, and he let himself be hugged. He was surprised by how good it felt.

"Jachin, thank you. I know you won't regret this." She backed away. "We're leaving tonight."

He corrected, "We're calling the police tonight." He seated himself and spent several opportune moments observing and fantasizing about Angela's soft lips. He came to the conclusion that he should discipline himself to think of her only in terms of physical pleasure and forget the unwanted emotional considerations.

"Precisely when and where is this transportation, or whatever, supposed to take place?" he absently asked Boaz.

Angela's heated blush made him wonder if she could read minds, too. Just in case, he let his mind wander deeper into the fantasy, all the time watching for her reaction. In his mind he placed one soft, teasing kiss on the corner of her upturned mouth, then moved to her delicate chin, going on to trail slow kisses down her arched neck, the end destination evident. As he watched Angela's embarrassment at being so blatantly scrutinized turn into what almost looked like a challenge, his body responded with a burning heat.

"Jachin!" Boaz said, bringing his fantasy up short. She snapped her fingers. "Yoo-hoo, over here. Did you even hear what I was saying?"

He frowned at the interruption. "What?"

Boaz gave him a knowing smile. "If you can, for just a moment, break the spell Angela seems to have over you...I was telling you that Marrion gave us some rules for Sena."

He gave her a dubious look. "What kind of rules?" He looked back to Angela, in no way having had his fill.

Boaz chuckled. "Angela, maybe you'd better tell him. I can't keep his attention."

Angela swallowed, her smile tremulous, as though struggling to recover from his imaginary kisses. She said, "Marrion told us that in order to keep the atmosphere on Sena pure, you must be careful not to take with you any kind of pollutants. Synthetic materials and electric devices are considered pollutants, and are banned from Sena."

Jachin felt his mouth quirk in a derisive smile, but he decided not to say anything snide. Soon enough he would be proven correct, and whether or not synthetic substances posed a threat to the mythical Sena would be moot. "Go on."

"Marrion explained that the environmental energy in Sena is in perfect balance." Angela's eyebrows dipped in concentration. "When someone or something 'borrows' energy from someone or something else, the total energy remains constant. But the molecular structure of synthetic substances interact negatively on both a small and large, long-term scale with Sena's energy. They take, but they don't give back." She blinked. "Does that make sense to you?"

Jachin shrugged noncommittally. He had no idea what she was talking about. She'd lost him when her eyebrows had quirked so charmingly with her intense concentration. The only thing he'd been aware of from that point was that her face was an artist's canvas, her changing emotions a study in honesty. He had the feeling Angela was one of those rare, guileless women who were incapable of telling a lie with a straight face, even if their life depended upon it.

"Does it make sense to *you?*" he asked.

At first Angela looked taken aback, then her expression turned to one of resignation as she shrugged. "I have to admit, I may be putting my faith in the existence of Sena simply because I want it to be real. But the certainty of your magic can't be denied, and logic tells me there must be a source. Because of that, I've come to believe what Marrion and Sean have told us. I know in my heart they were telling the truth. I try to trust my heart. It hasn't let me down yet."

He could tell by her expression that she not only believed in Sena but that he and Boaz were wizards. And he had to allow that something about the whole concept did touch a chord of truth deep inside him. It was as if he had at some place and time experienced Sena and its people. But that could simply be because Sena's description was so much like the place in his recent dreams.

"I haven't yet acknowledged any magic," he said. "The abilities Boaz and I have aren't unheard of in certain scientific circles."

He didn't believe a word he was saying. He'd never heard of anyone being able to transform clay into bronze or change the characteristics of metals. Or light candles with a breath. Except in fairy tales. But that didn't change the fact that he couldn't bring himself to accept an association with mythical people. When he'd been young, he'd often fantasized about his heritage. But the fantasies were limited to whether his dark looks denoted Italian, Spanish or Native American ancestry. His mind never wandered to the possibility that his roots were planted in another world.

Boaz shook her head. "Jachin, you could take a lesson from Angela. Try listening with your heart as well as your reason. The paradigm you and I have been raised with simply isn't true for us. It never has been, has it? We are not like the people we've been trying...and failing...to identify with. And that's not a bad thing. I don't know about you, but it makes me feel like I truly belong to someone, or to a people anyway, for the first time in my life. For me it's validating. I can say it out loud. I'm a white wizard. I'm good. My powers are good. Doesn't that feel liberating to you, too?"

Hell, no, he thought. If indeed he was a wizard, then he wasn't the white wizard Boaz was talking about. The darkness within him, which at times he only barely managed to contain, made him more like the wizard who had supposedly kidnapped Lilith.

He'd heard of 'good' and 'evil' twins. Why couldn't it work with triplets? Had he inherited all the darkness, while his sisters received goodness and light? Would his fears be born out if he tried to go with Boaz to Sena and they actually ended up in the Otherworld? If his powers were tested, would he fail? Would the dark power within him surface when he was needed most? There was a real possibility that instead of helping, he might ultimately destroy those who needed him. Even he didn't know the extent of the whirling vortex of darkness within him. He'd never allowed it to be tested because he was sure he wouldn't like the outcome.

Jachin looked at Boaz. "Like I said, I'll be with you when you try to cross over to Sena. But only to prove no such place exists."

Both women nodded reluctantly.

Boaz studied him. "Jachin, don't you want to find out who our birth parents are?"

He didn't have to think twice about his answer. "No. I accept that they didn't want us."

Boaz raised an eyebrow, saying derisively, "No issues to deal with, huh?"

"None." His voice was emotionless, just like he felt. Why should he care about people who hadn't wanted him or his sisters? He hadn't had the warmest upbringing, and by no stretch of the imagination did he consider himself 'family man' material. But even ' e couldn't comprehend how a mother could abandon her newborns to strangers when, as Boaz had said, there was a whole community of wizards who would have loved and cared for them. And to intentionally split up triplets—children who had shared the same womb—was downright heartless. "As far as I'm concerned, things turned out just fine."

"I had a good life, too," Boaz said. "But I need to know about my birth family."

"I don't." He wasn't about to tell her about his life. What purpose would it serve?

Angela noticed that the tension between Boaz and Jachin zoomed around the room like an electrified ping-pong ball as they discussed their adoptions, yet their conversation remained constrained. Angela could only guess that her presence was the cause. Deciding to give them time to talk alone, she said, "Sorry to interrupt, but may I use your restroom?"

Jachin never took his challenging gaze from his sister. He only nodded toward the hallway. "Help yourself."

Angela got up and padded in the direction he'd indicated, the immediate rise of Boaz and Jachin's agitated voices confirming her suspicion.

She peeked into the first room she came to, realizing it wasn't a bathroom, but some kind of a combination office and workroom. What she saw there caused her to stop dead in her tracks and a thrill to zing up her spine. In the center of the room stood a table draped in a tarp. And on the table sat a bronze bust. But it wasn't just any bust. She was staring at an uncanny replica of her own face.

The statue stared back as if to say, "Crazy, huh?"

"Loony toons," she whispered. She'd only met Jachin yesterday. How could he possibly have had time to do this piece? What she knew of the foundry process involved in making bronze sculptures told her this was impossible. The complicated process required hours of touch-up work even once the bronze molding was completed. How had Jachin accomplished this? The only conclusion she could come up with was that his power over metal was more extensive than she'd assumed.

Walking around the piece, she took in the details, suddenly not so sure she was the sculpture's subject. Scrutinizing the face, she couldn't find any distinct differences between her and the statue, but the woman before her was beautiful. She, on the other hand, knew the best adjective to describe herself, even with her new, sexy hair, was unremarkable.

What was it about the statue that made it look so different? Was this how Jachin saw her? Or had he taken the plain, uninteresting Angela Catherine Dawn, erased her flaws and turned her into the perfect woman? Was that Jachin Morgan's gift, to turn the mundane into perfection?

Typical man, she thought. Don't accept the flesh-and-blood woman for who she is, flaws and all, but instead turn her into a bronze image of idealized perfection. Didn't men know that with flaws came character? Sure the statue was gorgeous, but it wasn't her. He obviously didn't look for character in his women. He only created what he wanted to see.

She felt like she'd been complimented and slapped at the same time, and she didn't know which emotion to respond to, if and when she gathered the nerve to return to the living room. She decided that for the time being it would be best not indicate that she'd seen the statue. With what she was feeling, she wasn't sure she could contain her emotions. Knowing herself as she did, she was pretty sure any intense emotion directed toward Jachin could easily end up channeling into the incredible attraction she felt for him. And, from the moment she'd met the man, she'd had an unsettling need to kiss him to see if his lips fit over hers as perfectly as they had in her dream.

Once Angela could tear her gaze from the statue, she made an unnecessary trip to the restroom. She wanted to give Jachin and Boaz as much time alone as possible to debate their opinions about their adoption. While Boaz seemed more inclined to accept that her birth mother had a reason, Jachin seemed convinced that their mother was heartless.

Angela wasn't about to put in her two cents. Boaz already knew her opinion about adoption, and she was sure Jachin didn't care that she thought it was the ultimate selfless act. If someone couldn't, for whatever reasons, take care of her child, then giving it to a good home was an act of love. Sometimes Angela had wondered why her own parents hadn't made that decision instead of pawning her off on an already overcrowded family of cousins.

Upon entering the living room she was pleased to see that the tension between Boaz and Jachin had vanished. From what Boaz was saying about her bookstore, they'd obviously declared a truce and were catching up on each other's lives. As unobtrusively as possible, she headed for a far chair in the u-shaped seating arrangement.

Jachin's gaze broke from his sister's as Angela seated herself. If she hadn't already been seated, the look he gave her would have made her knees buckle. She hoped her smile wasn't as revealing about her reaction to him as it felt. No doubt about it, Jachin Morgan's media reputation as a lady-killer was well earned. His gaze was lethal, and she was certain the word *charisma* had been invented for him. She was pretty sure any woman, regardless of age or marital status, would be willing to sell her soul for the look she was receiving at that moment. It was a sensual look that said she was desirable, beautiful, and that he couldn't keep his eyes off her. She assumed Jachin's innate sexuality made him appraise every woman as a possible conquest. But knowing that didn't lessen the effect. With this man, she would have to stay on guard.

When Boaz got up, Angela realized her staring match with Jachin was rude. But Boaz's breezy, "I'm going for a run along the beach to work off some energy. Anyone want to come?" indicated she hadn't taken offence. In fact, her question about them joining her sounded like a tease.

Jachin shook his head. "Unless the vultures have gone, I wouldn't stand a chance of having a peaceful run. But you go ahead. Angela will keep me company."

She would? Angela had been about to get up and join Boaz, but the opportunity to talk to Jachin alone was too good to pass up. Still unnerved by the likeness of her that he had created, her curiosity won out. She was dying to question him about the piece.

"I'll wait here for you," she told Boaz, while her mind shouted, *Don't be a dope! Run!* But she ignored the warning. For heaven's sake, she'd had enough experience fending off unwanted advances not to feel threatened by Jachin's mere presence. And she hadn't made it this far with her virtue intact to let a womanizer like Jachin Morgan become her undoing. *Right? Right!*

"Okay," Boaz said, snapping her sport pack around her waist and retying her running shoes. "I'll pick up dinner on the way back."

"That would be great," Jachin said, turning his gaze back to Angela. His eyes were so wolflike she had the ridiculous feeling she'd just turned into Little Red Riding Hood.

Once Boaz was gone, the silence in the room felt like a vacuum. Jachin still looked at her like he could eat her alive. As she felt a hot blush creep up her neck, she decided maybe staying hadn't been such a good idea after all. And maybe she wasn't as brave as she'd thought. She half expected him to come over, pick her up and haul her off to his bed. Visions of them together mingled with memories of her vivid dream, and her blush intensified.

Hoping that the bright sunshine and sound of the crashing waves might snap her out of her fantasies, she jumped up and headed for the deck. "You don't mind, do you?"

Jachin's imposing presence behind her was a force she could feel without turning around. "You don't have to be afraid of me, Angel." His voice was deep, with a resonance that touched some deep pleasure center of her brain, causing her to want more.

She seated herself in a deck chair and looked at Jachin, who stood beside her, blocking the sun's glare. "I'm not afraid of you."

Her voice held conviction, and she realized the reason was because she wasn't afraid of Jachin. What she feared was something she'd always feared—her ability to think rationally once her desire was ignited. And, man-oh-man, was it ever ignited! She wasn't even going to correct his mistakenly calling her Angel. Had he meant it as an endearment, or had he already forgotten that her name was Angela? Her common sense said it was the latter.

He took a seat across from her, leaning back and closing his eyes to take a deep breath. He seemed to be relaxed and was obviously enjoying the sunshine, which bathed his already tan face, chest and legs. Chagrined, she acknowledged that the concerns she'd had about his desire to ravage her had been pure fantasy. No doubt the crazy dream she'd had about him, which gave her a sense of already having a physical and emotional relationship with him, was contributing to her instantaneous attraction. It was a responde that made her feel uncomfortably.. ...comfortable with him. Unfamiliar, yet somehow familiar. She wanted in the worst way to reach out to him as she had in her dream and touch the angle of his jaw, to feel the sharp stubble shadowing his chin. Instead she folded her hands in her lap.

His voice possessed a drowsy rumble as he said, "I'm glad you're not afraid of me. I want us to be ...," he hesitated then emphasized the word, "*friends.*"

Did this man's every word and glance have a double meaning? Or was she reading her own desires into his words and actions? She surprised herself by calmly responding, "I'd like that. And I'm sure Boaz would, too."

Thinking this wasn't going so badly after all, she decided to appease her curiosity. "Jachin, I took a wrong turn on my way to the restroom, and I couldn't help noticing a sculpture that looks ...." She couldn't finish the sentence. Suddenly, the very idea that Jachin Morgan, the famous artist, might have created something so beautiful with her in mind became just one more dream-induced delusion.

Jachin's eyes remained closed as he smiled and said, "That looks like you?" He put his feet on the railing, crossing his long, bronzed legs at the ankles. "It is you."

She shook her head, thrilled at the possibility, yet still doubtful. "But how is that possible?"

He opened one eye to look at her for a moment. Then with a

flourish of his hands he said, "Magic."

"Really?" She hadn't meant to sound doubtful. She'd already accepted the fact that extraordinary powers existed.

His chuckle was deep as he opened both eyes. "No. I was teasing." Then he grew serious. "You can call my abilities whatever you want, but I've never considered my work to be magic. The actual sculpting I do with my hands...and my heart." His look intensified, and she had the uncanny feeling he could see into her soul. "Transforming the clay into bronze is...a gift from the elements. But magic? No."

The sensuous way he stared at her caused a thrill to zing its way throughout her entire body, awakening every nerve ending. She swallowed around a suddenly dry throat. "How is it a gift?"

He hesitated for so long she began to wonder whether he would answer her. Then he said, "It's a matter of concentrating my own energy and then *asking* the clay to become bronze." She watched his mouth as he talked, fascinated by his lips and his perfect teeth.

The canvas chair beneath her irritated her suddenly over-sensitized bare legs, and her skin became prickly and uncomfortable. Had the mild afternoon suddenly turned airless and hot with an impending storm? She felt perspiration break out across the bridge of her nose even as her glance verified the cloudless sky, and she could feel a cool breeze waft across her skin. She said, "You 'ask,' the clay?"

Jachin squinted as if considering her question, and she got the feeling he'd never really thought about it before. Then he shrugged as he spread his hands out toward the beach. "I ask the air...the earth...everything around me. The universe, I guess. I suppose that includes the clay too."

"And it just *happens*?"

He nodded.

"How long have you been able to do this?"

The corner of his mouth drew up in a partial smile. "Just full of questions, aren't you?"

She shrugged. He seemed more amused than put off, so she further indulged her curiosity. "How long?"

"Although it's a bit after the fact, I want you to swear to me you're not associated with any newspaper or tabloid."

"I swear, Jachin. In all the years I've know Boaz, I've never told another living soul about her abilities."

Jachin roared with laughter, and Angela realized she had her hand up in the sign of the Scout oath.

"Okay, put your hand down." He was still chuckling. "To answer your question...from as far back as I can remember I've had some powers, but when I was small they were mostly spontaneous. I began experiencing controllable powers when I was around twelve. The older I got, the more I could do. I experimented and found that I could change metals. At first I tried coins, then eventually went on to old stuff my dad had in the garage. At sixteen I discovered a talent for sculpting and began trying my energies on the clay."

She thought about the beautiful sculpture in the office. He had actually created it in one day? She asked, "But why make a likeness of me?" The moment she asked the question she regretted her impulsiveness. She had a bad habit of asking whatever came to mind, and more often than not she'd find herself either with her foot in her mouth, or in an awkward situation. And in this instance, she wasn't sure she wanted to know the answer.

Jachin got up and moved to where she sat. Angela found her body responding as he leaned toward her. But all he did was take her hand to gently urge her out of her chair. "Come on, I'll show you 'why you.'"

He led her into the house, keeping hold of her hand. Although his large fingers caressed hers in a friendly manner, her body was reacting to his warm, no, *hot* touch with waves of fire and ice, as though she had a fever. Until now she'd never understood those young women who became so enamored of celebrities that they lost all sensibility. She forced down her newfound 'groupie' mentality, determined not to be quite so affected by him.

When she realized he was leading her down the hallway, she pulled back. "Where are we going?"

Wolfman gazed back at her with a predatory smile that curled her toes. But his chuckle was benign. "I want you to see yourself." He gently nudged her into the room she'd ventured into earlier. Her stomach fluttered.

Jachin could sense Angela's wariness. He decided not to tell her he'd created her likeness in *The Dance* before he'd met her. The ramifications to the statue's inception still eluded him. But he did want to show her something he sensed she was completely unaware of. He wasn't sure why it mattered to him, but it did.

"Look at that," he commanded, pointing to the bust.

"It's beautiful." She seemed to be in awe of the work, but he had the impression she wasn't accepting the truth of the image.

"Yes. And I only sculpt the beauty I see."

She looked pained. "It looks like me, yet it doesn't look like me."

Jachin studied her face. Obviously she didn't really see herself as the outside world did. "It looks exactly like you. What don't you like about it?"

By the horrified expression on her face she must have thought she'd offended him. She quickly said, "Oh Jachin, I love it. But …"

Moving toward her, he took her chin in his hand to tilt her face up. She didn't flinch or turn away, even though he knew she'd been trying hard to keep her distance from him. But beneath her cool exterior, he sensed the physical attraction he felt for her was mutual. "I see who you are, Angel, even if you don't."

She blinked up at him, swallowed, and then slowly licked her lips. The unconscious act was so sensual his body instantly reacted. "Who do you see?" she asked as if his answer was the most important thing in the world to her.

He looked deep into her eyes, stroking his thumbs across her cheeks just as he had earlier with the sculpture, only this time reveling in the feel of very warm skin. What he saw in her that moment was the same thing he'd seen in her likeness within *The Dance* as he'd worked the figure—the same qualities he'd experienced in his dream. He saw a woman of inner strength unlike anyone he'd ever met before. He saw innocence coupled with a natural and innate sensuality. He saw keen intelligence, which somehow managed to co-exist with a trusting heart. But he also sensed pain, making him wonder what in her life could have possibly hurt so much it had left emotional scars. Using more willpower than he thought himself capable of, he gently lowered his lips to hers for the merest whisper of a kiss.

But the moment he felt her soft lips beneath his, felt the same heated response from her he remembered from his dream, his good intentions flew out the window. He took her in his arms, pressing her slim, curvaceous body to his, and igniting a passion within him that belied his earlier energy drain.

As she opened her mouth to flick her tongue provocatively against his, her boldness surprised and further enflamed him. She moved her body against him, molding contours that fit perfectly. The roughness of her cotton shirt with the hint of full breasts beneath teased his bare chest.

He realized Angela had taken over the kiss, but rather than being put off, it only excited him more. When he pressed her closer, she laced her arms around his neck. He felt her cool slim fingers move across the bare flesh of his shoulder. A soft moan came from deep in her throat as his hands found their way beneath her blouse to caress her back. Her bra strap released with a flick of his fingers. She arched against him, pressing her hips to his as though she, too, wanted to relive the passion of his dream. Thoroughly aroused, his control threatened to crumble.

At the abrupt sound of the front door closing, Angela tensed in his arms. Reluctantly he released her, even as he fought against a primal need to sweep the workroom table clean and take her right here and now—outsiders, conscience, and world be damned.

Their gazes locked as she said breathlessly, "You never told me what you saw."

"Perfection." He spoke the truth, but by the shadow of disappointment he saw darken her eyes, he knew it was the wrong answer.

Her smile hinted at sadness, and even though he felt her emotional withdrawal, her kiss-swollen lips reminded him of the passion they'd shared only moments before and which still pulsed through his body. But the mutual closeness he'd felt disappeared, and although they were still in the same room, Angela had so completely shut herself off from him, they might just as well be standing in different worlds. Without taking her eyes from his, she fastened her bra. She then turned and left the room.

Frustration and rejection replaced his passion with anger. He stormed off to his room, wanting to get as far away from Angela as possible until he cooled down. He'd promised Boaz he'd be with her when she tried to 'cross over.' The sooner he proved his sister wrong, the sooner she would leave and take with her the one woman he knew could threaten the control he held on his emotions.

How could he have opened himself up to her like that? He'd shared things with Angela he hadn't told another living soul. And why? Had he let his guard down out of some kind of misplaced loyalty? Or simply because she was Boaz's friend and, therefore, already privy to certain family secrets?

No, he'd been taken in by her honesty and the feeling of trust instilled by her clear blue eyes. Even so, what on Earth had made him, after only knowing the woman a few hours, override a lifetime of resolve to never to let his guard down?

He stepped out of the shorts and turned on the shower, flipping the handle to the 'C' position. The shock of cold water did little to ease his frustration. Damn her, why did she have to be so beautiful? And those eyes! She had him under some kind of spell.

It was a spell he was determined to break. He allowed his anger to simmer just to the peak of his control. He would willingly take her to bed, but he wasn't about to let her get under his skin. But if she was truly like his dream lover, could he do one without the other?

***

As Angela returned to the living room, she couldn't help noticing Boaz's raised eyebrows. Standing at the counter that divided kitchen from living room, Boaz took from a grocery bag a bottle of wine and what looked like the ingredients for a salad. She eyed Angela and said, "You look a wee bit sunburned, girlfriend. You decide to hit the beach after all?"

Sunburned? Mortified was more like it. But Angela had never lied to her friend before, and she wasn't going to start now. With a backward glance toward the hallway, she whispered, "No, it's that brother of yours. He's just too damned sexy for his own good."

Feigning shock, Boaz said, "You didn't put the moves on my brother, did you?" She shook her head in mock seriousness as she washed the vegetables. "I can't leave you alone with a man for five minutes without you trying to jump his bones."

Although said in jest, when Angela didn't respond to the joke, Boaz stopped what she was doing to took a hard look at her friend. "Oooo! Angela Catherine Dawn, what did you do?"

She tried to think how she could tell Boaz about the kiss and still control her breathing. "Will you keep it down? He'll hear you." She made sure Jachin wasn't coming down the hall before she said, "He kissed me."

Boaz lowered her chin, waiting for the rest. When Angela didn't continue, Boaz asked, "And? Did you kiss him back?"

Angela began to pace the area in front of the counter. "Yes, I guess I did." She bit her lip.

Laughing, Boaz said, "So?" She shook her head. "You sound like you poisoned the Pope. It was just a kiss."

Angela came to an abrupt halt. Boaz was right. So what if she'd kissed Jachin? It wasn't the end of the world. It was just a kiss. Just because she'd had a teeny-weeny lapse of control didn't mean she'd signed her soul over to him.

But what a lapse! With the reminder of the out-of-control passion she'd felt, she resumed pacing. Jachin Morgan was exactly the kind of man she'd promised herself never to become involved with. She liked him far too much for her own good. Damn the dream! How easy it had been to mistake the flesh-and-blood Jachin for her fantasy man. She could give in to her passions to the man in her dreams with no qualms or repercussions. Somehow, she'd lost the ability to distinguish the dream man from the real one.

But, just as she wasn't the perfect woman Jachin had created in bronze, he wasn't the man in her dreams.

She reflected upon how easy it would be to let her mind accept him as her dream man and to give herself to him as she had in the dream. She also realized how easy it would be to get hurt when he discovered she wasn't the 'perfect' woman he'd imagined.

By tonight that point would be moot. Boaz, and hopefully Jachin, would be in Sena, and she would be on her way back to Arizona. So why was she still stressing? Surely she could survive with what was left of her dignity for a few more hours.

Angela took a deep breath and sat on one of the high bar stools at the counter . "You know, you're right. It was just a kiss. So what? I've kissed lots of men."

It was just a kiss, she mentally repeated. So, if it was just a kiss, why did she feel like her entire world had been turned upside down?

***

Even after a long, cold shower Jachin's temper still simmered. He dressed in slacks and a shirt. It was a good thing he'd used so much energy creating the sculpture that morning, or he was sure electric bulbs and circuits would be sparking all over the place.

His bedside phone rang, reminding him that he'd forgotten to unplug it after he'd called Mildred that morning. When he looked at the phone he was relieved to see the second line that exclusively linked him with his studio was flashing. At least it wasn't a reporter.

The moment he picked up the receiver and heard Mildred's sobbing, he knew something terrible had happened. "Mildred, what's wrong?"

"Oh Jachin, something...horrible has happened to one of your pieces. It's...*The Dance.* You've...got to come right over."

Mildred wasn't given to hysterics. In fact, he couldn't remember a time when he'd seen her anything but happy. He didn't need to ask for details to know he needed to get to his studio as quickly as possible. Had someone vandalized the sculpture with paint? It was the only thing he could think of. If that was the case, it was fixable. "I'll be right there. Calm down, Mildred. It'll be okay."

With his intended reassurance came renewed sounds of sobbing. A sick feeling took up residence in his stomach as he put the receiver down and strode down the hall.

Both Angela and Boaz looked up, concern on their faces. Boaz said, "What's wrong?"

"Will you both come with me to my studio? My gallery manager is upset." He wasn't sure which was more daunting, the problem with *The Dance* or Mildred's hysterics.

Boaz asked, "What about the reporters?"

"Damn the press," he said as he grabbed his car keys. "It will be easier to avoid them if we drive."

He led the women through the kitchen into the connecting garage, and they got into the Jeep. When he opened the automatic security gates he had to honk to scatter the small crowd of what he assumed were reporters and curiosity seekers. With a screech of tires he shot into traffic, the feeling of doom growing stronger by the moment. Surely nothing irreparable could have happened to the bronze. But what could possibly have so upset the unflappable Mildred?

Jerking to a stop in an illegal parking space two doors from the gallery, Jachin turned to Boaz and Angela. "Stay close and move fast until we're inside." In front of his shop the milling crowd of about twenty people became animated when they recognized him. Cameras started whirring and flashing, and eager faces gawked.

"Ready?" he asked Boaz and Angela.

"Ready," they said in unison, their hands already on door handles.

He got out of the jeep and hurried around to the women's side of the car. Putting an arm around each of them as they got out, he hurried them forward as the crowd surged toward them like a powerful wave. The flood of questions and the click of camera shutters drowned out all other noise. He felt Angela cringe as one reporter abruptly blocked her way, and only inches from her face, shouted, "Are you a member of Jachin Morgan's coven?"

Gathering Angela closer to his side, Jachin directed his anger toward the reporter's microphone and instantly the man jumped back from an electrical shock, dropping the instrument. *That ought to give them plenty to talk about for the next week.*

As soon as the stunned reporter backed away, another took his place and pushed so close Jachin could smell the man's sweat. He continued to move the women forward through the tangle of people, heedless of stepped-on toes and jostled camera equipment.

A puffy-eyed Mildred stood poised at the double glass doors, ready to turn the lock as soon as they got close. Finally they reached the doors and hurried inside. Jachin quickly turned and secured the doors behind him. Cameras pressed against the windows, but there was little he could do since the front of the gallery was entirely glass.

After a rush of introductions, he turned to Boaz and Angela. "Let's go into my shop."

"No!" Mildred halted their progress. The sad look she gave Jachin made his heart sink. "Jachin, you need to go in alone. We'll be fine here. I'll take your friends to the back of the gallery."

He noticed the flicker of recognition in her eyes as she looked at Boaz and Angela. They were *The Dance* personified. She hiccoughed back a little sob.

Boaz and Angela both appeared to be in shock from the media assault. But they let Mildred hurry them off to the small office at the back of the gallery, away from prying eyes.

Jachin braced himself for whatever had happened to *The Dance*. With dread unlike any he'd ever felt, he slowly opened the door.

At first the subdued light made it difficult to see any change to the sculpture. Or was the obscurity of the destruction the result of the denial screaming through his head?

He blinked, and the tragedy before him became hard reality. His sculpture had somehow been melted. He couldn't breathe. A horrific, misshapen mass stood where his prized piece of art had once been. The only thing that proved *The Dance* ever existed beneath the mangle of metal was one perfect hand, which reached out as if seeking help. With a sinking feeling he realized it was Angela's hand, her slim fingers untouched by the massacre. He'd finally found the source for the sense of loss he'd been experiencing all afternoon.

Once he absorbed the reality of what he was seeing and he could again breathe, his mind began to clear. And with the clarity came a building rage so intense, he felt the air crackle around him. He stood with clenched fists, the need to kill the responsible person so strong he couldn't control it. This time he didn't even try to subdue the darkness within him.

"Jachin."

The voice made him swing around, glad to have a focus for his rage.

But the room was empty. Then he realized the unidentifiable voice came from inside his head. Someone was telepathically communicating with him.

It had to be done, Jachin, the voice said.

Jachin raised his hand, ready to form a ball of energy with which to destroy …. Destroy what? He stepped back, running his hands through his hair. What had he been about to succumb to?

He lowered his arm, his thoughts disorganized. His rational mind told him to control his anger, that he didn't want to destroy anything. But the dark, menacing anger he'd subdued all his life now soared to freedom.

The anger had a life of its own, became a separate entity. And it wanted revenge. It struggled against Jachin's efforts to regain control, the mounting energy so great the air sizzled with electricity. A building wind began to swirl around the room. Sheets of canvas fluttered, and papers were whipped to the floor to commence a jerky dance.

With every ounce of willpower he managed to force back the feelings, fighting against the hate for the unknown monster that had destroyed his masterpiece. At last he felt his emotions begin to balance and the darkness begin to recede.

For a moment he stood there stunned, his unappeased fury

settling like a hot, red ball in his chest. His breathing still came hard and fast. But as he took a deep breath and concentrated on control, his anger lowered to the simmering point, and the wind in the room subsided. The ambient sparks of rogue electricity crackled several more times and then dispersed.

Jachin began to shake at the realization of what he had been about to do. He'd almost let his rage consume him. He knew that if he had waited a moment longer there would have been no turning back. His enemy—the dark side which held the capability to destroy without remorse—would have taken over. Rubbing his face, he willed himself to calm down. But fury still lurked just beneath the surface.

He looked at the mutilated sculpture again, commanding himself to let go of the anger, knowing the more he gave himself over to it, the more of his soul it would master. And once it had complete control, nothing would remain of the man he'd fought his whole life to become. Any chance at finding peace would be lost fc 'ever. Taking a deep breath, he leaned against the worktable.

Feel the power, Jachin. He knew the sinister thought did not belong to him. Someone, some *thing*, still had access to his mind. But the incredible power the voice spoke of did belong to him. The moment he'd given in to his anger, a force of absolute and horrible strength had suffused him. Even now it hummed within him, fighting to resurface. The intensity of it was unlike anything he had ever experienced, and it tempted him with a promise of limitless power.

Acknowledge and control the power, Jachin, the voice again spoke, this time as though it came from down a long tunnel. *The Dance can be restored, Jachin. Face your destiny...claim your heritage...and the power to restore true order will be yours.*

"No!" Jachin rasped as he concentrated on blocking his mind to the intruder. But even as he denied the dark force within him, he knew he'd already taken a step closer to it.

Maybe, as the voice suggested, if he went to Sena he could gain the power to restore the beauty and purity of *The Dance.* But at what cost? Was the dark power that destroyed the sculpture the only one capable of restoring it? If it was, would he be strong enough to deny its power at the cost of *The Dance*? He had no choice but to find out. As the voice said, it was time to face his destiny.

With the final acceptance of Sena and wizardry as fact, something Boaz had said at last became reality. Their sister Lilith was in danger. He had to discover a way to find her. He'd been such a fool not to believe Boaz. And his denial had been born out of what? Some misplaced loyalty to his adoptive parents and the world in which he'd been raised?

At that moment Jachin acknowledged who he was. *I'm a wizard.* And it no longer disturbed him that he was different from the people around him. Although he still didn't know what his destiny was, he was ready to face it. With that thought, his senses hummed to renewed heights, as though he'd never truly been aware of his surroundings before.

He looked around, for the first time noticing how dirty the workroom was. It might look organized and clean at first glance, but he now saw the finer details. Even the air, streaming down from the skylights, seemed filled with tiny particles of various impurities.

Then he looked at the plastic-covered blocks of clay sitting on the pallet against the wall. Why hadn't he ever noticed how they glowed with latent life, as though imploring him to set the spirits within free? He realized he could even taste the air. An earthy flavor of clay tinged with various metals made him salivate with the subtle flavor as he breathed in the miniscule particles. It was as if his senses were now attuned on a molecular level, and everything around him was alive.

He breathed deeply, his body and mind more vital than ever before. Did this acuity go along with the dark power he'd been avoiding for so long? If it did, he had to consider its consequences. Because this new, sharper awareness felt like pure, clean water to a parched throat. He wasn't sure he could go back to existing in drought conditions when he knew he possessed the means to quench his thirst.

Old doubts resurfaced, making him realize that any fantasies he'd been entertaining about a possible relationship with Angela were now out of the question. He was a wizard. And even if he and Boaz somehow returned from Sena to live in this world again, he couldn't expose Angela to the dangers he felt certain would follow him in his new life.

He felt the last of his anger evaporate, and his gut tightened with the acknowledgment that Angela was better off with her own kind. She should have a normal life, like the people he observed on a daily basis, but with whom he never felt he truly belonged. She was meant to have a husband, kids, a career—all the normal things normal people wanted. A little boring perhaps, but less dangerous than living among wizards who could annihilate her with the flick of a wrist.

Jachin picked up a tarp, shook it out and reverently covered the crumpled bronze. Then, without a backward glance, he left his workshop. He locked the door behind him then turned to face the three women at the back of the gallery.

He walked into the office and with a calm decisiveness that surprised him, he said, "Mildred, can you run things without me for an extended period?"

Turning from Mildred's shocked expression, he said, "Boaz, I'm going with you."

SIX

The 11th House Magician: The Trickster.
Stirring things up to make change.

Angela couldn't believe the change in Jachin since they'd returned to his home after their visit to the gallery. Mildred had told them what had mysteriously happened to his prized sculpture, and Angela wanted to cry every time she thought about it. Jachin must be feeling miserable, and Boaz was as subdued as she'd ever seen her friend.

Right after Jachin had told Boaz he was going with her, he had told Mildred she would have to run the gallery and fend off reporters as best she could. Mildred told Jachin to take as much time as he needed, that she and the gallery would be fine.

Now Jachin and Boaz were quietly packing and getting ready for the trip, deciding canvas backpacks and minimal belongings were in order. From what Marrion had told Boaz and her, their quest on Sena was going to be a test of survival skills, and they would need to travel light. Angela and Boaz had only brought backpacks from home anyway, thinking they would be away no more than a day. Boaz wore new cotton pants and a shirt, while Jachin chose cotton twill trousers and a gauze shirt. Angela looked down at the lightweight cotton dress and short-sleeved sweater she'd recently purchased. Not exactly the kind of thing one would wear on a trek through an ancient forest. But then she wasn't going.

Seated at the dining room table and going over necessary paperwork before he left, Jachin hardly looked at her. When he did occasionally look up, his expression was closed, his clenched jaw the only outward sign of emotion. She was sorry for the way she'd treated him after their kiss. He was fighting demons she couldn't even imagine, and she wanted to help. But by her own coldness she'd shut herself off from him.

The front door opened and Sean Scot walked in, greeting the three of them. Jachin hardly looked up from the papers he was sorting.

"The mob outside is quite open to befuddlement spells," Sean announced. "I used one to get in just now. When we are ready to leave, I will cast another one so we can depart unnoticed."

Sean walked to the bank of windows to look into the night. Then he turned to Angela. "I still feel you are meant to go on this journey."

Jachin surprised them all with a vehement, "No!" In a softer tone he said, "She's staying here. Where she belongs."

She was sure he meant here, as in *this world*, but she had the fanciful notion he was referring to his home. She said, "I'd like to go, Sean, but I don't think I'm ready for Sena."

"At least," Sean said, "go with us as far as the end of the pier. It will be nice to have a *bon voyage* party."

"I wouldn't miss seeing everyone off," Angela told Sean. "I have a redeye flight, so I've got plenty of time." She wasn't sure what she was supposed to watch for when she saw them off. They'd agreed they would get to the moonbeam steps to Sena by going to the end of a little-used fishing pier at midnight. They'd then climb down to the water using the ladder set in place for rescues. They would be out far enough to be past the breakers, yet not beyond the fourth or fifth wave. Sean instructed that it was imperative they go to the ninth wave to enter Sena properly. Did they just disappear at a certain point? Jachin looked up, but he didn't say anything. Although his eyes regarded her, they remained devoid of emotion. He went back to his work.

Boaz frowned and said, "Aunt Marrion told me she would be here to help us cross over. Do you know anything about that, Sean?" Boaz had told Angela earlier that she, too, suspected Sean might be the troll Marrion had warned them about, but that she wanted to bide her time and keep an eye on him for now.

Sean looked taken aback, but quickly smiled. "Oh, she decided it wasn't necessary. It takes an incredible amount of energy to teleport here in spirit and then manifest into the illusion-body."

Boaz looked confused. "But she is here. We saw her in Half Moon Bay just two days ago. In a lovely Victorian home."

"All an aberration created by Marrion." His smile said he was sharing a secret. "She teleported her spirit to the house, but the house itself must be one used when wizards come to this world. Most likely, it was an old neglected house that has been used by wizards for many years. She probably created the illusion of the house being warm and inviting. The images she created—the one's you saw—were a bit like one of your holograms."

"Remember, Boaz and Jachin, you must not take any kind of modern technology into Sena," Sean said. "Anything that gives off manufactured electrical energy can adulterate the energies in our world." He glanced at their backpacks. "Are you sure all your clothing is natural? Be sure you're not wearing synthetics of any kind. They can interfere with the natural balance."

"Check," Boaz said with renewed excitement.

Jachin only gave Sean a look of impatience as he said, "How are we supposed to find Lilith?"

"Guides...of a sort...will show you the way," Sean said.

"And how," Jachin asked as he stacked the papers in front of him and shoved them aside, "are we expected to rescue her from this Kadien if he's so powerful?"

Sean's smile was enigmatic. "There are many types of battles on Sena. Battles of the material. Battles of the mind. And battles of the spirit. You will only know what your battles will be once you reach Sena and the elements involved come together. As I said, guides will be there to help you on your journey."

Jachin folded his arms across his chest. "It sounds like we've been expected."

"You've been told about the prophecy then?" Sean asked.

Jachin nodded. "Boaz told me." He paused. "Let me get this straight. We can only fight this powerful wizard with The Power of the Triad, yet we have to get past the guy before we can reach Lilith to combine our powers. Sounds like a Catch Twenty-two."

Sean said, "The greater the challenge, the greater the reward."

Jachin looked disgusted. "I'm not looking for a reward. I just want this whole bizarre episode over and done with."

With a look of concern, Sean said, "If you don't give your destiny every part of yourself, if you don't go into this challenge wholeheartedly, you will be doomed before you begin."

Jachin looked at the watch he'd taken off and placed on the table. "It's eleven fifteen." Then he said derisively, "The witching hour fast approaches."

But Sean's tone was reverent as he said, "Midnight of a full moon is a great time of magic. Especially during Oestarra—the spring. It's a time for migratory animals to return home. And you and Boaz are returning home, Jachin.

Boaz came to stand beside Angela, putting her arm around her shoulders. Angela could feel the excited tension in her friend's arm as Boaz said, "It does feel like going home. Do you feel it Jachin?"

By the preoccupied look on his face Jachin seemed caught in an internal struggle. He didn't answer.

Sean said, "An entire people have long been awaiting this day...with great anticipation."

Jachin abruptly stood, and Angela's heart jerked with a quick infusion of adrenaline as she realized the evening's events had just been put into motion.

***

Marrion focused her inner light into a ball of energy, praying that her powers had been adequately restored between teleportations. It was time to return to the Lute world and help Jachin and Boaz cross over into Sena.

Mentally blocking her surroundings, the sights and sounds in her small meditation room faded. The comforting creak of wood, the scents of humus and fragrance from her flowerpots, as well as Emmeline's contented purr became like a distant memory. There, yet not there. She began to chant the ancient sound, *Ommmm*, to attain supreme consciousness and attain a state of bliss.

She let go of the tangible essence of life and retreated into the spiritually quiet place within herself. Taking deep, purifying breaths, she visualized her spirit body shifting ever so slightly from her earthly body, which sat cross-legged on a mat on the floor.

She felt her spirit's light gently release itself from her warm physical self, making her acutely aware of gravity's pull on her earth-body. The uncomfortable heaviness passed as she consciously chose to inhabit the spirit body. Even for an experienced wizard, disassociating one's physical and astro-etheric bodies required intensely concentrated focus. Her visit with Boaz had left her psychic energy reserves low, and she had to use Herculean effort to reach the highest level of concentration. She knew she would be able to gather the energies needed to transport, but would she be able to maintain the astral-body illusion for a sustained period in the Lute world? She wasn't sure, which meant she would have to find the children quickly and make sure Gaban didn't interfere with their crossing.

At last free, her spirit separated and flowed like quicksilver from her earthly body. Her spirit hovered, looking down for a moment. She said the ritual prayer for her body's safety, along with Emmeline, both of which she was leaving behind. Although she hated to be without her constant companion, she didn't want to utilize the energy it would take to transport the cat. Even now her energy levels were so low, she could very well find herself unable to return to her earthly body.

She turned her focus to the Lute world and Laguna Beach. Although she'd been able to pinpoint Boaz's life force there intermittently since their initial meeting, something or someone had blocked many of her efforts. With the speed of thought she was transported to the local cafe where she had last made psychic contact.

Even though midnight rapidly approached and she felt an overwhelming sense of urgency, she couldn't create the illusion of her physical body until the café's sidewalk was crowded enough that no one would notice her sudden appearance. With numerous people about, she could easily make them think she had just stepped out of a shop doorway.

She took in the sights and sounds of the bustling modern village, experiencing the amassed energy of numerous Lutes. Wanting to concentrate on the people, she ignored the trash on the stony footpaths and the pollution issuing from automobiles. She counted herself blessed that in this etheric-body she had no sense of smell.

Listening to the easy laughter of small groups, mingled with the caressing whispers of couples, she realized that far fewer Lutes than she'd imagined carried with them the shadow of darkness. The carefree gaiety reminded her of one of Sena's own festivals. Maybe Lutes weren't so different from those in the world of magic after all.

Once she materialized she concentrated on trying to locate Boaz and Jachin. She focused her intuitive powers, radiating them out like a lighthouse beacon.

Then she felt a concentration of magic so strong she knew it had to be coming from either Jachin or Boaz...She hoped both. The magic was about a ten-minute walk up the street, and she hurried toward it.

A short time later, she found the magic emanating from a house with iron gates. About fifteen people stood in front of the house, standing around as if they had been summoned and now awaited instruction.

Odd, she thought. They looked like they were under some kind of spell, yet she couldn't sense a spell at work.

"Is this Jachin Morgan's home?" she asked one of the men.

He blinked as he looked at her, a common enough occurrence with those who couldn't figure out the subtle differences between a material body and spirit body. Seeming to shake off his confusion, he scrutinized her, puffing up as if he needed to defend himself from her. "Jachin Morgan lives here, but you're wasting your time, lady. He's promised me an exclusive."

From the snickers and derisive chuckles she heard from other members of the group, she doubted the man's truthfulness. But she had the information she wanted. This was Jachin's home. "Thank you, then. I'll just be on my way."

The man favored his fellow loiterers with a self-satisfied smile.

As Marrion glanced around at the faces of the mulling crowd, a sudden look of confusion replaced each and every smile. She listened to their thoughts, discovering that all of them had turned their focus inward. A bearded man with a pot belly thought, "Why am I here?" Another, holding a bulky camera thought, "What is my last name? Cramer? No. Collins? No. Chandler? No ..."

Marrion realized that a befuddlement spell was at work, but who inside Jachin's house knew how to cast one? Certainly Jachin and Boaz hadn't had instruction in such fine arts. And she was positive Gaban couldn't have pulled it off, since she was certain even a troll who'd been given transient powers wouldn't be able to concentrate long enough to cast a spell. But then, Gaban shouldn't have any powers, and he was here, which required a lot of power.

She found herself moving with the crowd as they shuffled to the edges of the driveway. Evidently the befuddlement spell had thrown her off, too, because instead of taking advantage of the situation and entering the house, she stood there like a stunned idiot. Now, to her horror, she realized the garage door stood open and a vehicle carrying four people was roaring past them.

Quickly she cleared her mind. Then, despite the possibility

of the surrounding crowd's notice, she dematerialized. Without the additional energy drain of maintaining a physical image, she quickly caught up with the automobile and followed, gliding along at a vantage point just above the roof.

The foursome stopped a few miles down the beach, but Marrion decided to evaluate the situation before resuming form. The vehicle's occupants got out and walked toward a pier. She hovered above them, her heart fluttering as she saw her niece and nephew. Jachin was every bit as magnificent as Boaz, and he walked tall and self-assured. Both children exuded enormous amounts of power and magic even though they had yet to have formal training. If only her sister could see them, she would be so proud.

Boaz and Jachin stood with Angela and a Lute man. Marrion sensed Gaban's life force within the Lute.

She turned her attention to Gaban's human form. Funny, she thought as she divined the Lute's character Gaban had borrowed and found him to be unusually stalwart. Usually one didn't choose to inhabit such a sound individual because they were difficult to control and tended to resurface at odd times. Even odder, she got a fleeting impression that the Lute had willingly allowed Gaban to inhabit him. She had to admit it tickled her to think the Lute might be able to give the great mischief-maker Gaban some of his own medicine and could influence the unknowing troll.

But her mirth died as a disturbing thought came to her. If the Lute knew what he was doing, could he somehow be involved in the plot to sabotage the children?

***

As Jachin walked the pier with Angela, Boaz and Sean, he closed his mind to the memory of the decimated statue, knowing such thoughts would only provoke his anger, and he needed to maintain emotional control in order to complete his task. Only then could he return and restore *The Dance*. He also put away his feelings for Angela. He was certain the hungers she had ignited would die once he could physically distance himself from her.

By the time they approached the end of the deserted pier, Jachin had managed to reach an emotionless state, and waited for the events they had been told about to unfold. It was nearly midnight, and the beauty of the crystalline, indigo night and full moon beckoned.

Once the silent group reached the pier's end, Sean turned to them and handed Angela her backpack, which Jachin realized the man had gotten out of the car.

"Why did you bring my backpack?" Angela asked Sean, her expression confused. "I'm not going."

Sean smiled. "I thought you might change your mind at the last minute."

Angela looked at Jachin and felt her heart sink when she realized she would never see him again. She would never have the time to discover if the strange bond she felt between them was real or her imagination. "No, I won't change my mind. As Jachin said, I belong in this world."

Jachin looked away from the unanswerable questions in Angela's eyes. He knew instinctively that if his eyes showed the unfathomable feelings he had for her, she might change her mind.

"We still have ten minutes until the veils between the worlds part," Sean said. "Then we will climb down the ladder, step onto the moonbeam stones and walk out to the ninth wave. Once there, a shoreline will appear. More stones will lead us to the shore. Remember, once you step onto that first stone you can't go back the way you came."

As Sean began repeating his earlier instructions, his words became an incoherent jumble in Jachin's mind. He looked at his sister who stood tall and strong. Then he allowed himself a glance in Angela's direction, realizing it could be the last time he saw her. One freeze-frame of her to keep for the future was a small enough indulgence. But when his gaze locked with hers and he saw the silent farewell in her eyes, his breath caught. He had to use every ounce of willpower to keep from walking to her and pulling her into his arms.

Why did he feel as if there was a connection between them he was powerless to break? Only two days ago he didn't know she existed. Or did he? She had been in his dreams, and he had made her a part of *The Dance*. On some deep level he must have known about and felt connected to her for some time now, maybe his entire life. That's what it felt like when he was with her. Like they'd known each other forever.

Angela walked toward him, and he had to fight to control his rapid breathing. If she touched him, even to lay a hand on his arm, he would be lost. She looked up at him, her face iridescent in the moonlight.

"Jachin, I'm sorry for the way I acted after…" She looked away, nervous. "Take care of yourself and Boaz." Then she once again met his gaze, the nervousness gone. "Good-bye."

Good-bye. It was a word he'd used a million times with the casualness of knowing the parting would be temporary, or sometimes knowing it to be final but not caring. Yet at this moment, standing here trying not to touch Angela with either his hands or his mind, and knowing they could never be together, *good-bye* felt like a death-sentence. He chose not to repeat her farewell, but instead nodded a brief acknowledgement, then turned away.

Suddenly, and seemingly from nowhere, an elderly woman appeared next to Jachin.

Boaz rushed toward her. "Marrion, you're here!" But Marrion held up her hand to stop Boaz's approach. "I am only here in spirit. The physical body you see is an illusion. I have come to help you cross over." She shot Sean a scathing look. "And to tell you that this man is not who he portrays himself to be. He is not a wizard, but a troll named Gaban who has taken over this Lute's body. And I'm not certain who put him up to it, but he is trying to sabotage your mission."

Sean smiled nervously. "Marrion, how nice to see you again." He raised his hands as if surrendering. "No harm done. I was just having a little fun."

Jachin found himself shaking his head. The man before him was almost unrecognizable as the Sean Scot he *thought* he knew. Subtle differences changed Sean's face, making him appear wizened, and his posture shifted from dignified to cavalier. Why hadn't he noticed that before?

"I just thought it would be interesting if Angela went along on the journey," Sean said.

Jachin saw a fearful expression on Angela's face as she glanced at Sean, so he took a step closer to her, putting himself between them. He might not be able to have her, but he could protect her from these lunatics.

This time, Sean gave Jachin a nervous smile. "Oh, don't worry. The game is over. I know when I'm beat. I'll not cause you further mischief." He glanced at the moon. "I'm anxious to return home, and the time to depart is at hand."

Marrion dismissed Sean with the wave, and then turned to Jachin and Boaz. "Hurry. Gather your belongings. It's time to go." Moving to the end of the pier she passed her hand over the railing, and the section across the end of the pier disappeared. She then turned back to regard them. "Mind that you go to the seventh wave. It is the *proper* way," she emphasized as she shot another scathing glance in Sean's direction, "to enter Sena."

Jachin picked up his backpack, as did Boaz, and they walked to the pier's end. He avoided eye contact with Angela, but he kept her in his peripheral vision. He watched her pick up her own backpack, move to a point a few feet away from him at the pier's edge to look down into the water.

He followed her gaze and noticed that, just as Sean had said, the moon's reflection on the water created what looked like large, round steppingstones of light. Those lights led directly to the ladder they would descend. Although the rolling waves splashed over the edges of the stones, they didn't cover them completely.

Marrion said, "Go ahead children. I will be on the other side when you arrive. Remember...the seventh wave." The woman seemed to be fading. Not only had her voice taken on a far-away sound, she was almost transparent.

Jachin waited at the top of the ladder as Boaz gave Angela a long hug, and with a catch in her voice said, "I think a quote from Houdini is appropriate about now. 'If there is a way, I will come back.'" Their soft laughter held a note of sadness.

Angela said, "You'd better hurry. I don't want you to get halfway there only to have the steppingstones disappear." The fleeting panic in her eyes reminded Jachin that Boaz had earlier told him that Angela couldn't swim. He resisted the impulse to tell her to move away from the edge of the unguarded pier. He didn't like this new, protective side, and he quickly steeled himself against it. She could take care of herself. She didn't need him telling her to be careful.

Boaz squeezed Angela's hand and came over to stand next to Jachin. With a nod, she said, "I'm ready."

He helped Boaz down the ladder's first rung. As she descended to the water, he was suddenly concerned the "stepping stones" wouldn't have substance. But when she took a tenuous step onto the disc of light, he saw that her footing held securely, even though water lapped at her shoes. She now stood with both feet planted firmly on the stepping-stone, waiting for him. He needed to stop questioning this world of magic. Over the past two days, it had been proven beyond a doubt that it existed.

He took one last glance at Angela, assuring himself she would return safely to her own home. Then he went down the ladder and stepped onto the first stone. Although his footing was solid, the feeling of the stone beneath his shoes was unsubstantial, as though he was standing on a foam pad.

He glanced up at the pier, only to have his breath catch and his heart jerk. Angela stood close to the edge, waving as she secured the straps of her backpack. And just behind her, standing much too close, was Sean. He looked at Jachin as if to make sure he was watching. Then, as Marrion's fading figure mouthed a silent, "No!" Sean pushed Angela.

Jachin watched in horror as Angela tried to catch herself. But she was too near the edge. Boaz shrieked. Then the night went shockingly silent as Angela went over the side. Then she was falling through space in a graceful kind of slow motion as her outspread arms reached in vain for something to stop her fall. Jachin made a grab for her, but the night's darkness shrouded her, making it impossible to focus on her enough to catch her.

Then she hit the water.

Jachin shoved his backpack into Boaz's arms and dove in. The frigid, salty water engulfed him. Although it was merely bracing to him, he knew the cold would be a shock to terrified Angela.

Surfacing, he frantically searched for her. Only the ripple of inky waves and the sparkling reflection of the full moon met his gaze. He looked at the pier to more precisely gauge where she had gone in. The pier looked blurred around the edges. Taking a deep breath, he dove again. Even though he knew he would find only darkness, he opened his eyes.

For a moment he was blinded by the water's salty sting, but he blinked and the irritation subsided. He quickly looked around. *Angela where are you?* his mind yelled. Small shafts of moonlight pierced the surface, giving him a dim underwater view. He thought he heard Angela call out his name, but when he realized he must be hearing her telepathically, he was both startled and relieved. He'd never had a telepathic connection before. It felt like a door in his mind had opened to Angela, and he looked in the direction of the voice.

Then he saw her. She was about two feet under the surface, trying in vain to free herself from the backpack. She then kicked her feet, obviously trying to move upward. Even if she had been a good swimmer, Jachin knew the heavy backpack would act like a scuba diver's weight belt.

Hang on Angela, he mentally called as he swam. *I'm coming.*

Although his chest ached with the need for air, he didn't surface, fearful of losing sight of her. If his lungs felt like they would burst, Angela must be close to drowning. When he was within arm's reach of her, she moved away from the shaft of light, and he lost sight of her.

He groped for her. When he felt her backpack, he grabbed hold of it, relieved when he felt Angela's body weight come with it.

He shot upward, taking her with him. When they broke the surface and he could at last take in great gulps of air, Angela coughed and sputtered weakly as he pulled her to him. He felt only a limp response from her, and her eyelids fluttered closed.

Panic surged through him. Had he been too late to save her? He pressed his hand to her neck and heaved a ragged sigh of relief when he felt her thready pulse.

Holding her close, he swam toward the pier. But when he looked up to get his bearings, the pier had disappeared. A heavy fog clouded the shoreline, obscuring everything. Marrion's voice came to him from far away. "You can't go back the way you came."

He would have to take Angela with him to Sena. Sean had made sure of it. But why?

He swam toward Boaz, who stood expectantly on the moonstone, appearing farther away than before. And now Sean stood with her. When she'd stepped off the pier ladder, she'd been able to step directly onto the stone, but now she wasn't even close to the pier. Was the stone moving? From his vantage point the two appeared to be walking on water. Jachin struck out for the spot where they stood. He could feel Angela move weakly in his arms.

Before he could reach the stone, Angela regained consciousness, flailing as she coughed and fought for air.

He stopped swimming, knowing he had to calm her. "I've

got you, Angela. You're okay. I'm not going to let anything happen to you. I promise."

Someone was talking to her, but Angela couldn't bring the words into focus. Her mind was screaming at her, telling her that someone was trying to drown her. The sting of ice water bit at her skin as strong arms held her tight, and terrifying images of sharks and huge fish swimming just below the inky surface flashed through her mind. Panic tore through her chest and she fought to get away.

Sean had pushed her off the pier! She remembered the sharp pain when her leg had hit wood. Then she'd felt a cold so sharp she hadn't been able to breathe. Now she was able to breathe again, but someone was trying to hold her down. Was trying to drown her. It had to be Sean. She fought harder.

But then the man's voice penetrated her panic, and she realized it was Jachin holding her. And he wasn't trying to drown her. He was keeping her head above the water.

"Angel, stop fighting!" Jachin commanded.

Somehow she managed to subdue her panic enough to stop flailing, even though instinct told her she had to fight to survive.

"It's okay. You're fine now," Jachin said as he grabbed onto her shoulders and shifted her around so that he looked into her eyes.

It truly was Jachin. She felt the strength of his body against her, felt his legs brush hers as he treaded water. But no mater how she tried, she couldn't force her body to relax. She remained rigid in his arms. All of her childhood fears associated with water had suddenly become real. Well most of them, anyway. The sharks and the ominous fish had been in her imagination. She hoped!

Another grip of panic seized her as her mind conjured up a twenty-five-foot great white shark moving silently just inches below her dangling legs. Her heart hammered, and she gasped, unable to breathe.

Jachin gathered her to him, and she wanted to shrink into a tiny ball in his arms. Most of all she wanted to get her legs out of the water and away from the shark her mind's eye insisted was real. She tried to control her breathing and to relax, but it was a losing battle. Looking up at the stars she concentrated on the sweet, clean air entering her lungs, refusing to focus on the blackness beneath her.

Jachin's breath was warm against her ear as he said, "Try to relax and float on your back. I've got hold of you. I won't let you go under."

He maneuvered her so he had his arm around her chest, and she was on her back. A small wave splashed against her chin as if to challenge Jachin's vow to keep her safe. She jerked away.

"Angel, trust me! I'm not going to let anything happen to you."

Jachin's grip grew stronger. While part of her shouted that she was the only one who could save herself, that she had never been able to depend on anyone, another part wanted to trust Jachin.

She pushed aside her fears and put her life in his hands.

Although her teeth chattered uncontrollably and her limbs were becoming numb, she felt a glow of warmth begin in the center of her being. Jachin wouldn't let anything happen to her. As much as she hated the feeling of depending on someone else for her survival, she did just that.

"We're almost there," he said, smiling reassuringly at her as he swam. "Just a few more minutes."

Finally they drew up to where Boaz and Sean stood, and Boaz reached down to pull her onto the steppingstone. But as the night breeze permeated her thin, clinging dress she started shivering so hard she couldn't stand. She could barely think.

Jachin hoisted himself up to sit beside her, immediately putting a reassuring hand on her shoulder.

"She freezing," Boaz said and bent down to put her arms around Angela.

Instantly warmth permeated Angela's frigid skin. It felt so good it almost hurt.

Jachin said, "I'll take her, Boaz. Can you handle all three backpacks?" He then shot a murderous look toward Sean who now stood on the next steppingstone. "What in the hell were you trying to do, kill her?"

Sean seemed unrepentant. "It's important that Angela accompany you. It was the only way. I knew you wouldn't let her drown, Jachin." He looked at Boaz. "I would be happy to help you with the backpacks."

She straightened the two packs she had. "Yeah, right, Sean, like I trust you as far as I can spit."

Angela tried to tell Jachin thank-you, but her teeth were

chattering so hard she couldn't get her mouth to form the words. All she succeeded in doing was biting her tongue. And as absurd as she knew it was, she suddenly found herself fighting an overwhelming urge to sleep. Her eyelids became so heavy she had to fight to keep them open.

"Jachin," Boaz said, "I think she's going to faint."

Angela heard Jachin's voice, as if from far away. "Sean, I have a score to settle with you, but it will have to wait."

She didn't hear a response.

Vaguely she felt Jachin pull the backpack off her shoulders. The loss of the weight made her feel lighter than air. She tried to roll some of the tension from her aching shoulders, but was only rewarded with a violent shudder as her back was hit by the cold breeze. Her eyes flew open, and she didn't feel drowsy any longer.

As she watched Jachin hand her pack to Boaz, she finally managed to stutter, "Th-th-thank you, Ja-Jachin."

"You're welcome," he murmured, his voice sounding oddly hoarse as he gathered her into his arms.

The warmth that had begun in her center when Jachin had asked her to trust him, now ignited and began to radiate outward. She closed her eyes and leaned into him. How could he be so warm? He'd also been in the water, but the bare skin covering the bulging muscles of his arms seemed to burn her fingertips. And how could he hold her so effortlessly, with no sign of fatigue after his swim to save her?

Save her. The words echoed in her head as she blinked, but was unable to reopen her heavy lids.

Jachin said, "Come on, Boaz, we need to get her to Sena for help." The flat, unemotional tone was back in Jachin's voice, and Angela wondered if she'd only imagined the caring she'd heard earlier. *What happened to you calling me 'Angel' in that deep, sexy voice?* she groggily wondered. *Why have I suddenly become an indifferent 'her'?*

Darkness engulfed her before she could find an answer to her question.

Jachin noticed that Angela's lips were a dark shade of blue. He couldn't tell if it was from the moon glow or the cold. He noticed, too, what looked like a dark fluid mixing with the rivulets of water streaming down her leg. She must have cut herself during her fall from the pier. As he felt panic surfacing at the memory of her near drowning, he pushed away the unwanted emotions and focused on what needed to be done. He needed to get her to some kind of shelter before she went into hypothermia.

If Marrion's claims about them not being able to go back were true, then they needed to get to Sena as fast as possible.

"Let's go," Jachin told Boaz, nodding toward the stones ahead of them. As he took the lead he asked, "Did you count the waves, Boaz?"

"Yes," she said. "As close as I can tell, we've passed the third one. Four more to go. I'm guessing one wave per moonstone."

Although he didn't think this was a good time to guess, he didn't say anything. After the distraction of Angela falling into the water, and the ensuing chaos, he wasn't sure he'd have been able to keep an accurate count.

He saw the next wave begin to crest at the stone before them. When it subsided, they walked to the next stepping-stone, and Jachin mentally counted, *four*. Glancing over his shoulder he watched the fog roll in behind them, as if it waited for them to take the next step before it moved.

"I think you're wrong," Sean said, now looking like the Sean Jachin remembered, not of the troll, Marrion had called Gaban. Was this just another trick?

"I believe we are only at the first wave," Sean continued. "You need to count the pattern of the breaking waves, not each wave as it comes in. The first wave is essentially a series of waves that break at the same spot."

This couldn't be easy, could it? Jachin thought, chagrined. But then, if crossing over to Sena was easy, anyone could do it. He'd just have to rely on gut instinct, and his gut told him they were now on the fourth stone. When he'd observed the waves and the stepping stones from the pier, he could see a definite pattern of one breaker per stone.

Ignoring Sean, he adjusted the now motionless Angela in his arms and led the group to the next stone. *Five*.

Again, he looked behind him, and the fog, which had been several yards away, was now encroaching at an alarming pace. He said nothing, but stepped onto the next stone. *Six*, he mentally counted as the others followed him.

Without warning, the fog overtook them, and he felt his heart jolt as Boaz, who was only two feet away disappeared into the mist. "Boaz!"

"Jachin!" Her panic was clear, even though her voice seemed to be coming from a great distance.

Jachin took a step in the direction he'd last seen her, only to see her being pulled away by Sean as the man said, "Follow me. I know the way."

Jachin had no choice but to follow. The eerily illuminated fog was so thick now that he couldn't see his feet, and worse yet, he couldn't see where to step. One false move, and he and Angela would be back in the water.

"Boaz, where are you?" He called as he took a cautious step, feeling the spongy surface of the stone beneath his soggy shoes.

"Jachin, this way." Her voice sounded too calm considering the panic he'd heard just moments before. And now it was ahead of him.

He followed her voice, taking cautious steps. The only movement from Angela was an occasional shiver. Otherwise, she remained limp in his arms. It was probably better that she was unconscious. He needed to focus on advancing through the fog without stepping off the stone, and holding a panicked woman would be extremely distracting.

After several steps he saw a flash of movement, so he hurried his pace. Several more steps and, again, a bit of movement. Or was it the fog? It swirled around them like grasping arms.

Then he saw Boaz hurry away. "Dammit, Boaz! Stand still and wait for me."

Why was she following Sean, whom she knew would sabotage them if he could? Had Sean put some kind of spell on her?

"Jachin, this way." The excited tone of his sister's voice held no indication she'd even heard him, let alone that she had stopped her progress.

Heaving a frustrated sigh, Jachin followed the sound of her voice. He had no idea where they were. He only knew that he'd crossed at least one stone, possibly more. And if it hadn't been for Marrion telling them they couldn't go back the way they'd come, he'd be wondering if they were going backwards.

Other sounds now reached through the mist to mingle with his sister's plea of, "Hurry, Jachin!"

He could hear a woman's eerily unsubstantial laughter, then a quick rush of wind, although no breeze blew past as he hurried on. He heard the strumming of a harp mingling with a low rumble of indistinct conversation, and a peacock's eerie cry joined the unearthly melee.

Suddenly Boaz stood directly in front of him, looking confused. She stood with her head tilted to the side as though listening, and she started when she saw him.

"Jachin, why didn't you wait for me? I called and called to you. Couldn't you hear me?"

"Me wait for you? You told me to follow you."

She rolled her eyes. "Jachin, I was right behind you." Then she looked uncertain. "At least, I thought it was you. It looked like you. But you wouldn't answer me, and you kept rushing on ahead." Boaz frowned, stating the obvious. "Sean."

Jachin nodded. "No doubt some kind of trick."

Sean had evidently been able to imitate their voices as well as change his appearance enough to fool them. And Jachin knew Sean's ruse had most likely worked. They had probably gone to the ninth wave instead of the seventh. But he wasn't sure their route of entry mattered all that much. All he had was Marrion's word that they must enter at the seventh wave because it was the 'proper' way. To hell with proper, he just wanted to get to dry land and get Angela some help.

Jachin looked around. Sean, or Gaban, or whoever he was, was nowhere in sight. The fog was turning spidery and allowed some measure of visibility.

"Look!" Boaz pointed to an area to his right. "I see trees! I think we made it." Her voice held a note of awe. "Sena."

As the mist receded, a broad, moonlit beach flanked by trees came into view, and Jachin realized they were no longer standing on the moonbeam steps, but were on a sand bar which lead to a cove. Even with the moon's brightness, more stars than he had ever seen were visible. Great sweeping trails of stars formed constellations that, until now, he'd only seen clearly in drawings.

Angela moaned softly, and he strode toward the beach, scanning the thick forest for signs of life. He saw only variegated darkness through the trees.

So this was Sena. Would the forest beyond the beach resemble the one in his dreams? Something told him it would, and his mind whispered, "You're home."

But he still felt that this might be some kind of elaborate trick.

"Isn't it just like you'd imagined?" Boaz asked.

Jachin let his irritation show when he answered, "No. I haven't *imagined* Sena. I'm not even sure this is Sena," he said. "We could be in Long Beach for all I know."

They needed to get Angela to a warm, dry shelter, not dwell on the fact they were in this strange place. Besides, he didn't want his dream world to exist, even though his heart told him it lay just a few yards before him. Too many dark images came with the reality of Sena.

Boaz shot him a sidelong glace, but didn't comment on his rudeness.

He fought the urge to clench his jaw. "We've got to find some kind of shelter for Angela." He nodded his head toward the trees to indicate they should move in that direction.

Boaz's expression turned apprehensive. "I sense something dark in the forest."

He snorted. "Boaz, everything in the damn forest is dark. It's night." He knew he needed to reassure her, but the best he could come up with was a gruff, "We'll be fine."

They started toward the trees, Boaz straightening her shoulders and walking beside him, instead of holding back as he'd anticipated. He had to give her credit. She had guts.

Suddenly Angela stiffened, then tried to push away from his arms. He stopped. "Hold up a minute, Boaz. Angela's awake."

Obviously Angela had regained full consciousness and now struggled weakly to free herself from his arms. "You can put me down now, Jachin." Her voice was a hoarse croak.

"Oh, Angela, you had me so scared," Boaz said, tossing the backpacks on the sand.

Jachin held onto Angela. "It's okay, Angela. I've got you, and you're safe. It's okay."

She pushed harder, her lack of strength evident in her feeble attempt. "No, it's not okay. I want down."

As she struggled with Jachin, she also self-consciously tugged at her wet dress, pulling the clinging material away from her full breasts and flat belly. The clinging folds of wet fabric, along with the moonlight, had turned her beautiful body into an artistic masterpiece, outlining enticing curves and chilled nipples. Jachin couldn't help smiling, but he kept his thoughts to himself. She was distressed enough, and he knew instinctively that if she realized it was too late for modesty, she'd be mortified. He lowered her to her feet, noticing how wobbly she was. She wouldn't last two yards. He'd have to carry her.

Picking up his backpack, he noticed that Angela's was missing. It must have fallen off Boaz's arm in the confusion. *Oh well, no big deal*, he thought as he adjusted the pack's straps over his shoulders.

"You might as well stop fighting me on this, Angela," he said "I *am* going to carry you." He turned to Boaz. "Angela's pack is missing. Give her something dry to put on."

"Are you always so c-c-controlling?" Angela hugged herself, her teeth chattering as she waited for Boaz to get the clothes out of her backpack. Boaz handed her a soft cotton dress and positioned herself, arms crossed, between him and Angela.

"It's one of my better traits," he said as he turned away to get a dry shirt for himself.

A few moments later he heard Angela sigh and say, "Thanks, Boaz."

He turned, seeing her button the last button on the dress. Stepping around Boaz, he scooped Angela up and started walking toward the forest, hoping she wouldn't put up a fight. No such luck.

"Put me down!" Angela pushed against him, but she was too weak to do much good.

Boaz grabbed the wet dress and the remaining backpack and hurried to keep up with them. "Angela, don't be silly. Let Jachin carry you. You need to conserve your energy and body heat." She fumbled with one of the packs.

Jachin could feel her body warming against his. He had enough body heat for the both of them, but he was still concerned she might get hypothermia. Although the air was mild, her core temperature had dropped.

She finally gave up struggling, but remained stiff in his arms, mumbling, "I guess I don't have much choice in the matter."

Jachin said, "No, you don't."

Boaz said, "He's only trying to help you, Angela."

Angela looked up at him, her stubborn scowl relaxing. "Thank you."

"You're welcome." He looked straight ahead and filed away a mental note that Angela Dawn was not a woman who liked to depend on others. He wanted to ask her why, and was stunned to realize he really wanted to know. More than that, he cared about what had made her the way she was. He cared about her safety. And he cared about what she thought of him.

Dangerous thoughts, he warned himself.

***

With the full moon as her lantern, Marrion hurried through night. She needed to reach the children before Kadien intercepted them. As it was, they had entered Sena the worst way possible. They'd come onto unconsecrated, impure ground, and worse, with a Lute, endangering their unenlightened spirits and leaving them wide open to Kadien's influence. They needed to be taken to the compound to undergo the purification ritual and become enlightened to their powers. As for Angela...Well, she still wasn't sure what the ramifications of having Angela in Sena would be.

She was almost to the shore at which the three had reached land. Hurrying through a grove of moss-covered pines she could just make out three figures standing uncertainly on the sandy shore. There was no sign of either Gaban or Kadien.

Thank the stars, she wasn't too late.

Jachin held Angela in his arms, making Marrion wonder how badly the poor thing had been hurt when Gaban pushed her off the pier. When it had happened, there was no doubt in Marrion's mind that Jachin would save the girl and be forced to bring her to Sena, as indeed he should. He couldn't let her drown. But Marrion had an uneasy feeling about Angela's presence.

The novelty of a Lute could cause a distraction to the others on the island. That could compromise Boaz's and Jachin's mission to find Lilith, so the triplets could rejoin and get ready for the prophesied battle with The Darkness. But then, the triplets would be a novelty, too, since no one except herself and Gaban had seen them before.

"Jachin, Boaz!" Marrion called out as she walked into the clearing. The yielding sand slowed her progress, and she gathered her long skirts to keep from tripping. The soft splash and lap of waves was the only sound on the beach. Marrion could sense creatures large and small observing from the forest, as if they knew the importance of this particular crossing.

Boaz and Jachin turned in unison to look at her, relief in their expressions when they realized who she was.

Jachin spoke first. "Angela is hurt. We need to get her warm." First Marrion did what she hadn't been able to do as telepathic image in the Lute world. She rushed up to Boaz and hugged her tight, and Boaz hugged her as if to make up for lost years. Their spiritual connection was instant.

From Boaz's mind came a rush of emotion, allowing Marrion to feel the pain and sense of abandonment Boaz had buried her entire life. Marrion gave her niece one last squeeze and then gently disengaged her arms. There would be time for healing the child's spirit. Right now they needed to get to the compound.

Marrion noticed tears in Boaz's eyes, but the girl's smile was happy.

Turning her attention to Jachin, Marrion gave him a hug, as best she could with Angela in his arms. "Welcome home, children. This is indeed a momentous night."

What Marrion felt from Jachin upon the embrace was a confused jumble. She could discern emotions that were completely shut off, yet at the same time she sensed a dreamy kind of lethargy. There was a darkness lurking just beyond the reach of her telepathy, too, and its cool fingers chilled her. Then she realized she was intercepting Angela's vibrations as well as Jachin's. Of course. After all, she'd touched them both. But which of the children harbored the darkness?

Boaz interrupted her worried thoughts. "It really does feel like home, Aunt Marrion." She looked around the beach and at the forest, all the while stroking her arms as if to bring the touch of her surroundings to her.

"Well, don't get too comfortable, my dears. Through no fault of your own you entered Sena on unconsecrated ground. You should have been purified and enlightened, for your protection as well as Sena's. You still have Lute energy about you, and it can affect the balance, causing who knows what kind of disturbances."

Marrion noticed Jachin shifting Angela in his arms, not as though she might be a burden, but more as one might to comfort a loved one. He looked quite comfortable in the role of Angela's protector, and the thought disturbed Marrion. Jachin must not be distracted from his mission. But then, she reminded herself, the role each of them had to play in this drama wasn't hers to decide. Marrion knew that all would be revealed, even Angela's place in the prophecy, and there had to be a place for her, or she wouldn't have ended up in Sena. With that thought came a sinking feeling. Would Angela be a friend or a foe?

"Come with me," Marrion said as she quickly led the way toward the forest path.

A short time later they arrived at the ancient healing village where the children should have arrived. Marrion's relief at reaching them before Kadien was immeasurable. She still wasn't sure why Kadien hadn't been at the ninth wave to meet them at crossing over. Surely he knew of their arrival.

***

Gaban shed his host, leaving the man to doze peacefully under a large willow tree, then laughed at the little joke. The enlightened ones called the willow *Li Ambi*—hue of the lifeless. This mortal lay in a deep slumber resembling death. Only The Master's magic, through Gaban, could release the man from his slumber. But Gaban wasn't about to let the man go just yet. He might need him later. But for now it felt good to be rid of the cumbersome Lute body and clothing and to stretch. How did humans manage with such short limbs? He'd had the devil of a time maneuvering the Lute's arms.

Bypassing the labyrinth surrounding Kadien's fortress, Gaban hurried toward the hidden portal to the underground tunnel and shortcut to his master's lair. He didn't take time to look back to see if the others had made it to shore. Where else could they go? Besides, he'd done his job. He'd tricked them into entering Sena on unhallowed ground, just as his master had demanded. No mater that he had no idea of The Dark One's plan or reason. He could congratulate himself on a job well done. The fog had helped with the disguises his master had instructed him to use, but he alone had come up with the idea of imitating Boaz's voice to confuse Jachin into moving to the ninth wave. All that mattered to him at that moment was that he'd fulfilled the sentence set down by his master. Surely now Kadien would forgive past transgressions and leave him in peace.

Gaban chuckled. He had something with which to barter, should The Master hesitate. During the chaos in the fog, he had taken one of the backpacks. It held all manner of Lute magic. A cell phone, which he had become accustomed to seeing on his visit. It also held a small black leather folder with holographic credit cards. Surely The Dark Lord would be pleased, but he didn't want to reveal his sleight of hand until it was absolutely necessary. If he was freed without giving up the treasures, he might be able to use them himself. Who knew what powers they contained. The white wizards were afraid of the magic within the Lute items, so it must be powerful.

He noticed the hurried retreat of creatures as he moved through the forest, which suited him just fine. Trolls preferred their own company to that of silly fairy folk and animals, anyway. The other creatures on Sena were nothing more than casual diversions to be toyed with when the mood suited him.

At last he approached the huge, twisted oak tree and pushed through the panel of curtain camouflage made to look like ancient tree bark. His troll's eyes quickly adjusted to the tunnel's darkness, allowing him to easily make his way through the earthen passageway. Before he went to see The Master, he needed to hide his treasures.

Within an hour—a journey that would have taken days if he'd gone by way of the maze—he arrived at The Master's chamber door. He knocked carefully, but even then the huge door's rough wood abraded his knuckles. Sucking on them, he tasted both sweat and blood. It was then he noticed the moisture dripping onto the stone floor. Visiting The Master always made Gaban nervous, and The Dark One would not be pleased if Gaban slimed up his chamber. He rubbed his arms along his breechcloth, but it did little good. The more he dabbed, the more profusely he sweated.

The door to the chamber suddenly whipped open, and he started shaking, unable to move. Before him stood The Master, taller than any human Gaban had ever seen. The wizard's title of The Dark Lord did him justice. He was dark, from his shoulder-length hair to his black eyes. Gaban restrained a shiver of apprehension, feeling a rivulet of sweat tickle its way through the folds of skin on his throat.

"Well," The Master's voice was so restrained Gaban had to lean toward him to hear. "I see you have returned. I've viewed the travelers, and I must say …" He paused, his nostrils flaring. "What is that stench?"

Gaban knew that others found troll sweat to be offensive, but the more he worried about offending Kadien, the more he oozed. He would have fled, but there was something he needed to know. Instead of following his instincts, he said, "Am I free to go, then, Master?" He didn't mean just for the moment, he meant was he pardoned to return to the forest as a free troll.

Kadien's smile wasn't friendly.

Cringing down as far as his long legs allowed, Gaban lowered his head. The Master's smile surely meant displeasure. He was about to be destroyed with a bolt of lightning and a ball of flame. But the strike never came.

As he opened his mouth to bargain for his life with the purloined Lute treasures, The Master said, "I am so well pleased with your performance, Gaban, that I feel compelled to request you grant me additional...favors. And this time I am prepared to make you the offer of an exchange."

Straightening a bit, Gaban hazarded a peek at Kadien, then quickly ducked his head. "An *offer*, Master?" His curiosity hummed like an agitated bee. Did he have bargaining power with The Dark One?

As The Master moved across the room, he touched his fingers to his nose, reminding Gaban of his offensive scent. "Troll, I am willing to bestow upon you certain powers...*permanent* powers...if you will once again assume your Lute body and assist me."

Powers? *Permanent* powers? To a Troll? It was unheard of. For a moment, Gaban felt lightheaded with the wonder of it. If he had permanent powers he would be the most powerful troll on Sena. Just having the temporary powers Kadien had given him had been intoxicating. What if they were his forever? He would be the only troll ever to achieve such greatness!

He stood to his full height, cricking his neck painfully as he looked up at Lord Kadien. "What would you have me do, Master?" He didn't ask why The Master was requesting instead of commanding. Or why he was asking a troll when he had legions of dark wizards to do his bidding. He knew better than to question The Dark One's motives.

"You are now familiar with the Lute ways. This will aid you as you go about your tasks."

Just then the door opened and an under-wizard in dark robes entered. Gaban wiped at his dripping face as he saw what the man held. The Lute satchel! The man handed the pack to Kadien, bowed and then backed toward the door. Just before he closed the door, Gaban saw the look of repulsion the man shot his way.

"I...I can explain, Your Darkness." Gaban hiccupped when Kadien raised his hand for silence.

"You forget, Gaban. I can see your every move whether you are here before me or lurking in the deepest cavern."

Gaban felt his foot begin to slide on the stone floor. Quickly he righted himself, wishing he could stop the flow of sweat.

The Master went to the table and picked up a candle. *This is it*, Gaban thought. To be annihilated in a burning ball of fire was a troll's worst fear.

Kadien's laughter was like a low growl. "I'm not angry, Gaban." He made a large circle around Gaban as he talked, all the while casually holding the candle. "I don't expect you to act contrary to your nature." He held onto the strap of the Lute woman's pack with one finger, swinging it back and forth. "I know what this pack contains. And as much as I hate to deprive you of your 'treasures,' I would ask you to return them to their rightful owner."

Gaban's mouth dropped open, a stringy line of drool escaping before he quickly closed his mouth. He hurriedly tried to brush his foot across the spot on the floor where the spittle had landed, but since his foot was covered in sweat, he only made the wet mark larger. "To the Lute, Master?"

"To the Lute." Kadien tossed the backpack to Gaban, as if even he didn't want to touch it too long. The magic must be powerful, indeed.

"Be warned, Gaban. If you do not follow my directions in this task as well as the others I set forth ...." He waved the candle in a circle.

Gaban felt both feet slip from beneath him.

SEVEN

**Void-Of-Course Moon: A time to rest and recover.
Plans will be altered, new and strange experiences
will manifest. False starts abound.**

As Angela looked around the right-out-of the-middle-ages
bedroom, she had difficulty assimilating the fact that she was
actually on the mythical isle of Sena—Avalon. But this was no
myth. Everything around her felt as solid and real as her own
world.

A sloping ceiling ran down to leaded-glass windows, which
stood open to the mild morning breeze. There was a carved bed,
a sturdy dresser and a rocking chair begging to be sat in. Drying
herbs hung from the ceiling beams, giving off a pleasant aroma.

Even though the air was a comfortable temperature, a fire
blazed in the hearth. After last night when she thought she might
never thaw out, it felt wonderful for her toes and fingers to be
toasty. She'd been well taken care of by a kind young woman
who lived on Sena. *Sena.*

She couldn't believe it. Her lifetime passion for myth and
legend now had substance, and she was smack dab in the middle
of it. How many more life forms and worlds existed? She couldn't
imagine.

Still shaky and a bit weak, she eased from beneath soft muslin
sheets, only to find that she was completely naked. She
remembered now how, after a steaming bath in a wooden tub,
she'd been herded into bed. Ailleann, the young woman who had
helped her, seemed to take no notice of her nudity, and hadn't
offered her a nightgown. The last thing Angela remembered
thinking as she put her head on the pillow was that it was
impossible to keep her eyes open.

Now she wrapped the sheet around her as she eased her legs
over the side of the bed. Surprisingly, her legs were strong once
her feet touched the wood floor.

A glass of milk and a luscious looking peach sat on the dresser,
and her stomach growled in anticipation. As she ate, she looked

around for her clothes, wondering where Boaz and Jachin might be. The last time she'd seen either of them was shortly after they'd arrived at the house.

A young woman had met them at the door as if they'd been expected. Marrion had talked to the woman, and then told Jachin to take Angela upstairs to one of the bedrooms. After Jachin had put her down, he had hurried off as if he couldn't wait to be rid of her. She'd been left with Boaz, Marrion and Ailleann. Marrion had told Angela that she was in Marrion's home, and that Ailleann, along with her eight sisters, were healers. Ailleann would take care of her. Then Marrion and Boaz had also left.

A gentle knock at the door snapped her out of her memories, and she scrambled to wrap herself more securely with the sheet.

"Come in." She felt a twinge of trepidation as she sat on the edge of the bed. After all, she wasn't exactly an invited guest. But then, no one had really been given a choice in the matter. Once Sean had pushed her off the pier and then Jachin had jumped into the water to save her, all choice had been eliminated.

The door slowly opened and Ailleann came in. "How are you feeling?" Her words carried a gentle brogue. She was dressed as the night before, in a dark blue, caftan-like dress, with a gold rope-like belt. Her hair, which she wore down her back in a thick braid, was a shimmery gold, and her eyes were a clear, vivid blue. Angela tried not to stare at the delicate starburst tattoo along the woman's temple.

"I'm fine...thanks to you," Angela said.

Ailleann walked over to stand next to her. "May I look at your leg injury?"

It was then that Angela realized the pulsing pain from the previous evening was completely gone. "Sure." She sat back and pulled the sheet up to reveal her bandaged shin.

Ailleann glanced at the sheet Angela held clasped around her. "Are you cold?"

"No." Cold or not, it wasn't in Angela's nature to walk in the buff in front of complete strangers. Anybody, for that matter. The look the woman gave her was one of concern, as though she didn't understand the need for the cover. Angela was left feeling like she should explain.

But then Ailleann's eyes twinkled, and she smiled. "Oh, yes, I think I understand. I have heard that many of your people feel shame in revealing their bodies. Our worlds are very different. But you do whatever makes you comfortable."

Ailleann removed the bandage and ran her hand just above, but not touching, Angela's injury, causing a warm tingling on her shin. Ailleann's tone was wistful as she said, "I would love to visit your world."

She closed her eyes as if to concentrate, and Angela felt little shooting pains radiate throughout her leg as the woman went on, "But the elders have long forbidden it."

When she took her hand away, Angela was shocked to realize her leg felt and looked like it had never been injured.

She stared at the spot on her shin, which just the night before had been covered in ugly gouges, and she was amazed to discover that she couldn't tell where her injury had been. Marrion had said Ailleann was a healer, but Angela could hardly believe what she had just experienced.

She put her wonder on hold and focused on the woman's statement. It was forbidden to leave Sena? "But surely you could leave Sena if you wanted to."

The woman shook her head. "Long ago, all creatures on Sena traveled freely between the worlds, but that changed when the great divide occurred and we fled persecution in our homeland. That was hundreds of years ago, when our people were betrayed and forced to retreat to Sena."

"And in all that time, no one has either left or come to Sena?"

Ailleann seated herself in the rocking chair, her aura of calm suddenly slipping as she rocked quickly back and forth. "A selected few of the elders become *travelers.*" She gave special emphasis to the word. "They wander through the other worlds and gather knowledge. But it is forbidden for the rest of us to leave."

"What would happen if you did?"

Ailleann shrugged. "I don't know." She looked up. "There was one white wizard, Seumas, who left. I don't know where he went. And several friends have disappeared, but we are not sure they crossed over. There are many other worlds besides yours and mine, and while we now know that Vivian took her babies to the Lute world, Seumas and the others could have gone anywhere. None has ever returned."

She looked sad for a moment, but then shook her head. "I

long to be a traveler, but my destiny is in the healing arts. If I ever dared to leave Sena, I fear I would not be able to return."

Angela was about to ask about the other worlds, but the young woman had questions of her own. They sat for over an hour, Ailleann growing more and more excited as she asked one question after another about Angela's life in the Lute world. And while they were talking, Ailleann worked more magic by brushing Angela's short hair and arranging little flowers in it.

Just when Ailleann began winding down and Angela felt free to ask questions of her own, the door opened, and Marrion entered carrying a small bundle under her arm. Ailleann got up and, resuming her initial manner of serenity, said good-bye to Angela and left.

"So, my dear. Are you feeling better?" Marrion asked.

Angela felt a bit uneasy with the woman since, being a Lute, she wasn't exactly an invited guest. If Marrion was upset by her being there, she didn't show it. "I'm a little overwhelmed." She motioned to take in all of Sena. "But, physically I'm fine." She moved the sheet aside to show Marrion her shin. "Amazing, but you'd never know I'd been hurt." Then she looked at Marrion. "Where are Boaz and Jachin?"

Marrion chuckled. "It seems Boaz and Jachin won't find peace until they see for themselves that you're alive and well. Jachin has been pacing like a caged griffin. Here, put these on, and we shall join your friends." She handed Angela the bundle from beneath her arm. "I have returned Boaz's dress to her. I think you'll find these quite comfortable."

The bundle contained an incredibly lightweight, gauzy chemise, a dark blue dress similar to the one Ailleann had worn, and a gold tunic overdress with a rope-type belt. The dress was soft and had long, slim sleeves and a floor-length hemline. She looked at Marrion. "What about my underwear?"

"Both of your undergarments were of synthetic fabrics and could be a threat to our environment. We had to seal them in crystal so as not to upset the elemental balance here on Sena. Besides, it's much healthier and less restrictive to the body and spirit to go without. I'm sure you'll quickly become accustomed to the freedom."

The fact that her brand-new designer bra and panties were an environmental hazard was cause for chagrin. Angela slipped the chemise over her head then put on the dress. Marrion helped her with the tunic and belt.

When she was dressed, Marrion smiled as she gave Angela the once-over. "I think we're ready to go downstairs. Why, you don't look like a Lute at all."

Angela thought about all the synthetic things in her backpack. "Do you know where my backpack is? I have a cell phone, a plastic camera and several other plastic items in it."

Marrion looked alarmed. "We'd better go ask the others what happened to it and dispose of the synthetic items as soon as possible."

As they hurried downstairs, Angela could feel the unaccustomed brush of cotton against her breasts and bottom. It wasn't unpleasant. In fact, it was rather sensual. And she felt a bit risqué knowing she wore no underwear beneath the dress.

The pleasant awareness was intensified the instant she made the first floor landing and found her gaze captured by Jachin's. Her pulse raced into overdrive, and all rational thought went out the window as he slowly looked her up and down, giving every indication that he was Superman with x-ray vision instead of a wizard. She fought the urge to cross her arms over her breasts. Suddenly she felt up to the challenge, although what exactly the challenge was, she wasn't sure.

Boaz bolted from her seat at the table and ran across the room to hug Angela, breaking the magic spell Jachin had cast over her. "I was so worried," Boaz said. Then she looked down at the dress Angela wore and reached up to touch her hair. "What a hoot. In that getup you look like you're right out of a fairy tale." She bowed. "Princess Angela."

Angela chuckled. "I think women are supposed to curtsy." She glanced over at Jachin only to see that his closed scowl had returned.

"Children," Marrion said, "do you know what became of Angela's pack and the items inside?"

Boaz looked pained. "I'm sorry Angela, but your backpack got knocked off my shoulder when we were trying to find each other in the fog. It must have fallen into the water."

Marrion let out a deep breath. "Thank heavens. Well, at least we won't have to worry about that."

"It's okay," Angela said. "In fact it's better off where it is. I had a whole bunch of stuff in there that isn't allowed in Sena."

Boaz looked relieved.

"Take a seat, children." Marrion indicated the long table as she went to a cupboard beside the stone fireplace and retrieved a large, leather-bound book.

Angela and Boaz took seats along the benches on either side of the table, and Marrion's cat, Emmeline, jumped up to stride in front of them, giving each a blinking acknowledgement. Jachin, on the other hand, acted as though he hadn't heard his aunt. He remained standing.

"Hello, kitty," Angela said, and the cat looked at her as though to return the greeting.

"Emmeline, you can get acquainted later," Marrion stated as she set the book in the middle of the table, then sat down. She scooped the cat into her lap and then turned to look at Boaz and Jachin. "As I told you before, Jachin, you've been raised in a world where your powers were not allowed to flourish. That's easily enough remedied now that you're here. Among other specific qualities, we all—all people of our race, that is—have the ability to access generational memories. All knowledge about our people is stored in your subconscious. We only need to bring those memories to the surface."

Jachin broke his brooding silence. "You're saying that I know everything our ancestors did? As far back as …?" He let the sentence hang, doubt strong in his voice.

Marrion nodded her head. "Although the further back you go, the more energy and skill it takes, you can go back to our lineal beginnings."

He began to pace in front of the fire. "And what are our beginnings? Exactly what *kind* of people are we? I know you call us wizards, but that doesn't explain anything. Why are we so different from the people in my world?" His tone was hostile.

Marrion frowned. "This is your world, Jachin."

Bracing his hands on the end of the table, he studied Marrion. Angela was unnerved by his anger, but Marrion seemed completely unfazed by it as he said, "I guess they're both my worlds, then, because as soon as we get Lilith away from this Kadien person, I'm going back."

Marrion only smiled. "We'll see. Who knows where your destiny will lead you."

"You haven't answered my question about who we are," he said, ignoring her comment. "And don't tell me we're from another planet." He crossed his arms, making Angela wonder if he really wanted to know.

"Would it make a difference?" Marrion's chuckle said she was only teasing, but her answer was as obscure as her letter to Boaz had been. "When you're ready to acknowledge the truth of your heritage, you will make that journey into your memory."

Jachin frowned. "Figures."

Marrion chuckled again. "Jachin, there are no easy answers, no matter what world you inhabit. Each of us must follow our own path to the truth."

Jachin's only response was to roll his eyes and look out the window.

Boaz said anxiously, "Let's get back to this generational memories thing. Do you mean we could tap into our memories to discover what happened to our mother?"

Marrion shrugged, seeming to think that over. "Perhaps. You would only possess your mother's memories up until the time you were born. Her actions after that would no longer be connected with you. The ancient memories have had generations of reinforcement, so they're stronger. The newer ones are quicker to retrieve, but they aren't always solid. But I think it might be worth a try. I, for one, would be much relieved to know the reason for my sister's actions."

Jachin said, "So why can't you just 'remember' it?"

"The memories," Marrion said, "are passed...well I guess the Lutes would say 'genetically.' For example, Boaz got the gene for blue eyes from her mother, and you, Jachin, inherited your black hair from your maternal grandfather. And you both inherited from your ancestors the genes enabling your powers. I don't possess the direct genetic link to my sister, only to our parents, grandparents and so forth, so I can't tap into her memories."

Angela realized she was gaping and immediately closed her mouth. But to be able to retrieve from your own memory the events of your ancestors was incredible. One of the ancient North American tribes she'd studied had based their religion on that very thing. They worshiped their ancestors and had 'dream visions' of them in order to recall the ancient ways. Angela always wondered if such a thing was possible. It would be great to "go back" and find out about the supposed curse her uncle had told her about. Or to relive through memories what it had been like for her ancestors hundreds of years ago.

"Enough about memories," Jachin said. "What we need to do is find Lilith. You don't seem to be in such a hurry now that we're here."

"I've been observing her, and she is fine for now. For some reason Kadien hasn't tried to break the spell I put on her. He could if he wanted to." Marrion puzzled as she made that announcement, and then she shook her head and looked at Boaz and Angela. "We must wait for the proper moon cycle to begin this new journey. For the moment we are in the "void-of-course" moon—a time between cycles. This is a time to rest and refresh, not the time to begin journeys."

Marrion touched the book. "This is your mother's book of light, Boaz. After you have been purified, I will give it to you. It will then fall upon you to protect it and the knowledge within it."

Marrion turned to Jachin. "The first thing we must do is purify all of you as well as enlightening you and Boaz so that you are able to tap into your powers. My use of the word *enlighten* in this instance refers to teaching you the meditation techniques that will allow you to recall your powers."

"Then let's get to it," Jachin stated. "The sooner we get this whole thing settled and I can return home, the better."

Marrion looked worried. "I'm afraid you are all bound here until the next Wizard's Moon a year from now, no matter what the outcome of facing Kadien."

"But Sean told us about some kind of maiden boat or barge or something," Boaz said.

"Yes." She squinted at Angela, and Angela felt her throat go dry. "I didn't think to look before, but I do sense in Angela the purity required." She looked at Jachin. "That is an option. Angela is a virgin, and as such, could call the maiden's boat to take you back."

When Angela looked at Jachin it was to see him staring at her in astonishment. All she could do was smile weakly and shrug her shoulders. Since when was being a virgin a crime? It might be a bit odd, especially to these people, whom Marrion had said took many lovers before they found their lifemate. Even so, it wasn't like she had two heads, for heaven's sake!

"Stop staring," she told Jachin, but he didn't look away.

Boaz began to chuckle. "Yes, our girl is one of a kind."

Marrion petted Emmeline. "Angela will remain here," she said to Jachin, "while you and Boaz go to your sister. Then—"

"No." Jachin cut her off. "Angela stays with us."

Marrion shook her head. "Impossible. The dangers would be too great for all of you."

Angela stood up. "Hello? Do I have a choice in the matter? I know I'm an uninvited guest, but I am used to making my own decisions."

"Of course you have a choice, dear," Marrion said, "but in this instance, the triplets' safety could be jeopardized."

Jachin began to pace irritably. "Enough of this. I'm going after Lilith, and both Boaz *and* Angela are coming with me. Just tell me where Kadien is and what I'll be up against." He looked like he was ready to bolt for the door.

Marrion stood up, wringing her hands in distress. "First you must be purified and enlightened."

"Then do it." He looked just like Boaz did when she experienced her EOD—Energy Overabundance Disorder—spells.

"Yes, well then, come with me, children. All has been readied to perform the purification ritual for the three of you. Tomorrow, Boaz and Jachin, you will be helped toward enlightenment before you leave on your journey."

Marrion returned the book to the cupboard and walked to the door, explaining, "The villagers know you haven't been purified, so all but the healers and elders will avoid you until after the ceremony. Then you are free to mingle and get to know your community. Angela, you came here through no fault of your own. You will be treated as an honored guest."

Angela followed them, noticing Jachin held back, taking up the rear. He was uncomfortably close to her, and his energy seemed to radiate like a heat lamp.

Jachin knew he shouldn't have been so abrupt with Marrion, but once the words were out he couldn't retract them. At least he was outside now. He felt the tension ease in his chest. He needed to get his anger under control. It wasn't Marrion's fault that he could never live up to her expectations. Would she be in such a hurry to do this purification ceremony if she knew the darkness dwelling inside him? It would take more than a ritual to wash it away.

As they walked past a myriad of what seemed to be deserted buildings, he found himself focused on Angela's slim neck. A pair of doves cooed to each other from the treetops, and she tilted her head as if listening. He couldn't believe she was a virgin. She certainly hadn't kissed like one. The way she had pressed her body to his gave him every indication she knew exactly what she was doing and where it could lead. His memories of the passion they'd shared in his office mixed with those of his dream, and he had to caution himself not to confuse the two.

Marrion led them into a windowless stone structure. "A word of caution, children. This is a sacred site, and as such the energies of creation within are at their highest. When you enter, you will become an integrated part of the energies of the land. The thoughts you have will be transferred to the energy in the room. Those thoughts and feelings will be amplified and returned to you. For this reason it is important to watch what you think when you enter. Keep your thoughts positive."

A moment before they stepped over the threshold, Marrion closed her eyes and intoned, "Let all who find themselves in a space of negativity or darkness allow light to come into their minds, bodies and spirits."

When they entered the building, Jachin felt an immediate calm wash over him. It took a few moments before his eyes adjusted to the dimness within the large, steamy room. Candles offered diffused light. And a fine mist of steam came up from two rectangular pools, giving everything fuzzy, indistinct edges.

"What is this?" Jachin wasn't in the mood for a sauna. Scents of spice and forest filled the room.

"This," Marrion said, "is where we conduct our purification ritual. In order to stay in Sena, your mind and body must be cleansed of the influences of the outside world. This ceremony will also open your minds to enlightenment."

"What about Angela?" Boaz asked.

"Everyone coming to the Light side of Sena is purified and sanctified, so that their minds, spirits and hearts will be open to The Light. It will help protect you from those on Sena with dark intent...that is, unless you *willingly* open yourselves to outside dark forces."

Jachin thought, *What if that dark force comes from within?*

Then he remembered Marrion's warning about his thoughts being amplified, and he quickly buried the thought.

"So, what do we do?" Boaz squinted through the fog, her body slightly swaying. Evidently she, too, was feeling suddenly enervated.

Just then, the group of women Jachin had met the night before walked through the door. They held white towels draped over their arms. All nine of them took up positions standing along the walls.

"You will disrobe and then immerse yourselves in the water," Marrion said. "One pool is for you, Jachin, the other for Boaz and Angela."

Jachin felt drowsiness overtake him. He was fast becoming a sleepwalker—aware of his surroundings, but detached. Taking a deep breath, he smelled flowers and herbs.

Three of the women left their places, one going to each of them. Boaz and Angela were led to the far pool, while the woman next to him indicated he should follow her. She showed him the location of the steps leading into his pool. From his vantage point, he saw Angela and Boaz as ghostly, blurred images.

Marrion said, "Please disrobe and enter the water."

Normally, he would have balked at such an order, but the sooner Marrion had her way, the sooner he could be on his. He stripped then stepped down into the water until he was up to his waist. Evidently the pendant he wore wasn't a problem, because no one had mentioned it, and he could see Boaz's glittering from across the room, so he knew she still wore hers.

The water was hot but not uncomfortable. Looking at the other pool, he saw that Boaz was already in the water, but Angela seemed reluctant to let the woman help her off with her dress. The woman said something, and Angela's head slowly bobbed an acknowledgement. Finally the woman lifted the dress over Angela's head, and Jachin was given a steamy view of her perfect body. It was just how he remembered it from his dream.

Lazy thoughts drifted through his mind, and he wondered if she actually had the clover-shaped birthmark on her left thigh. From this distance, he certainly couldn't tell. He realized his mind was becoming as foggy as the room. He went under the water and let the calm feelings wash over him. For the first time in his life he knew what the word 'euphoria' meant.

As he came to the surface, Marrion began to speak in a monotone cadence. "Breathe deeply. Clear your minds and relax." Several moments passed. "Cultivate nothingness...Breathe deeply."

Over the years he'd become adept at meditation to help him control his excess energy, so following her commands was an easy task. He felt himself respond to her words, and his mind peacefully focused on everything and nothing.

After a few minutes of blissful silence, with only the sound of water softly lapping against the side of the pool, Marrion spoke. "Dismantle your emotional filters and fears...and discover your infinite energy."

Jachin found himself doing just that. He let the energy flow through him.

"Breathe deeply," Marrion intoned. "Maintain balance and harmony."

The other women began softly singing, "*Geebyrt geearee fys ...*" Jachin couldn't understand the words, but was swept away with the serene harmony. The grotto-like room gave the voices a slight echo, which reverberated through his entire being.

"Bring your soul into The Spirit."

Again the singing, and he felt himself being transported to another self. A peaceful self he hadn't known existed.

"Recognize that you are born of The Great One. Breathe deeply, letting negative thoughts leave with the breath."

He let go of the fleeting feeling that this was turning into a religious ceremony. After all, weren't most ceremonies based on spiritual beliefs?

"Uncover the majesty of who you are."

The power within him hummed to life, bringing with it the certainty that he was, as Marrion said, a member of one of the royal families of wizards. As full acceptance came to him at that realization, so did more peace and sense of purpose than he'd ever experienced. He had an important part to play in The Great Prophecy. Although what part he would play hadn't been revealed, for the moment it was enough to know he was a part of it.

"Know that all are one."

"*...er yn aght cosoylagh...*," the women sang.

He concentrated on opening his mind and memory to the words. If what Marrion said was true, it might be possible to recall from his "generational memory" what the words meant. As easily as it was to think the thought, he understood the words. The women were merely repeating what Marrion was saying, but in an ancient language.

All material and energy in the room, in the world, became recognizable as a whole. He realized that when he took the elements in the air and earth to make bronze, he wasn't accomplishing such a great feat. He was just asking the *whole* to reorganize.

"Oh Great One," all of the women murmured, "Let the eyes of the blind be opened. Let those who are lost find the true path. Dissolve the boundaries of fixed ideas. Purify their spirits and their souls. Let them be reborn."

Jachin felt as though, with very little effort, he could float out of his body. But he couldn't let go of the final thread of control. What, if in doing so, he allowed the darkness within him to emerge? Even now that darkness crouched like a tiger ready to strike. Ready to destroy.

***

Seumas succeeded in rousing himself from the weak spell he had allowed the troll to place on him. He granted himself a few moments to revel in the luxury of being *home*.

Taking in the forest surroundings—the morning sky peeking through the treetops, the echoed songs of birds, and the scent of pine—he felt reborn. He ran his hands across the soft moss at the base of the tree, feeling the true, pure energy of his homeland caress his spirit. Ecstasy.

After thirty years he'd almost forgotten the deep, vivid blue of Sena's sky. A lump of gratitude closed his throat as he realized that after three long decades of exile, he was truly back. The fates had deemed him ready to return.

Thanks to circumstance—and the most unlikely of aids, Gaban—he had been able to make it back home undetected. No longer would he refer to himself as the Lute Sean. The powers he had abstained from in order to remain undetected by those of his kind, and which he had only recently used to destroy Jachin's sculpture, he could now restore to freedom. And the Lute persona he had invented could now be put to rest. He was sure that most wizards on Sena thought him long dead. That was good. He needed to remain unobserved for as long as possible. He must find a certain pool deep within a secret cave where he could perform the purification ritual unobserved.

He was back. He had his powers.

And Seumas Scot had a promise to keep.

***

Angela picked a variegated yellow and green squash and added it to her basket as she spoke in a low whisper so Jachin, who stood at the opposite side of the compound yard, couldn't hear her. "Boaz, is it me, or does Jachin seem to be running hot and cold since The Big Jacuzzi this morning? One minute he's almost pleasant, the next he's doing his Heathcliff routine again."

She looked across the yard to where Jachin stood listening intently to the blacksmith, and she wondered for the hundredth time why she hadn't been embarrassed about getting naked in front of Jachin during the ritual bath. At the time it had seemed perfectly natural. She'd felt drowsy and perfectly at ease. Although, if truth be told, whenever she was around Jachin, words like naked, hot, steamy and sex tumbled through her mind like the wheels on a Las Vegas slot machine.

Boaz glanced up as she snipped some herbs to add to the overflowing basket of vegetables they were gathering for the welcome home party being held in Boaz and Jachin's honor. Boaz and Angela wanted to help even though Marrion said it wasn't necessary. Everyone seemed to have a job or task to do. Several other women were gathering vegetables in the garden along with them, but they stayed a respectful distance away, as if they didn't want to intrude unless invited. Angela couldn't help noticing that they all had tattoos of various patterns, some on their arms and some on their faces. In fact, everyone in the village, including the children, wore tattoos.

"For some reason, Jachin's still fighting hard to keep his barriers up," Boaz said. "But I can tell he's more attuned with the surrounding energies. How about you? Do you feel different?"

Angela shrugged as she picked a ripe tomato and held it to her nose, inhaling the rich acid tang. "I guess." She couldn't in all honestly say she felt any kind of special 'energies' around her. Not like Boaz obviously did, anyway. But then, she hadn't when they'd been home, either, and Boaz always seemed to be tuning into some weird vibration.

Angela stated, "I do feel relaxed, like I've been given the full treatment at a day spa." She added the tomato to the basket as she looked back at Jachin. "Why do you think Jachin needs barriers? It's wonderful here, but most of the time he acts as though he doesn't like it."

Boaz leaned toward Angela confidentially. "I've been unintentionally picking up on some of his thoughts. Probably because of Sena's heightened energies. Anyway, I know he's pretty much come to terms with what we are, but he's still fighting to control the wizard part of himself. For some reason, he believes the powers are evil-based and dangerous. I think he just needs more time to adjust. He'll come around." Boaz straightened, dusting the rich, dark mulch, along with an enormous wriggling earthworm, from her gauzy dress.

In an effort to get a better look at Jachin, Angela craned to look past Ailleann and the cow she was leading through the yard. He did have a harsh, sinister look about him at that moment, but that could be due to the fact that he wasn't wearing sunglasses and the setting sun was at a glaring angle. Or was he right about himself? Were his powers dangerous? Just because Boaz's were good, didn't mean his were. But even as her doubts surfaced, her heart told her he couldn't possibly use his powers to hurt anyone.

Just then a group of three small, squealing children darted from the side of a building and directly into the path of Ailleann and the cow. The shrieks and sudden movement startled the huge animal, which bolted blindly past Ailleann and headed directly toward the children. They froze in terror.

Her heart pounding, Angela caught up her long skirt and rushed from the garden, her mouth open to cry a warning. But the sound stuck in her throat as she saw there was no way to stop the cow or get to the children in time.

A sudden blur of movement caught her eye. Jachin had somehow reached the children. Quickly he scooped up all three and instantly hauled them safely out of harm's way. The cow immediately calmed and trotted off with Ailleann in pursuit.

When Angela breathlessly reached the kneeling Jachin, the three wailing toddlers were clinging to him as if they would never let go. His strong arms held them tightly, and Angela heard him whispering, "It's okay. You're not hurt. You're fine."

He repeated the soothing chant until they began to calm. One little girl, a tiny brunette with huge blue eyes, was shaking so hard Angela feared she might be hurt. She had her face pressed hard against Jachin's cheek, her arms locked in a death-grip around his neck.

Two women rushed to claim the children, thanking Jachin profusely. One of the women tried to disengage the little girl from Jachin's neck. "Come, Guendoloena, we'll have a nice cup of cider to sooth your nerves. Jachin must prepare for his journey."

But the little girl, her nose running and her eyes red with tears, refused to let go. She pressed herself even more tightly against Jachin's cheek.

"It's okay," Jachin said to the woman. "Give her a few minutes."

He stood and shifted the little girl to a more comfortable position, which was no easy task since she seemed determined to become part of his face.

The woman took a handkerchief from her skirt pocket and wiped the girl's nose. "Very well. But you be mindful, Guendoloena. Understand? And you come into the family house when Jachin tells you to. We must wash up before the festivities."

The little girl nodded, but never moved her cheek from Jachin's. Her fingers remained locked behind his neck.

Boaz, who had joined them, chuckled. "Looks like you might have a friend ...or an added appendage...for life." She reached up to stroke child's face, eliciting a shaky smile from the girl who looked to be about three or four years old.

Jachin seemed to shrug off his sister's comment and headed back to the blacksmith's barn with Guendoloena still attached.

Boaz looked down at her basket of vegetables. "I'll take these into the kitchen, but I think you should go with Jachin. He doesn't look all that comfortable with the little monkey around his neck. Besides, you've always been great with kids...in case he should panic."

She chuckled again as she walked off.

Angela shook her head in wonder as she headed toward the barn. She and Boaz had just been talking about his supposed 'dark powers' when, in the very next moment, he'd shown them all that his instincts were to help, not hurt. He'd saved her as well. He might grouch and complain, and even say he had no intention of helping, but she was sure it would go against his nature to let something bad happen.

When she entered the barn, she saw Jachin standing next to a huge open furnace, talking to the blacksmith. She caught his sideways glance and look of pleasant surprise when he noticed her, but he turned his full attention back to the man. The blacksmith was explaining about the knife he had just made and why he used a forge as well as magic.

The man held the long, dangerous-looking knife at an angle, eying the blade as he talked. "I have made the blade true and sure to pierce the toughest of hides. You'll have no trouble skinning any animal made available to you on your journey."

"Available?"

"Yes," the man continued. "I think you'll soon see that the entire animal kingdom on Sena will make itself available to you on this most important of quests. Don't hesitate to take the gifts offered, but remember to thank the spirits who offer themselves to you as sustenance."

"You mean," Jachin said with a disbelieving smirk, "animals will just walk up and say, 'I'm dinner. Kill me?'"

The man chuckled. "No, but you will see that when there is need, the opportunity for fulfillment will present itself. When we take food, it is our custom to thank the food's spirit for its sacrifice." He handed the knife to Jachin, who easily held the heavy-looking weapon with his free hand.

Angela noticed that the man kept glancing at Jachin's pendant, and she could have sworn she saw a hint of excitement in his eyes.

The blacksmith went on. "Procuring a new blade for you was necessary. Metals take on the spirit of their owners as well as the spirit of what it has been used for. If I were to give you someone else's knife, it could possess any bad vibrations its previous owner might have possessed, or any evil deeds for which it was used. That negative energy could transfer itself to your hand and work against you when you need the knife to do your bidding. Once you have attained your full powers, you will design your own sword. It will hold more power than the knife I have made for you. But for now the knife will have to suffice."

Again he glanced at Jachin's pendant. What was it about the pendant that was so interesting? Angela wondered. First Marrion had given Boaz's and Jachin's pendants strange looks but said nothing. Now this man was staring at Jachin's as if it was the lost

Ark of The Covenant.

Angela found her gaze turning to little Guendoloena, who had comfortably settled into Jachin's arm, her legs straddling his waist. She was happily playing with the lightning-shaped pendant, twisting and turning it, then pressing it to her lips as if feeling its smooth texture. He appeared not to notice, his intent stare focused on the knife blade.

As Jachin handed the knife back to the blacksmith, he said, "I think I know what you mean about the metal's spirit. I work in bronze."

The man looked delighted. "I had hoped one of my immediate family would inherit metalwork."

Jachin looked confused. "Your family?"

"Yes, I'm your Uncle Illan. Marrion wanted those of us who are your immediate family to introduce ourselves as the need arose. She feared that for us to introduce ourselves all at once would be too overwhelming. We are many."

"You're my uncle?"

Illan nodded. "Your mother and Marrion are my sisters. Many of the men in our family have been metalworkers, gifted with the transforming of such."

At Jachin's incredulous stare, the man said, "Yes, it's inherited." Then he hastily added, "But only by the men. Our women have never been gifted with metalwork, just as our men have never inherited the power to heal."

A spark of excitement flared in Jachin's eyes. He turned. "Angela, would you take the child?" He looked at Guendoloena who nodded her reluctant compliance.

"Sure." Angela smiled reassuringly at the little girl.

He eased Guendoloena into her arms, helping the child to get settled on Angela's hip. His hand lingered long moments on Angela's shoulder as he smiled down at the little girl. Angela felt her heart catch as an unbidden picture of what it would be like to be a family struck her with the force of a Mack truck. She had to swallow back the lump in her throat. It was a foolish thought, and one she shouldn't connect in any way with Jachin Morgan. She was only a visitor in his world. Tomorrow he and Boaz would be on their way to find Lilith. Once they did, she would return home. She was sure that if Jachin returned at all to her world, it would only be long enough to put his affairs in order.

Angela said, "Come on, baby doll, let's get prettied up for the party, shall we?"

The child nodded eagerly and said, "Oh yes, please."

Angela turned with Guendoloena and walked back toward the main house, having the strange sensation that Jachin's heated gaze followed her.

***

Gaban couldn't understand what had happened to his Lute. Looking around the small clearing, he scratched his head. Then his arm flopped back down to swing at his side. He was sure he'd left the man peacefully sleeping under this very *Li Ambi* tree. Had someone stolen his Lute?

***

As Jachin entered the huge hall he gazed at the crowded room. Flickering candles softly illuminated the room and seemed to be dancing to the lively music. He glanced at the musicians, recognizing a harp, a lute, a pan-flute, a fiddle, and an instrument that looked similar to an obo. The remainder of the instruments were strange. Children wore bells around their wrists and kept cadence with the music as they danced and played.

Boaz rushed up to him. "Jachin, finally. The party is in our honor, you know. So many people want to meet you." She then proceeded to drag him around the room, introducing him to at least fifty people whose names he would never remember. How on earth did Boaz?

After wading through the sea of faces, Boaz turned to him and said, "Well, you're on your own now. I'm in the mood to party." She hurried off to join the throng on the dance floor. Evidently partners weren't necessary.

He spotted Angela dancing in a circle with a group of children. She wore a long white dress and had a wreath of flowers in her hair. Slim ribbons fluttered down her back as she swirled. The look on her face was one of abandonment and joy. She was so much like his rendition of her in *The Dance* that it left him mesmerized.

He never considered joining the merriment. Instead, he walked over to take up a spot along the wall and out of the limelight where he might not be so easily observed. These people, having known about him for so long, might easily accept him. But he was having trouble with the adjustment. He still felt like an outsider. Or like someone who has been away far too long. At least he felt he could let his guard down a bit since they knew who and what he was, and he appreciated the fact that no one fawned over him because he was a famous sculptor, or even because he was wizard royalty. Their only concern seemed to be living for the moment, reveling in the merriment and rejoicing in life. It *almost* tempted him to do the same. Although tonight he felt less of his usual reticence, it just wasn't in his nature to let himself go as these people did so easily.

The lively tune ended to be replaced with a dreamy number, and Jachin took advantage of the changed mood. He could handle a slow dance, and he crossed the room to claim the only woman with whom he wanted to dance. Angela.

Her startled look as she caught sight of him approaching twisted his insides into a hard knot. She was beautiful. And sexy as hell. The thin white dress hugged every curve, and in just a few moments she would be in his arms. To hell with concerns about where they might be tomorrow. At least that part of the party mood had rubbed off on him. He was going to do what he damn well pleased and dance with his *Angel.*

As he came up to the group he recognized one of the children as Guendoloena. "Hello, Guennie. How are you this evening?"

She giggled and shook the bells on her wrist at him. He noticed the tattoo on her arm. All of the children of Sena had the markings. Marrion had told him that their people were called The Painted Ones, and that they had long ago begun marking themselves so the outside worlds would know them as people of magic. He wasn't sure why the tradition had continued if they no longer went into the outside worlds.

He said to Guennie, "Do you mind if I steal Angela for a few minutes? I'd like to dance with her."

Guendoloena said nothing, but she took Angela's hand and put it in his. Then she ran off to be with the other children.

He didn't ask Angela's permission because he wasn't about to take no for an answer. Instead he merely pulled her body to his and began swaying to the music. It wasn't exactly a waltz, but close enough to improvise steps.

Angela looked up to meet his gaze, and what he saw in her eyes made his breath catch. An honest, pure affection coupled with passion flared there.

He found himself clearing his throat. "Doesn't Guennie talk?"

A smile dimpled the corner of Angela's mouth, but she didn't break eye contact. "Not much. I understand she hasn't spoken more than a few words since her parents disappeared or died...I'm not sure...a year ago."

Angela's announcement startled him. For some reason, he'd had the impression that people on Sena never died. "I've seen what the healers can do. So what happened with Guennie's parents?"

She shrugged. "I don't know, only that they're gone. All three children you saved this afternoon are orphans. A group of six people who live in what's called the 'family house' raise all orphans on Sena."

The word orphan made Jachin tense against the flood of unwanted feelings. But, then he hadn't really been an orphan. He'd had parents from almost the moment he was born. And although his father was detached, his mother tried her best to make up for her husband's shortcomings by pouring her love into her adopted son. She'd never considered him anything but her real child. It was when she died that he truly felt like an orphan.

Jachin brought Angela closer, the feel of her warm body against his a comfort against the bitter memories. Her curves molded to his without restraint, and her smile was enticing. He leaned down and kissed her, his entire body coming alive as he realized that no other woman had ever felt like she truly belonged in his arms.

When the music ended and they parted, they were both breathless. Angela's eyes held unshed tears, which she blinked back as she smiled. The sadness he read in her eyes reminded him that they belonged in different worlds, and his stomach plunged.

He pulled her against his side, and they walked across the room. He wasn't ready for her to leave him. As the throng around them milled about, waiting for the next tune, Jachin found himself telling Angela, "I don't want to leave you tomorrow. Come with us." He didn't know why he said it. Even before the words were out of his mouth he knew the request was impossible. And her response was as expected as it was impossible to accept.

"I can't." She still never broke eye contact.

"Then let's go back home together." What was he saying?

He couldn't go back. And for what? He hardly knew Angela. Why was he so ready to give up his newfound home, where he truly fit in, for a woman he knew nothing about? A voice inside said he knew everything about her.

She shook her head. "And leave Lilith to Kadien? You couldn't do that if you wanted to, Jachin."

"Then come with me."

Marrion approached with two tankards, handing one to each of them. "This is Maisy's famous *fraoich*. It's wonderful heather ale. I want you to try it."

Jachin accepted the mug, but didn't take a drink. "Marrion, Angela is going with us tomorrow."

Marrion's eyes widened as she looked at Angela. "Oh, but you can't. Even having you here this short time goes against our laws. But we are defering to Jachin's wishes because they have expressed a wish to return to the Lute world and will need you to do so. When Jachin and Boaz leave on their journey tomorrow, you will remain here. The elders feel it is important that you interact with our world as little as possible, for your own safety as well as ours. You do see that this is necessary, don't you?"

"*I* do," Angela said.

"Well I don't agree. She's staying with me." Jachin stood his ground, all the while wondering why it was so important. Sure, he wanted to be with Angela, but he'd already established that it was impossible for them to have any lasting relationship. Still, he couldn't bring himself to let her go. The thought of something happening to her and his never seeing her again made him feel empty. He captured Angela's gaze. "She's going with us."

Their conversation was interrupted as the musicians began playing again, but this time the crowd turned toward the group of minstrels instead of dancing. From the back of the hall the wail of a bagpipe began, the first, strong note drawn out in a mournful sound. Then the crowd parted as the piper made his way to the front of the room. A man stood and began to tell a story, his loud, clear voice easily heard as it echoed from the rafters. The crowd stood in rapt attention. Even the children became silent.

Marrion held onto Jachin's arm, as if to put their conversation on hold. He had no other choice than to listen to the story along with the others.

"*Long ago,*" the man stated, "*before the great divide, all creatures freely roamed the worlds."*

Jachin saw confirming nods from the crowd.

"The fairy folk and the enlightened ones were free to work their magic."

More nods, and a murmur of agreement.

"We gathered the heather for ale. We hunted our food. But always we gave to the land more than we took." He looked across the crowd. *"Our painted bodies marked our kind to let others know us."*

Jachin found himself rubbing the tattoo on his arm.

"We defended our highlands from those who would pillage it...first the Vikings, then the Scots." The cry of the bagpipes filled the room.

Jachin could feel the tension coming from the crowd. And from somewhere deep within, he felt a kindred spirit to what the man was relating. He felt the connection to a far-away land, to the heather-covered hills and to maintaining the balance of the earth. And he knew the land that the man was talking about was Scotland.

"Then came the worst of the pillagers. One man...a man with half our blood running through his veins...a painted-one like ourselves...a man named MacAlpin. MacAlpin, the great betrayer."

The crowd roared in unison.

Jachin looked over to see Angela turn white. She looked like she was having trouble breathing. She was so focused on what the man was saying, Jachin couldn't get her attention.

"In the Christian year of 841, when our nobles gathered in Scone to make a lasting peace between our people and those of MacAlpin's father...to unite the peoples in friendship...MacAlpin secretly planned our destruction. His hidden army murdered our noble elders...forcing we of magic to take sanctuary on Sena."

The name "MacAlpin" was whispered throughout the room, and Jachin got the feeling that these peaceful people were ready to do battle.

Angela had begun backing out of the room, her glance darting frantically around her. Marrion still had hold of his arm. He looked down at his aunt and excused himself to follow Angela, but when Marrion released him and he turned back, Angela was gone.

He walked through the crowd, searching for her as the narrator went on, "*That day all MacAlpins and their ancestors brought upon themselves a curse. Until our homeland is regained and the worlds restored as one, the name of MacAlpin will live in infamy.*"

"Yes!" The crowd shouted in unison.

Instantly the lively music began again, and the throng heartily joined in a riotous dance.

Jachin still couldn't find Angela. He spotted Guennie, but Angela wasn't with her. Then he saw Boaz rushing toward him.

She was breathless as she said, "Where's Angela?"

"She took off." He motioned to the room.

Boaz took hold of his sleeve. "Jachin... Angela's mother's maiden name is MacAlpin!"

EIGHT

**Birch Tree: New beginnings and opportunities.
Many magical adventures**

Kadien looked down at the sleeping woman. Lilith. One of
Vivian MacCuill's triplets. One of three who, according to legend,
would attempt to conquer him.

A rapping on the open door broke the silence. His high
counsel, Nudd, entered. "My Lord, she still sleeps?"

Walking to the window, Kadien pushed back his cape and
looked into the darkness. It called to him. As much as he wanted
to go, he had things to deal with. His brittle laugh gave away
none of his concerns. "Yes, she remains under Marrion's puny
spell. I have toyed with the idea of breaking it...an easy enough
task. But I think the better choice would be to let Vivian's child
sleep." He reflected upon how unlike the mother the young woman
was. Vivian had been purity itself, and Kadien could sense her
daughter had the scent of the corrupted Lutes about her.

As Lute-like as she was, he wondered which powers she might
have inherited from her wizard parents. "You know, I wonder
what the full extent of the woman's powers are?" he mused aloud.
"Surely her father, whomever he might be, could have bestowed
powers different from those of her mother. Vivian's powers
focused on telepathy and healing."

"You said the daughter was a healer among the Lutes," Nudd
said.

Kadien nodded. "Yes, she has knowledge of the healing arts,
but I wonder if Lilith might have inherited powers from both
parents." Kadien's curiosity wasn't strong enough to tempt him
to break the spell to find out. Whatever the powers of Vivian's
three offspring might be, he was certain that, once reunited, they
would be almost matchless.

What would it be like to capture that power for himself? It
would not be an easy task. He would need to find out each of the
children's weaknesses, desires, and what they coveted most. Only
then would he have bargaining power. But the rewards would be

infinite. Darkness would at last conquer Light, and he would rule all the worlds.

Nudd jerked his head toward Lilith. "It was difficult to get a sense of her powers. Transporting her from the Lute world to Sena seems to have been a shock to her entire being."

"An understatement." Kadien chuckled as he looked back to the peacefully sleeping Lilith. For the moment he was relieved not to have to deal with the woman's struggles. "It seems she had no knowledge of her heritage or her birthplace. She'd only just begun to have the glimmer dreams. I am certain she had no knowledge of their significance."

Looking at her, he wondered, and not for the first time, what had become of Vivian. Discovering that Vivian's triad had been abandoned to the Lutes had filled him with a sense of disbelief— a foreign sensation for him. Even now he had trouble shaking this new concept. Why would Vivian do such a vile thing?

He looked away from the sleeping woman, putting aside his useless thoughts of Vivian. She was the only one who had the answers, and apparently she was dead. "I need to focus on keeping the triad apart for the time being," he said to Nudd. "The remaining two must not easily reach my fortress. I wish to observe them for a time."

Kadien wanted their powers enhanced to their highest level before he took them. He sensed Boaz knew and accepted the many spirits within her, while Jachin had the farthest to go on the journey of discovery. How strong would Vivian's son become once he acknowledged his many sides, regained himself as a full wizard and became complete? Just as Kadien had planned, the journey to find Lilith should accomplish that. And the stronger their powers, the stronger Kadien would be once he captured those powers for himself.

Nudd looked impatient. "Why don't you just destroy them? Surely it would be a small enough task for you. You said yourself they have yet to recover their full powers. Once they do and are reunited..." He left the sentence unfinished.

Uneasiness crawled like a spider across Kadien's skin. Dismissing it, he allowed the dark power within him to build, a reassurance of its strength. "I know. But I don't want them destroyed." He turned to Nudd.

"Not yet."

***

Angela ran through the night, more afraid of the people she'd just left than the unknown elements her imagination told her lurked in the surrounding forest. A bright moon illuminated traces of the seldom-used path they'd come down the night before. Since she didn't know the layout of Sena or where the nearest shore might be, she had to try to find the place where they'd come ashore. For the moment, Marrion's warning about unconsecrated ground seemed a moot point. She needed to catch the next fog out of town.

Movie scenes of people being tarred and feathered—or worse, burned at the stake—came to mind. Although she had no idea what kind of retribution the crowd might have in mind for her, a MacAlpin, she wasn't about to stick around to find out.

So much for her one and only adventure. It seemed even this mythical world had the cold slap of reality to wake you when you dared to dream.

Plain and simple, she didn't belong. Big time. Whatever had made her think that she would fit in with these people? Her only means of defending herself was a series of self-defense classes she'd taken. They were a laughable weapon against people who could probably melt her with a glance.

She pushed on in the direction she hoped the shore stood, ignoring the dwindling trail. The salty tang of an ocean breeze indicated she was close. At the shore she would call the maiden's barge.

Her heart pounded harder as she ran, the echoed memories of the crowd's words repeating themselves in her head. *A curse on the MacAlpins*! *A curse on the MacAlpins*! Her uncle had been right. It didn't matter that she had no idea what kind of curse it was. She wasn't sticking around to find out. She was a MacAlpin, and as such, she was a big-time enemy to the White Wizards of Sena. It's all she needed to know.

A painful stitch in her side made her stop. She leaned against a moss-covered tree, fighting to catch her breath. Not such a good idea, she realized. The pause gave her time to consider her surroundings. And what she saw caused her to stop breathing altogether.

The branches of the huge oak trees now draped like long arms across the trail, completely closing it behind her. And if she wasn't mistaken, the trees themselves seemed to be glaring at her in disdain.

She blinked hard. The image stayed the same. The trees didn't move. The knot-hole eyes didn't blink back, but she got the distinct impression the tall oaks were purposely blocking the path. Even if she had wanted to go back, which she didn't, she now had no choice but to head in her original direction.

A loud crashing of underbrush on the other side of the tree-barricade had her grabbing her up skirts and darting down the trail. Something was coming! Something loud and big. A mythical monster of some kind? Well, she wasn't about to wait around to see if the trees let whatever it was through. She ran as if her life depended on it, which it probably did.

As she ran, darkness crowded in on either side of the trail. She had the strange feeling she was being watched from within that darkness. The trees again? Or was it something more menacing?

A sudden thought startled her to a stop. *I'm living out the exact dream I had last week!* Same trees. Same trail. Same feeling of panic as the forest seemed to close in around her. But, if she was reliving the dream, then it wasn't a monster chasing her. It was Jachin.

She stood frozen, staring into the forest's gloom. The moon's glow painted the long, sinuous tree branches blue, and what was left of the trail glowed eerily in the darkness. Her knees shook as she fought to remain standing, praying that she was living her dream, that Jachin would soon burst through the trees and not some mythical monster come to devour her.

Her heart thumped hard and fast against her chest, and her every muscle tensed, ready to run. The crashing grew louder, now coming from only a few feet away.

Please God. Let it be Jachin.

Her rational mind took over just moments before whatever it was burst through the branches. She turned and ran. Why had she believed it could be Jachin? Just because she'd had a silly dream strangely similar to what was happening now? It had only been a dream. And now she had wasted precious moments.

The noise grew closer, and she forced herself to run even faster, gathering the long dress higher to keep it out of the way.

Then, with a stunning force, something huge knocked her

off her feet. She landed hard, the air slammed from her lungs. She'd been knocked sideways and now lay off the trail.

The mossy forest floor had only slightly cushioned her fall. One thing she knew for certain, she hadn't experienced pain in the dream. Afraid to look back at what had attacked her, she attempted to scramble away, intending to go deeper into the forest where the *thing* couldn't see her. But something immediately grasped her leg, bringing her break for freedom to a jerking halt. A prickling rush of adrenaline coursed through her body as she felt a hot touch against the bare skin of her ankle. She tried to kick free, but the touch just tightened. At last, she was forced to look at what was attacking her. The moon gave just enough light to see the silhouette of a man. Instantly she knew who her attacker was.

"Jachin!" Her screech was tempered by breathlessness.

"Shush!" Jachin whispered as he quickly scrambled up beside her to cover her body with his at the same time he clamped a hand over her mouth. "Something is following me."

She realized she was still hearing a rustling sound in the underbrush even though they were both still. The scratching sound came to an abrupt halt, and her shallow breathing thundered in her own ears. Surely, whatever the *something* was it could hear her. Or smell her fear. She'd heard that animals could do that.

In her dream Jachin had appeared, and she had gone freely into his arms, the hot and heavy sounds of their lovemaking soon filling the night. But the only heavy breathing in this scenario had to do with fear and the fact that Jachin was practically smothering her. Something was stalking them, and the damp forest floor hard against her back assured her this was definitely no dream.

Her lungs aching, she bit Jachin's finger, feeling more than hearing his surprise. But he let go, and she slowly filled her lungs with welcome air.

As they waited in tense silence for *the thing* to make a move, Angela became acutely aware of Jachin's body pressed hard against hers. Something rigid jabbed her side. Heedless of the dire situation, her mind went right ahead and blithely paraphrased the old joke, *is that a sword in your pocket, or are you just glad to see me?* She tried to shift away from him, but he held her tight. Given the situation, she thought it was damned inappropriate for him to be aroused. But she had to admit, she wasn't completely sure if the renewed pounding of her heart had to do with the nebulous *whatever* that was stalking them, or from the erection pressed intimately against her side.

Jachin moved to place his lips next to her ear, his warm breath sending chills across her skin as he whispered, "Don't move. I'm going to see what it is."

"No!" she whispered back. But he had already crept away from her. Her arms felt...What? Lonely. At Jachin's abrupt release, a release she'd been fighting for only moments before, she realized she liked having his strong arms around her. She liked the feel of his body pressed to hers. Now she just felt vulnerable and alone.

She watched his crouched silhouette move toward the path. She didn't dare look at the forest surrounding her, sure she would have a heart attack, or at the very least faint, if so much as a twig cracked or a tree branch moved in the breeze. She figured she was better off not knowing if something was about to pounce on her.

Just as Jachin overtook the moonlight on the path, a great hissing and growl reverberated from a few feet ahead of him. She couldn't see what it was, but it sounded like a combination of a cougar and an alligator. The smell of rotten eggs filled her nose. Whatever it was, it smelled awful! Angela held her breath, her hand to her throat, holding back the scream she wanted so badly to release.

Jachin stood boldly facing whatever it was—his legs apart, feet firmly planted on the path. Only then did Angela realize he held the long knife his uncle had given him, and she felt foolish. It had been the knife within its sheath jabbing her in the side, not Jachin. She scolded her over-sexed imagination.

Jachin seemed to be staring down the thing. And she heard the animal move with a crashing of branches and underbrush. Then a huge shape rushed past Jachin, green scales glittering in the moonlight. It raced down the path in the direction Angela had been going. *God, what is it!* It was too big to be an alligator. Too long and stiff in its movements to be a cougar.

She let her breath out when she saw Jachin still standing on the path. The moonlight was strong enough to assure her that he was unharmed.

She watched his shoulders relax slightly. And that was the

only sign she needed. She bolted from her spot and, holding her skirts, darted toward the safety of his arms.

The next thing she knew, those arms were enveloping her in an embrace that made her lose her breath all over again. It felt so safe, so wonderful to give her fear over to his strength.

Jachin moved his head back and looked down at her. "Did you see that thing?" His voice was steady but held a note of awe.

She closed her eyes tight, not wanting to relive the terror. "No, and I don't want to." Then she peeked down the trail. "What was it?"

"Beats me. Some kind of big lizard." He took a deep breath, the first sign of nervousness she'd sensed in him. "A really...*really* big lizard."

He suddenly held her firmly at arm's length. His eyes were so dark she could have sworn they were black instead of brown. "And what the hell were you thinking running off like that?"

Remembering the scene at the great hall, she straightened her spine. When she spoke, she intended for her voice to be strong and clear, but it came out shaky. "I'm going home." She glanced down the trail in the direction she had to go, the smell of rotten eggs a reminder of the animal, which could even then have been lying in wait.

Jachin chuckled, pointing his knife in the direction the animal had gone. "You sure?"

"Yes." She looked around. "But there must be another way."

"Come back with me."

She put her hands on her hips. "Didn't you hear them?" She caught herself glancing around at the thicket of trees, an immediate chill of apprehension causing goose bumps along her arms. Were people out there who could hear them talking? If they found out the truth about her...She lowered her voice and whispered, "I'm a MacAlpin."

Jachin waved away her concerns. "So, you're a MacAlpin. And so they cursed all MacAlpins. Plenty of people have cursed me, and I'm still here."

Angela looked around. "Yeah...*here*. I think that pretty much proves my point." She could swear she heard the hum of chorused whispers through the woods, like a hundred voices were engaged in muted conversation.

Nah, she told herself, *it's only the wind.* But there was no wind.

Not even one leaf fluttered to indicate any kind of breeze. She returned her attention to Jachin. "Besides, I'm sure when they find out the truth about my ancestry, they'll kick me off the island...at the very least."

Jachin frowned as he moved closer. "Would it make any difference if *I* wanted you to stay?"

Trapped in his gaze, she could only whisper, "Why?"

He didn't respond. Evidently she was supposed to read his answer in his hard, soul-wrenching stare that held questions of his own. But all that did was renew the weakness in her knees.

Finally he said, "Let's go." He put his arm around her, leading her back the way they'd come. Quickly Angela made a decision. She would have to take her chances with the wizards instead of the big lizard. For the time being, anyway.

As she looked up the path, she realized it now stood open, the trees noncommittal in the drape of their branches. She shook her head as she accepted the change. *Dorothy, you're most definitely no longer in Kansas,* she reminded herself. She had to stop questioning the strange happenings in Sena.

She had to admit, she liked the feel of Jachin's arm around her. Neither the shadowed forest nor the prospect of the lynch mob seemed quite as menacing when she had Jachin by her side.

When they walked into the common room, the music and gaiety had reached a heightened level. She saw Boaz dancing and flirting with a hunk. *Some things,* she mused to herself, *are the same no matter where we go.*

"Look around," Jachin said. "No one except Boaz, Marrion and me knows you're a MacAlpin. Let's just leave it for now and enjoy the evening."

Angela had the feeling he was saying this for her benefit, since he didn't look all that inclined to dance, either. She tried to smile in response, but it was hard since she feared that at any moment the lively crowd could turn on her.

Boaz spotted them, left her dance partner and hurried over. "Angela, are you okay? Where did you go?"

Angela shrugged. "I thought I'd better get off the island before..." She lowered her voice. "...anyone found out I'm a you-know-what."

Boaz smiled at her brother. "Thanks for bringing her back. I was worried."

Jachin shrugged, folding his arms, his mouth turning up at one corner. "I wasn't about to lose our ticket out of here."

Marrion hurried over. "Angela, it's not safe for you to wander about the forest at night. You don't possess the wizard skills to deal with Sena's night creatures."

"Speaking of creatures," Jachin said. "We saw a big lizard of some kind. What was it?"

Marrion looked worried. "A dragon? However did you escape? They feed at night."

Jachin shrugged. "I just sort of stared it down, and it took off."

With that Marrion positively beamed. "Well done. You called upon your powers."

"I guess," he said.

Boaz said excitedly, "What was the dragon like?"

Angela touched her nose. "All I saw was something big...and it smelled awful! Then Jachin scared it off."

Marrion laughed. "Yes, they do smell rather awful." She turned to Jachin. "Did it breathe fire?"

He looked surprised, while a thrill of apprehension zinged through Angela's middle. It could breathe fire?

"No," Jachin said.

Nodding her head, Marrion said, "Then it was a male. A female would most assuredly have defended itself."

"They really breathe fire?" Angela asked, awed.

"Yes," Marrion said. "Just as certain wizards are able to do." She looked at Boaz. "Just as Boaz is able to do."

Looking startled, Boaz said, "But I can't really breathe fire. I can only light candles with a breath."

"Same principle. The fire doesn't come from within you. You only ignite existing elements in the air," Marrion said as the music stopped and the crowd quieted.

People began to disperse, and Marrion nodded to the three of them to follow. As they walked across the courtyard, she said, "It is now time to conduct the ceremony of recall. Angela, feel free to go where you please within the compound, but I'm afraid this particular ceremony is highly sacred and restricted to only those of magic. It takes intense concentration, so it will be conducted with only Boaz and Jachin. And, of course, I will be there to facilitate the ceremony."

"I'll just go on up to bed, if that's all right." She'd had enough of this cockeyed world for one day. She wanted nothing more than to fall into a sleep-induced coma and wake up when the world had righted itself. Maybe she would wake up to discover this was all a dream and that she wasn't her host's archenemy after all. And maybe after a good night's sleep, she would have a better perspective on the enigmatic Jachin and why he ran hot and cold.

***

Jachin and Boaz bowed low, ending the ceremony. When Jachin rose to his full height, it was as if he'd awakened from a long sleep. The ritual to recall their heritage and their powers had been a lengthy one, although it had been physically, emotionally and spiritually exhilarating. It had taken place in Marrion's home, with several elders in attendance.

All the elders except Marrion quietly left.

Boaz said, "I had no idea."

Jachin smiled at his sister as she voiced his very thought. A strange sense of peace had taken up residence inside him, along with the knowledge of the immense power he possessed. It was like a humming engine. He knew instinctively that Boaz felt the same sensations. Innate skills and powers he had never dreamed he possessed had been set free.

"Jachin, come close," Boaz said.

As he did as she instructed, he felt his powers begin to heighten, as if the closer they got the stronger their powers became. This was what Marrion had been talking about when she'd referred to them working together to challenge The Darkness. If their powers were enhanced when he and Boaz were together, what would it be like when they joined forces with Lilith?

Suddenly, it all became clear to him. Kadien had taken Lilith to prevent the joining of their powers. But to what end? Did he intend to defeat them one by one? Or was Lilith bait, to lure him and Boaz to Kadien's fortress, where he had the upper hand? Only Kadien knew his real agenda, but Jachin knew that it was critical that Boaz and he get to Lilith as soon as possible.

"We must rescue Lilith," he said.

Boaz nodded.

Marrion went to the cupboard and brought out the book she'd showed them yesterday. The Book of Light. Even the knowledge of its importance had become known during the ceremony. He knew that it was to be held by the women of the tribe, for their people were a matriarchal society and had been from their beginnings. Glimmers of those beginnings flashed through his mind. One day he would take the time to bring forth those memories. But the ceremony of recall had told him that for now he needed to focus his attention. He was part of the great triad. He and his sisters had a destiny to fulfill. And they couldn't do it without Lilith.

"Tomorrow the two of you will begin your journey." Marrion looked serious.

Feeling calm and confident with his newly recalled knowledge, Jachin said, "Angela is coming with us."

Marrion looked concerned, but said nothing, as if she wasn't sure how to respond. Their relationship had subtly changed during the ceremony. He and Boaz now shared much of Marrion's knowledge. She must realize he no longer needed to defer to her for knowledge of their people and what they could and could not do. Although the ceremony had not brought total recall, and they would have to complete a more in-depth ceremony to recall specific past incidents, they now knew the shared history and ways of the wizards of Sena.

Even the knowledge of The Prophecy whispered through his mind like an ancient memory. The task he and his sisters were destined for was clear on one point—they must challenge the Darkness. Just how and when that was to occur was still up in the air. But he knew that their success or failure would determine the future of mankind. Either the encroaching Darkness would conquer The Triad, win their powers and rule with absolute power, or The Triad would win, restoring the balance between light and dark.

He felt frustration about when, exactly, that battle was to take place. The Prophecy was vague. It only said it would happen during a general timeframe. That could be any time between this very moment and six years from now. But he did know his first challenge would be to rescue Lilith and combine their powers. He also had a feeling that his statue, *The Dance*, was in some way connected. He must restore the bronze to its original perfection, or his mission would be incomplete.

His thoughts were interrupted when Marrion said, "I don't

think it's wise to take Angela with you."

"No one, not even you, know in which world the challenge between The Triad and The Dark One is to take place. It's possible that Kadien brought us all here because it's meant to take place in the Lute world, and if we're stuck here, he can defeat us. I want to know we have a way off the island when we need it.

"Also, when we get Lilith, I fully intend on returning to the other world to restore *The Dance*. Something tells me that its restoration is critical to our success. So, Angela is coming with us."

He didn't mention that he had another reason to keep Angela with him. Just as he had during his dreams of her, he now had a fierce need to protect her. Although he now knew the tribe would only shun her if they discovered she was a MacAlpin, he feared she might try to leave again if he left her here.

Marrion still looked reluctant, but she said, "As you wish."

***

"But I don't want to go!" Angela's heart beat wildly. Jachin had come into her bedroom without so much as a knock and announced that she was going with them. She would be going with them to find Lilith. He now stood in the doorway, arms crossed.

She felt as helpless as when her parents had dropped her off at her aunt and uncle's house to live. She was losing control over her own destiny. And there was the effect Jachin had on her to contend with. She didn't think she could be around him day after day and control the passion he stirred inside her, and she had to control it or lose not only her self-respect but probably her heart.

She looked out the window. She couldn't think or talk straight when she looked at Jachin. He was just too knee-meltingly handsome. And his eyes sent tickling sensations all through her middle. "Jachin, I have to admit...after our Jurassic Park encounter last night, I'm *afraid* to go with you." She pointed outside. "Who knows what else is out there...as if dinosaur-sized lizards aren't enough."

"Don't worry. They won't hurt you as long as I'm with you. And it wasn't a lizard. It was a dragon. A fire-breathing dragon at that."

"Oh, that makes me feel better." She wasn't sure if the dragon or her feelings for the unattainable Jachin held more threat. She felt like she was under one of Sean's befuddlement spells when she was around Jachin.

"Besides we need you to get back home. I want to make sure I have a way out of here once we find Lilith."

"I can't believe there isn't another adult virgin in all of Sena." He shook his head. "Nope. I get the feeling that taking your first sexual partner is a rite of passage into womanhood. I suspect that anyone who might be a virgin wouldn't admit it."

How was she going to tell him that if she went on this quest and was alone with him for any length of time, she might not qualify for too long? Both the familiarity she felt toward him because of the dream and her spontaneous physical reaction to him threatened the very resolve that had kept her a virgin and made her their ticket out.

"Jachin...I would like to help, but ...." She wrung her hands as she looked around the room.

"What have you got to lose?"

She swung toward him. "Oh, nothing important. Just my life."

"Your chances of getting eaten by a dragon have to be less than getting hit by a car back home."

She glared at him. "You have statistics to prove that?"

He arched an eyebrow. "You're afraid of me, aren't you?"

His intense gaze gave her every reason to nod. She was afraid of what he did to her. Mostly, she was afraid that he was the one man in her life who could, without a second thought or any kind of commitment, unlock the passions she had fought so hard to keep under control.

He put his hand over his heart. "I, Jachin Morgan, make a promise—I assure you, a white wizard never breaks a promise once he has given it—that if you'll go with us, then get us off of Sena, I will keep my hands off you." His eyebrow arched. "But, you'll have to promise me the same."

Her face burned as she remembered their kiss in his office when s*he* had become the aggressor. Embarrassment turned to frustration, which then turned to anger. "Don't flatter yourself, Jachin Morgan. I'm not one of your groupies." Her mind went back to the magazine articles she'd read about his conquests. "Or one of your mindless models. I...I ..." She let the air out of her lungs in a rush, needing to let go of her fears about overreacting to Jachin's charms. This journey was an adventure of a lifetime.

Suddenly, she decided she wasn't going to let her own fears rob her of it.

She looked into Jachin's eyes, knowing she could tell if he was lying. She wanted him to restate the oath. "You promise?"

Again he put his hand over his heart. "I, Jachin Morgan, promise to leave Angela Catherine Dawn's virtue intact."

She saw a strange glint in his eyes, but she let it go unchallenged. After all, he'd given his word. And he really did need her virtue intact if he wanted her to get him back home.

She stuck her hand out. "Okay, I'll go with you."

Jachin slowly took her hand. For a moment she thought he was going to pull her into his arms. But he merely smiled as he bowed over hand and, in a totally non-threatening, courtly manner, grazed his warm lips over her knuckles.

Even as she gave a sigh of relief, she had to bite back disappointment. No doubt about it, she was safe with Jachin. Which meant *she* was the only threat to her peace of mind.

NINE

**Roan Tree: An assembly point for warriors.
Also pertaining to visions and divination.**

Angela felt like a fraud as she stood with Jachin, Boaz and
Ailleann, accepting the blessings of the villagers. It looked as
though every white wizard from the island must have come to
stand beneath the grove of smooth-barked trees to see the four of
them off on their journey. She was certain these tattooed people
would not be so nice to her if they knew she was a MacAlpin.

Marrion and Illan stood together, evidently the ones appointed
to give instruction.

Marrion handed Boaz the large book she'd showed them
before. "It is time for you to take your mother's Book of Light.
You are now the keeper of the knowledge held within its pages. It
will help you on your journey. Although through the remembrance
ceremony you now know our history, the knowledge held within
these pages is for your use only and unknown to the rest of our
people. Trust is placed upon you to use the power wisely."

Boaz nodded and carefully put the book in her backpack.
When she was done, she kicked a pebble from her sandals then
flipped back her long cape and adjusted her cotton tee shirt.

All three of them had been given a flask for water and a
lightweight cape in place of a bedroll, but that was pretty much
it. And while she and Ailleann wore a typical Sena dress, Jachin
and Boaz wore their Lute street clothes beneath their capes.

Angela felt as if they were headed off on one of her and Boaz's
frequent overnight hikes through Arizona's Oak Creek Canyon.
Almost. This would be no walk in the park, where all you had to
watch out for were a couple of skittish snakes along the trail. She
shut her mind to images of mythical beasts with glittering scales.

She watched Jachin as he listened to his uncle speak, noting
that his gaze came back to her every few seconds as if he was
worried she might take off. And her gut was telling her that was a
great idea. Even the dreaded fire-breathing dragon wasn't quite
as daunting as the unknown dangers they might encounter on

their trip.

Illan said, "Jachin, your knife is all you will need."

"What about food and more water?"

"Food and drink will present themselves as needed. Listen to your senses and follow them."

Listen to your senses? Angela knew if she took that suggestion to heart, she'd be out of here faster than Superman could fly. She was a bundle of nerves and second thoughts. She was sure her underdeveloped Lute senses weren't up to the task. What if she became separated from Boaz and Jachin?

"And shelter?" Jachin asked. "You said it would take at least three days to reach Kadien's fortress."

Marrion answered with a maddeningly simple, "Take what is offered. The nights are mild and pose no threat to comfort."

There she went again. *What* exactly was going to be *offered?* And by *whom?* This wasn't the way Angela liked to travel at all. When she went camping, even on overnights, she had a checklist a mile long. *A flashlight would be nice,* she thought as she pushed the strap of her flask over her shoulder then crossed her empty arms. But Jachin and Boaz were both nodding as if they knew what everyone was talking about, so she didn't say anything. She would just have to trust that between the survival skills she and Boaz had learned from years of camping and hiking, and Boaz and Jachin's powers, that they would make it to Kadien's fortress. Then what? She didn't even want to think that far ahead.

Illan said, "You may need to use the Book of Light to decipher the signposts. They are in the ancient Ogham writing of our people. Be warned, they are in riddle, and since you are not familiar with them, they may seem at first strange. Just remember that you must answer the riddle to determine the direction you must take."

Angela spoke up, "You mean there are actually signs to this Kadien's fortress?" She got a mental image of a brightly colored sign reading *This Way To Oz.*

Shaking her head, Marrion said, "No, not directly to Kadien's fortress. But we do have markers in different areas. Once you begin your journey, the trail won't be direct. Journeys within Sena are not like those in the Lute world. They are both physical and spiritual. If one is in search of his or her inner self…" she glanced pointedly at Jachin, "…detours of discovery will present themselves. The decisions you make will determine the length—

and success—of your journey."

Boaz chuckled uneasily. "Kinda like those *Choose Your Own Adventure* books we used to read as kids, huh, Angela? Where the outcome of the story depended on what page you selected when you were given the option."

Angela couldn't help the slightly derisive tone in her voice as she replied, "Yeah, but who is choosing this adventure? You, me, or Jachin? The outcome will affect us all."

"There will be guides along the way," Illan said. "It is not for us to determine to whom the lesson belongs. Ailleann will accompany you. She knows much about what the forest has to offer. She is also proficient with herbs and knows which plants are edible."

Angela noticed that Illan continued to glance at both Boaz and Jachin's pendants. She still couldn't figure out why he didn't just ask them whatever it was he wanted to know about the pendants. Obviously he knew something about them that he didn't want to share with either their owners or the rest of the white wizards.

Ailleann stepped forward, and Angela noticed she was attaching a small cooking pot to her belt. "But this is not my journey of discovery. It will be up to Jachin and Boaz, and perhaps even you, Angela, to read what the forest has to offer. I only go as a healer, to help cook, and because I know the forest as a friend."

Jachin sheathed his knife, gave Angela and Boaz a long hard look. "Are you ready?"

Boaz nodded, but Angela only shrugged, her nervousness manifesting itself in an internal singing of munchkin voices telling her to follow the yellow brick road. She wasn't sure if the others were Dorothy, the Tin Woodsman, and the Scarecrow, but she was definitely the Cowardly Lion.

When Jachin continued to stare at her, she finally said, "I guess."

They started off down the trail Illan had indicated would lead away from the compound and across Sena. The villagers quieted.

Then a child shouted, "Wait!"

They turned to see Guendoloena rush toward them. She flung herself against Jachin's legs.

Jachin smiled at the little girl, and Angela's heart caught. He bent down to her. "We'll be back. You keep a lookout for us, okay?"

She hesitated a moment, but then nodded and smiled.

Once again, they began their journey. Jachin walked at the head of the group, followed by Ailleann and then her, with Boaz bringing up the rear. She took a deep breath as they left the crowded village behind. The scents of the forest floor rose up to surround her, and she suddenly felt the sense of relaxed adventure that she experienced when she and Boaz took their hiking trips. The sun warmed her shoulders, helping to ease her tension. Maybe everything would be okay.

"I feel really strange not having a backpack or a flashlight," she said, suddenly realizing she was the only one who wasn't carrying anything other than her water flask.

Boaz chuckled, "Count yourself lucky. This book is heavy. Remind me to put it on disk when we get home."

Jachin walked on in silence, like a man on a mission, which he was.

After following the trail for half an hour, Angela said, "Jachin, do you know where to go? I haven't seen any signposts yet."

He looked back, "Illan said we go to the end of the obvious trail, then read the signs from there."

Ailleann dropped back to talk to Boaz. The young woman asked question after question about the Lute world, just as she had when she'd helped Angela that first morning.

They followed the trail for quite some time, and Angela wondered if any of her companions felt as anxious as she did. When they came to the end of the discernable trail, Jachin stopped so abruptly that Angela almost bumped into him.

"Oh!" She backed up, but not before she felt the heat emanating from his cape like a radiator. It reminded her of how hot he had been the few times she'd touched him. Boaz said she ran hot, too. Must be a wizard thing. Whatever it was, it certainly made her all hot and bothered whenever she was near him. She took another step back.

Jachin didn't say anything, only gave her a searching look. Then he pointed to a three-foot tall wooden plank marker. "Our first signpost."

While Boaz and Jachin and Ailleann inspected the marker, Angela sat on a large rock alongside the trail, noticing that the forest was very close around them. She couldn't see any trails, let alone a choice of them.

Boaz said, "It's Ogham all right. Do you know what it says, Ailleann?"

"It will take a few moments to translate," Ailleann replied.

Angela could see the markings from where she sat. From her studies of the ancient European cultures, she recognized the characteristic vertical line with various marks on either side as Celtic or Pictish. "Are you Picts or Celts? Or are they the same? I can't remember?"

Boaz closed her eyes as if trying to recall something. Then she opened them and said, "Picts."

Angela got up to look more closely at the marker. Questions that could never be answered in her previous studies ran through her head. "I can finally know where the Picts came from. No one I've ever met knew for sure, although I heard speculations ranging from France to, well ..." she glanced at Ailleann, "outer space."

A look crossed among the three wizards.

Boaz said, "We didn't go back that far into the memories. Marrion said we needed time to adjust to our new way of life first. I got the feeling she doesn't think we're ready to know the truth." She looked at Ailleann. "Do you know?"

"Yes, but I must defer to Marrion. You will remember when you are ready." She again studied the signpost.

Angela sat back down, feeling both disappointed and tired of what was becoming a refrain. *All will be revealed when you are ready.* She had the feeling there must be something shocking in their origins. Why else hesitate to tell them? But what could be more shocking than finding out they were wizards?

They all stared at the board, trying to decipher the marking. Angela was sure both Boaz and Jachin knew more than she did because they had done the recall ceremony and had gained so much knowledge about their culture.

From where she sat, she was getting more a sense of Jachin than she was the Ogham. She still had trouble believing all that had taken place in the last few days. She was in the ultimate fairy tale world of fairy tale worlds, complete with Prince Charming and the evil entity in the fortress. There was even a sleeping princess in a tower! She was as excited as she was scared about every element of the whole crazy world. But she realized that the most exciting element of the fairy tale was definitely Jachin

Morgan, himself. Just being near him gave her a gut-wrenching sense of panic, terror and elation all at once.

Angela blinked, realizing Jachin was staring at her. She tried to smile, but the solemn look on his face deflated her attempt like a burst party balloon.

She found herself going for honesty by asking, "Why do you keep looking at me like that?"

Boaz turned to listen to his reply.

"I just like looking at you." He continued to stare.

"Well, it makes me...nervous."

He didn't apologize or even stop staring. For some reason, she didn't expect such a blunt reply, and it made her even more nervous. *He liked looking at her.* Simple. Direct. And way too honest. It sent a thrill coursing through her body, and she suddenly recalled the sensations she'd experienced in the dream. The look he was giving her right now was the exact one he'd given her then. It was a soul-searching look that made her want to open herself to him, revealing everything—from what she liked for breakfast to her deepest fears.

"Ahem!" Boaz said with a chuckle. "I can only decipher a few words on the signpost. How about you, Jachin?"

Angela blinked to break Jachin's spell, and they both looked at the marker.

Boaz went on. "Ailleann, correct me if I'm wrong, but I think that everything in Ogham is on three levels—physical, mental, and spiritual. The wood and carvings are the physical level." She touched the marker, running her fingers over the notches. "Then there is the mental, which is the word or letter that the mark makes you think of. And the spiritual level has to do with all the associations you make regarding a specific letter or word."

"That's correct," Ailleann said as she continued to study the marker.

Angela sighed. "This couldn't be easy, could it? You have to read it on three levels?"

Jachin nodded. "It gets better. The writings are riddles. After we decipher the words and their spiritual associations, we have to figure out the riddle."

"You can do that? Just from that one recall session you had last night?"

"With Ailleann's help, we can try," Boaz said. "It isn't meant to be easy. It's a secret code of sorts, that only our race is supposed to be able to understand." She slid her backpack off her shoulder and retrieved the book, opening it and scanning pages.

Angela tilted her head as she looked at the signpost. Maybe the markings would make more sense if she looked at them sideways. Nope. They were still chicken scratch. "So?" She looked expectantly at Ailleann. "Anything?"

"Not enough yet to know the riddle," she answered.

Jachin and Boaz also continued to study the panel.

Since it appeared this was going to take some time, Angela decided to be brave and investigate the forest close to the path. They had been so intent on making fast progress that she hadn't really had a chance to take in the sights. In the light of day, nothing looked in the least bit intimidating. The trees looked like trees, the rocks looked like rocks, and she didn't see human characteristics in anything inanimate. She decided she'd been foolish in her fears. Marrion said that the dragons fed at night, so she was safe on that score. The daytime seemed safe enough.

As she wandered over to a beautiful, gnarled oak to gaze up into its twisting branches, her stomach rumbled, reminding her they hadn't eaten since early that morning. Almost the moment she thought of hunger, a flash of red from deeper in the forest caught her eye. A small cluster of apple trees stood several yards beyond the stand of oak trees. Marrion had said food would make itself available when needed, and here it was.

She shrugged. It could be a coincidence. After all, didn't Avalon, the other name for Sena, mean the island of apples? There were probably apple trees everywhere.

***

Gaban stood behind the tree and yawned, almost giving himself away to Angela by snorting as he closed his mouth. Just as she was about to take a bite from an apple she looked in his direction, and he ducked back.

He'd been following the travelers for the past three hours and was wondering what he should do with the opportune unguarded moment. The Dark One had instructed him only to watch and to wait until ordered to return Angela's backpack. But Gaban had never been good at resisting temptation. Where was the harm in one little game?

He masked his voice to sound like Jachin's and called,

"Angela!"

He listened after he shouted the name, knowing that the ever-present but invisible wood sprites had the ability to capture and repeat shouted words. Immediately he heard an echoed, "Angela!" and he knew his ruse had worked.

"Angela!" came the repeated call.

Instantly she headed deeper into the forest, hurrying in her effort to locate the sound's source. He chuckled, the sleep deprivation tiredness from last night's dealings with the fairy folk evaporating like a puff of dragon smoke. The Lute was heading directly toward the Bewilderment Stone. If he could coax her closer to the stone, she would become confused. And if she stayed long enough, she would forget who she was altogether. Wouldn't it be interesting if the Lute lost her memory?

***

Jachin looked around, his stomach tightening with dread when he saw that Angela was nowhere in sight. "Angela!" he called out through cupped hands.

Several odd sounding echoes came back to him. "Angela...Angela...Angela!"

"What the hell is that?" he muttered.

"When you shout, the wood sprites can capture your voice," Ailleann explained. "Then they repeat it. We'd better go look for her."

"Stay together," Jachin said, then blew out a frustrated breath. "Why would she leave the group?"

"Maybe she's just making a pit stop...you know, *nature calls*," Boaz said.

"She should have told someone."

He saw his sister roll her eyes. "Why? You going to escort her? Besides, I know Angela. I'm sure she wouldn't go far."

Still, he didn't see a sign of her anywhere.

"Boaz, you can use your telepathy to connect with her," Ailleann said.

"Oh, yeah." Boaz closed her eyes, concentrating. Then she opened them, frowning. "I'm getting confused images. I can't connect."

Even though Jachin knew male white wizards didn't posses the women's telepathic gifts, he remembered connecting to Angela when she had been under water. Maybe he could do it again. He closed his eyes and pictured her. His mind called her name, *Angela*! A voice like a far-off whisper called, *Jachin?* Suddenly, he knew the direction she had taken, but why had she wandered so far?

"This way," he told Boaz and Ailleann. They followed as he raced down the path and past an old oak tree which led to an apple grove.

He noticed Boaz quickly grabbing fruit and storing it in her backpack as they passed the trees, but he didn't slow down. Angela's scent lingered, drawing him forward like an invisible hand.

Ailleann warned, "Be mindful, Jachin. I sense an evil one close by."

"I feel it, too." Boaz caught up with him and grabbed his arm, jerking him to a stop. "Whoa Trigger, ever hear of the word *caution*? What if this is some kind of trap? Who knows who or what is out there watching us?"

Jachin also sensed the evil presence. It felt like the darkness that dwelt within him, only this evil came from an outside source. The urgent need to find Angela had clouded his newfound perceptions. He needed to slow down and take in all the signs, not just depend on his inexplicable telepathic connection with Angela. With his hand on the knife at his hip, he moved forward, looking in all directions and using all of his senses. Then Angela's scent was replaced by the sharp tang of kerosene. *Gaban*!

"Keep your eyes peeled for Gaban. I smell a troll," he told the women.

"No shit, Sherlock," Boaz said pinching her nose with her fingers.

He looked back to see a quizzical look on Ailleann's face. He was sure Boaz's crude slang was lost on the woman.

"Remember what Marrion said about trolls being flammable, especially when they sweat? I'm tempted to barbeque the guy."

Jachin looked into the forest. Where in the hell was Angela? If Gaban had hurt her, Jachin would be the one to torch the guy.

***

Angela wondered how and why Jachin had gone so far ahead of her into the forest. Still, she could hear his voice, so she knew he was just ahead. "Jachin!" she shouted, only to have her voice come back to her in a myriad of echoes.

She stopped, suddenly feeling dizzy and overheated. She unhooked the cape and dropped it to the ground. Then she pulled her overdress off and draped it over her arm, sighing in relief when a breeze caressed her heated skin through the thin, gauzy chemise. She pushed on in the direction she'd last heard Jachin's voice.

Coming to a large boulder etched with a circular design, she rested, leaning against its hard, cool surface. But the rest didn't seem to help. Her dizziness increased. She dropped the overdress to the ground then slid down to sit on it.

The forest is so beautiful, she found herself thinking as she looked around, enjoying the peaceful clearing. Birds sang above her head, and she could hear the rustling of small animals in the underbrush.

Where was I going? She couldn't remember. Didn't she have to be somewhere? She shrugged when nothing came to mind. The stone cooled her back, and she leaned her head against it to gaze up at the sky. *What would it be like to fly? To soar through the air, weightless?*

With an abruptness that rudely startled her out of her daydream, three people entered the clearing.

"Yes?" She asked, offended that these strangers had disturbed her peaceful musings.

The woman with red hair rushed toward her and gave her a hug.

"What do you want?" she asked.

"Angela!" The red-haired woman gushed. "Why did you wander off?"

Angela. The name sounded familiar. She shrugged her shoulders, not really caring who Angela was, only that the woman stop calling her by that name. Her name wasn't Angela, it was …? At the moment she couldn't quite remember. She just wanted the people to go away and leave her in peace.

The other woman spoke softly to the others. "Quickly, we must get her away from the stone. We must all leave. See the ancient markings? It is the Bewilderment Stone. We shall all come under its spell if we linger."

The frightening-looking man with black hair and a dark scowl walked to her and grabbed her arm, pulling her to her feet. Then he did the most astonishing thing. He picked her up and carried

her into the forest! *Now why would he do something like that?*
As much as she liked the coolness of the rock and the idyllic
clearing, she *loved* being held by this man. She looked up at him.
"I want you to hold me forever."
At least that got a smile out of him. His smile was funny, like
he wasn't sure her suggestion was a good idea, so she snuggled
against his chest and listened to his strong heartbeat. She felt her
body respond to his in a way that made her insides sing. Wanting
the material of her shift and his shirt out of the way so that their
skin could touch, she began working open the buttons down his
chest. She pushed aside the thin material, running her hand over
the springy hair on his warm skin. His hard muscles flexed at her
touch. Just as she was about to put her lips to his chest, he came
to a halt.

When she looked up it was to find his dark eyes boring into
hers. She liked it. The heat from his body and the passion in his
eyes made her feel like she was standing in front of a roaring fire.
She said. "Take off your clothes. You'll be cooler." She pushed
the cape off his shoulders.

Giggles from the two women made her skin prickle. "Make
them go away," she told the man. He was the only one she wanted
to be with.

She found herself being gently lowered to stand on the ground.
Immediately her arms ached for his, so she slid them inside his
open shirt to bring him close again. But he didn't seem to want
her. His push was gentle but firm. She didn't understand. She had
felt him respond to her.

"You don't want me?" she asked, confused. Their bodies had
felt so right together, like they had known each other forever.
Why was he pushing her away?

The man cleared his throat, his eyes saying he was angry. He
asked the quiet woman, "What do we do? How do we snap her
out of this?"

Snap who out of what? Or was it 'whom' out of what? She
couldn't remember.

The quiet woman bit her lip, slowly shaking her head. "We
can't."

The man looked angry. "It *will* wear off."

Again the woman shook her head. "I'm afraid not."

"Ailleann, you're a healer. Fix it," he demanded.

"I can't. It's a spell, not an illness, and it's an unbreakable spell cast by a great wizard. The ancient stone was at one time a dark wizard. He broke our laws by continually trespassing in our village and casting bewilderment spells. He was captured by one of our ancestors, and his essence imprisoned within the stone. His powerful bewilderment spell is also embedded in the stone, so the stone was marked as a warning to those who might happen upon it."

"Well, why in the hell hasn't some kind of fence or barrier been put up around the stone to protect people?"

"Because the stone moves. Very slowly, to be sure, but the wizard within is a strong one, and he is able to move several fathoms during the course of a year."

"So people who come in contact with it spend the rest of their lives bumbling around like idiots?" His look was incredulous.

Ailleann shrugged. "Maybe it's their deepest wish...to go through life without a care."

Confused by the conversation, she turned her attention to the man. *Your hands are hurting me*, she thought as she tried to pry his fingers off her arm. All she wanted to do was make love to him, so why was he being so difficult?

"Well, I don't think Angela wants that," the man said. "And I don't accept it. Boaz, look in that book. See if there's a way to break the spell."

Boaz, she thought to herself. *What a pretty name. Boaz, Ailleann and Jachin.* All their names all sounded nice, although Jachin was kind of grumpy.

The woman called Boaz hurriedly looked through a big book as if she were searching for a recipe.

I really like the way he smells, she thought, leaning in toward the man. *Clean and salty and warm. Like the beach on an early spring day.* He had relaxed his grip, so she took advantage of the moment and moved against him and put her nose to his chest. Ahhh, she loved that scent. Just one little taste ....

He grabbed her by the arms and held her away from him again, but she could see by the heat in his eyes that he didn't really want to.

Boaz looked up from her book, looking like she was going to cry. "Nothing, Jachin. I don't think we can do anything for her. It says the spell of the Bewilderment Stone is unbreakable."

"To hell it is."

Growing bored with the talk about spells, she said, "You're angry again. Don't you ever laugh or smile?" He looked taken aback, and she felt bad that she'd hurt his feelings. "I'll bet that if you kiss me you won't be so angry." She tilted her head back and puckered up.

He pulled her close, and she thought for a blissful moment that he was going to kiss her. Instead he stared into her eyes. *Ah well, we take what we can get,* she thought with a deep sigh. She licked her tingling lips and stared back. Her body felt like warm liquid, and she wanted to melt into him, but he kept her in place, just staring into her eyes.

Jachin focused on connecting with Angela's mind, heedless of the fact that as a male wizard, he wasn't supposed to have telepathic abilities. If he had reached her subconscious before, surely he could reach it now.

Angela, he thought, *come back to me.*

She blinked as if she had heard him, looking confused for a moment. Then she returned to her idyllic staring. God, her mouth was inviting, and every subtle movement of her body said she wanted him. He felt his body respond, but he held it in check. Now was not the time.

Angela, he repeated with his mind. *Come back to me. Your name is Angela Catherine Dawn. You live in Sedona, Arizona. You came with your roommate, Boaz Hamilton, to find me, and then we all crossed over into Sena. We are in Sena now. Angela, wake up!*

"It's not working," he muttered to himself.

Boaz and Ailleann stood several feet away. Seeing that Boaz was shaking her head, he realized that their negativity was interfering.

"Oh ye of little faith," he muttered as he pulled Angela past Boaz and Ailleann, to take her deeper into the forest.

They started to follow.

"Meet me back at the signpost," he said in a tone that said he wasn't going to debate the issue.

Both women nodded and walked away, Boaz throwing a worried look over her shoulder. He pulled the complacent Angela along until he felt clear of Boaz and Ailleann's negative energy.

As soon as he stopped, Angela curled against him like a kitten drunk on catnip. For a long moment he indulged himself and let his arms go around her to hold her close. Her sensual sigh worked its own kind of confusion spell, making him momentarily lose sight of his mission. Reluctantly he held her away.

"Angela, listen to me." He focused his gaze on hers, which was difficult with her standing there in that transparent slip.

"Yes, Jachin?"

"You know who I am?" Maybe the spell was already broken. She nodded with a little giggle. "You are Jachin."

"Jachin who?" he tested to see if she knew his last name.

Her eyebrows jerked up along with her shoulders. "Just Jachin, I guess." She smiled like it didn't matter. "Kiss me. You know you want to." Her playful look turned sensual, and he knew if he didn't concentrate on getting her back, he, too, would be lost.

"No, Angela. I'm not going to kiss you."

She pouted and looked away.

This wasn't working.

"Okay," he said. "Just one kiss, then you have to do something for me, okay?"

She smiled, nodding as she drew out the word, "An-ny-thing."

The next thing he knew she was in his arms, her head tilted up to him.

"One kiss," he reminded himself.

"Stop talking, Jachin," she teased as she pulled his head down to hers.

He had intended to make the kiss brief, a light touch of the lips to fulfill his promise to her. Then he would be free to focus on breaking the confusion spell. But the instant his lips touched her warm, moist mouth, he was swept into a vortex of sensation he never wanted to leave.

She moaned, and he was lost. Deepening the kiss, he wrapped his arms around her and held her close, unable to get enough of her. Her soft breasts pressed against his bare chest, and she ground her hips against his, nearly undoing his resolve. With a shaky breath, he broke the kiss and reluctantly stepped back.

"Ummmm," she murmured. "More?"

He cleared his throat. "You promised," he reminded in a surprisingly strong voice given his shaky state of mind. "One kiss. Then you would do as I say."

A dimple appeared at the corner of her mouth as her chin dipped coyly. "I'll do what you say."

This wasn't going to be easy. He took her by the arms, more to keep himself from pressing his body to hers than to keep her from jumping him.

"Okay," he said. "I want you—"

"I knew it!" She tried to push past his arms, giggling.

"Angela! Be serious."

She gave him an exaggerated look of seriousness, and he had the feeling she was trying to imitate him. Then she burst out laughing. "Oh, Jachin, lighten up. Smile." Then she did get serious. "If you don't laugh or smile for me, I won't play your game. I don't play with fuddy-duddies." She crossed her arms and pouted.

TEN

**MERCURY RETROGRADE: Communication upsets,
a time to look back, things seen in a new light.**

Angela felt heat flood her face every time she looked at Jachin.
What had she done? They were all once again standing by the
signpost with chicken scratches on it, and Boaz edged up to her,
saying, "You go, girl. You want my brother, you go for it. I must
say," Boaz went on mercilessly, "Sena seems to have brought out
the sex goddess in you. You run with those wolves. I always knew
you had it in you. Finally, you're putting my lessons into practice.
But, dear, eager pupil...next time you might wait until you and
Jachin are alone." Boaz burst out laughing, causing Jachin and
Ailleann to turn and look at them.

Angela smiled at Jachin through gritted teeth as she
whispered, "I was under a spell, for God's sake!"

"Which *God's sake,* would that be? Or goddess, should I say?
Venus?"

Jachin glowered at them. "Do you two mind? This is difficult
enough without you two acting like eight-year-olds."

Angela felt her spine stiffen. She was about to reply with a
witty retort, which she hadn't quite yet formulated in her mind,
when Boaz said, "Oh lighten up, Jachin. You have to admit it was
funny. The big, powerful wizard, Jachin Morgan, trying to fend
off the evil temptress. She almost had you, too." She giggled
again, making Jachin glower more, if that was possible.

"No, I don't think it was funny. Angela might never have
regained her memory. Would you be laughing then?"

Angela felt Boaz's arm go around her, and she knew her friend
wasn't done teasing.

"My poor baby," Boaz crooned. "I would have taken care of
you, idiot that you would have been." Boaz took a sharp breath.
"Oh! We could get one of those kiddie leash things, so you
wouldn't wander off."

Angela found herself chuckling at the image. She knew, too,
that despite Boaz's teasing, she really would have stood by Angela

if her memory hadn't returned. She gave her friend a hug.

"Jachin," Boaz said. "I think you have some serious issues here. Like having no sense of humor. When did you lose it? Or did you ever have one?"

Jachin folded his arms, and Angela could see a sibling connection pass between them—him stubborn, Boaz baiting. Angela had seen the same thing many times between her cousins. They felt secure enough in their familial bond that their tease-and-challenge routine held no threat.

Jachin said, "Acting like a child serves no purpose. And we've got to figure out this riddle, or we're never going to get anywhere."

"Serves no purpose!" Boaz was hopping up on her soapbox. "What about as a tension-reliever? What about endorphins? What about giving your spirit a little freedom? You can only do that with a sense of humor, and if you let your inner child out of his cage once in awhile. Acting like a child is like freeing your spirit." She nodded in satisfaction.

"Enough Jungion psychology, or whatever you're spouting. Help me with this." He looked back to the signpost, effectively putting an end to the discussion.

Angela wasn't sure why it was an issue with him, but Boaz's words had definitely pushed his buttons. Come to think of it, she had noticed that Jachin didn't have a sense of humor. He was sexy as hell, intelligent and confident. But someone or something had stolen his laughter.

Ailleann was saying, "I'm translating this from the old words, so the riddle may not have the rhyming cadence it should, but I feel the meaning is the same." She looked to the marker. "The first part could mean either, *I am darkness*, or, *I am your greatest fear.* The rest is clear. *Only find me by facing yourself. As you look to the source of life, keep the serpent on your right shoulder.*" She shook her head, indicating she hadn't solved the puzzle.

"Okay," said Boaz. "We've got the words. Now we need to look at it on a spiritual level. Your greatest fear would mean something different for all of us, depending on whose spiritual journey this is." She looked at Jachin and smiled broadly. "You seem to have the most hang ups, so let's start there. What's your biggest fear?"

Jachin snorted. "The fear of this thing taking forever. It's a sign for anyone who happens upon it. Surely it's referring to the greatest fears of the population at large. And I'm sure *you've* got 'spiritual' issues to deal with, right along with the rest of humanity."

Ailleann said, "The sign will mean different things to different people. And it will lead each of them on a different, individual journey. That is why you must interpret it on your own spiritual level. She studied Jachin. "What *is* your greatest fear?"

Jachin sighed. "Greatest fear?" He shrugged. "Facing Kadien, I suppose."

Boaz smiled. "That wasn't so hard, was it, Brother?"

They began going over the rest of the words, trying for different meanings.

Angela couldn't understand why they couldn't get it. It was obvious. She found herself saying aloud, "The darkness is Kadien. Facing yourself, means to turn around. The source of life is water. The serpent is the winding river. As riddles go, it's pretty simple. If we want to find Kadien, we have to turn back the way we came, find the river, then follow it, keeping it to our right."

They all stared at her as if she'd grown two heads.

"You're right," Jachin said. "That's what it means."

Boaz executed a cheer. "Angela, Angela, she's our man, if she can't do it, no one can! Woohoo!" she said, ending it with a cheerleader jump.

Ailleann put her hand on Angela's shoulder. "Well done."

Angela shrugged and kicked the dirt, going along with her friend's silliness. "It was nothing. My uncle used to break up the monotony of long car trips by giving us brain teasers and riddles."

Boaz chuckled. "Well, that shoots the whole 'spiritual journey' thing." She gave Angela an exaggerated stare. "Unless it's your journey we're on." Then she turned to Ailleann. "Guess the Lutes have a handle on our ancient, secret language."

Ailleann smiled as she looked at Angela. "So it would seem."

They headed back the way they'd come, Jachin once again taking the lead, with Angela next, and Boaz and Ailleann chatting behind her. Soon Boaz and Ailleann were far enough behind that she felt they couldn't hear her. She stared at Jachin's wide shoulders and strong back, saying, "Jachin, thanks for what you did back at the Bewilderment Stone."

She saw the slight jerk of one shoulder, as though he hadn't given it another thought. She decided to pursue it, finding it much easier to talk to his back than to look in his eyes. Curiosity about his reaction to her advances made her push on. "I'm sorry, too, for...the way I acted."

His step faltered, but he kept walking. "I knew you had a sensuous side. You just do everything in your power to hide it. The Bewilderment Stone allowed you to be yourself."

She stopped at that then hurried to catch up. "That...that, *wasn't* the real me!"

"Yes it was." He kept walking.

"No, it wasn't. I don't go around trying to...to," she whispered, "*rape* men."

Jachin turned so abruptly that she was forced to stumble to a stop. He looked into her eyes, and her stomach turned summersaults. His body leaned toward hers. "You...*Angel*," he said on a low growl, "are a sensualist at heart. But you are afraid to admit it, even to yourself."

The combination of him calling her Angel in that deep whisper and the realization that he had her pegged kept her from responding. She just stood there like an idiot. She felt a wall go up. It was a wall she was used to. She didn't want to be sensual. Not until the right man came along. And by "right" she meant someone who wanted her for the rest of her life. Mr. Right, not Mr. Right Now.

Jachin Morgan might be the sexiest man in any world, and he might make her insides melt with wanting him, but he was about as far from her idea of Mr. Right as a man could get. She wasn't so far gone into the fantasy world of Sena to forget she had a life to return to. And she wanted to be true to herself, not be swept away in the moment only to regret it the rest of her life. Jachin Morgan might want to sleep with her because he had some misguided notion that she was as perfect as the statue of her that he had created. But once he realized how unspectacular she was, he would walk away without a second glance. She had no hope of ever being special enough for him to commit himself to a lifelong relationship with her.

Boaz and Ailleann caught up to them, and they all began walking again, Jachin obviously not as shaky from their encounter as she was. Angela took a deep breath, silently saying, *Oh Lord, protect me from myself.*

Just then a little Scotty dog bounded toward them, yapping

playfully then rolling on its back in a submissive posture.

"Is this one of the 'guides' Marrion told us about?" Jachin asked derisively.

"One never knows," Ailleann replied. "We must be open to all creatures and all elements. Maybe the little dog is a guide. Or perhaps he is just a dog seeking companionship. Dogs can be wonderful trackers, able to follow by scent as well as follow what you would call a *psi* trail."

"What's a *psi* trail?" Jachin asked.

"A trail left by someone's spirit, the energies we radiate. Some people read them as an individual's own personal scent, while others, like dogs, can perceive the spirit force that lingers after we have moved on." She chuckled. "I'm afraid you won't find that your Lute laws of physics apply to this ability. The *psi* trail operates outside time and space, your theory of relativity, and even your laws of thermodynamics. We on Sena have long accepted it as fact and don't try to explain it. It just *is*."

"I'm afraid that won't help us much in finding Lilith, or Kadien for that matter," Boaz said. "We have no way of letting the dog know who we're looking for. We didn't bring anything of Lilith's that we could use as a lead.

"Let's just observe the dog," Ailleann suggested. "He may already know what we're looking for."

Angela said, "Come here, boy." She crouched down and patted her knee, holding out her hand. She'd always been a sucker for animals, especially dogs.

The dog stayed close to the ground as he approached her outstretched hand. Then, after licking it, he sided close to her, wagging his tail furiously. She was in love. "He's so adorable. Let's just let him follow us, and if he wanders off, so be it."

Boaz got a comical look of concern on her face. "Oooo, you're turning into one of us. 'So be it?' The pod people have taken over Angela."

Jachin heaved an exaggerated sigh. "Not this again. Let's go. Forget about the dog. If he follows, fine. If not, fine."

Angela threw her hands up and said to Boaz, "Isn't that what I just said?"

Boaz shrugged. "Oh, honey, rule number one in the book, The Way to a Man's Heart...instituted during the 50's I believe...says, 'Make your man think it is all his idea.' It makes him feel manly, or virile or something." She tilted her chin to her chest, raising her eyebrows knowingly. "And act like you're an idiot who can't complete a sentence, let alone come up with an original idea."

The three women burst out laughing, while Jachin walked off, shaking his head.

Boaz sighed, saying to no one in particular, "Don't you just want to get him down on the ground and tickle him until he screams uncle?"

Angela chuckled, "I don't think he's ticklish."

"What about it, Ailleann?" Boaz said. "Are all male wizards born without a funny bone?"

For a moment Ailleann looked puzzled. "Oh, I see, funny bone is a figure of speech. I'm learning that you have many that I don't understand."

"Yeah," Boaz said. "It means a sense of humor."

Ailleann shook her head. "All white wizards are raised to take great joy in life and to know that laughter can heal. We spend much time in joyful activities, and we balance that with serious tasks. Jachin seems...well, like he is afraid to embrace the laughter, as if he sees it as a weakness."

Angela thought about that. So, they both had fears. She of letting her passions wreak havoc on her life, and Jachin of frivolity of any kind. Why? What happened to him? Hadn't he ever been a child?

***

, Marrion and Illan sat in Millie's tavern, sipping *Fraoch* and munching on pine nuts.

Marrion said, "I've observed the children. Their progress is slower than I had hoped."

Illan patted her hand. "It is not for us to say. It will take as long as it takes. You said yourself that Jachin has much to learn about himself. You can't rush that kind of journey."

Running her finger around the edge of her mug, Marrion said, "If the children had been left in Sena, Jachin's spirit journey would have been taken long ago." Instantly she held up her hand, knowing what her brother was about to say. "I know. We can't hope to know The Master's plan. Only The Great One knows the purpose for past events and the events now unfolding. And only The Master knows how to prepare The Triad for the confrontation with darkness. Everything has a purpose, this I know. It's just difficult to sit idly by and watch."

"Maybe our part in the plan is complete. Let us rejoice in the part we have played." He raised his mug.

Marrion did the same. "Blessings be to The Light. Thank you for allowing us the honor of partaking in this great journey."

They brought their mugs to within an inch of each other, not touching, lest the blessing be broken.

"And to the children. May lightness follow them and protect them," Illan said.

If things were progressing as they should, Marrion thought, why did she have such a powerful sense that something was terribly wrong?

ELEVEN

Alder Tree: Represents Facing up to the things about yourself and your place in the Green World.

Jachin heard the stream before he saw it. He veered off the path, making his way down the bank to the swiftly moving water's wide, mossy edge. Dog, as he'd named the terrier, trotted alongside him. He didn't need to look to see if the women followed him because the sound of their non-stop chatter was getting closer and closer.

For the past hour Ailleann, Boaz and Angela had been exchanging information about their worlds as if they were new sorority sisters, telling each other about their hometowns. He simply didn't get the whole female 'bonding' ritual. Although he'd seen it before, most of the women he knew looked at other women as adversaries, not buddies.

"I'm starving," Boaz said as she stepped to the edge of the riverbank and peered into the water. "I say we eat and rest a bit. The stream is loaded with fish." She held out her arms. "Sushi anyone?"

Jachin snorted. "You think they're just going to jump into your outstretched hands?"

"Why not? You know, Jachin, you're a pain-in-the-ass brother." She smiled. "But I love you anyway."

"Gee, thanks," he said. Having the word *brother* applied to him still gave him a weird feeling.

"Angela," Boaz said, "I'd kill for some of the incredible guacamole you'd make for our weekly Thank-God-It's-Friday get-togethers. And some fresh, hot tortilla chips. Ummmm."

"Yeah. If anyone's listening." Angela peered through the treetops. "I'm putting in my order for guacamole, chips and icy beer." Her expectant gaze was met with a gentle rush of wind through the trees.

Boaz sighed. "Right now I'd settle for a PB&J."

"Or just the peanuts. Anything," Angela said.

Jachin looked around for something to use as a lure or a trap.

"Maybe we can catch some fish."

Angela began gathering wood, explaining, "If we do, I'm not about to eat it raw. I only like tuna sushi, and I doubt we're going to find tuna in fresh water."

Jachin noticed she looked like she knew what she was doing, selecting only the dry pieces of wood. He shrugged, heading over to a row of bamboo to slice a thin pole to use for a spear.

He looked over to see Ailleann and Boaz asking the river to provide sustenance. They finished by bowing with their hands folded. He *recalled* that the way of his people was to ask a simple request of nature. Then to thank nature for what was provided. He got up and went to the edge of the water and thought, *We are hungry. We ask for food to nourish our bodies.* He didn't know if he would ever be comfortable saying words like that aloud. For now, his prayers would have to be silent ones. He bowed with his hands together.

He looked over to see Angela doing the same thing. Their eyes met and she smiled, causing his stomach to tighten. He wanted her, and it was becoming a gnawing hunger that grew whenever he looked at her. Quickly he began cutting the pole's tip into a sharp point. Only one hunger could be appeased. That was, *if* he could catch a fish.

Taking off his shoes, Jachin rolled up his pant legs and waded into the cool water. There were enough fish, so he shouldn't have a problem spearing one.

He glanced over to where the women worked, noticing that Angela had already set up a pretty amazing fire pit. A ring of rocks held a sizable stack of wood set in the shape of a teepee.

Still chatting, Boaz and Ailleann were rummaging through a large cluster of cattails near the water's edge.

He returned to his task.

After about the twentieth miss, he finally speared one. Although it wasn't huge, it looked big enough to give them each several mouthfuls. Foolishly enough, he felt like a warrior, bringing food home to his tribe. He flipped the spear over to hold it up for everyone to see.

But instead of congratulations and pats on the back, Boaz and Ailleann were squealing like stuck pigs as they gushed over Angela. She was standing just upstream, looking like a water sprite with her skirt tucked between her legs and looped through her belt to hold it up. She was holding something up for the others to see. A fish, Jachin saw with chagrin. She had evidently caught it with her bare hands. He shrugged, his pride not nearly as wounded as he thought it should be. In fact, he was as close to laughing as he'd come on this trip.

He silently thanked the fish for giving its life for the nourishment of their bodies, and he noticed that Dog sat quietly beside the bank, his head lowered as if he too were saying a blessing.

While Jachin cleaned the fish, Boaz started a fire. He'd forgotten she had the gift of fire and, with one breath, could condense the needed elements in the air and breathe the spark of life to ignite them, just as he called on the elements to gather and form into metal.

On a flat rock he left the fish remains and some meat for Dog, which the animal quickly devoured.

"Look what Ailleann found," Boaz said as Jachin took the fish to the fire circle. "Wild herbs, mushrooms, and cattail sprouts. She said the sprouts taste like cucumbers."

"And," Angela said, her eyes wide, "I found *avocados*. I thought they were indigenous to the Americas, but I'm not going to question a gift from the gods."

Boaz rubbed her hands together. "What a feast!"

As they each held a skewer of fish over the fire while the vegetables boiled in the pot, the women talked.

"I am confused about the land you grew up in," Ailleann said. "Sometimes I think you like it, and at other times I have the feeling you do not."

"Don't you feel a little bit like that about Sena?" Angela asked.

The young woman seemed to think about it. "Yes, I guess I do. I love Sena and my people, but I want to explore other worlds. As a healer, I am not permitted to leave. I don't have the knowledge to return. Only The Seekers, who go to other worlds to keep abreast of their ways, know how to freely travel from world to world. They would be banished if they revealed their ways to others." She sighed.

"But, our mother left Sena with us," Boaz said. "How is that possible? Was she aided by a Seeker?"

Ailleann shook her head. "We do not know. There are but a few ways to leave Sena. All, with the exception of The Wizard's

Moon, are so perilous that none but the Dark Ones dare use them."
She looked around as if she were afraid of being overhead.
Then she leaned in toward the group and murmured, "Please
don't think me a heretic, but I am sympathetic to those who feel
that if the People of Light crossed over more often between the
worlds, we could help in the struggle against The Evil Ones. One
man, from long ago, Seumas Scot, tried to rally the enlightened
ones to this cause. He was shunned and chose self-banishment.
Who knows? Maybe he went into your world to fight for his
cause. He would recognize the Dark Ones among the Lutes."

"There are wizards in the Lute world?" Boaz asked. "Don't
tell me...our political leaders, right?"

Again, Ailleann shook her head. "Your leaders aren't wizards.
They, among others, are only influenced by them. Your world's
miseries are instigated by The Dark Ones. The dark wizards
influence your world's leaders to fight and to create weapons of
mass destruction. They turn people's hearts against one another
so that darkness can enter. They enter lonely young people's minds
to coax them to violence and hatred. They urge your scientists to
create new viruses, which, once released, cannot be controlled.
They turn people's hearts away from faith, so the great religions
are dying."

Jachin said, "If we have so much power as white wizards, it
seems criminal not to help."

"From what Ailleann says," Angela murmured, "I don't think
it's a good idea to voice that opinion too often around here."

Jachin said, "I won't censor myself because the white wizard
community might not agree with me." He felt the darkness within
flair at the thought of being repressed.

Go with the anger, an internal voice urged, but he knew they
weren't his own thoughts. He shivered as the voice said,
"Acknowledge the darkness. Then you will have all that you seek."

The women seemed lost in thought, while Dog was staring at
Jachin as though the thoughts were coming from him. It had to
be his imagination, because he sensed no magical abilities from
the dog. Someone was trying to influence him. Ailleann had said
that the Dark Ones used their influence to cause destruction. He
had to conclude that a dark wizard knew where he was and was
trying to get him to release his own dark side. Marrion had said
that all wizards, white and dark, operated on the principal of free

will. The Dark Ones could not have him unless he willingly gave himself over to them, so he closed his eyes and concentrated on shutting his mind to outsiders. A quiet calm overcame him, and he knew he had succeeded.

For now, his own conscience murmured, forcing him to recall how he'd spent his life controlling the darkness within him. But he knew that the darkness itself could entice him with promises of incredible power, because he could sense that incredible power lurking inside him. Would he be strong enough to resist the urge to let the darkness control him?

He had to be, because if he wasn't…. He wouldn't let himself finish the thought.

Instead, he opened his eyes and saw Angela staring at him with concern. She made a motion of drawing on a frown, then a smile. He realized he had been scowling, and he made an effort to soften the look. She got up from her side of the fire pit and came to sit next to him. Boaz and Ailleann took no notice since they were once again engulfed in their ongoing discussion.

"A penny for your thoughts," Angela said.

"You don't want to know my thoughts, Angel."

She looked startled, then smiled. "Why do you call me Angel sometimes?"

He shrugged. "To me you seem like an Angel." He wasn't about to share his dream with her, or the fact that she had been in his now-destroyed sculpture. What was the point?

She looked suspicious. "Why would I seem like that to you? Believe me, I'm no Angel. Just ask my parents."

"We all act the angel to someone during our lifetime." He looked deeper into her eyes. "Maybe you're mine."

He saw her swallow then lick her lips. "What do you mean?"

Moving closer he said, "Let me show you." He lowered his lips to hers.

At first she pulled her head back. Then she moved forward so that their lips barely touched. As soon as his lips brushed the softness of her mouth and he felt the warmth of her rapid breaths mingle with his own, he began to fall under a spell every bit as bewitching as the Bewilderment Stone.

He pulled her into his arms, immediately feeling her heated response. Their hearts, so close that they beat against each other's chests, took up one rhythm. He felt her body arch against his in a way that made him lose all reason.

He deepened the kiss, their tongues playing out the act they ultimately wanted but had no right to consummate. Her hands clawed at his back, grabbing handfuls of his shirt, and he resisted the urge to pull her closer. If they got any closer, their bodies would take over and there would be no turning back.

With every ounce of remaining willpower, he began to pull away. But Angela's tongue flicked out for one more taste, and her teeth took hold of his lower lip and tugged gently. The sensation sent electric shocks through his entire body. If the other two women hadn't been there, he was sure his willpower wouldn't have withstood the provocative invitation.

A soft breeze brushed between them when they parted, and a feeling crossed between them that he could only call awareness. They were as close to reading each other's thoughts as a wizard and Lute could get. Now he knew why he had insisted she come on the journey, even though he knew they could never be together. He wanted, no, *needed* to be near her for as long as possible.

At that moment he realized what he'd been denying since they met. He and Angela were spiritually connected. Their hearts, minds and souls were attuned in a way he thought could never happen. And he sensed that she felt it, too.

She gave him more than friendship, beauty, and emotional complications. She gave him a depth of passion and feeling he'd never before experienced.

But that didn't erase the reality of their separate worlds. Feeling spiritually connected to Angela didn't change the fact that they couldn't be together. His people would never accept her once they learned she was a MacAlpin. And he couldn't ask her to give up her normal, all-American life, even if the wizard community might grow to accept her. He could visit her from time to time, but what would that accomplish? It would only serve to remind him he had to live without her.

He had responsibilities in Sena and to his people. And, although he hadn't asked to be one of the "chosen ones," he couldn't turn away from all that the title entailed. The remembrance ceremony had shown him the truth of The Triad and his and his sisters' obligation.

He had already decided that once The Great Confrontation, whatever that was, was over and the balance of power restored, his only course would be to return to Laguna Beach. But only long enough to settle his business affairs and restore *The Dance*. Then he would return to Sena forever.

To punctuate that point, he heard Boaz say to Ailleann, "I don't know what to do. I know I have an obligation to our people here, but I also have a life back home. I can't just travel back and forth between the two worlds. You said yourself, it's almost impossible. That would be some heavy-duty commute," she threw in with her usual humor. "I have to make a decision. And the only answer I can see is to stay in Sena. I don't want to turn away from my birth family now that I've found them, or from my responsibilities as part of The Triad and the matriarch of the white wizards. I guess neither can Jachin and Lilith. It looks like Angela is the only one who can return to the Lute world and stay."

Ailleann looked sad. "Our people and creatures once crossed between the worlds with little trouble. But with the betrayal of the MacAlpin and our retreat to Sena, an impenetrable veil was placed between the worlds. All but a few of our people's villages were wiped out by MacAlpin and his Lute warriors. We have been slowly rebuilding our numbers, but as you can see, we are still a small clan."

Jachin looked down at Angela, who wore a pained expression. He knew she was still worried about being found out.

Ailleann looked toward the sky then turned her attention to Jachin. "Might I make a suggestion? Dusk nears. It would be wise to set up camp here until tomorrow. To continue our journey during the dark hours could be perilous. Mischievous creatures, night-feeding animals and The Dark Ones roam the night. We can place a protection spell around our camp for safety. The creatures will not harm us."

Jachin rubbed his neck. "I'd hoped we would make better time. At this rate, who knows how long it will take to reach Kadien's fortress. I don't like the idea of Lilith being there any longer than necessary."

"Each journey takes as long as it is ordained," Ailleann replied. "There are lessons, and they will be offered as you open yourselves to them. Once the lessons are learned, you will be better able to face The Dark One. One would not want to go into battle as half a warrior."

"You're starting to sound like Aunt Marrion," Boaz

bemoaned. "But in a weird kind of way, you make sense. We need to be spiritually balanced in order to make the best decisions during the confrontation."

"Yes," Ailleann replied, her smile warm.

"Whew! Maybe I should become a motivational speaker after this is over," Boaz teased.

The thought that they still had lessons to learn along the way made the journey seem to stretch out ahead of them like an endless road.

"Okay," Jachin conceded, "we stay here for the night. Let's figure out sleeping arrangements." He covertly winked at Angela as they all got up. She pretended not to see, although he saw her suppress a smile. He knew they couldn't sleep together, but they could enjoy thinking about it. Her kiss, coupled with flashbacks to their dream sex, had him envisioning their bodies entwined against a soft, green bed of forest moss ...

"Hello, Jachin? Are you ignoring me?" Boaz stood with her hands on her hips, Dog at her feet, his tail wagging.

"No. Did you say something?"

"Among other things, I *said*, we should all sleep close together and take turns keeping watch."

"Oh, sure."

She shook her head in disgust. "I thought the phrase 'sleep together' might get your attention, but you must have been out in la-la land." She gestured toward the forest. "As I said, the protection spell will work against the little forest munchkins and whatever, but it can probably be broken by some of the more skillful wizards. If someone wanted to get to us, night would be the best time. We need to keep vigilant."

"Someone already knows where we are." He told them about the voice in his head, but he didn't reveal that the voice had urged him to *give in to the darkness.* "And," he said, "I sensed Gaban's presence when Angela went to the Bewilderment Stone. Although I haven't sensed or smelled him since then, he's probably lurking around for who knows what reason."

"So, you think whomever it was that telepathically talked to you might be waiting for dark to do something?" Angela asked as she rubbed her arms then gathered her cape around her.

"My instincts say they're only observing us for now, but we should definitely stay close together at all times."

"Speaking of that," Boaz said, pointing to a cluster of boulders. "I claim a spot behind those rocks as the little girl's room. Anyone else need to use the facilities?" She looked at the confused Ailleann and said, "Privy."

Angela and Ailleann nodded, and they all headed for the rocks.

"Don't wander off," he said to their retreating backs.

"You and Dog keep the camp safe," Boaz said.

He turned back to the campfire, adding a few more branches. They were almost out of wood, and they needed more since they'd be staying here for the night. He had gathered enough wood by the time the women returned, and they immediately set out selecting spots on which to spread out their capes on the soft, mossy banks.

***

Angela sat next to the fire and watched the fireflies flicker as Boaz took her book from her backpack and began to flip through the pages. Jachin and Ailleann each seemed lost in thought.

Shaking her had, Boaz said, "I still can't believe I can actually read what's in this book. It's in Gaelic, but ever since the remembrance ceremony, I feel like I've known the language forever."

Ailleann said, "You have. Our people believe that all beings are in possession of Eternal Knowledge. But we have lessons to learn before we can acknowledge the truths, and sometimes we need help recalling the knowledge. The ceremony is only one of many ways."

She turned to Angela. "I have heard that the Lute's method of recall is through taking classes from skilled teachers. It is a slow process."

Angela teased, "You mean somewhere deep inside me, I know quantum physics?" If she did, it was buried way, way deep in her subconscious.

Ailleann nodded. "All knowledge is there within you. You only need help in recalling it and organizing it."

Boaz seemed to have found what she was looking for in the Book of Light, and she stood up, holding the book balanced in one hand. Looking around at them all, she said, "Okay. Wish me luck. This is my first spell."

She raised her free hand toward the sky and began reciting as she read from the book.

As far as Angela was concerned, Boaz might as well have been speaking Greek, although she'd said it was Gaelic. Angela was once again amazed by Boaz's growing powers and knowledge. But if all creatures had Eternal Knowledge, why did she feel so completely clueless here on Sena? Her *truths* were obviously buried deeper than those of the white wizards.

"*Fainey shee...gardey...fainey airhey,*" Boaz intoned as she turned slowly in a circle. Then she bowed. "There," she announced. "How'd I do, Ailleann?"

"Beautifully. I've never heard that particular protection spell before, but I can feel its strength." She smiled toward one of the darting fireflies that bobbed close to the fire. "But, I see one of the night creatures made its way into our camp before you cast the spell."

"I love fireflies," Angela said. It was one of the things she missed most about the Missouri farm where she'd been raised. But this one looked bigger than any she had seen as a child.

Ailleann got up to walk toward the light, chuckling. "But this isn't a firefly." She put her hand out. "It's a night fairy. Let me see if I can coax it to land. They're quite friendly. As a child, I used to play with them."

The tiny creature, with its wings outspread, was about the size of a quarter, and it landed in her palm. Its illumination cast a light on Ailleann's pale skin, and she shielded the tiny creature with her other hand as if it might blow away as she moved. She brought it toward where they were sitting.

They all peered into Ailleann's hand, and Angela gasped. Ailleann was holding a tiny woman with wings, just like one of the fairy pictures she'd had in her childhood books. Delicately lacy, transparent green wings, like those of an insect, fluttered at her back, and her tiny, perfect body seemed covered in a wispy membrane that looked like a transparent leaf. Her entire being was illuminated with a blue-green light, as if she'd been dipped in florescent paint. She smiled at them.

"She's beautiful," Angela breathed.

"Wow," was all Jachin said.

"Will she come to me, do you think?" Boaz held out her hand.

Ailleann said, "It's up to her. They're incredibly delicate, so I don't want to pick her up. She will have to go to you herself."

Boaz got close, and the little creature smiled up at her, the glow of her body growing brighter. She fluttered her tiny wings then took flight, alighting on Boaz's open palm.

"I can hear what she's thinking!" Boaz whispered in awe.

"Yes," Ailleann said. "Night fairies communicate telepathically."

"What's she saying?" Angela asked.

Boaz looked startled. "She says she is here to help protect me."

Angela watched a doubtful expression move over Jachin's features. He spoke in a low voice, as if afraid the night fairy might overhear, as he asked, "How is she supposed to protect you? It looks like a strong wind could crush her."

Boaz and the fairy looked intently at each other, and Angela could have sworn she saw the little woman frown in concern. Boaz said, "Her name is Brigid. She says she can move freely among the night creatures, even the dark wizards, and will return to tell me if they intend us harm."

Ailleann said, "It is true. Night fairies are considered harmless to the creatures of Sena and insignificant to the dark wizards who do not appreciate their gentle beauty. She could do as she claims, although I've never known of a night fairy helping a wizard before. They play with us when we are children, but begin to shy away when we grow up."

Boaz was still staring intently at the little creature. "She says her people know of the upcoming battle between darkness and light. She is their leader. They want to help."

Angela looked around to see hundreds of bobbing lights just outside the boundary of their camp, as if all the night fairies in the forest waited in anticipation of the meeting's outcome.

Jachin said, "Do they have any powers?"

Ailleann said, "Besides telepathy, they do have limited magical powers. Fairy magic has been known to transform the ordinary into the extraordinary. She can freely move around the forest and perhaps, as she said, alert us to potential dangers."

"You're sure she's not tricking us?" Jachin asked.

Ailleann said, "Night fairies are truthful by nature."

Angela stifled a yawn. "I'm dog tired." She smiled at Dog. "I'll bet you are, too. Ready to hit the leaves?"

Dog headed to the makeshift bed Angela had made up, as if he understood what she had said and was glad to share her sleeping arrangement.

Jachin said, "Boaz, you and Ailleann take first watch. Angela and I will take the second."

Boaz shrugged. "Sure." She watched as the night fairy flew up to sit on her shoulder.

Angela noticed then that only a few lights bobbed between the branches of the forest now. Evidently most of the fairy folk had gone elsewhere.

Boaz and Ailleann walked a distance from the fire to sit down and lean against a large boulder. Dog must have changed his mind about sleep, because he followed them.

Darn! Angela thought. She was hoping to keep Dog next to her as a chaperone of sorts. Sleeping next to Jachin on a balmy, romantic, star-studded night was going to be the biggest challenge of all. All she could think of as she rearranged the leaves to form a long mound was the way Jachin kissed. She felt her toes curl and warmth tingle across her skin. Taking a deep breath, she lay down.

Jachin had set up his own bed within inches of her own, and he now stretched out facing her. "You okay *way* over there? All by yourself? In the dark?"

She chuckled. "Are you trying to scare me into your bed, Jachin?" It was very close to working. She was as tense as a board, hoping the protection spell held. She didn't relish the thought of dealing with another dragon or heaven only knew what else.

"How about I just ask. Would you like to come over here and sleep with me? I'll keep you warm."

"I'll bet. But, thank you, no," she said, although she would like nothing more than to lose herself in those wonderful arms and re-ignite the passion they'd shared. "Go to sleep, Jachin."

He didn't respond, but continued to watch her. The flickering light from the fire painted orange streaks across his face, distorting his features just enough to make him look slightly evil. But she knew in her heart she had nothing to fear from him. Her eyes began to get heavy, and as she worked at willing her muscles to relax, she began to fade.

Jachin watched her drift off. They'd had a long day of walking, and he was tired as well. But he wanted to lie there and watch her while she wasn't aware of him. The slight frown on her face eased as she fell deeper asleep. The air was mild, and the rhythmic chirping of crickets and far-off sounds of night birds began to soothe him to sleep. He lowered his eyelids for a few moments and when he opened them it was to see Angela looking back at him. He heard the song of a bird along with the gentle gurgle of the stream nearby.

It wasn't until Angela stood and began to remove a flowing, white gauzy dress that he realized he was dreaming. He vaguely noticed she wore some sort of medallion around her slim neck. He looked toward the bank where Ailleann and Boaz were supposed to be, but the spot was empty. The fire danced and flared with the rhythm of his quickening heartbeat.

Angela now stood before him, completely, beautifully naked, her hair a mass of wild curls accentuating her high cheekbones. He felt his body respond. It was just a dream, he reasoned. What the hell. What harm could there be in allowing his passions free rein in a make-believe world?

Her body was just as he remembered it from his past dreams. Perfect. Her slim neck tapered down to small, full breasts and taught nipples. His eyes followed the curve of her waist to the flat belly that urged his eyes still lower. He moved close as he stripped off his shirt, all the while watching the flickering invitation in her sultry eyes. The medallion against her chest glittered orange in the firelight. He realized it had the astrological sign of the scorpion engraved on it.

As he looked at Angela, he felt as if they had been lovers forever, and her expression said she waited with barely contained anticipation for him to come to her. Untying the rope belt at his waist, the last barrier between them fell away, and she breached the short distance to him.

He enfolded her in is arms, his skin growing hot at each point of contact with hers. His erection pressed hard against her belly, and she responded by grinding against him provocatively.

"Make me yours, Jachin," she whispered. Her tongue flicked out to lick his nipple, and her teeth took hold, sending zinging sensations radiating out from that point.

His breath caught. "You are mine." At least in his dream. He bent down to capture her heated lips with his, their tongues devouring each other.

"Jachin!" A voice shouted at him, jerking him out of the dream.

Only instead of lying on his cot of leaves, he was standing, completely naked, holding an equally naked and horror-stricken Angela! He didn't know whether to keep hold of her or step back, given his state of arousal. She answered the question by roughly pushing away from his arms.

He turned away from Boaz as Angela scrambled for her clothes. He felt his pants hit his leg as she threw them at him, and he caught them, putting them on.

"What the hell happened?" Angela asked.

Boaz chuckled derisively. "Seems pretty obvious to me. And I wouldn't mind, but your virtue is our only way off Sena, and we still might want to leave." The little fairy sat on her shoulder and Dog sat at her feet, giving Boaz the look of some modern day deity.

"But...but I ...," Angela sputtered as she straightened her dress.

Tying the belt at his waist and feeling ridiculously like a teenager caught making out in the backseat of his parent's car, Jachin found himself explaining. "As far as I knew, we were dreaming. It was just like one of those glimmer dreams Marion told us we were having. At least for me. I didn't think it was really happening."

" Vell, I certainly wasn't awake!" Angela said in a shaky voice. "I thought I was dreaming, too. I wouldn't..." She motioned toward Jachin. "...I swear."

She put her hands to her face, and although it was too dark to see if she was blushing, Jachin was sure she was.

"After we complete what we have to do here," Boaz said, "knock yourselves out. But, Jachin, we need Angela unsullied, so to speak, if we want to get back home. And I need to go home and settle some things before I move back here permanently."

"And I don't?" Jachin could feel his frustration rise toward anger. "I know Angela and I can't be together. But tell that to my dreams. And hers, for that matter."

"Okay, okay," Boaz said. "We'll just have to keep you separated while you're sleeping."

"You three take watch together, and I'll take my shift alone," Jachin said. "That way Angela and I will be asleep at different times."

"Well, it's been about four hours," Boaz said with a yawn.

"It is your turn. Angela, go back to sleep. You can join our watch tomorrow night."

Jachin put on his shirt and shoes and headed toward the rock.

Angela was afraid to go to sleep. She gripped the front of her shift, telling herself, *Don't take your clothes off. Don't take your clothes off.*

But despite her fears, her eyes closed, and the next thing she knew she was awake, fully clothed, thank God, and the sky was turning gray. Jachin was already busy taking the fire pit apart. Ailleann and Boaz were stretching as if they too had just awakened.

They quietly ate a quick breakfast of oranges and avocados that Jachin had found nearby. She would have loved a cup of coffee, but the clear, cool water from the stream tasted wonderful and was quite satisfying.

They filled their flasks before they left, then headed upstream as the signpost had told them to do.

***

Seumas trotted behind the group. Jachin had done a remarkable job of keeping his anger at bay since he had been in Sena. The energy outbursts Seumas had witnessed over the past few years had been disconcerting, and he had wondered at the cause. It wasn't like a white wizard to be so angry—so unbalanced. And Seumas had to wonder if that anger would help or hinder Jachin when he confronted Kadien.

The only intense anger he had ever felt was when he was shunned for believing that the veil between the worlds should once again be lifted. And even then, he hadn't felt the need to hurt or maim as Jachin often did. Maybe it was simply the fact that Jachin hadn't had a lifetime on Sena and that the Lute world had corrupted his inherently gentle soul.

Whatever the reasons, Seumas knew for certain that Jachin fought a daily battle with the darkness inside him. And Seumas was both intrigued and frightened by it. When fighting a dark wizard, you always knew their intent. But fighting a white wizard whose soul hid an unnatural darkness would be more difficult, because there had never been such a wizard before, and no one knew how Jachin would respond to any given circumstance or even the extent of his dark powers.

For now, he would continue to observe. Not only was he not

ready to reveal himself to Sena's inhabitants, he wanted to be able to covertly observe Jachin and Boaz to best know how to handle them when the time came.

***

Angela walked along, daydreaming of a long, hot bubble bath. A glass of iced tea wouldn't be too bad, either. And a steak—a big, beautiful, tender, juicy, pink-in-the middle steak. Her mouth began to water.

She turned to Boaz, who was walking behind her, and jokingly whined, "Mom, are we there yet?" It had been four days, and she wasn't getting a sense that they were any closer to Kadien's fortress. For all she knew they could be walking in circles.

Boaz shook her head. "I don't think we're even close. Illan said once we saw the hill to Kadien's fortress we would have another full day of walking. Either we're reading the signs wrong, or we're not learning the lessons Aunt Marrion told us about."

Angela's stomach growled. "Do you think there's a Burger King up ahead?"

"Don't I wish," Boaz said.

Ailleann caught up to them. "Remember, journeys in Sena aren't like the hikes you are used to. They are physical, mental and spiritual journeys. We will be tested on all counts. Nature will offer us what we truly need. It may be that our spirits need to be nourished before our bodies. It could be that the one among us—the one whose journey of discovery this is—might not be open to accepting the lessons. Until he or she is, we will just keep walking."

They hadn't been offered any protein since the fish their first night out, and the fruit, mushrooms and roots they'd found along the way just weren't cutting it for Angela. She was beginning to feel weak and she knew she'd lost some weight. They all had. Jachin's muscles were more delineated than before, and Boaz and Ailleann had hollows beneath their cheeks that weren't there when they had started their journey.

"So," Angela said, "what do we have to do to let the-powers-that-be know we're ready?"

"The universe knows," Ailleann said, looking thoughtful. "Sometimes the lessons *are* forced upon us before we're ready. That may be the only way we will discover whose journey this is." She stopped and bowed her head, closing her eyes. "I will take a few moments to pray about it."

Angela and Boaz walked a respectful distance away then waited for Ailleann. Jachin had already rounded the next bend in the forest and was out of sight.

"What do you think about what Ailleann said, Boaz?" Angela lifted her dress to let the breeze cool her legs. The under garment was dust-stained and needed a good washing. She did, too. In fact, they all needed a good bath.

"I can't be sure, but I get the feeling that it's Jachin's journey," Boaz said. "And he still has a wall up against accepting who he is." She picked up a stick and drew an intricate design in the dirt. "I don't mean about who we are, you know, wizards and all. I think he is confused about who Jachin Morgan the man is. He's shared very little about what his life has been like, but I have the impression he's carrying around a ton of baggage about his adoptive parents, about his powers, and about our parents and why they abandoned us."

"Or this journey could be yours," Angela responded. "Maybe you're the one keeping us walking in circles with your denial. Maybe you have the baggage."

Boaz looked startled. "Do you think so?"

"Not really." Angela smiled at her friend. "I was just trying to deflect the responsibility from me. I thought you were going to go down a list of my issues next."

"I guess it could be any one of us. Even Ailleann."

Angela doubted it. Spiritually, Boaz and Ailleann were the healthiest women she knew.

"If anyone's holding the group up, it's probably me," she admitted. "I've had enough psychology classes to realize I resent my parents for loving their lifestyle and vocation more than they loved me."

Boaz gave her a speculative look. "I thought you said they were great and that you were proud of them."

"I do think they're great, and I am proud of them. I also think that a child is more important than some ancient civilization full of dead people. They took me with them on their archeological expeditions the first few years of my life. But then they decided I needed a formal education, so they left me with my aunt and uncle. And their *five* kids."

Boaz said, "That seems to have worked out for you. I've

seen you with them, and you're a part of their family. They're great people."

Angela released the hem of her dress and smoothed it across her knees. "Don't get me wrong. Aunt Sara and Uncle Tim are wonderful people, and so are my cousins. But I never felt like I fit in completely. They didn't treat me like a guest, or anything like that. But even as a small child I always felt like I was imposing on a family already bursting at the seams. One extra kid, and one they hadn't planned for." She straightened. "I guess I've never really admitted this to myself before, but I'm angry at my parents for leaving me."

Boaz put her hand on Angela's knee. "I really thought you were okay with their lifestyle."

Angela shrugged. "I'm realizing that I'm not okay with it. Heck, you know that they hardly ever call. From the time I was little, their excuse has always been the same. They move around a lot, from dig to dig and research project to research project. I guess they figure I have my own life now. I get birthday and Christmas cards, but they haven't made the Christmas get-togethers for over four years. I just go to my aunt and uncle's to visit with my cousins. I know I should have told you, but I guess I was in serious denial. I realize now that they never did want me."

Angela looked over to see huge tears in Boaz's eyes. She quickly put her arm around her. "I didn't mean to make you cry. I'm okay, really I am." God, now she felt awful. She had probably reminded Boaz of her own birth mother's desertion.

Boaz sniffed and smiled. "Sorry. But that's just too sad. Your parents abandoned you, too, didn't they?"

Angela got up. "Enough of that. Anyway, you can see why I think I might be the one holding us up."

Boaz stood as well. "But you're facing your feelings about your parents and your past. I don't think this journey thing works on people who have already acknowledged their feelings."

Angela shrugged. "You may be right. It was just a thought."

Ailleann came up to them join them just as Jachin reappeared.

Jachin scowled as he said, "You might give me a shout the next time you stop. I don't think we should split up."

"Sure, Jachin." Boaz seemed pensive as she studied her brother.

Jachin looked at Angela. "Is there a problem?"

She looked him straight in the eye. It was easier on her nerves than looking at his bare chest. As they hiked, he liked to take his shirt off and tuck it into his waistband and sling the cape over his shoulder. "Evidently one of us isn't fessing up to their problems. This 'journey of discovery' just isn't happening, and both Boaz and Ailleann think it's because one of us doesn't want to face their issues. I agree."

He snorted softly, never breaking eye contact. In a low, slow voice that threatened to curl her toes, he said, "I take it you all agree it's me?" His eyes were conducting an entirely different conversation, and her body was answering.

She only nodded, afraid her voice would be as wobbly as her knees.

"Maybe," he moved a step closer, "my issues are too complex, too twisted, and too dark, even for the powers of Sena to fix."

She swallowed hard, her throat suddenly dry. Heat flooded her face as images of them standing naked upon waking from their mutual dream flooded her mind. Clearing her throat she said, "I don't believe you're irredeemable."

At that Jachin did laugh. But it was harsh. "I wouldn't count on it," he lowered his voice, saying for her ears only, "*Angel.*"

Ailleann said, "Jachin, if you will just acknowledge to the universe that you have lessons to learn and are willing to take this journey of spirit, maybe the universe will open the book of knowledge to you."

Jachin glanced toward Ailleann, and Angela realized she'd barely been breathing. She stepped away from him, folding her arms across her breasts, acknowledging even as she did so that folded arms wouldn't protect her heart from this man.

"Fine. You want me to open my spirit, I'll open it. But if it is indeed my journey, you may regret the outcome. No journey of my spirit is going to be a walk in the park."

"I'm not afraid," Boaz declared.

"I will gladly accompany you, Jachin," Ailleann said.

"Well, you're not leaving me here alone," Angela added.

Without another word, Jachin walked off in the direction he had taken before. Angela and the others followed.

They had gone another hundred yards when Angela heard a distant sound. She stopped, hoping what she was hearing was just a trick of the forest and not what she thought—the screaming of a child!

The others stopped as well.

"What's wrong now?" Jachin asked.

"Don't you hear it?" Angela could hear the sound quite distinctly now, and it raised goose bumps along her arms.

"I don't hear anything. What is it?" Boaz said.

Ailleann shook her head, indicating she couldn't hear anything unusual, either.

"It's a child!" Angela's heart raced now as the child's terror-filled screams cut through her. She started running toward the sound.

"Angela! Stop!" Jachin shouted.

But she had to help the child. It was either hurt or in some kind of horrible danger. She'd never heard such terror! Tree branches grabbed at her dress as she rushed toward the screams, which were getting louder as if the child, too, was running toward her.

TWELVE

Willow Tree: Acceptance of one's place in the scheme of things, and participation.

As he ran, Jachin felt his senses go on alert, heightened by the imminent danger. His body strained as his muscles readied for battle, and his mind focused on finding the threat. As soon as he began chasing Angela through the forest, he too could hear the child's distressing screams. Whatever was happening to the child he didn't want to happen to Angela as well.

He broke through the dense foliage and into a clearing. What he saw made his heart stop. Then it thudded hard.

Angela stood between a huge reptile and a little boy. The monster was at least three times the size of the one he'd come across the night of the party. This one now slowly circled his prey, its mouth opened enough to show rows of sharp, alligator-like teeth and its fat, pink tongue. The little boy seemed rooted to the spot, his eyes wide with terror.

Angela stood her ground against the beast, staying between it and the child. Jachin knew that with one lunge it could have her within its huge jaws.

It opened its mouth wide, emitting a hissing sound, followed by a low, drawn-out growl. Angela glanced over her shoulder at the boy and shouted, "Run!" But the child remained frozen.

Jachin unsheathed his knife as he ran across the meadow, the dark force within him surging forward until his vision became tinged with red. He felt the darkness threaten to take control, and he fought to restrain it. The air crackled with electricity.

A voice within him said, *Let yourself feel the power. Use the darkness."* But he ignored it. Losing himself to the darkness now wouldn't help either Angela or the little boy. And he still had several yards before he would reach them.

Let the power help you, the voice said. As the voice whispered the words, Jachin knew that if he gave in to the darkness and let it take hold, the dark magic would allow him to breach time and be with Angela in a split second. But he also knew that if he gave in to the darkness, he would be forever controlled by it.

He forced back his soul's blackness. If this was his time to die, then so be it. He wouldn't even use his dark powers to save himself.

Jachin watched as Angela, in a darting movement, turned, grabbed the child and ran. For a moment the animal stood still, its belly close to the ground. Then it opened its mouth again. This time, a huge plume of fire shot from the creature's gaping jaws, sounding like a furnace erupting.

In his peripheral vision Jachin saw Angela and the child fall as the plume struck them. If either of them screamed, he didn't hear it. The only sound in his head was a high-pitched hum. He ignored the instinct to head for Angela and kept running toward the beast. He had to kill it before he could let himself worry about her. If she was injured and needed help, he couldn't do anything if the beast wasn't dead.

The creature suddenly raised up on all four legs and whipped toward him, jaws chomping. But Jachin didn't allow himself to hesitate. A stench of sulfur came from the monster's open mouth. With a strength he didn't know he possessed, he bounded over the creature's head and landed on its back. He grabbed hold of its neck, feeling the animal's monstrous strength as it whipped its body back and forth.

Jachin raised his blade, going for what looked like a vulnerable part of the dragon's throat just below its jaw. No protective scales covered the spot. With the first slice, he felt the beast's tendons ripple beneath his shoes. Without hesitating, he again drove his knife deep. And the blade sliced through the creature's hide as if it were butter. Again and again he plunged the blade home, cutting and ripping with a savageness that both terrified him and energized him.

With one last jerk, the animal's legs buckled, and it collapsed to its belly.

Fighting to catch his breath, Jachin stood atop the motionless mound of green scales. It was then that he remembered he had seen Angela fall. Frantically he looked around until he saw her. She was attempting to stand. Sparks of electricity still glittered in the air, and he knew the threat of darkness remained close, waiting to claim him. He calmed himself, not willing to give in to the evil force, especially now when it would do no good.

When his vision cleared, he jumped down and ran toward where Angela knelt next to the child. When he got to within a few feet of them he saw that Angela was crying and trying to soothe the little boy who lay so still. Maybe he was only in shock and not truly hurt.

When Jachin took the last few steps toward Angela she got up and flung herself into his arms, still crying. "Jachin," she sobbed against his chest. "I thought you were going to be killed!"

"Me!" He realized he was still angry. Angry with the child for luring Angela into danger, and angry with her for putting herself in harm's way. "What in the hell did you think you were doing? Playing Joan of Arc?"

He took a deep breath, trying to focus, but the darkness threatened with each pounding heartbeat. Angela could have died. The thought of her once again putting herself in such danger made him want to kill all over again.

Instead he held her closer, running his hands through her hair as he cupped her head. Her soft cheek and silky hair brushed against his bare chest. And as she finally stopped crying, he felt the darkness begin to subside.

But when he looked down at her, his stomach clenched and his heart nearly stopped. Her left sleeve was charred, and the flesh on her hand and forearm was blistered and bloody. He closed his eyes, but the vision of burned flesh where perfection had once been had seared itself into his brain. Looking once again, he heard a surreal voice say, *It's your fault, Jachin. You could have saved her and the child from any injury.*

"Are you hurt anywhere else?" He was afraid to look.

"No." She was obviously doing her best to ignore her blistered arm, which she held close to her body protectively. She gently pushed him away with her good hand. He wanted more than anything to take hold of that hand and bring her back into his arms, but she said in a pained voice, "Jachin, the boy's hurt really bad. Hurry and go get Ailleann."

"But your arm." A sick ache began in his chest as the voice again said this was his fault, and it kept repeating the condemnation over and over again. Whoever was telepathically communicating with him was right. If he had used his dark powers, he could have reached her in time to save her and the boy from any injury, but then his soul would have been lost. It was a selfish thought that made the ache worse when the voice murmured, *Isn't Angela worth losing your soul?*

Angela jerked him out of his morose reflection as she said, "The boy, Jachin. Get help for the boy."

She knelt beside the child, stroked his head and murmured, "It's okay, we'll take care of you. You're safe now."

The child was awake, but seemed unresponsive to her touch. Jachin found himself turning away, unable to bring himself to look at the boy for more than a few seconds. Guilt, yes. But there was something else he didn't have time to examine.

Fetching Ailleann and Boaz and bringing them back to Angela and the boy couldn't have taken more than ten minutes, but it seemed like hours. Imagining what horrible pain both Angela and the child must be going through made Jachin feel helpless. What good were his powers? They hadn't helped destroy the animal. The knife's blade had done that. They hadn't prevented the creature from almost killing Angela and the little boy. They hadn't prevented Angela's horrible burns.

As they approached Angela , she said. "Ailleann, I think he's only burned on his chest, but I was afraid to move him. What can you do?"

As Jachin watched Ailleann evaluate the frighteningly still boy, he now saw that the angry flesh on the skinny little guy's chest looked far worse than Angela's injury. A large, irregular patch of black lay over the area of the boy's heart.

Boaz watched, saying to no one in particular, "He's so thin. Where'd he come from?"

The scruffy looking, black-haired child was bare-chested and wore filthy, torn pants. Jachin could see that his ribs poked out and that dark circles shadowed his sunken eyes. He reminded Jachin of one of the neglected, unwanted orphan kids he saw on news reports. How could a child go uncared for in Sena?

"Look at him," Angela said. "He looks like he's been alone and starving for a long time."

She blinked back tears, and Jachin knew they had to be in part due to her injuries. He had to do something to stop her pain.

He wondered if Ailleann had read his mind when she looked at him and said, "My healing powers are limited. Without rest to renew them, I can only heal one at a time."

"Angela first," he said, knowing it couldn't be that way but unable to accept it.

Boaz and Angela scowled at him, and he raked a hand through his hair in resignation as he said, "Of course, you should heal the boy first. But how long will Angela have to suffer?"

"I can't be certain until I sense how deep the child's injuries are." As Ailleann ran her hands above the boy's body, her gaze jerked to Jachin. She quickly studied Jachin, making him uneasy with her directness. Then she looked back and forth between him and the boy several times. Finally she let out a long breath and nodded some kind of acceptance as she closed her eyes, focusing inward.

Jachin moved next to Angela, caressing her neck. She didn't move away, but shakily smiled up at him. Together they watched as Ailleann began chanting ancient words over the boy.

With eyes still closed, Ailleann seemed to go into a trance. She rocked back and forth as she slowly moved her hands over the injured child's chest, and a humming sound rang in Jachin's ears as he noticed a light begin to radiate from Ailleann's hands. Then her whole body suffused with a soft glow. Ripples of light flowed into the boy, but he never looked at Ailleann or even acknowledged what was happening to him.

The wrinkled black patch over his heart began to smooth, the skin glowing from beneath. Then the darkness faded, and the child's chest appeared healthy and unburned. Jachin felt an empathetic warmth form in his own chest.

With a final nod, Ailleann bowed over the boy then sat back and opened her eyes.

The boy looked fine, but he still hadn't moved.

Angela asked, "Is he okay?"

Ailleann gave her a sad smile then looked directly at Jachin.

Why the look of pity? Jachin wondered. He wasn't the one injured.

Still looking at him, she said, "I hope he will heal completely."

She walked over to Angela. "The child's injuries did not take a great deal of energy to heal, since they were not purely on the physical plane. I can help you now." She gently held Angela's arm up so that the injuries weren't touching anything.

What did she mean, not on the physical plane? Jachin saw Angela flinch and take in a sharp breath at the movement.

Again Ailleann chanted the words, and the light emanated

from her to surround Angela's arm. Sweat broke out on Ailleann's forehead, and Jachin realized this healing must be more difficult than the boy's, although his burn had looked worse.

When Ailleann opened her eyes, Jachin quickly inspected Angela's arm. Except for a small, irregular patch on her palm that looked like a slightly raised scar, her skin was a beautiful, healthy pink again. Jachin found himself laughing with relief.

"Do you hurt anywhere?" he asked her.

She looked down at her palm, shaking her head. Then she held her palm up toward Ailleann. "Why did this scar when the rest looks untouched?"

"I do not know," Ailleann replied. "I just accept that it is."

Jachin didn't care about the scar, or the reasons for it, just as long as Angela was okay. He hugged her to him, and she began to laugh and cry at the same time.

Boaz said, "It's getting late. We'd better set up camp before it gets dark. How about we head back to the stream?"

"Sure." Jachin glanced back at the animal's lifeless form. How on Earth had he killed the huge beast? Or jumped over its head? All he could remember was a blur of red and black and struggling to contain the darkness of his soul.

Shaking off the thought, he turned to watch Angela say to the little boy, "Come on, sweetheart. I won't hurt you."

But the boy moved away and began crying loudly.

At least he was moving, Jachin thought, but the kid had it backwards. He should have been wailing when he was burned, not now that he was fine.

Angela coaxed. "You can't stay out here all by yourself. Are your parents nearby?"

The boy looked sideways at her but kept crying.

Jachin studied the little boy, realizing he looked vaguely familiar. Although Jachin didn't remember seeing any kids with black hair at the compound, it was the only place he could have seen him. But could such a small child have traveled so far alone? He must be about four or five, judging by his size, but it was difficult to tell in his emaciated condition.

"Is this child from your village, Ailleann?" Jachin asked.

Ailleann shook her head, opening her mouth to speak, but closed it again when Angela spoke.

"What's your name?" Angela asked the child.

Jachin noticed that Ailleann had taken up a quiet stance a few feet away. Why wasn't she helping? She of all people should have some clue as to where the boy came from. Just as he was about to ask, the sobbing increased in volume.

"We have a little dog traveling with us. Do you want to see him?" Angela coaxed, pointing toward the forest. "Just call out, Dog, and he'll usually come. I don't know where he's gone off to."

The boy didn't seem interested in the dog.

She shrugged, looking at Jachin. "Should I try to pick him up? I don't want to traumatize him even more."

"What do I know about kids? Do what you think best." Jachin himself felt like taking a step back from the situation and the child. What *did* he know of children? Not one damn thing. Thanks to his powers, he hadn't been allowed the luxury of ever being one.

When Angela reached for the little boy, he jumped and gave her a startled look, as if she had struck him.

At least he stopped crying, Jachin thought.

The mournful wailing began all over again, and Jachin's chest tightened with emotions so strong his entire being ached. Why was he empathizing with the boy on such a dramatic level? Whatever it was, Jachin had to do something to stop it. These were emotions he wasn't prepared to deal with.

Jachin glared at all three women. "*Do* something."

Angela shot him a scathing look and again moved as if to take hold of the boy. This time her reward was for the child to raise his hands as if to protect himself from her.

"This is crazy," Jachin mumbled to no one in particular. "I'll do it!"

He approached the boy who suddenly stood stock still, a calmness coming over his features. Jachin felt his insides calm as well. He picked the boy up, surprised by how unsubstantial he was. This child had been starving for a long time.

"Jachin, he likes you," Angela said.

"He's probably just afraid of me," he muttered in response.

Irritatingly, the little boy tried to cuddle against him, but Jachin kept rearranging him so that he wasn't so close. He'd never been particularly fond of kids, but he hadn't disliked them. In fact, he'd developed a soft spot for little Guinnie. Why then did he feel an actual disdain for this child? He didn't even know him. He was as disturbed by the thought as he was by the child.

The sound of Dog barking led them back to where they'd left the trail. Dog sat wagging his tail as if he had been standing guard over something.

Jachin said, "And where were you when we needed you?"

The dog sat up and begged.

"Stupid dog." He quickly set the kid down on a flat rock. The little boy put his elbow on his knee and his chin in his hand. Now he just looked depressed, Jachin thought.

As Angela excitedly explained to Ailleann and Boaz what had happened with the big lizard, the women and Dog kept looking back and forth between him and the kid like they were watching a tennis tournament. Only there was no ball. In fact, both *players* were as still as stone statues.

Jachin interrupted. "You'll have to tell the rest of it later, Angela. It's getting dark and we need to get settled. If all of you will s t up camp, I'll take care of the food for tonight. I don't want anyone leaving camp without me for any reason."

He shot Angela a look he hoped looked stern, even though he was mostly feeling residual fear over what could have happened because of her impulsive dash into the forest. And then there was that little matter of him not being able to prevent what happened.

"Stay close. I'll be back." He walked back toward where he'd left the dead animal.

***

Angela blew out a deep breath and walked to where the little boy sat completely ignoring them. She said over her shoulder to Boaz and Ailleann, "You should have seen Jachin. He was so...so ...."

Boaz finished for her with a breathless, "So...*wonderful.*" Her sigh was exaggerated. She walked over to put her arm around Angela. "I'm glad you two have the hots for each other. Really I am. I don't want to lose you when this is all over."

"We'll all be going home," Angela said. "Only I'll be staying there, and you and Jachin will be coming back here."

Boaz soothingly patted her on the shoulder and teased, "I can't see you going back to your boring little life." She cocked her head. "I think there's more of your parents' need for adventure in you than you'll admit. Heck, you've been obsessed with this place half your life, even if you did think it was a myth. Besides, I can't see either you or Jachin with anyone else."

When Boaz began to gather rocks for the fire pit, Angela gave a wry shake of her head. Why try to convince Boaz of something they both already knew? She *would* be going back, and even though she and Jachin had the "hots" for each other, that didn't change the fact that he was the invincible wizard, and she was a mere mortal. She was sure he would settle down in Sena with a woman of his own kind. And she would try her darndest to find some nice guy who could make her forget all about Jachin Morgan.

By the time Jachin got back they had the camp set up, and Ailleann had once again gathered delicious tidbits from the surrounding area. Tonight it looked like they would be having some kind of squash and herbs to go with whatever Jachin had found.

"What's for supper, Jachin?" Boaz asked.

"Meat," he said as he handed Boaz his shirt wrapped around something oozing wetness.

Angela watched as Boaz cocked one eyebrow and held the parcel away from her. "What kind of meat?"

"Whatever it was I killed back there."

Ailleann said in a mater-of-fact tone, "Dragon."

She and Boaz stared at her, openmouthed, and Ailleann nodded and repeated, "Dragon."

Angela said, "It *did* breathe fire. But it didn't look like any dragon I've ever seen in books. It looked more like some kind of dinosaur. Did it look like the dragon you saw in the forest, Jachin?"

He nodded. "But about three times the size."

They all looked at the shirt as Jachin opened it to see what it held.

"What," Angela asked warily, "does is taste like, Ailleann?"

"Enough!" Jachin said before Ailleann could answer. "If we don't cook it pretty soon, we won't have dinner. Boaz, would you please start the fire?"

"Sure." She went over to the little boy. "Want to watch me start the fire?"

He looked past her as though he couldn't see her. Jachin seemed to be the only person he would acknowledge.

Boaz shrugged her shoulders and said, "Ailleann, do you think there's anything wrong with him?" She went over to the wood and slowly breathed until it lit with a small *poof!*

Angela handed Jachin the sticks she'd found for skewers and he began threading the meat on them.

Ailleann cautiously approached the boy, but didn't touch him. Then in a calm tone she said, "He isn't of this world."

Jachin swung around from where he had been gathering wood. "Then where the hell's he from?"

Ailleann smiled, "I'm not sure. But he isn't of this world. Nor the one you came from."

They all stared at the little boy, but he only looked at Jachin.

They followed the boy's stare, and Jachin scowled. "Well, don't look at me. I don't know who he is or where he came from." He looked at Ailleann. "Surely you must have some idea?"

Ailleann got up and went to Jachin, placing her hand on his arm. "Jachin, I believe he is here to help you. To guide you. He may be your lesson on this journey."

Jachin jerked his arm away from her. "That's crazy. He's just some lost kid."

"Deny him if you will," Ailleann said, "but you are the only one who can help him. And if you don't, I fear he will die."

Boaz went to the little boy. "What's your name, little guy?"

He looked at her and tilted his head in question. But when she reached for him he scrambled away from her touch.

Angela tried again to touch him, but she couldn't get any closer than Boaz had. One thing was for sure. For such an emaciated child, he certainly had boundless energy when it came to avoiding contact.

Boaz said, "Jachin, you try."

"No. We've got to get the meat roasting. Will you put a protection spell around the camp as far as the river? We'll need water."

"No problem."

As she had since she had joined the group, the little fairy Brigid appeared and fluttered around the camp just as the sun's rays disappeared. Her green light bounced to and fro as she checked out her surroundings and watched Boaz put the spell in place.

As they became busy preparing their meal, other dancing lights appeared just outside the protection barrier, and Brigid went over to them, but not past the barrier.

Angela was amazed that the child hardly took notice of the twinkling fairies. Nothing seemed to excite him. It just wasn't right. But if what Ailleann said was true, and the child wasn't of this world, then maybe he wasn't completely aware of his surroundings.

***

Jachin couldn't shake the kid. Wherever he went, the kid went. When he washed up at the stream, so did the child.

He worked around the fire, setting the skewered meat and vegetables on the stone rests they had set up. The little boy took one of the meat-studded branches from him, and without a word began helping skewer the meat. Did the kid scowl *all* the time? And why in the hell had he attached himself to Jachin?

Boaz broke the group's pensive silence by cheerfully saying, "How about some songs around the campfire while 'Puff' cooks?" She laughed at her reference to the fairy tale dragon and immediately started in on the song, "Puff The Magic Dragon."

Jachin watched as Angela joined in, obviously practiced at singing the song with Boaz because they harmonized beautifully. As it got dark, he noticed more and more lights gathering just outside the protective barrier. And there were other creatures as well, because he could feel hundreds of little eyes watching them. He sensed they meant no harm, but only wanted to listen and observe.

When the song ended, he noticed Angela looked more relaxed than she had in the past couple of days.

"How about a dance?" Boaz stood up and grabbed Angela's hand to dance her around the fire, starting in with another of their favorite silly songs. Angela joined in with an abandon that Jachin had to admit he envied. It was a treat to see Boaz and Angela getting such a kick out of the song. An ache began in his chest as he realized they were in almost the exact poses as in his sculpture, *The Dance.*

Ailleann sat and clapped her hands as Boaz and Angela sang, and Dog raced back and forth wagging his tail.

Angela tried to coax the little boy to join in their dancing, but he scurried over to Jachin and clung to his cape, as if Angela had asked him to jump into the fire pit.

Jachin moved the child an arm's distance away. "You're fine."

He almost added, *quit being such a baby*. But he realized the kid was still a baby. He gentled his tone. "They're not going to hurt you."

The child glanced sideways at the women, but Jachin could tell he wasn't convinced.

"Meat's done," Jachin said.

Boaz and Angela were laughing and out of breath as they sat down.

Angela said to the child, "Come here, I'll help you with the meat. It's going to be hot."

The child acted like he hadn't heard her and took a huge bite of the sizzling meat, immediately spitting it out and fanning his mouth.

Jachin grabbed the skewer from the boy. "Hey, Angela said it was hot. Here, blow on it like this."

The child responded by following Jachin's instructions and giving him a disconcerting smile.

Boaz said, "Looks like you're the only one who can reach him, Jachin."

"Great." Jachin tried to soften the harshness he heard in his voice. After all, the kid was sitting right here. "What do I know about kids?"

Boaz said, "Obviously nothing. But, he won't let any of us near him, so, dear brother, it seems you're it."

Ailleann took a skewer from the fire. "The child is Jachin's lesson, not ours. He must find out what the child needs...or what knowledge the child has to impart."

They each took a skewer of meat from the fire, and Jachin noticed the look of concern on Angela's face. "You go first, Boaz," Angela said. "Then tell me what it tastes like."

Boaz blew on the meat then slid a piece off the stick to bravely pop it in her mouth. She chewed, looking thoughtful for a moment. Then she laughed as she said, "It tastes like chicken."

Angela rolled her eyes then took a small bite. Then another and another. Evidently she liked the taste.

Jachin wasn't a big meat eater, but he was hungrier than he'd ever remembered being, so he took a bite. "It does taste like chicken." He chuckled, and so did the child.

Boaz was nodding, her mouth full and a rapturous look on her face. She swallowed. "Ailleann, have you ever eaten dragon before?"

"Yes. While we don't go out of our way to kill them, we do take what is offered if one threatens our compound. That has only happened a few times, so we have a festival when it does. One dragon can provide much meat and many other supplies to our people. We can use the hide for shoes, and the bones for utensils."

Angela said, "What will happen to the rest of the dragon Jachin killed? We can't take it with us, and I'm sure it will spoil."

Ailleann motioned to the forest beyond the glow of the fire. "The creatures will take what they need. It will not go to waste."

Jachin shook his head, still amazed he had killed the thing. It had felt like the natural thing to do, with Angela and the child threatened. Living on Sena wasn't like living in California. Danger here came not only from the animals in the forest, but also from the wizards themselves. It reminded him to keep his distance from Angela. She belonged in her world, and he belonged in Sena. But thoughts about abandoning Sena and going back to the Lute world to live out his life with Angela kept intruding on his resolve.

***

Kadien handed Angela's backpack to Gaban with a warning. "Be sure you don't open it or touch anything inside. I want you to return the bag to Angela and only Angela." He walked across the room where Lilith slept to look out the window at the labyrinthine forest surrounding the hill. "Angela is becoming an increasing threat to Jachin. She may coax him into leaving before his quest is complete. She needs to be removed from the group." He laughed. "It's time to see just how resourceful Jachin and Boaz are." Striding over to the sleeping young woman, he added, "And it is time to awaken Sleeping Beauty."

He waved his hand over Lilith's still form, releasing her from Marrion's weak spell.

As Lilith awoke, she sat up with a start, her gaze darting around the room. "Where am I?"

Kadien felt her terror's energy wash over him, and he gladly absorbed the power as his own, breathing in her essence. She might seem demure and gentle to others, but the strength he felt emanating from her was intense and true. The moon pendant around her neck began to glow, its brightness intensifying as she became more fully awake. What was the source of its power? He had noticed that all three children wore pendants of different signs, but he had never seen them glow before now.

He instinctively backed away. It was time to observe and try to discover who had provided the children with the amulets. He would know soon enough the pendants' significance and whether or not he need concern himself with them.

***

Angela was having a difficult time keeping her grumpiness to herself. She wanted a bath. She wanted clean clothes. She wanted a comb. And she wanted her own American-Dental-Association-approved toothbrush and mint-flavored, tartar-control toothpaste instead of the twigs they had been using. And real toilet paper! What a treat that would be. How much longer was this "quest" going to take, anyway?

She conjured an image of a tall glass of iced tea, but that only made her mouth seem drier than ever. Drawing the flask to her mouth, she swallowed the last few ounces, but the water was tepid and barely quenched her thirst. It didn't help her feel refreshed. The dust-covered dress she wore had been bearable until the dragon incident. Now it smelled of smoke, and she felt hot and sticky.

"Sorry, but I've got to rest and refill my flask," she said, heading toward the stream they'd been following. Out of the corner of her eye she thought she saw someone head in her direction. Most likely Boaz, who usually accompanied her whenever she left the trail.

The sound of gently rushing water was too tempting. As she neared the bank she hoisted the flask's strap over her head and dropped the flask to the ground. Next she pulled her dress over her head and discarded it. The chemise fell to the ground, and she stepped out of it and walked right into the water. The stream bed was sandy, and the occasional large rock was easily avoided.

God, the water felt wonderful! She quickly waded to the deepest part but still had to bend her knees to submerge. Relishing the water's cool, clean feel, she wanted to take huge gulps of the crystalline liquid, but she wasn't ready to give up the feeling of rejuvenation, so she stayed submerged.

Why didn't I do this before? she thought as she ran her fingers through her tangled hair. Jachin had convinced them it would be safer if they only washed up at the water's edge.

A sudden crushing force around her ribs had her sucking in

water, then coughing and sputtering. Then she realized a breeze was chilling her wet skin. Through rivulets of water she saw an equally wet but fully clothed Jachin.

"Jachin!" She had to cough past water in her throat before she could go on. "What in the—"

"Angela, what were you thinking!" As angry as she'd seen him in the past, she didn't think she'd ever remembered his eyes flashing so brilliantly. "You don't know who or what could …"

Sparks of light flashed before her eyes, and she had to blink. But the lights weren't a problem with her vision. They were coming from Jachin!

He let her go. By the pained look on his face, she figured he must be trying to control his temper, but he wasn't having much luck. Lights continued to dance in the air.

A breeze chilled her bare breasts, and realizing she was naked, she dipped into the water to her shoulders, feeling mortified. "I'm sorry, but I couldn't help myself."

But she wasn't sorry at all. The danger, whatever it might have been, had been worth the feeling of being clean.

He closed his eyes and took a deep breath, and she watched droplets of water drip from his face. The gauze shirt clung to his strong chest and shoulders, making her want to reach out and touch him. But maybe this wasn't a good time, since he looked like he was about to explode. At least the lights had stopped flashing.

When Jachin opened his eyes, the only remaining sparks were within the burgundy depths of his gaze. He took hold of her shoulders, his fingers biting into her flesh. Although she knew he wouldn't hurt her, she realized he was pretty darned mad.

She was about to open her mouth to apologize again when he brought her out of the water and crushed her to him. His mouth captured hers in a hard kiss, and she had to fight not to cry out with pleasure as her body reacted to the sensual assault.

Her chilled skin stung at every point of contact with his. He was so hot! And she could feel his heart thudding against her breasts, matching her own frantic heartbeat. She felt wonderfully plundered and adored. At the same time as his kiss gentled, he caressed her back and bottom. A delicious, tingling sensation started at her lips and then traveled throughout her to enflame her most sensitive points. Of its own accord her body moved against him, wanting more. Wanting all of him.

Traitor, she wanted to shout at her body, but her mouth was much too busy. She moaned instead. If this was so wrong, then why did it feel so right?

With the very last ounce of willpower she possessed, she tore her mouth from Jachin's. Then she pushed away from him, covering herself and shaking her head.

Just then Boaz walked up. "I guess as wet as you are, it wouldn't do much good to hose you two off." She laughed. "Sorry, Angela, but Jachin said he would follow you and see if you were okay. And when he didn't come back, I got to thinking about the other night and figured I'd better check on you myself."

"Nothing happened," Jachin snapped. He looked down at Angela. "Go ahead." He nodded toward the shore.

Her teeth were chattering now. "Af-f-ter you." She wasn't about to prance up the shore in her birthday suit!

"No, you go first. If it will make you feel any better, I'll turn around. Although I've already seen—"

She cut him off by turning him away from her. "But, you don't have to stare." Then she scrambled to Boaz who was holding her discarded clothing.

Once she had the dress and chemise in her hands, she remembered how dirty they were. "Oh, Boaz, I just can't put these back on."

"Here," Boaz said, strategically arranging the bundle in front of Angela. "Jachin, you can come out."

He turned and walked out of the water, his clothes clinging to him like a second skin, revealing every ripple of muscle.

"We're going to stay down here and wash our clothes," Boaz said, "so you might as well set up camp a little further up the road. Will you please let Ailleann know so she can clean up, too?"

"Sure, but keep your eyes open. Gaban could still be close by. I have a feeling he's been following us again."

"This is going to take some time," Boaz pointed out. "Do I have your permission to read your mind to keep in contact?" She chuckled. "Hey, we've got our own built in wizard walkie-talkies!"

"That's fine. But how will I know all of you are safe? The batteries in mine are dead."

Boaz laughed. "Jachin, was that a joke?" She turned to Angela. "Did you hear that? Jachin made a funny. His telepathic batteries are dead."

Angela gritted out a smile, not thrilled with the delay, since she was having trouble keeping the bundled clothes in place.

Boaz smiled at Jachin. "You seem to be able to connect with Angela for some reason. I think you'll know if anything is wrong."

He gave Boaz a funny look. "Boaz, what's up with your pendant?"

Angela saw that the half-sun medallion was glowing. Jachin's lightning bolt pendant was as well. She had noticed it when she was in the water with Jachin, but she'd thought it was just a reflection from the sun. Now she could see that both pendants were glowing as if they were hot to the touch.

And as Jachin moved toward Boaz, the light from the pendants grew even brighter.

Boaz said, "I think they're connected somehow."

Jachin shrugged. "Since we both have them, I kind of figured that. But mine has never glowed before. I can feel energy coming from it."

"Me, too." Boaz held her pendant between her fingers. Then she looked up at Jachin with a start. "Lilith is awake. I can feel it."

Jachin said, "Believe it or not, I can feel it, too. She's awake and scared."

Boaz closed her eyes, holding her pendant. "I sense fright, but I also sense determination and strength." She opened her eyes again. "Poor thing. I don't think she even knows about us yet, let alone that we're coming to get her."

Angela saw a renewed look of determination clench Jachin's jaw. He gave her a unfathomable look that made her stomach tighten, then walked toward where they had left Ailleann and the boy.

Boaz began to take her clothes off. "My turn for a bath." She turned to Angela. "You might as well go back in the water and wash your clothes."

"You don't have to ask me twice." She headed toward the water. It was a good thing the air temperature was mild, because both she and her clothes would have to air dry.

***

When Jachin reached the boy and Ailleann, they both stared at his wet clothes. "I guess we're going to take the afternoon off.

You can join the women and bathe, Ailleann. If you can, take the boy with you and try to get him cleaned up."

Dog barked at Jachin, but Jachin ignored him.

Ailleann said, "It's you who must care for the boy, Jachin. He has made that clear. Try to find the caretaker inside you."

He put his hands on his hips, tired of the games. "Why, Ailleann? Why, do I have to deal with the kid? What is the great lesson he's supposed to teach me? That kids are a pain in the ass?"

She smiled, evidently not offended by his cross words. "When you were little, Jachin, how did you want to be treated? Just do the same for this little one."

When he was little, he just wanted to be left alone. No, that wasn't true. He wanted his parents to want him. And they hadn't. At least his father hadn't. That's why he'd attempted to run away when he'd been about five. He'd lived on his own for two days before his father found him and let him know how frustrated he was with him. Then it struck Jachin that he was treating the little boy exactly like his father had treated him, keeping him at arm's length and speaking to him as if his very existence exasperated him.

Ailleann nodded with a smile and headed toward the stream. Had she read his mind?

"Come on," he told the boy in a gentler voice than he'd previously used.

"Sure," the boy said in a whisper, imitating the way Jachin said the word.

Jachin was so shocked that it took a few moments to recover. "You can talk?"

The boy shrugged noncommittally.

What was with the kid, anyway? Either you could talk or you couldn't. Again, he focused on controlling his frustration. It wasn't the kid's fault he was alive. No kid deserved to be ignored.

He reached down and took the little boy's hand. The child smiled, and Jachin forced himself to return the smile, finding it wasn't as difficult as he'd imagined. Dog followed them to the stream.

Once the little boy was cleaned up, Jachin noticed he didn't have a tattoo like the other inhabitants of Sena. It made him recall Ailleann's declaration that the kid had come from another world.

Where? And why was he here?

When they returned from the stream, they easily found the women by the sounds of their singing. Now, even Ailleann was humming along as they set up camp close to the river.

The singing stopped when the women caught sight of them.

Angela said, "That can't be the same little boy." Shock showed on her face.

Boaz said, "What'd you feed him over the last two hours? He looks like he's gained weight."

Jachin looked at the kid. "He looks the same to me, only cleaner."

Boaz shrugged. "Must be a trick of the light. We caught some fish, picked some cattail flower heads, and found some apples. Ailleann gathered some cattail pollen to use as flour and has promised apple melba for dessert! Let's get to it. I'm starving."

The little boy said, "I'm starving."

Boaz walked over to him and crouched down. She said softly, "What's your name, little guy?"

The little boy just stared, unresponsive.

"Why don't you just give him a name, Boaz?" Jachin arranged the wood in a dome within the fire pit.

Boaz studied the boy again, her fingers on her chin as she squinted in concentration. "He looks like a Jake."

Jake was what Jachin's mother used to call him. "He looks like," Jachin quickly said, "a Tommy to me."

All three women gave him a funny look and simultaneously shook their heads.

"No," Angela said, "I think you're right, Boaz. He looks like a Jake."

Ailleann nodded, making it unanimous.

Jachin rolled his eyes. He was outvoted, so he might as well resign himself to lending the kid his childhood nickname.

"Jake," Angela said to the boy.

Immediately, he turned and smiled at her.

Boaz nodded. "Jake it is."

Jachin took his time cleaning the fish, showing Jake how it was done. It was a task Jachin's father had been too busy to teach him, and one Jachin had purposely taught himself when he was about seven. He had a two-inch scar on the inside of his palm to show for his unsupervised foray into the world of fishing.

The more Jachin did with Jake, the more responsive the child became. By the end of dinner Jake was actually looking and acting like a normal child except that he would only respond to Jachin and a bit to Angela. He still wouldn't allow Angela to touch him.

When it was time to go to sleep, Jake stood next to the matting of leaves and the cloak Jachin had set up for himself. Jake said, "I'm afraid. I want to sleep next to you."

Jachin looked to Angela for help.

"Sorry, Jachin. He won't let me get anywhere near him. Besides, Boaz and I have first watch tonight. Go ahead, he won't bite. He's a kid. He's scared of the dark. He needs an adult to cuddle up next to."

Try as he could, Jachin couldn't get comfortable with the kid next to him. And cuddling was out of the question. Finally by resting Jake's head on his arm and lying on his back, he found comfort. Looking up at the stars, Jachin wondered if he would ever have a child of his own. If his treatment of Jake was any indication, he wouldn't be a very good father. So when Jake, who had fallen asleep within minutes, moved his arm over Jachin's chest and took hold of the pendant, Jachin didn't push his hand away. Instead, he took the child's hand in his own and held it. As sleep overtook him, he wondered if the child could feel the power emanating from the metal.

***

Angela awoke with the dawn to find Jachin and Jake already breaking up the fire pit and cleaning up camp. Although Jachin was gruff with the boy, it was in a funny, gentle way. And Jachin was taking great care with his instructions to Jake. She sat up to brush leaves from her dress then put her shoes on.

Jake looked so much like Jachin that it made her heart ache. They had the same scowl, the same bouts of silence. The same rare, reluctant smile. They even said, "Sure," in the same way. Unrealistic fantasies of Jake being their child began to swirl through her sleepy head. With a little practice in patience, Jachin could be a good father. The approving way he was looking at Jake as the child returned the fire pit rocks to where they had found them told her Jachin had potential. She hoped he someday found someone to love and had a family.

Angela realized Jachin had caught her staring at him.

"Good morning," he said in a quiet, sexy way that made her

imagine they'd spent the night in each other's arms.

"Good morning, Jachin. Good morning, Jake." She nudged Boaz with her toe.

Boaz swatted at her. "Go away. I'm dreaming of Mel Gibson." "I thought you only had glimmer dreams. Does this mean Mel's in your future?"

Boaz blew out a frustrated breath, sat up and sighed. "Wouldn't that be nice? But, no. I was only daydreaming about him."

Ailleann had her shoes on and was stretching luxuriously, as though she'd spent the night on a feather bed. Angela's hip was numb from the hard ground.

"Privy call. You ready?" she said to Boaz and Ailleann.

Nodding sleepily, they all headed to their designated spot several yards away.

When they returned, camp was returned to the way they'd found it. Jachin handed each of them an apple. "Let's get going. I have the feeling we're finally getting close."

By early afternoon Angela was amazed to see that Jachin actually seemed to be enjoying Jake. The little boy would point out things of interest, and Jachin would comment on them and add bits of information about birds or plants. For a few hours they seemed to forget everyone else and simply enjoyed each other's company.

At one point, Jachin hoisted Jake onto his shoulders and began teaching Jake the words and clapping sequence to the children's song, *Bingo*.

Boaz grabbed Angela's arm and said, "I can't believe it."

Ailleann joined them and said in a low voice, "I believe Jake will be leaving us soon. Look at him. He is healthy. He is whole. Fear and shame no longer motivate him. His time here is at an end."

"But, where will he go?" Angela looked at the little boy, alarm racing through her.

Ailleann put her hand on Angela's arm. "He won't be alone. Never again."

The healer's touch felt warm, and Angela believed her. All fear about Jake's welfare vanished, and she trusted Ailleann's words.

"Jachin," Ailleann's voice was strong and sure, causing Jachin to stop and turn around.

He set the boy down, and Jake walked over to inspect a huge red and yellow toadstool, delight showing on his face.

Ailleann looked at Jachin for a long moment. "I sense that it is time for Jake to leave."

Jachin didn't understand. "Leave? Where to?"

"Return to his own realm. He came because you needed him. You no longer need him. His work is complete."

"And how do you know that?" Jachin looked skeptical.

"I am trained to heal the mind as well as the body." She nodded to where Jake had stood.

He was gone.

Jachin shouted, "Jake!" and strode to the spot to look for him in the surrounding forest.

Ailleann hurried after him. "You won't find the child." She put her hand on Jachin's arm, just as she had done with Angela, and Jachin's face finally registered acceptance.

He looked around and ran his fingers through his hair. "You're sure he's okay?"

"More than...okay." She smiled as she used the modern slang. Her hand moved to his heart.

"Hey, look!" Boaz shouted. She ran to where Dog stood barking at a large parcel. She picked it up and turned toward them with what looked like Angela's lost backpack held high.

Angela got a sinking feeling. The backpack was supposed to be at the bottom of the ocean. What was it doing here? Marrion had told Angela that the things inside it were dangerous in Sena. Dog's barking turned sharp and aggressive.

As Angela opened her mouth to remind Boaz of Marrion's warning, her friend flipped open the pack and pulled out the little red cell phone.

"Dog, shush! Hey, I wonder if there's a roaming charge for Sena?" She laughed as she began punching numbers with her thumb.

"No," Ailleann shouted as she grabbed Boaz's arm.

With a snapping sound and a bright flash, Boaz and Ailleann disappeared!

THIRTEEN

**Ash Tree: Giving the ability and the confidence
to sail forth into the unknown.**

Jachin couldn't believe his eyes. Boaz and Ailleann were
gone! First Jake had vanished into thin air then so had his sister
and Ailleann. Dog ran to where they'd stood and sniffed the
ground.

Angel looked like she was about to faint. Her gaze was fixed
on the spot where Boaz and Ailleann had been standing. Slowly
she shook her head and swallowed hard. "Jachin. Boaz… Ailleann
…Are they…?" Tears filled her eyes.

He hurried to her and took her in his arms. "I'm sure they're
all right." But he wasn't sure. He had no idea what had become
of them. Although he had readily enough accepted Ailleann's
claims that Jake was okay, that he had returned to where he
belonged, Boaz and Ailleann's disappearance was different.

Gently releasing Angela, he turned a slow circle, searching
for clues. He ran his hand through his hair. Could they be dead?
"What the hell happened?"

Angela said, "We were warned that anything from the Lute
world could act differently here. Especially anything made with
synthetic materials." She clutched her throat. "Boaz dialed my
cell phone."

Jachin could feel the pendant growing warm against his chest.
He held it, immediately getting a sense that Boaz was safe. The
feeling was strong and sure, almost as if her voice was inside his
head, assuring him of their safety.

Dog barked at their feet, then backed up to a spot a few feet
away. As Jachin and Angela watched his antics, something began
to happen to the dog. At first he sat up on his hind legs, in a
begging position. Then he began to change.

***

Damn! Seumas thought as he began to change. Although he
wasn't ready to reveal his identity, he needed his human form to
help undo the mischief Gaban had caused by providing Angela's

backpack to Boaz. Surely a confusion spell had been cast on it and its contents, or Boaz would have remembered his and Marrion's warning.

As he regained his human form, he saw that Angela stared at him with a look of horror, but Jachin stood calmly beside her. By the look on his face, he knew exactly what was happening and wasn't the least bit surprised.

"Sean," Jachin acknowledged him. "I should have known. The dog smelled like a combination of wet dog and vanilla, but I kept telling myself that what I was smelling was just some forest flower. Still, we should have sensed your magic."

"I'm known as Seumas here on Sena." How good it felt to have human vocal cords again, and to breathe instead of pant. His heart pounded true and strong, and slower than it had over the past few days. He couldn't help stretching, reveling in the feel of human muscle and agility. "And don't feel too bad about not being able to sense my presence. During my years in the Lute world, I perfected disguising my aura to be sure I wouldn't be detected by other wizards."

Jachin's eyes were filled with hostility. "Sean. Seumas. Gaban. Dog." His voice was harsh. "Which is real and which is illusion?"

"I am of your people. I am a white wizard...Seumas Scot," Seumas replied. "My gift is that of a shapeshifter. I have been observing you for years, Jachin. I realized what Kadien was up to when he sent Gaban into the Lute world, so, I manipulated the troll into my body, letting him believe he was taking over a Lute body when he went into your former world to sabotage your journey. You must believe me when I say I am your friend."

By the look of distrust and fury on Jachin's face, Seumas knew their previous friendship in the Lute world only increased Jachin's sense of betrayal. And Seumas had to admit that he had been forced to trick Jachin more than once. But he'd only done what he'd had to do to ensure the success of a mission he'd committed himself to nearly three decades ago.

Angela was shaking her head in disbelief. "What is it you want from Jachin? And why trick him? If you're his friend, why didn't you tell him who you really were?"

The young woman held a firm grip on Jachin's arm, her eyes bright with loyalty.

Good, thought Seumas. He had watched the barely controlled passion between the couple over the past few days, but he hadn't been able to discern the depth of their emotional commitment to each other. By the way Jachin's arm protectively held her at his side, and by the defensive spark in her eyes, Seumas got a very clear picture of what these two meant to each other. He was certain, however, that neither of them were ready to acknowledge their feelings yet.

"My dear, I only want to ensure the successful outcome of Jachin's journey."

"Successful," she said, "being the key word. That could mean two different things to two different people. Is reuniting Jachin and his sisters your idea of success? Or keeping them apart?"

Before Seumas could respond, Jachin asked, "Did you cause what just happened to Boaz and Ailleann?"

Seumas noticed that Jachin's free hand tightly gripped his knife's hilt. "I admit that I may have indirectly caused what happened, but it was never my intent. I could have been more careful with what became of Angela's backpack when Gaban took it, but just like you, I lost sight of it and assumed it had been dropped into the ocean when we crossed. I was not at all times fully aware of my surroundings when Gaban inhabited my body."

"You're lying." Jachin said.

"No. I can only give you my word that I am not." Realizing that Jachin didn't know that Seumas' word was his sword, he couldn't expect Jachin to believe him. He'd have to work at earning his trust.

"I took the shape of a dog in order to keep the fact that I had returned to Sena a secret as long as possible," he explained. "I am no match for Kadien, and once he knows I have returned, he will try to destroy me. We have unsettled…issues."

"So why put yourself in danger by taking your true form now?" Jachin asked suspiciously.

"To help you find Boaz and Ailleann."

One of Jachin's eyebrows rose above his scowl. "How are you going to do that? I thought male wizards weren't telepathic. How can you find them, if you can't connect with them?"

The boy had so much to learn about his world. "Male wizards are capable, with the use of spells and tools, to *see* events and people. And you should do this now for your peace of mind. But I intend to physically find Boaz and Ailleann and ensure their safety. I frequently take the shape of an owl and can easily fly unnoticed over Sena."

Angela looked hopeful, "They're still on Sena?"

"I believe so. But, let us make sure." He pointed toward the backpack containing The Book of Light and said to Jachin, "You have the means to discover her whereabouts yourself. I'm sure your mother's book contains a scrying spell."

Jachin walked to the pack and extracted the book. He gently unwrapped it from its protective fabric and opened the first page.

The sight of the large book brought back painful memories that, even after thirty years, caused Seumas' chest to ache as if his heart was paralyzed. Images of Jachin's mother, Vivian, ripped through his mind like a dagger, and for a moment he couldn't breathe. She was the only woman he had ever loved. As he looked at the object she had never been without, the inconsolable loss he'd felt upon learning she was forever outside his reach once again felt sharp and new. For a moment, an intense need to avenge her loss almost overtook reason, and he was tempted to change into a ferocious monster and fulfill his wish to insure the death and destruction to those who had caused her downfall. But then he recalled Vivian's soft smile, and it calmed the beast within him. Now was not the time for revenge.

He looked up to see Jachin and Angela with their heads drawn close as Jachin leafed through the book's pages.

"Here," Jachin finally said, "this could be it. I need something reflective." He looked around and immediately headed toward the stream, taking Angela with him, his hand holding her tightly, as if he feared she too might vanish.

Seumas followed them.

Over a shallow pool formed by an eddy, Jachin began chanting the ancient words of *sight*. He read the words from the book, but by the natural way in which he pronounced them, Seumas knew Jachin had been quite successful in his Recall Ceremony.

Both Jachin and Angela peered into the glassy water as Jachin chanted and moved his hand over the surface. When he stopped speaking, Seumas knew Jachin had succeeded, so he walked over to look as well. Boaz and Ailleann were indeed still on Sena.

Seumas said, "They're in The Forest of Tranquility on the other side of the island." He stepped back, readying to *change*. "I will go to them and help guide them to Kadien's fortress. You continue your journey and meet us there."

He began to transform. Just before he felt the blackness of the transformation take hold, Seumas saw that Jachin was about to reject his plan. He still didn't trust him, and why should he? Although the change took but a second, Seumas felt every aspect of the metamorphosis. He felt a moment of excruciating pain as his body's molecules and DNA rearranged. With a hard beat of wings, he became a Great Grey Owl.

With his new, keen raptor sight, he viewed Angela and Jachin, their figures glowing with life-giving heat. Hunger and a need to hunt raised his wings, but he remained aware of his ultimate goal. His sharp talons closed as he took flight, but he knew they would be ready to snatch prey at a moment's notice. Moving silently through the air, he headed in the direction of The Forest of Tranquility.

***

Angela sat down on the ground with a jolt that would surely leave her behind bruised. But what was physical pain compared to the turmoil her mind was going through? She'd had enough magic for one day, and felt as dizzy as if she'd just gotten off an out-of-control merry-go-round.

"You okay?" Jachin knelt next to her, his hand resting on her knee.

Was she okay? No, she'd just been subjected to one disappearing "Other-realm" child, two vanishing friends, and a wizard who, in the blink of an eye, had changed into a huge bird of prey. Jeez, the talons on that thing looked like meat hooks! The only response she could come up with was, "I'm afraid of what might happen next. I wouldn't be surprised if you turned into Batman and flew off to join everyone else."

Jachin chuckled. "Batman didn't fly."

She looked into his eyes. There went that new sense of humor again. She could tell it still wasn't comfortable for him, but she instinctively knew he was trying to ease her fears by joking. The least she could do was go along with it.

Angela wished she could crawl inside his gaze and be safe. "I guess you're right. Superman flies, not Batman."

Jachin smiled as he offered his hand then pulled her up when she took hold.

"Come on," he said. "Let's get a couple more hours of walking in before we lose the light."

She wasn't nearly ready to give up looking at that rare smile, but she had to ask, "Do you trust Sean, or Seumas, or whatever his name is? Do you think he'll help Boaz and Ailleann?"

Jachin's perpetual scowl returned, and Angela stifled a sigh of regret.

"I can't be sure. Who the hell knows what his motives are? I don't even know whose side he's on. If he *is* on a side. He seems to have his own agenda. For now, whether or not I trust him doesn't matter. He's on his way. But I think Boaz is resourceful enough to handle Seumas Scot. Anyway, it's out of our hands at this point."

Shrugging, he put his arm around her. "And, for the time being, we're on our own." He winked at her. "Think you can keep your hands off me?"

She knew the words were meant to lighten the mood, but she was having trouble returning his smile. She wasn't at all sure.

So instead of answering his question, she said, "How can we decipher the Ogham markers without Boaz to read the book?"

"I can read them. I just left it to Boaz because she had the book to help translate." He nodded toward where Boaz's backpack sat. "We have The Book of Light. We'll be fine. I just want to rescue Lilith and have this whole episode over with."

Jachin picked up Boaz's backpack and readjusted his water flask, then nodded toward the trail. They began to walk side-by-side.

He took her hand, running his thumb across the top of it as he confessed, "I need to hold onto you. I want to make sure you don't disappear on me, too."

She found herself smiling, feeling a foolish giddiness at his confession and his caress. This trek had gone from dangerous to downright delightful. Too bad it couldn't last.

Knowing if she thought about their eventual parting she'd get depressed, she asked, "What happens after you find Lilith and get her away from Kadien?"

He looked down at her, holding her gaze for a long moment before he answered. "I don't know. I have things to settle in your world." He looked straight ahead as he chuckled derisively. "I guess it's my world, too. Funny, but for the first time in my life, I feel like I do belong in the world we left behind. I know I am accepted for who I am here, but I'm beginning to realize a connection to the Lute world that I never felt when I lived there. I can't see myself staying in Sena forever. There are things I would miss."

"Like what?" she said.

"Watching Lakers basketball." A smile curled one side of his mouth. "Ice cubes."

She laughed. "Me, too. I'd love an iced tea. And I miss the sunsets in Sedona." The laughter went out of her voice. "And I miss my family, even though I hardly ever see them. It's the thought that I might never see them again that makes me want to."

Jachin said, "You'll see them again."

She deepened her voice, imitating a God-like tone of authority, and asked, "What do you think about 'The Great Prophecy'?"

He shook his head. "I still don't believe the three of us are some kind of all-powerful messiahs come to save the world. I figure we'll get Lilith, and then we'll go home. I'll clean up the media mess and get back to my sculpting. The Darkness can take care of itself."

"Do you miss your work?" She stopped long enough to reach for an apple hanging from a branch over the trail, but saw Jachin's hand reach above hers.

He gently twisted the apple from its branch and handed it to her. Then he picked one for himself. "I do miss my work. It's hard to explain. It's what I am. Creating bronze sculptures is what makes me whole." He chuckled. "Well, it's part of what makes me feel whole. Sena has given me a part of myself I never thought I'd have. I think half of me belongs in the other world, and half belongs here. So, where can I ever really feel whole? There is no in between." Then he laughed outright. "Enough psychobabble. I'm not sure what will happen when this is over."

He stopped and turned to her, running his hand over the apple, but not taking a bite. "What about you, Angela? What do you go back to?"

She sighed in resignation and shrugged. "I'll go back to teaching and…" She found she couldn't go on, that what she was saying was no longer her resolve. Squaring her shoulders in determination, she said, "I'm going to make some changes in my life. I'm going to go out and see the world instead of teaching other people about it. The security I was looking for before seems foolish now. I realize nothing is forever, security is an illusion, and I'd better live while I can."

He smiled, nodding, and they started walking again.

They came to a signpost, and Jachin took the book out of the backpack as Angela sat down on a grassy patch under a tree and leaned back to rest.

She opened her eyes with a start, realizing she'd dozed off when she heard Jachin say, "Can you make this out? It says 'I see the division of the Dark Realm ahead. First you must find me. I fall and I fall and I fall, and I stay where I am.'"

She closed her eyes and thought for a moment, recalling some of the riddles her uncle Tim had told her about. "*Division* could mean a wall, a barrier, or some kind of spiritual separation. *Dark Realm* could mean something as simple as Kadien's fortress, or the darkness within ourselves."

She opened her eyes and smiled at Jachin. "The rest is easy. It's a waterfall we need to find. It falls and falls and stays where it is. I say we look for a waterfall, and then we should be able to see Kadien's fortress."

Jachin put the book away, giving her a sideways look. "Why are you're so good at riddles?"

She shrugged. "Thanks to my uncle's riddle games, my mind stores all kinds of useless information. But I can't remember really important stuff, like people's names, or directions."

A twinge of homesickness made her swallow back a lump in her throat. She realized she loved her aunt and uncle. They had been wonderful surrogate parents. She had been the one to remove herself from the family circle because she had felt as if she was imposing on them, not because of anything they had said or done.

"I'll have to thank your uncle if I ever meet him," Jachin said. "I never would have figured it out."

He smiled, and Angela's stomach did a crazy little dance. He'd changed over the past few days. He smiled now, and occasionally even showed a wonderful sense of humor. Somehow, seeing this new side of him made him even more accessible. And even more dangerous to her peace of mind.

Through the trees, Angela could see the sun dipping low, and her stomach danced again with apprehension. Heaven help her, she and Jachin would be alone tonight.

***

Kadien sat at the head of the long table, forming his hands into a tent as he looked at the woman at the far end. Her gaze darted around the cavernous room and to the shadows, which the candlelight caused to flicker across the walls, but she maintained an aura of serenity.

"Lilith, my child, you're not eating," he said, concerned. And he was concerned. He wanted her to be strong in mind, spirit and body when she reunited with her siblings. At the prospect of what their combined powers might be like, anticipation gnawed at him. "I sense that you dislike me. And I've gone out of my way to be hospitable."

He'd hoped to feel something more powerful than dislike from her, but the woman seemed incapable of truly dark feelings.

"You know," he said, running his fingers over the smooth table,"you are very much like your mother."

At that her head jerked up, but her demeanor remained serene. "You know my mother? What's your name? Maybe I've heard her mention you."

"I'm not talking about your adoptive mother, but your true mother. And your true mother *was*," he drew out the word, "my nemesis. Our paths crossed many times."

"Was?"

"Was," he repeated, purposely keeping his tone flat. Let her know the truth.

The flawless serenity of her expression faltered, and he knew she understood.

"You know for certain that she is dead?"

He nodded slowly, deliberately, never breaking eye contact. Nothing but death could have kept Vivian from her children. He remembered the brilliant, mesmerizing power he had sensed in The White Queen. Like a flame, it had been dangerous even to him, threatening to draw him to her like a fairy is drawn to a moonbeam's magnetic radiance. He had even been foolish enough to once—only once—try to capture that radiance. But it had almost cost him his life.

Lilith turned toward a noise at the door, her expression guarded as his high counsel, Nudd, entered and announced, "Gaban has answered your summons. Where shall I put him?"

This should be interesting, Kadien thought with a devious thrill he hadn't felt since childhood. "Show him in, Nudd."

Kadien took note of Nudd's quickly covered look of disbelief. He couldn't quite hide the disapproval.

A subordinate entertaining disapproval? Kadien would have to keep a careful eye on Nudd.

"In the dining room, Lord Kadien?" Nudd's tone held a note of restrained censure.

Pushing his plate away, Kadien looked at Lilith as he said. "It seems our guest has already lost her appetite, so there is no threat. Show Gaban in."

"As you wish, my lord." Nudd turned and walked from the room.

Still another breach of etiquette! Nudd should have backed from the room. Kadien narrowed his eyes, his senses on alert. Nudd would have to be dealt with later.

Almost immediately Kadien could smell Gaban's sharp stench. From the way Lilith held her napkin to her nose, she too could smell the offending troll. Gaban entered, slipping and sliding on his own sweat as he timidly made his way across the stone floor. Finally, he stood before Kadien.

"Lord Kadien," he said and attempted a bow. It was a difficult task for a troll since their heads were so out of proportion with the rest of their body that they sometimes toppled when they leaned too far forward.

Lilith stared at Gaban with an expression of disbelief and disgust.

Kadien could see that Gaban was in his usual agitated state. His saucer-sized eyes shot nervous looks from Lilith to Kadien to the candles. Wouldn't it be an amusing after-dinner entertainment if Gaban burst into flames?

"Gaban," Kadien began, careful to keep an eye on Lilith. He didn't want to miss her reaction to what he was about to say. "Since you bungled my last assignment and Boaz was transported instead of Angela, I need to change my strategy." He rubbed the tips of his fingers together. "I want you to enlist the help of the fairies."

"By what magic?" Gaban asked, as if the task was impossible.

"No magic. They know the importance of the Triad coming together. I want you to use your cunning to convince the fairy folk that Jachin cannot leave Sena without Angela's virtue to call The Maiden's Barge. You must convince them that Jachin and

Angela's joining is the only way to keep Jachin on Sena. Then let
the fairies do their magic."

"But, my lord, will their spells and potions work if Jachin
and Angela resist?" Gaban asked.

Kadien's sharp laugh echoed around the room. "I assure you,
Gaban, that they will not resist."

***

Angela began collecting wood as Jachin gathered rocks.
Together they built a fire pit and started their dinner. Tonight they
would be eating a quail Jachin had caught, as well as avocados
and strawberries they'd picked along the trail. The best thing
Angela could come up with for herbs was a handful of mint leaves.
Without Boaz to put the protection spell on the camp, Angela
was feeling jumpy. Every bird screech or frog croak in the forest
caused her heart to skip a beat and her muscles to tense.

They had decided on a spot next to a gentle waterfall leading
to a pool, and although it was enchanting, Angela couldn't relax.
As she was looking for two sticks suitable to use as eating utensils,
Jachin came up behind her and began massaging her neck. The
heat from his hands and his strong fingers was powerful magic
against her tight muscles.

"Ummmm." She gave herself over to his touch. What harm
could there be in a little shoulder massage?

As his fingers moved lower on her collarbone to stroke the
sensitive skin just above her dress's neckline, she realized precisely
what a little shoulder massage could lead to. But Jachin knew as
well as she that their ability to leave Sena depended upon her
virginity. He wasn't about to jeopardize his only means of leaving
the magic realm.

As if he could read her mind, he moved his hand back to a
more neutral spot at her neck. But then his fingers stopped and
his arms slipped around her waist to hug her close against him.

In her ear he whispered, "Angela, I want you more than I've
ever wanted anyone in my life."

Ripples of tingling warmth radiated out from where his breath
brushed her ear. Just his breath against her skin drove her crazy
with wanting him, and she found herself leaning back against his
chest while her hand stroked his arm. The springy hair prickled
her sensitive fingertips, and she could feel the movement of warm
muscles beneath her touch.

She wanted him, too, but she wasn't going to tell him that. If she did, she was certain they would both be lost.

"Your heart's beating so fast," he whispered, moving his hand to a spot just above her breast.

She fought the impulse to move his hand lower. Instead she cupped her hand over his. That seemed safe enough without giving up the incredible sensations by moving away from him.

But Jachin shattered her idea of 'safe' by moving his hand, along with hers, even lower. The two layers of soft fabric she wore seemed to melt as she felt their hands cover her breast. She pressed his fingers tightly against her, and her nipple hardened. Her entire body reacted with heat to his touch, her knees threatening to buckle. But still his hand moved lower, splaying against her belly as he pressed her more tightly against him

Don't turn around, she told herself. *If you do, you'll be lost. Don't let him kiss you. You won't be able to stop yourself. You'll be lost. Lost.* The word repeated itself over and over again as logical thought struggled to survive.

She'd been worried about the dangers of the surrounding forest, but that didn't compare to the terror she now felt at the passion within her that Jachin threatened to release. She knew if she gave herself to him, not only would they lose their only means of leaving Sena, she would be forever lost to a man she could never have.

Her greatest fear had presented itself like a fire-breathing dragon, and Angela was afraid she wouldn't survive this attack with only a few scars because it wasn't only her body threatening to surrender to Jachin. It was her soul.

As his fingers slid to the juncture of her thighs and pressed against her intimately, she fought for the strength to stop him. She was drowning, and she couldn't swim.

"Nooo," she said in a pitiful whimper even as her hips arched toward his hand.

Jachin's entire body stilled. She could feel his rapid breathing, warm against her ear as he whispered, "I'm...sorry."

Then he roughly moved from her. "No I'm not, dammit! I'm not sorry. Why should I be sorry for wanting you?"

Angela turned to him, watching his anger replace his passion.

His eyes challenged her as he said, "If we were in our world, we would only have each other and our consciences to answer to." He raked his fingers through his long hair as he turned his back on her.

Angela gave a weary shake of her head. What Jachin didn't know was that she would be fighting the same battle back in the safety of a non-magic world. Just like here, she would lose herself if she allowed herself to make love to him. Even though he had made it clear he wanted her, without true love and a lifetime commitment, she wasn't about to give her soul to any man. Besides, she knew a man like Jachin wanted—no, needed— perfection in a woman, just as he did in his art. She was only a mortal, and a MacAlpin at that. She had too many flaws for the great and powerful wizard Jachin Morgan.

Shakily she walked to the fire pit, only then realizing that without Boaz, they couldn't start a fire. She pointed to the pit. "Jachin, how are we—"

Her words were cut off as Jachin pointed angrily toward the pit, and a bolt of electricity arced from his finger to the wood. Instantly, flames appeared.

His action only intensified the realization that she didn't belong with Jachin, in this world or any world.

***

Gaban chuckled as he moved through the forest. The fairies had been so easily manipulated into believing that they needed to procure a passion spell for Jachin and Angela. All he had to do was convince them that Angela wanted Jachin to leave Sena and that, without Jachin, Kadien and the powers of darkness would conquer the power of light. As beings of light, they had been horrified at the mere mention of such a plight. Immediately they set about working their spell.

***

Angela and Jachin ate in silence, and even though she saw no sign that his sense of humor had returned, at least he no longer seemed angry.

Firefly fairies darted here and there. She hadn't seen Boaz's little fairy, Brigid, but others now fluttered about. Jachin threw the last of the quail bones into the fire, wiped his hands on his pants, then reached down at his feet for Boaz's backpack. He withdrew the Book of Light and, holding it so the fire illuminated the pages, he began to read.

After a few moments he said, "I think I've got the protection spell figured out. But I don't think I can do anything about the fairies close by. They seem to be hovering closer than usual."

He looked at the page again, then stood and chanted some words Angela didn't understand. As he did, he held his hand out and moved it in a circle.

Closing the book he said, "I'm sure it worked. I put a spell from the other side of the falls to just the other side of those trees." He indicated a circle of about thirty yards.

Immediately Angela felt herself relax. All the trolls, dragons and dark wizards of Sena would just have to wait until morning if they wanted to get to them.

"I still think you should sleep close to me. I promise," he said, holding his fingers in a Boy Scout oath as he grinned wickedly, "not to touch you."

She moaned, rolling her head back. She had mixed emotions about his sense of humor resurfacing. This was going to be a long night. *Promise away*, she thought to herself. The question was, could she keep her hands off him?

"Jachin, we need some kind of wizard's magic-spell-oath." She was only half joking. "Something ancient and unbreakable. There must be something in that book because I'm pretty sure the Boy Scout pledge isn't going to cut it."

Jachin smiled. "I'm irresistible, aren't I?"

She only nodded. "And humble."

"And humble," he repeated, his grin widening. "Now, if you can keep your hands to yourself, we need to get some sleep. We will be leaving at daybreak."

Like a prisoner going to the gallows, Angela walked to a soft, mossy patch of ground near the fire and spread out her cloak. She sat down on it.

Jachin's look became serious as he stood next to her. "I mean it, Angela. I won't touch you. I want to be able to leave Sena."

As she got as comfortable as possible, Jachin added a large log to the fire pit. Then he stretched out next to her, offering his arm as a pillow. With his other hand he raised three fingers in a silent promise.

She rested her head on his arm, staring up to watch the fairy lights dance high above, becoming at times indistinguishable from the zillion stars. An illusion was created by the moving lights, making it seem like sparkling dust shimmered through the air.

Her eyelids grew heavy, and she realized she was more tired that she had thought. No matter how hard she tried to keep them open, her eyelids kept closing.

***

It was a dream. It had to be. Jachin blinked at the sight before him. A glowing mist surrounded the camp, illuminating everything with a soft light. Fairy lights twinkled with a diffused brightness through the haze, looking like dancing cotton balls.

He jerked and turned to his side as he realized Angela was no longer beside him.

Instantly he was on his feet, his hand readied at his knife. He could hear distant, echoing music playing, but he couldn't tell where the lilting tune was coming from or how far away it was. It seemed all around him, yet not substantial enough to be real.

Then he saw Angela. She was standing next to the pool, looking toward the waterfall. Only she wasn't dressed in her blue dress. Instead she had on a long, gossamer white gown. This dress had long, tapered sleeves. As delicate and wispy as fairy wings, the fabric clung to her body, revealing full breasts, rounded hips and a tiny waist. The dress's neckline cut straight across, and Angela's shoulders were bare.

Slowly she turned, and he noticed she had flowers woven throughout her hair. Definitely this was a dream. But a glimmer dream? A dream of the future? Whatever it was, he was going to enjoy it.

Angela came toward him with slow, deliberate steps, the gown fluttering about her as if touched by a breeze. She began to sway to the gentle music, her smile provocatively inviting.

Jachin picked up his cloak, knowing they would need it for a bed, and he went to her, no longer held in check by reality. Still afraid he might awaken, he dropped the cloak and gently took her in his arms. This might only be a dream, but he was going to savor every moment of it.

***

Not remembering how she'd come to be standing next to the falls, or why she was wearing a different dress, Angela felt as if she were sleepwalking as Jachin took her in his arm. She couldn't think of a reason to stop him as his mouth touched hers.

His kiss was maddeningly gentle, skin barely touching skin. She wanted more, but he only teased her with soft kisses along her jaw and down her throat, his fingers fluttering down her back to send goose bumps of pleasure racing along her skin. The gauzy dress did little to diffuse the sensations shimmering over her body.

"Kiss me, *Angel*," he murmured, his lips so close to her mouth that his warm breath mingled with her own.

Feeling a freedom and wantonness she'd never before experienced, she drew her tongue along his parted lips, tasting mint. She slowly nuzzled her own aching lips against his, her tongue flicking out to tease. Finally she gave in to the building passion and pressed her lips to his in a passionate kiss.

Jachin's arms wove around her, his hands caressing her body. She broke the kiss.

"Love me, Jachin." The deep, sensual voice she heard couldn't be her own, but she knew it was.

Jachin spread the cloak at the pool's edge and then lowered her to his makeshift bed. As he came over her, his mouth once again found hers in a kiss that said everything she wanted to hear but knew he would never say. He moved his kisses down her throat, his hand cupping her breast to send pleasure spiraling throughout her body.

She felt his fingers draw the dress's bodice down until her breasts were revealed. At first he only lightly ran his fingertips over her sensitive flesh, and her nipples reacted instantly to the sensation. Then he took a nipple into his mouth, and Angela cried out with pleasure.

A thousand pleasurable sensations rushed her toward a cliff, and she knew that when she reached its edge she wouldn't be able to stop herself. But that was fine because she didn't want to stop. She pushed his hands away to tug at his shirt. In one fluid movement, she pulled it over his head. Next she discarded his knife, which was quickly followed by his pants.

His body was magnificent. And fully aroused. He was huge, and she wondered if she could take all of him inside her. But, as eager as she was to find out, she wasn't ready to give up the teasing pleasure his hands and mouth promised. Besides, she had only begun her journey of discovery of his lean, muscular body.

She kissed her way from his mouth to his chest, stopping to lick a nipple and tease it with her teeth. She was rewarded when he moaned with pleasure.

"Ummm," she said. "You like this?"

"Yes!" His breath caught as she did it again.

She let her hand travel down his chest and across the firm muscles of his flat stomach. "And this?" she asked.

His answer was a sharp intake of breath as his stomach muscles jerked. As she started to move her hand lower, he grabbed it. She felt giddy with feminine power.

Angela stood up and, enjoying the feeling that she was the reason for the passion in his gaze, slowly eased the dress from her body. She delighted in the way his eyes devoured every inch of her as the fabric dropped to the ground.

As Jachin reached out and reverently ran his hand up her calf, rational thought tried to kick in, to warn her that she couldn't do this, but she pushed the warning aside. Her decision had been made. She wanted to give herself to Jachin, even if it meant that in doing so she would lose a part of herself to a man who could never love her in return. She loved him. It was as simple as that. And she wanted to be with the man she loved. The only man she would ever love to the depths of her soul.

Eagerly she rejoined him on the soft cape, only briefly acknowledging the possible consequences of what they were about to do. But the passionate nature she had fought to deny her entire adult life took control as she began to explore his body. He was magnificent, and her fingers and lips wanted to know every inch.

Jachin stopped her movements by taking hold of both her wrists to still her. "My turn," he said as he moved her to her back.

His expert hands and adoring kisses left no part of her body untouched, and she thought more than once that she would die if he didn't release the exquisite tension building within her.

"Now, Jachin. *Please.*" She took his head in her hands and looked into his eyes, her breathing coming fast and hard. "I love you."

For a brief second denial flickered in his gaze. Then his mouth came down on hers in a claiming kiss that left her breathless. He raised his head and parted her legs with his. "I'll be as gentle as I can, Angel."

But she didn't want gentle. She was hot and wet and ready for him. She put her legs around him, feeling his rigid muscles tense. "Jachin. Love me." It was an urgent plea.

She felt the tip of him against her. He paused for a moment, then drove into her. She bit his shoulder with the brief, stabbing pain. He lay completely still, and she knew he was holding back, giving her time to adjust to him.

Over and over again he kissed her lips, all the time murmuring, "I'm sorry. I'm sorry."

But her pain was quickly replaced with incredible pleasure as the building tension responded to the hot fullness of him within her. She arched against him, wanting him deeper still.

"Look at me, Angel." It was a soft command.

She opened her eyes to meet his gaze.

Their eyes remained locked as he slowly moved deeper inside her, causing her breath to catch in sweet pleasure. Her eyes fluttered and threatened to close again.

"Look at me, Angel," he repeated.

She obeyed, her breath halting with the sweet torture of his controlled stokes. All the time his gaze bore into her, branding her soul with his. She willingly gave him the very piece of her own soul she had been so afraid of losing.

The sweet tension where their bodies joined became unbearable, and her breathing grew frenzied as she fought to hold onto the sensations.

Then Jachin's lips covered hers, and he drove into her completely. She could feel him deep within her, hot and throbbing.

He began moving faster, and her breath came faster. Pleasure took her to the brink again and again, until she thought she would go mad. Her moans filled the night.

Jachin kissed her throat, his teeth grazing her sensitive flesh. Then, with a deep moan, he began taking her even faster and harder. She went higher and higher with him until she was perched on the edge of an incredible cliff. With a start, she cried out as wave after wave of pleasure crashed over her. She felt Jachin's shuddering climax meet hers, and he held her tight.

They remained joined as Jachin's heated lips gently caressed hers until their bodies quieted and their breathing calmed. "You are magnificent, my Angel," he said, all the while holding her close.

No regrets, she reminded herself as she kissed his neck. It was a done deal. Whether he wanted it or not, her love was his. For her, at least, there was no turning back. They would soon be separated by different worlds, but no matter what happened, she loved him and always would.

***

Jachin awoke in the night with Angela in his arms. He chuckled. The dream had been so real, he could almost...He looked at her sleeping form. She was naked, and beside her was the dress in his dream!

It hadn't been a dream at all.

Oh, God, what have I done?

FOURTEEN

Hawthorn Tree: Represents a negative period, which could be put into a positive use. It only appears negative or positive depending on your reaction to it.

Angela awoke slowly and stretched, cool morning air brushing parts of her body that her dress should have been covering. She looked down, realizing her chemise was draped over her as an inadequate blanket, and she was lying on a soft blanket of some kind. She glanced down and frowned. No, it wasn't a blanket. She was lying on Jachin's cloak. Slowly, she sat up and saw that she was no longer by the fire, but at the edge of the pond. What was going on?

Suddenly, the memories of the night before came flooding back. Had she really made love with Jachin, or had it been a dream?

No, she was naked, so it couldn't have been a dream. But where was Jachin?

She turned her head toward where they'd built the fire. He was pacing next to where the fire pit had been the night before. He'd obviously cleared the camp.

She studied his face, and her heart plummeted. His distracted scowl was as fierce as she'd ever seen it, which could only mean one thing. He regretted last night.

She brushed her hands over her bare arms, remembering the feel of his touch. Although she knew she might regret her actions once she was back home and alone, for now she allowed herself the pleasure of remembering the closeness they had shared. She'd never in her life felt the physical and spiritual bond she'd shared with Jachin last night, and she was glad she had put aside her fears to give herself over to the passion.

Still, she didn't remember how she came to be wearing the beautiful dress, which lay beside her. What she did remember in intimate detail was Jachin's and her lovemaking. And if she'd thought for a moment that it had been a dream, certain aching parts of her body assured her it wasn't.

She saw Jachin glance her way, his stare unreadable. She didn't try to hide herself. It was too late for that.

He continued to stare. "We need to leave."

Unashamed, she stood and turned to test the pool's shallow water with her foot. She wasn't going anywhere without a bath. Jachin Morgan could wallow in regret and give her all the dark looks he wanted. The only thing she regretted was the realization that by making love to him she had destroyed any hope they had of leaving Sena until the next Wizard's Moon.

She didn't hesitate as she slipped into the cool, clear water, the shock momentarily taking her breath away. Her body adjusted quickly, and she leaned back to wash her hair. As tiny white flowers floated to the surface, images of the surreal night she'd spent in Jachin's arms made her shake her head. She knew some kind of magic was at work. Although she'd been fully aware and in total control of her actions from the moment Jachin first kissed her, the time before that was fuzzy and dreamlike, as if she'd been under a spell. But what a spell!

When she finished bathing, she waded to the side of the pool. "Jachin," she called, and he turned toward her. "Could you hand me my blue dress?"

"I couldn't find it. I guess you'll have to wear...the other dress."

She smiled, but his expression remained closed.

She decided she wasn't going to let herself be put out by his foul mood. Last night had been the most beautiful night of her life, and she wasn't ready to give up the euphoria.

Blinking water from her eyes, she reached across the grass to finger the dress's delicate material, wondering again where it had come from. It was like nothing she had ever seen—a gauzy, thin material that was light as air yet strong as silk. The shimmery threads were so tightly woven she could hardly see them, yet, when she held the dress up to the light it was almost transparent. She'd definitely have to wear the chemise underneath.

She got dressed and joined Jachin, running her fingers through her wet hair. She felt a bit silly wearing such an elegant, impractical gown while traipsing through the forest, but she didn't have much choice.

"Are you ready?" His tone held none of last night's tenderness.

Her stomach growled in response.

Jachin got an apple from the backpack and tossed it to her. He walked off.

With a lump in her throat, Angela looked at the shiny red fruit. She got the distinct impression that he wished it were poisoned.

How could he act like last night had never happened? Worse, for the past few days, he had been wonderfully attentive to her, and at times even seemed lighthearted. Now he was back to the scowling Jachin she had first met, making her feel like she was imposing herself in his life.

The last of her euphoria vanished with the thought. She glared at his back as she hitched up the train of her dress and hurried to catch up. Passing him, she turned and stopped. He stopped inches from her, still looking at her with hard eyes.

"Jachin Morgan," she began, but her throat closed. She cleared it. "How can you act like last night never happened? Didn't it mean anything to you?"

She had to blink away tears, but she refused to look away from his hard gaze. She wanted to see the truth in his eyes. Let him deny that he had shared with her more than the passion of his kisses and the tenderness of his touch.

She saw the slightest softening in his eyes. Then guilt. Her heart soared. He wasn't angry with her. He was angry with himself!

His crossed arms were like a barrier between them as he stated, "Last night was a mistake."

Angela couldn't deny that it was true in part. Her chin tilted up, and even though she knew the answer, she asked, "Why was it a mistake?"

What she really wanted to know was whether or not Jachin felt for her even the tiniest twinge of what she felt for him. She was too new to lovemaking to recognize the intent behind his tenderness. Maybe he was that way with all his lovers. The thought that he'd had other lovers made her feel ill.

Jachin took her by the arms and brought her closer. Her breath caught, and her skin tingled where his heated touch scorched her through the thin dress.

"I'll tell you why." His gaze bored into hers. "Because of my stupidity, we're stuck here for who knows how long. I know now that I willingly gave myself over to what had to be wizard or fairy magic, but that's no excuse. I took advantage of you because

I conveniently allowed myself to believe it was a dream. Now I've ..." his eyes searched hers. "I've ...." He crushed her to him. "I'm sorry."

Although his arms felt wonderful, she gently she pushed away. "But, Jachin, I don't want you to be sorry. Not for me, and certainly not for what we shared." She boldly looked into his eyes. "I love you."

The truth was so easy.

He closed his eyes, and his jaw tightened, misery creasing his forehead instead of joy.

"Listen to me." She jerked his arm so that he opened his eyes. "No strings attached. I love you. It doesn't mean you have to love me back. It doesn't have to *mean* anything to you."

In his eyes she saw that he did care a little. Maybe even more than a little. She squeezed his arm as she fought back tears. "I know there is no future for us. I accept that. But that doesn't mean I regret last night. I never will."

She felt her throat close again as a single, renegade tear sprang from her eye and skidded down her cheek to land on Jachin's arm.

She slowly brushed the wetness from his skin as she fought to regain her composure. "Jachin, I gave myself to you because I wanted to, not because you seduced me. And not because of magic." She smiled, remembering the bliss. "At least not wizard or fairy magic." Another tear escaped, trailing down her cheek.

He followed the tear's trail with his finger. "What if," he said gently, "you're pregnant." He chuckled mirthlessly. "I don't think the protection spell works for sex."

Pregnant? God, she hadn't even thought of that! She was speechless. Surely she couldn't get pregnant the first time.

Denial! her mind shouted. She knew enough about reproduction to know she certainly could. Quickly she counted back to her last period. God, she was in the middle of her cycle.

Even if she was pregnant, it wouldn't change anything between them, she told herself as her mind raced through myriad questions. If she was pregnant, would the child have powers? How could she raise the child? Would she be a good single mother?

Good heavens, if she was pregnant, she'd be having...A baby. *Jachin's* baby. What would she do?

Before the questions could overwhelm her, she pushed them

aside. The chances of her being pregnant were miniscule. Why borrow trouble?

She shook her head, looking down. "It isn't the right time of the month." If her words held conviction it was because she prayed that by saying it aloud it would become fact. "I can't be pregnant."

When she looked up and saw the look of relief on Jachin's face she had to bite her lip to check her emotions. His expression said everything. The thought of her carrying his child was abhorrent to him.

She was glad she had lied. If their lovemaking had created a child, she would love it just as she did its father. A part of her desperately hoped she was pregnant. Although she could never have Jachin, she would have a part of him with her always. If she was pregnant, the part of her soul she'd given to him was a fair exchange for what she would be getting in return.

A child. Angela mentally shook the thought from her head. It was a selfish thought. Unfair to the child and to Jachin. Chances were she wasn't pregnant, so dreaming about raising Jachin's child was a fruitless fantasy. Besides, if she was pregnant, she'd never tell Jachin. He might feel obligated to stay with her, and she didn't want him out of obligation.

But if you are pregnant, you won't be able to hide it from him, an inner voice murmured. *A pregnancy only takes nine months, and because you're no longer a virgin, you're stuck on Sena until the next Wizard's Moon.*

Oh, God, what am I going to do! she inwardly wailed as Jachin put his arm around her and they walked up the trail.

***

Marrion helped the smaller children with the wands they were making while her friend Maisy sorted various stones into small piles along the table. They were outside, the bustle of the busy compound allowing a momentary sense of well-being.

"Maisy, I know I shouldn't interfere, but things have gone from bad to worse," Marrion said.

"The journey is not yours, my dear. Let it go. What will be will be."

Marrion took a handful of the rose quartz crystals, allowing the calming radiance to enter her. She set the stones back on the table.

"There, that's better." Then she said with resolve, " I will not question the workings of the universe."

Maisy helped little Guendoloena wrap the thin leather strap around the stone to secure it to the polished oak branch. "The prophecy isn't ours to fulfill. Only The Triad is ordained to complete the cycle. The outcome is up to them."

"But the children still don't completely believe in The Prophecy. I felt it during their recall ceremony. Both Boaz and Jachin believe they are only on a journey to find and rescue their sister."

Maisy stopped what she was doing, and Guendoloena gave her an impatient look. "My dear friend, you are too close to be objective. For all you know, this very journey may culminate in the prophecy's fulfillment. Let Jachin and Boaz reunite with Lilith and see what happens. We are only observers."

"True." What would Marrion do without her wise friend? Maisy never hesitated to keep her focused. "The children may have a short road or a long road to their confrontation with The Darkness. It is not for me to question when the event will take place."

Maisy nodded. "They will certainly have to confront Kadien in order to get Lilith, but we can't be certain that Kadien is the darkness which they are prophesied to face."

"True as well." Marrion took the wand offered by a child for her inspection. She waved it before her, sensing the balance and easy feel. Smiling at the little girl, she nodded. "Truly inspired job, my dear.

"The travelers are drawing near to Kadien's fortress," she added. "I shall call a prayer vigil this night. I have had a premonition that only with the assistance of others will they free Lilith and unite at last."

Maisy looked as concerned as Marrion felt, and by the way she was avoiding eye contact, Marrion could tell she had a secret she wasn't ready to share. "What is it, Maisy?" she asked, alarmed.

Her friend shrugged uneasily. "I too have a feeling they will need assistance to take Lilith from Kadien. But I do not believe the aid will come from me or you, or any one in this compound, for that matter."

She pulled Marrion away from the children, and her voice was a whisper as her gaze darted around the grounds. "Brace yourself. Seumas Scot has returned to Sena. I saw him yesterday when I viewed the children. At first I didn't think anything of the little dog with them. But, then I saw the dog change into a wizard. And as sure as I am standing here, it was Seumas Scot himself!"

Confusion rang through Marrion. "Seumas Scot? Why would he be with the children?"

Maisy shook her head. "I do not know."

"I don't know what to think of it." Marrion scratched her head.

"Maybe," Maisy said, "he is aiding Kadien."

"Oh no, not Seumas."

"But, he never really fit in here," Maisy reminded.

"Only because he wanted to return to the old ways and weaken the veil between the worlds. That doesn't make him evil. Just misguided."

"Seumas Scott was always a troublemaker. That carries with it its own evil. If he has returned for the betterment of Sena, then why has he not shown himself to us? There is deceit in that." Maisy gave a sage nod as she made the pronouncement.

"Now stop, Maisy," Marrion scolded. "Seumas' only fault was that he had an opinion opposite to the rest of our people." A feeling of sadness swept over her. "That and his great, unrequited love for my sister."

"Maybe he has deceived us all in that matter as well. Maybe he knows what became of Vivian."

A thread of hope pulled at Marrion's heart. "This could be possible."

Maisy again whispered as she said, "There are those among us who believe that Seumas Scot is the father of the Triad and the reason for Vivian's desertion."

Marrion shook her head. "Then why would she leave? And take the children with her?"

"To be with Seumas."

"No," Marrion said. "My sister would not have abandoned her children to the Lutes only to be with Seumas Scot. I heard her profess many times of her sadness over being unable to return the affections of so ardent a pursuer."

They walked back to the children, and Marrion reiterated, "No, Maisy. Seumas Scot did not lure Vivian away from her home, her children and her responsibilities. We may never know what, or who, did."

***

Seumas maintained his owl guise for the entire night, unable to break through the strong barrier Boaz had place around their camp. By morning he'd had his fill of field mice, and now sat in the large oak tree, cleaning his beak against a tree branch. His talons held him secured to his perch.

Even when the young women awoke and released the barrier, he held back his transformation, wanting to observe their strengths and weaknesses now that they no longer had Jachin's help. He was pleased to see they seemed quite capable and sure of themselves.

Raising his wings, he beat them just enough to keep him aloft as he moved from the tree. He stretched his wings, splaying his feathers as he swooped down to a low branch next to where the women sat.

They both looked at him in awe.

"Hi, pretty bird," Boaz said. Then he saw the spark of possible recognition in her eyes. "Do I know you?"

With a low, reverberating *whoooo, whoooo*, he hopped down to stand before them and quickly transformed, regaining his true form. He had chosen to procure from the elements a fine cape of blue as well as the same kind of linen pants and shirt he most favored when he had lived on Sena.

"Sean!" Boaz looked suspicious. "Or is it Gaban?" She sniffed the air, her expression changing to caution when she couldn't detect the troll's odor.

He bowed. "I am known on Sena as Seumas Scot. Sean was my Lute name."

Boaz looked at Ailleann for confirmation, but the young healer only shrugged. "I have never seen this man before, but I have heard tell of the great shapeshifter, Seumas Scot." Her eyes brightened when she said the name. "You were shunned for advocating the lifting of the veils between the worlds."

Evidently enough years had passed that he was no longer thought of in damning terms by everyone on Sena.

"I am indeed that man."

Boaz eyed him. "And why are you here?"

"To help you find Kadien. I know the way. Although you are very close and could surely find it on your own, I would like to accompany you and help as I may." He picked up Angela's backpack. "And to safely dispose of this. I'm sure you have by now deduced what happened when you operated the cell phone."

Boaz looked uncomfortable. "I should have known better."

"I am positive there must have been a spell on the pack to inhibit your deductive powers."

She eyed him. "How do we know it wasn't you who put the spell on it?"

"Because I say I didn't. I want you to believe me. I am here to help."

Boaz looked at Ailleann, who had been quietly observing. "What do you think?

"He is a white wizard, and as such will have only our best interests at heart. And I would like to hear more about the views that caused his exile."

He added, "Self-exile, my dear. I was only *shunned* for my beliefs. My exile to the Lute world was self-inflicted...and for reasons which I cannot divulge at this time."

"Don't forget," Boaz said to Ailleann, "he lived in the Lute world for a long time. Maybe some of that world rubbed off on him. Maybe he has some weird agenda of his own going on here."

Ailleann gave her a startled look. "Do you sense this, Boaz?"

Boaz shook her head. "I don't sense anything about him, except the need to be cautious."

He felt a fleeting moment of pride in the young woman's sharp mind. And once again he wished her mother could observe the daughter she never knew. She, too, would be proud.

But that pride was not his to own. And regrets that he had not been allowed to raise Vivian's child as his own only served to diffuse the focus he needed to achieve his true purpose.

Seumas nodded in agreement. "It is always good to be cautious."

***

Jachin would never forgive himself. As he walked through the forest with Angela at his side, he fought an internal battle. It might have been easier if she had told him she hated him for what he had done. Even now, images of her beautiful body left him breathless and his resolve weak. But he had to be strong.

If she would just get mad at him and tell him she blamed him for what had happened, he might feel better. As it was, she kept looking at him with that horrible look of acceptance. And love.

How in hell was he supposed to respond to that?

"Jachin," she said, interrupting his unsettling thoughts. "There has to be another way off Sena besides my, umm, you know." She bit her lip. "When is the next Wizard's Moon?"

"In a year." A year of danger for Angela, and it was his fault she was here. And since she didn't have magical powers, she didn't have a way to defend herself from the constant danger.

"I think there might be another way off," she murmured, her expression far away, as if she were lost in thought.

He thought back to last night. There was no forgiving the fact that he had taken something from Angela that she had saved for one special man in her life. It made him feel so guilty he could barely look at her. Thank God she couldn't be pregnant. He had never in his life been so careless as to leave a woman unprotected during sex.

But he'd thought he was dreaming, and he had to admit that at the moment he entered Angela, he had acknowledged in the back of his mind that there was the potential of starting a new life. He'd always thought that something like that would scare the hell out of him, but it had only enhanced the fantasy, the pleasure, and the feeling of ultimate closeness he'd never felt with any other woman. But the pleasure only lasted until he woke up and realized that it hadn't been a dream, that the fantasy could very well become reality. How could he have allowed himself to jeopardize her like that?

When he felt his emotions start to take hold, he breathed deeply and brought himself back to the present. He had to stop thinking about making love with Angela.

He turned his thoughts to what she'd just said. "What makes you think there's another way off Sena?"

"Well, how could Kadien have kidnapped Lilith and brought her here before the Wizard's Moon if there wasn't another way?"

"Marrion told us that there are 'dark' ways to travel between the worlds." He wasn't about to unleash the dark forces within himself just to return to the Lute world.

"Oh." She ran her fingers down the dress's long, tapered sleeve. "From the mythology I've read, there are several ways off Sena. Maybe they're not all by way of dark forces."

"I think Marrion would have told us if that were true."

"Maybe she doesn't know everything."

He laughed and hugged her against his side. "Okay, Miss Mythology Guru. What do you know about Sena that Marrion doesn't?"

"You ever hear of *The Cave of Rebirth*?"

He chuckled. "No. Sounds like some kind of psychoanalytical retreat."

"Bingo! Did you ever study Carl Jung, the psychologist?"

"A bit in college."

She stopped and turned to face him. "The Cave of Rebirth is supposed to be the center of the collective unconscious, you know, like Jung was always referring to. You go into this cave, and you tap into the collective unconscious. But to get to its center, you have to go through chambers where you will be confronted by your fears, and you must conquer them."

She'd lost him. "So you think old Dr. Jung was a wizard from Sena? And how will this cave get us off Sena?" he teased.

"Be serious." Her frown was so severe it was almost comical. "This cave is not only a trip through your individual unconscious and the collective unconscious. It's supposedly a way *out* of Sena."

He tilted his head to the side. "And?"

She looked at him like he should be getting it by now. "And?" She opened her hands in a gesture of hopelessness.

"And, aren't you going to tell me why it's call The Cave of Rebirth? Or are you talking about a mythical psychological metaphor?"

She cringed. "Well, according to the myth, you have to die and be reborn in order to get out."

"Reborn? As in baby?"

"No. The guys in the legend only went through a spiritual death and rebirth."

"Great." He tried not to laugh. She was obviously reaching for a solution. But since he didn't have any better ideas, he shouldn't dismiss hers so offhandedly. "Can we walk while you tell me about this?"

"Yes. But think about it, Jachin. If there was such a place, we could leave Sena."

"Don't you think Marrion would know about this cave if there was one?"

She shrugged, her bared shoulders drooping. "I guess she would have told you if there was such a place."

Coming to the top of a small rise, Jachin came to a stop. Angela followed his gaze. In the distance stood a hill. And at the top of the hill was a large, ancient-looking fortress surrounded by what looked like an unbreachable wall.

Angela shook her head in awe. "It looks like a picture I once saw of Edinburgh Castle. Only it was a picture taken at night when the castle was all lit up. I don't suppose Kadien turns on flood lights at night." Her laugh was nervous.

"I doubt it." Jachin suddenly wanted Angela as far away as possible from the danger he sensed. She was here because he had selfishly insisted she come. He'd done enough damage, and the thought that he might put her in further danger made his powers hum to life.

"Jachin?" He turned and saw her looking at him strangely as she asked, "Are you okay?"

Would he ever be okay again, he wondered? A voice inside his head said, *You are corrupt. Angel is purity and honesty. You will destroy her.* He couldn't tell if the thoughts were his own. But since he'd had them before, he suspected they were. He was well aware that his feelings for Angela could only destroy her.

He looked at her. She was dressed up like a princess in her fairy garb, and her face was aglow. Then he looked in front of him, to Kadien's fortress, and he saw the complete antithesis of goodness. A presence of evil darkness emanated from the fortress like the breath of hell.

You cannot protect her, said the voice. Jachin wasn't sure about that, but he did wonder how he could protect Angela and confront Kadien to retrieve Lilith. Somehow he knew one would prevent the other. Someone would lose in the upcoming confrontation. Was it to be him, Lilith...or Angela?

She is in the way. She will force you to make a choice that will destroy you and everyone around you.

Suddenly he wished he'd never met Angela. From the moment they'd met she'd been like a match to his dynamite. The all-consuming feelings of protectiveness he felt for her could very well override his duty to his sister and jeopardize her release. If he had to choose between the lives of the two women, could he? If Angela wasn't here now, he wouldn't be asking himself that impossible question.

Angela or your sisters? Choose.

"Jachin?" she repeated as she took his arm.

He involuntarily shook her off, and he regretted it the moment he did. She backed up a step, hurt etched in her blue eyes, which rapidly filled with tears. She swallowed and backed up another step, her posture stiffening. "Never mind."

He had to fight hard to subdue the emotions Angela triggered. The more he fought, the stronger his powers became, as if fueled by the suppressed energy.

Good, he thought to himself as he pushed the emotions deeper. The stronger his powers, the better chance he would have against Kadien. It was long past time to kill his foolish daydreams and focus his energies.

He renewed his resolve to keep his dark side under control. Because if anyone could release Jachin's demons, he knew with inevitable certainty it was Kadien.

Or Angel, the voice taunted.

* * *

Lilith sat at her room's open window high in the fortress and closed her eyes to better focus her thoughts. Even though she knew there was a chance she was being telepathically watched, she wanted the confirming contact she'd previously made with her newfound brother and sister.

Ever since Kadien had told her about her heritage and that she was one of the so-called Triad of ancient prophecy, she had concentrated on connecting with her siblings. Almost immediately she'd had success. Although the connection wasn't reciprocal, she had been able to get a strong sense of both Jachin and Boaz. She'd also connected with Ailleann, who, Lilith was delighted to learn, was a healer like herself. And she had formed a psychic bond with the woman Angela as well, so that now the woman felt every bit as much a sister as Boaz. And there was something about Angela that touched Lilith deep inside, a trait she found herself wanting to emulate. She had gotten a sense of innate incorruptibility and goodness from Angela that radiated like a halo. The woman's spirit was as good as any Lilith had ever encountered.

Since awakening and being told of siblings, Lilith had been contacted by someone as well. In a dream, she had been visited by a woman she now knew as her aunt Marrion. Marrion had taken her back through time to visit her ancestors and to learn about her heritage. When the dream had ended, Lilith felt complete for the first time in her life. She knew who she was and who her people were. And she knew the source of her powers. The realization of the origins of her people still amazed her.

A loud knock at the door abruptly destroyed the pleasant images of distant ancestors in white robes.

Kadien strode in, and Lilith had to wonder why he had knocked in the first place. "Jachin and Boaz are near. I think it best I keep you close."

With a calm that surprise her, Lilith said, "Lord Kadien, may I ask why you haven't killed me if that is your ultimate goal?"

His smile accentuated his predatory handsomeness. If he lived in her world, Lilith knew the charismatic man would have legions of followers blindly following him, never seeing him for the evil entity he was.

"I don't want to kill you, dear Lilith." His voice was compelling. "I admire you greatly. I believe you and your brother and sister are the most powerful wizards born this millennia."

"Then what do you want?"

He studied her. "I simply want your powers." His gaze was not malevolent, even though his words were. "And those of your brother and sister."

"Is that possible? How does someone take powers that another is born with?"

Then realization dawned that people in her world did it every day through manipulation and intimidation, and a gradual eating away at the soul. They stole energy and robbed people of their inner light, feeding upon their weaknesses until nothing of the true person remained.

He smiled. "Very good. I see that you do understand."

She held the glowing pendant at her neck. "I will not willingly give you my powers."

He walked to where she stood and touched her face.

His touch wasn't unpleasant, although she expected it to be. Surprisingly, he was extremely gentle. Alarms went off in her head. This man's touch was false, his words and manners false. Lilith closed her mind and spirit to him.

She locked gazes with him and repeated, "I will not willingly give you my powers." It became a mantra she began repeating to herself.

"We shall see." He offered her his arm, nodding toward the door.

***

Angela entered a large meadow with Jachin trailing a few feet behind. Movement at a copse of oak trees caught her attention.

"Boaz! Ailleann!" She waived her hand high in the air. "Over here!"

Jachin walked up beside her, but his expression remained set in stone. *If you're not careful, Jachin Morgan*, she wanted to say to him, *you'll turn into one of your statues.* Instead, she ran ahead to greet Boaz, so relieved her friend was safe that she felt tears spring to her eyes. God, but she was doing a lot of blubbering lately. It had to stop.

"Angela!" Boaz and Ailleann ran to meet her.

They came together with group hugs and teary laughter.

Ailleann immediately fingered her dress, her expression awed. "Fairy silk! Where did you get it?"

Angela shrugged. "The fairies, I guess. I just woke up with it on."

"Cool!" Boaz said as she, too, ran her fingertips over the fabric.

Then Boaz turned toward the fortress. "Did you see the castle? I keep thinking we're going to see troops of armored knights on horseback break through the trees and descend upon us!" she finished in a British accent.

Seumas walked up. "Kadien will wait for you to come to him. It's his way. It gives him the upper hand if you play the game on his own chessboard. Then the rules are his."

"So what are we supposed to do? Walk up and knock on the door? We aren't equipped to storm the gates," Jachin drawled sarcastically.

"You have the power to destroy Kadien's fortress, Jachin, but it won't stop the wizard. His be a battle of the minds, to be sure," Seumas said. "I will present myself to Kadien as your emissary, and find out what he wants."

Jachin scowled and gripped his knife as if he was ready to do battle. "I don't have anything he wants."

"You sell yourself short, Jachin Morgan," Seumas said. "You have much Kadien desires."

The knowing look Seumas directed toward Angela caused a

blush to creep up her neck. Jachin's gaze followed the older wizard's as the man finished, "And he will use whatever means it takes to get it."

Thankfully, Boaz missed Seumas' innuendo because she said, "Jachin, it's best to be cautious. Let Seumas go see Kadien."

Angela didn't like the look she saw in Jachin's eyes when their gazes met. It was as if this whole thing with Kadien was her fault, and he hated her for it. He was still looking at her when he said, "Seumas and I will both go. This is my fight."

"No," Boaz said. "I have some say in this. Lilith is my sister, too. And you're my brother. We must fight Kadien together, but not until we know what we're up against. You forget, I can read minds. I've read Sean's...I mean Seumas'...and I trust him. Let him go alone."

Jachin eyed Seumas disparagingly. "Trust him? I've only seen deceit and lies. Is he Sean, Gaban, Seumas, or someone else? And he admitted he can block wizard's from sensing his true powers." He put his hands on his hips, his legs braced apart as he challenged Seumas, "Why are you here? Now? At this particular time? You have your own agenda, and it's not to serve as our emissary. So, what is it?"

Angela watched the man look Jachin directly in the eyes. "Long ago I wronged your mother terribly. Because of me, irrevocable damage was done before I could stop an event I put into motion. As penance, I swore to your mother that I'd devote my life to serving her. She took pity on me and allowed me to help her. She then asked me to do something for her. I made a promise to your mother. Although I have sworn never to reveal the particulars of that promise, I am honor-bound to carry out her wishes, and I have now returned to Sena to fulfill the promise."

"When did you make this promise?" Boaz asked.

He suddenly looked old, and Angela's heart went out to him as he said, "The day you were born."

With that, Seumas turned and walked toward the fortress at the top of the hill.

Jachin gave Angela that long, hard look again, and she wanted to belt him one right in the stomach. And if he wasn't so damned handsome even when he was being an insensitive jerk, she would have. "What!" she demanded. "What did I do?"

Boaz put her arm around Angela's shoulders protectively.

"You two have a fight?"

Angela felt her face grow warm. "Not exactly."

"Then what's going on?" Her gaze shot back and forth between them.

"Let's just say …." Angela tilted her chin up, although the bravado was false and her knees were weak. "I'm no longer your ticket home."

Boaz looked at Jachin through narrowed eyes. "And you think it's *her* fault?"

"Of course not," Jachin said. "I take full responsibility."

"Damn right you do!" Boaz tightened her hold on Angela until Angela felt certain her shoulder would have permanent fingerprints.

Angela removed her friend's hand and stepped away from her. "What happened isn't Jachin's fault. It's mine. I seduced him. He knows it, and he's angry with me."

Boaz laughed out loud. "Sorry, Angela, but I think the position of the last great martyr was filled by Joan of Arc a long time ago." Her tone gentled. "Honey, you forget that I know you. If you believe little old you broke the iron-clad virtue of the great womanizer Jachin Morgan, then you're kidding yourself. He's been after you from the moment he saw you." She glared at Jachin. "I'm not blind."

Jachin glared back. "I said I was responsible."

"Then quit giving Angela the evil eye."

Jachin stormed toward the edge of the clearing.

Angela shrugged at Boaz and Ailleann.

"Jachin isn't angry with you, Angela," Ailleann stated. "He is afraid *for* you."

The healer reached out and touched Angela's arm, her soft smile instantly replaced by a look of shock.

"What!" Boaz said.

For a moment Angela was frightened by Ailleann's expression. Did the healer sense an illness? It had been over a year since her last checkup, but she felt fine. A moment of anxiety rushed through her.

Ailleann never broke eye contact with Angela as she said, "I feel great joy and great sorrow from Angela."

Whew! Angela felt relief that Ailleann had only tuned in on her inner struggle over Jachin.

"Oh, honey," Boaz said as she once again crushed Angela in a hug. "That brother of mine and his temper. He's what's causing your joy and your sorrow, isn't he?"

"Please don't blame Jachin. I think Ailleann was right when she said Jachin is just afraid for me. I feel better now that I know he's not angry with me. Being afraid for me is a good thing, right? It means he cares."

She looked at both women for confirmation, although in her heart all the doubts remained. "I don't want you to be upset with your brother, Boaz." She wasn't about to make Boaz take sides. Angela moved back so she could look into her friend's eyes. "I swear Jachin and I are A-okay."

***

Jachin was grateful for the silence. Everyone seemed lost in individual thoughts as they quietly began setting up camp just inside the wooded area next to the stream they had been following. They were just finishing up when Seumas returned.

Jachin hurried to meet the man. "What happened? Did you see Lilith?"

Seumas looked gray, and Jachin wondered if he had made the right decision in letting the older man go in his place.

"Lilith is a fine, strong wizard. Kadien is playing the gracious host and has not harmed her, of this I am sure." Seumas looked sadly at the others as they gathered around him.

"What does he want?" Jachin held back his anger. He would need every ounce of reasoning power, and that meant he couldn't let his temper control him.

Seumas looked at him and then Boaz. "Kadien will come to you, but beware. Kadien's motives are never what they seem."

Jachin looked at Seumas, his chest aching with a sickening feeling of impending doom. "When will he come?"

"He wouldn't reveal a time."

Boaz's frustration was showing as she said, "And we're just supposed to wait here until Mr. High and Mighty decides to come to us? And that feels right? Not!"

Seumas said, "I believe he means to take your powers, but he may not tell you that."

"Take our powers? How can he do that?" Boaz looked confused. "Do you mean by killing us?"

"Kadien's ways are not as obvious—or direct—as that,"

Seumas said.

"I don't get why he hasn't just picked us off one at a time," Boaz said. "He already has Lilith. Seems to me, we've been pretty easy marks. He's had plenty of chances."

"He's playing a game," Seumas said. "It's a game he has perfected, and only Kadien knows the rules."

A flash of light to Jachin's left momentarily blinded him, and he reflexively grabbed Angela, holding her close.

There, standing not ten feet away, was a man equal to Jachin's height, dressed in a long, richly embroidered white cape and white clothes. Although Jachin saw no weapon, he felt danger, and he knew he'd found the focus of the evil he had only sensed before.

Kadien.

Jachin's hand went to the hilt of his blade, his muscles tensing to face the enemy.

Arrogantly the man assessed them one by one. Jachin stood ready, as did Boaz. But when Kadien's gaze rested on Angela, Jachin noticed a slight glitch in Kadien's arrogance.

It was as if he recognized her. But that was impossible.

FIFTEEN

Oak Tree: Represents a successful spiritual journey. You are now ready to embark on your true journey with the protection of the High One.

Jachin moved Angela to his side, and Boaz came to stand next to him. He could feel his sister's energy connect with his as they stood close, and the medallion resting against his chest seemed to come to life, its heat scorching his skin. The pain only served to galvanize his resolve.

Kadien acknowledge them. "Boaz. Jachin. It is my pleasure to...at long last, meet you both."

Then Kadien bowed slightly, his eyes fixed on Angela. "*Angel*," he said as if they were lovers.

Jachin's anger rushed to boiling, and his blood pounded in his ears. How dare Kadien use Jachin's nickname for Angela!

"What do you want, Kadien?" he demanded, feeling his powers building. He knew he had to maintain control. If he didn't, Kadien would win whatever game he was playing with them.

He gave Jachin an aggrieved look. "For the present, I only want to meet you. Nothing more."

Jachin stepped forward. "Release Lilith."

Kadien smiled. "My dearest houseguest may leave whenever she pleases. I do not hold her against her will. It is not my way."

"I can't believe she *wants* to stay with you," Boaz said suspiciously.

Kaiden's eyes darted toward Angela. "For the time being Lilith has *selected* to accept my hospitality."

Why the emphasis on the word *selected*? Jachin wondered. Was she really given a choice? If so, what would the consequences be if she left? He began to understand what Seumas meant by Kadien playing a game.

With a slow bow that Jachin was sure Kadien meant for Angela alone since he was looking right at her when he made it, the wizard disappeared in another flash of light. Only the tang of copper remained to remind Jachin that the man had ever been there.

"Well, goodbye to you, too," Boaz said. "Don't let a bolt of lightning hit you in the ass on the way out." She turned to them. "What a *lovely* man. We must have him to dinner some evening."

Jachin realized Angela was trembling violently. Forcing back the raging, dark force within him, he took her in his arms and cradled her against him until her shaking stopped. If only he could hold her forever and keep her safe. But he knew his very existence threatened her safety.

At some point, he realized the others were preparing food, and that the fire had been started. Angela finally looked up at him, and with a tenderness his racing heart threatened to override, he leaned down and gently kissed her. Her lips molded perfectly to his, and her arms went around him. As her curves fitted intimately against his hard angles, he knew he'd found the perfect woman. God, why was he forced to shut her out of his heart? Why was he being forced to reject her in order to save them all, when what he really wanted was to lose himself in her arms for the rest of his life?

Knowing that the answer was simple, that he had to reject her in order to protect her, he broke the kiss as gently as he could.

She gazed up at him with a sweetness that clawed at his heart. "I love you, Jachin Morgan."

God, would she stop saying that! She couldn't love him. He wouldn't *allow* her to love him. But he knew it was already too late. For some unfathomable reason, she did love him. But if loving him would have been dangerous in her world, it was deadly in his.

She stepped back, a sad smile on her face. "I meant what I said before. No strings attached."

Before he could respond, she turned and walked toward the others.

A voice inside his head said, *She may say her love is without conditions, but she wants a piece of your soul. Be careful. She doesn't know what unconditional love is. And, just like the other women in your life, she will sooner or later betray you.*

Jachin shook his head, shutting his mind to the morose thoughts. He had no intention of letting Angela into his soul, so why keep fretting over the fears of what could happen if he did?

As he walked to the fire, he overheard Boaz murmur to Seumas, "Did you see the way Kadien looked at Angela? And why did he call her Angel? Especially in that …" She paused and shivered. "…creepy way?"

Jachin moved closer to the whispered conversation. He wanted to hear Seumas' opinion without alarming Angela who stood with Ailleann next to the stream.

"I …," Seumas didn't meet their eyes. "I'm not sure."

"Take a guess," Jachin said. "You know more about the guy than we do."

"It may simply be that Kadien recognized Angela as a Lute. A Lute in Sena would seem very unusual, I'm sure, even to Kadien."

Jachin wasn't buying it. That was not what he had seen in the dark wizard's eyes.

But he couldn't question Seumas further because Angela and Ailleann chose that moment to join them.

Angela looked at Boaz. "Do you think the protection spell will work against Kadien?"

Boaz shook her head. "The Book of Light says the spell can only be broken by calling on the dark powers. I'm pretty sure Kadien has a direct line."

So much for getting any sleep, Jachin thought.

Later that night, as the others slept and Jachin stood watch, he gazed up at the field of stars. The fire had burned low, allowing an undiffused view of the brilliant lights. It was then that he realized that certain *other* lights were missing. He looked at the trees around the camp. The fairies were gone. Most likely they didn't want to be around in case Kadien decided to make a return visit.

Seumas rose from his sleeping pallet and walked to where Jachin stood several yards from the fire. They were silent for long moments before Jachin asked a question that had been on his mind, but one he was reluctant to ask because of where it might lead. "How well did you know our parents?"

Instead of answering, Seumas gazed through the trees toward the clearing, making Jachin nervous. Did the evasive gesture mean he was about to avoid the truth, or tell an outright lie?

"Why do you want to know?" Seumas finally asked. "What purpose will it serve? Will it change anything?"

He was avoiding an answer, which meant he had something to hide. "It will serve to satisfy my curiosity. I want to know what part you played in what happened thirty years ago." His stomach clenched with the fear that Seumas might admit to being their father. Jachin was fairly certain he was, and part of him was reluctant to acknowledge that fact. If Seumas was their father, then the man had the answers to questions that had plagued Jachin most of his life. But did he really want those questions answered?

"The part I played," Seumas repeated as he bent his head. When he looked up again, Jachin could see the hard line of his clenched jaw work before he answered. "What happened thirty years ago was my doing. I am the reason your mother left."

Jachin folded his arms. "Are you the reason she left us with strangers?"

Seumas nodded. "She had no choice. You were in danger here."

"Everyone has a choice. Why were we in danger here?"

"Because of who you are. She knew the dark wizards would do everything in their power to destroy you before the time of prophecy."

"Fine." He could feel old wounds open and anger wash over them. "Devoted mother that she was, she took us from Sena. So what was her excuse for separating us and dumping us on the doorsteps of people who knew nothing of our ways or our powers? What was her motivation to leave us unprotected in another world?"

Seumas looked at him with stark shock. "Surely you don't think she had anything but your welfare in mind?"

"How would I know that?" Jachin's breathing came faster, and he could feel the darkness moving inside him.

Seumas stared at him soberly. "You must trust me on this. Vivian loved the three of you more than life itself. She ..." His face became tortured. "She gave up her very existence for you."

"I don't believe you. I think you and she went off together and didn't want to be saddled with three infants."

"No, no, you're wrong." Seumas looked genuinely distressed, but Jachin wasn't about to believe a man who had already shown his actions only served his own secretive purposes.

Seumas continued. "I only helped her take the three of you from Sena. As I've already told you, I had betrayed her. She took pity on my misery and let me help her. After that I never saw her again. She...left, as she knew she must. She knew that the dark wizards could find you by discovering her whereabouts. Or if they found her, they could work their dark magic on her to make her reveal where you were. There was only one solution. She must cut off all contact with you, and she must...cease to exist so that no one from Sena could find you."

"But they did."

"Of course. She knew that as you approached your thirtieth year and began having the glimmer dreams, your whereabouts would certainly be detected. You would also be at the height of your powers and be better able to protect yourselves. Her fate was to sacrifice herself to keep you safe so that you could fulfill your destiny. Now that time is at hand, and you and your sisters must fulfill the prophecy and restore balance throughout the worlds. Vivian knew this could only come about if she kept you safe."

So, even as babies, they had all been pawns in some wizard power trip. He was once again forced to control the anger simmering inside. As he began to feel calm enough to go on, he asked, "Are you our father?"

"I would like nothing more than to claim that privilege." He looked away. "But sadly, I am not. Your father died soon after your conception, and I have sworn an oath to Vivian to never reveal his name. It would serve no purpose. " He glanced back at Jachin. "I'm sorry to dash your hopes, if you had wished to find either one of your parents."

Seumas wasn't their father? Then who in hell had been? And why was it such a big secret? Jachin shook off his concerns. Like Seumas said, the man was dead, so it didn't matter. He closed the book on his birth mother and father. He needed to focus on what was happening now.

He looked toward the fire pit. Angela slept beside it.

***

Jachin and Seumas led the group to the base of the hill leading to Kadien's fortress. All the while, Jachin's thoughts were onAngela, when they should be focused on finding a way to Lilith.

As they neared the rise, he looked ahead and saw two men standing in the forest. One was Kadien. He was dressed all in white again, and he held a long scepter with a clear crystal globe at the top. Sunlight glistened off the rounded orb.

Seumas said in a low voice, "Kadien himself has come to meet us, and with only one ally. I know this man. His name is Nudd, and he is Kadien's high counsel."

Jachin stopped and turned to the women. "Stay back. Seumas and I will meet with Kadien."

"Don't think so, Hercules," Boaz said. "You and I are in this together, and you know as well as I do that we have to stay together so our powers are at their greatest."

"I don't want Angela or Ailleann put in danger," Jachin stated.

Boaz shrugged. "Then I think they would be better off with us than alone, don't you?"

He knew Boaz was right, but he still wanted to argue with her. Yet no amount of arguing would change the facts. He needed Boaz close to draw on her power, and they didn't dare leave Angela and Ailleann alone because they'd be in as much danger alone as they would with them.

Frustrated by the Catch 22, he reluctantly nodded. They all walked forward, and Jachin had to admit that he felt physically, spiritually and emotionally stronger with Boaz beside him. Their powers were definitely enhanced when they were close. He began to believe that together they could defeat Kadien in a battle of powers.

As they drew closer to Kadien, he could see that the dark wizard's scepter had a dragon carved down its sides. It looked like the dragon was slithering up the long stick, its tongue reaching out to lick the crystal.

He studied his opponent. Kadien's smile from last night was gone, and his gaze kept flitting to Angela, making Jachin want to take a step in front of her to block her from the man's line of vision.

Instead, he said, "So, what's it going to be, Kadien?" He still didn't know if this was supposed to be a battle of physical, magical, or emotional strength, but he was ready on all counts.

Kadien's eyelids lowered. "Your choice, Jachin. Either you and I battle wizard-to-wizard...or I will have Lilith killed."

I will force you to use the darkness. In doing so, you may kill me, but I will win all the same. You will be one of us. Your soul will be mine, Kadien added mentally, and the words pulled at the darkness within Jachin, stirring it to life.

"I will never become one of you," Jachin said, knowing he had to voice the sentiment aloud.

"We shall see," Kadien said with a smug expression. "I believe the battle you wage within is greater than the one about to take place between us."

"What happens if I win?" Jachin asked.

"Lilith is released."

"And if Jachin loses?" Boaz asked.

"The same. If Jachin dies, your sister will be released."

"Where is this battle supposed to take place?" Boaz asked next.

"Here." Kadien nodded to the peaceful meadow just beyond the tree line. "And now." With a wave of his scepter, the meadow was shrouded in darkness, and the sky turned into red and black ribbons of roiling clouds. The sun turned black as if in full eclipse, and there was a red halo surrounding it. In the center of the field, large squares of red and white had replaced the meadow grass, making it look like a huge chessboard. Along the circular bank of trees stood stone statues of serpents and gargoyles, perched as if ready to take their place on the board.

As Kadien's white cape took on a red glow, Jachin decided Kadien's show was a bit theatrical, but he knew there was real danger present.

"Beware, Jachin!" Seumas said. "The battle has begun. There are no rules. He is trying to trick you into believing it is only a game of the mind. But he will use the physical, the magical and the mental in his battle."

Jachin glanced at Seumas. "I figured that one out on my own."

One thing was for certain, Jachin wasn't going to be the defensive player in this game. He ran toward the meadow, gathering strength as he went. All the feelings he had submerged since his arrival in Sena surged to the surface with a humming power. Each stride he took gathered more and more strength, so that when he finally stood in the center of the chessboard he was energized.

He didn't wait for Kadien to make the first move. He raised his hands to gather the electricity from the air. Instantly, an arcing ball of white light formed between his hands. With all his strength he hurled the ball at Kadien, who had just begun to turn and face him.

The instant before the charged ball hit Kadien, he raised his hand, and the ball stopped mid-air. Laughing, Kadien motioned the ball high into the red sky, where it exploded into a burst of sparkling light.

Jachin focused on the elements around him, bringing them together as he did when he formed clay into bronze. He aimed the charged elements at Kadien. The ground shook as the swirling mass struck. Jachin felt a moment of exhilaration as he saw a bronze statue of Kadien where the flesh-and-blood man once stood.

But his victory was short-lived. The statue exploded, leaving an unharmed Kadien smiling at him.

Enough games. Kadien's voice reverberated through Jachin's head as Kadien raised his hands, and the black clouds began to churn high above their heads. Shadows like flickering flames billowed across the chessboard and the trees. *Do you know what I'm going to do with Angel* to Angel *after you die?*

Thunder rumbled as Jachin's anger grew at the implied threat. He threw a bolt of lightning at Kadien's feet, and the ground split open. Kadien levitated above the opening, moving to an undamaged spot on the chessboard.

Do you know what will happen to your sisters? Surely you know they must die. Kadien raised his hand, and as he lowered it, a portion of the whirling sky fell toward Jachin.

Tiny bolts of electricity connected with his skin, making him feel as if a shower of white-hot knives stabbed him. He fought against the pain, the urge to cry out, and most of all, the internal darkness that was even now clouding his mind as it struggled to come forward. Finally he recovered from the assault and shook off the pain, wondering why Kadien hadn't attacked again while he was incapacitated. The fact that he hadn't made Jachin even more wary. What was the man up to?

Give in to your nature, Jachin. Become one of us. You can save them, and you can kill me if you use the power.

At Kadien's mental encouragement, Jachin suddenly understood exactly why Kadien hadn't attacked. He wasn't trying to kill him. He was trying to get him to give in to the darkness, and Jachin fought even harder to control the evil entity inside him.

The sky continued to convulse with a hot, sulfurous wind. Through ear-piercing cracks of thunder, Jachin heard Seumas' voice inside his head, as he also encouraged, *Acknowledge the darkness within, my son. It is part of you. To deny it is to live in fear. The fear can control you. If you look at your fears and accept them as part of you, you can control them.*

Jachin's temper flared higher and hotter. He had been right not to trust Seumas. The old wizard also wanted him consumed by the darkness, to be destroyed by the evil darkness inside him.

Well, he wasn't about to give in to either of the wizards! He fought harder to control his raging anger and the power it held, all the while keeping Kadien in sight.

*You cannot win without using the darkness, "*Kadien taunted. *Feel it, Jachin. Know it. It is who you are. You are one of us. Join forces with me. We can control the world.*

Kadien's voice seemed to be whispering over his shoulder, and Jachin jerked around to see Kadien standing behind him and laughing.

At the edge of the chessboard, there was a flash of light that made even Kadien flinch, and Jachin watched Seumas morph into a monstrous winged dragon. But instead of heading for Kadien, as Jachin expected, the dragon raced across the meadow toward him.

As the dragon drew close, scorching heat came from its mouth, and its jaws gaped, revealing sharp, gleaming teeth. Only by leaping to the side did Jachin avoid the torch of flame that suddenly shot from the dragon's mouth. A patch of burned black grass sizzled where Jachin had stood.

Let in the darkness, came Kadien's chant.

Face the darkness, he heard Seumas chant.

As the two men's minds bombarded his with their insistent chanting, the ball of energy inside him threatened to break free, but he held tight to the control. He wasn't going to give in to the darkness. He wasn't!

But even as he made the vow, he felt an immense pressure inside his chest as his dark powers fought to consume his light powers.

The dragon growled, low and menacing, its intake of breath a long hiss. The beast's tail swished, the tip flipping from side to side as the rest of its body remained tensed as if preparing to pounce.

Its eyes glittered, and steam rose from its iridescent scales as Seumas mentally ordered, *Destroy me, Jachin. Only by facing the darkness in your soul and owning it can you conquer it. Don't let it control you. You must control it.*

The dragon opened its mouth, but instead of the expected blast of fire, it turned and raced toward the women.

Jachin knew instinctively that Seumas was giving him a choice: kill Seumas, or Seumas would kill the women.

You can't do this! You can't give in to the power! his conscience railed at him, but Jachin didn't listen. If he had to lose his soul to the darkness, so be it. He couldn't—wouldn't—stand by and let the women die because of him.

He gathered a ball of electric energy from the surrounding air and directed it at the dragon, cursing when it missed. The monster relentlessly pursued the women, and it would reach them within a few seconds if he didn't so something to stop it.

He gathered the elements he used for creating bronze and threw them at the dragon, but the animal easily deflected the energy and progressed unharmed.

You can reach them in time if you use the power. He was no longer sure whose voice was echoing in his head. Was it Seumas', Kadien's, or his own?

When he realized all the women stood frozen directly in the animal's path as if under some kind of enchantment that wouldn't let them move, his fear combined with his anger until it reached the boiling point. As he began to run, he realized he was reenacting the exact scenario as the last time he'd faced a dragon to save Angela. Only this wasn't a real dragon. This was a powerful wizard with the capacity to kill them all. He couldn't believe he had let himself be duped by Seumas. Obviously the man had been aiding Kadien all along, and now he was working with Kadien to ensure that Jachin forfeited his soul to the darkness.

Save them, Jachin. You're their only hope.

At Seumas' taunt, a swirling vortex of power began to stir within Jachin, and with it came a feeling of invincibility. His vision became focused and tinged red. He could see Boaz struggling to keep the dragon back with her powers, but she wasn't strong enough alone. He had to help her, but the only way he could reach her in time was to do as Seumas said and give in to the darkness.

Even as he made the admission, he still struggled against it. But the harder he fought, the stronger it became. It wanted control. It wanted out. It was like a separate entity, and Jachin was losing the battle against it.

Control the darkness, Jachin. Don't let it control you. It's part of you. Acknowledge it. You don't have to lose yourself to it.

Like the lightning flashing around him, Jachin realized with a jolt that Seumas was right. What he had been fighting his whole life was a part of himself that was never going away. He needed to face it, acknowledge it, and learn to control it. Until he did, he would be easy pray for Kadien and those like him.

Suddenly he was no longer afraid, and for the first time in his life, he let the darkness have complete freedom. Then he mentally grabbed hold of it and directed it to obey him.

As the dragon got to within a few yards of the women, Jachin blinked, transporting himself to a spot between it and where the women stood. He felt waves of power radiating from him like an aura. Holding his hands out toward the animal, he willed the beast gone.

In a puff of mist, the dragon disappeared.

Instantly the sky cleared and the wind died. The meadow now glistened as if it had just rained.

As he stared around him in wonder, Jachin felt whole for the first time in his life. No longer was he afraid of the destructive forces within him. He knew how to control them without a struggle. Simply by acknowledging them as part of his whole, and choosing whether or not to use them, was all within his power.

He looked around for Kadien.

The dark wizard walked toward them, a satisfied smile on his face. "Jachin, you are more clever than I ever dared hope." He bowed. "Our battle seems at an impasse. You have conquered your dark side. For the time being. So, I have a proposition."

Jachin eyed Kadien suspiciously. He knew instinctively that Kadien's and his powers were equal on all levels. They could continue their battle for hours, or even days, and the result would be the same. An impasse. Without joining his powers with those of his sisters, he could not conquer Kadien. He had to come up with a way to save Lilith. Only when she had joined with him and Boaz could they defeat Kadien.

Jachin said, "I'm not really in the mood for bargaining, Kadien. Release my sister, and release her now."

Kadien said, "On one condition."

"What condition?" Jachin asked, growing even more suspicious.

Kadien knew the condition he was about to propose would never be acceptable, but he was already anticipating the turmoil and conflict it would ensure. Jachin might be equal with him in power, but he was still vulnerable in one area—matters of the heart.

Kadien almost laughed when Jachin said, "No conditions. Just release her."

The boy was obviously reveling in his new sense of power. "You know you cannot take her. And you also know that I would be a fool to release her so that you could combine powers with her."

"And you know that you're risking too much to keep her." He walked to Boaz and draped an arm around her shoulder. Kadien marveled at the immediate increase in magical power flowing from them. "We will do everything in our power to get Lilith."

Now was the time he had been waiting for. His move to checkmate. He knew what he was about to do would break Jachin's newfound spirit. Shrugging, Kadien said, "Only one person here has it within her power to secure Lilith's freedom."

Before Jachin could respond, Kadien turned to Angela, relishing the look of fear in her eyes as his gaze met hers. "Angel, if you will agree to become my lifemate, I will release Lilith."

He watched for her denial, her horror at his suggestion. Even one as pure as Angela would not sacrifice herself, he was sure of it.

To his surprise, her look of fear was replaced with calm acceptance. Without hesitation she walked toward him.

She is bluffing, Kadien thought. *She's hoping Jachin will rescue her. Little does she know that he cannot. And the test she sets for him is one he cannot and will not pass.*

When she reached him, she held her hand toward him. "Kadien, I will give myself freely to you if you promise to release Lilith and let the others go unharmed."

Ailleann rushed forward to grab hold of Angela's arm before the slim fingers touched his. "No, you mustn't do this, Angela!

You do not know what you are doing! I beg of you, do not give yourself to Kadien!"

The foolish healer had tears in her eyes. Kadien smiled smugly and held a summoning hand to Angela. "I will forever be your slave, my pet."

Before their hands could touch to seal the bargain, Jachin rushed forward, grabbed Angela and held her to him. Angela raised her face to look into Jachin's, and Kadien saw such radiance in her expression that his heart stilled.

She was serious in her commitment! Could she really love the boy so intensely that she was willing to sacrifice herself? He didn't believe it. It wasn't possible. She was a Lute!

"Let her come to me, Jachin." Kadien kept his eyes on Angela, still unable to believe what he saw. She had to be playing a foolish game that she couldn't possibly win.

"No," Jachin growled. "Kill us if you have to, but you're not getting her."

Angela struggled to free herself from Jachin's arms. Once he lost his hold, she stood on tiptoe and quickly kissed his cheek.

Then she turned and hurried toward Kadien before Jachin could stop her. She took hold of his hand, and Kadien felt a surge of pure love run through his fingertips. Love for Jachin. The feeling both amazed and angered him. The boy wasn't worth this woman's love.

Angela's words held no hint of martyrdom, only quiet resolve and determination, as she said, "I give myself willingly to you, Kadien."

Kadien had expected tears, or trembling, but Angela's touch was strong and true and never wavered. Her purity raced through him with incredible power. He realized he wanted that power more than he wanted that of The Triad. And he made a vow to have it. But now was not the time to fulfill that vow.

"No! You're coming with me," Jachin yelled as he took hold of her arm.

As the three of them stood linked together for that moment, Kadien felt the strength of their love move from Jachin through Angela and then through himself. He felt the truth of Angela's willingness to sacrifice herself for Jachin, and he felt Jachin's determination to die before he let Angela go to Kadien.

Inwardly, he laughed victoriously. He may have lost the battle, but the war was far from over. He hadn't been able to corrupt any of them, but once he did manage to do so, the victory would be even sweeter. The power would be even greater because he'd also be absorbing the unmatched power of true love.

He patted Angela's hand. "Nudd, bring Lilith to us. The battle has ended."

Angela bravely pulled her arm from Jachin's grasp, and Jachin looked so devastated that for a moment, Kadien was almost sorry for the man. Allowing himself one last look at Angela and the aura of her pure soul, Kadien raised his staff over her head and called on the dark forces. He chanted the ancient words, and with a crack of thunder Angela was gone.

Jachin stood in shock, his breath coming in short, strangled gasps. Boaz bit her finger in distress, and Ailleann released a sob.

"Angela is not dead," Kadien said, suddenly tired of the game. "I have merely sent her back to her own people. She does not belong in our world."

Kadien could tell that Jachin didn't believe him. The look of grief on his face was utter devastation. This was good. As long as the boy was grief-stricken, he wouldn't be concentrating on destroying him.

"Lilith will join you shortly, and then you may go," he told the group. "The time for the final battle is still ahead. You must go home and prepare yourselves. And do not delude yourself that your powers are equal to mine. I allowed you to win today in order to assess your true heart, Jachin. I want your powers to be at their strongest when you give them to me, and you will give them to me, of that you can be sure."

With that, he waved his staff and disappeared.

***

As Jachin watched Kadien disappear, he knew the wizard was telling the truth. Angela wasn't dead. He could feel her living spirit within his heart, but he still felt emptiness and grief because he also knew he would never see her again. Although it was for the best, his heart wasn't listening to his head.

Before he could sink further into his morass of grief, a figure approached through the trees. The moment he saw her, Jachin recognized his sister, Lilith. She was the exact image of her portrayal in *The Dance.*

Boaz rushed past him to embrace Lilith, and with a sudden

need to be connected to both of them, he walked to the two women and put his arms around them. Their powers fused, swirling around them like a whirlwind.

Lilith smiled at him and then at Boaz. "What took you so long? I've been waiting thirty years for you two to show up. We have a job to do."

***

Angela felt like she'd been hit with a stun gun. Dazed and with every nerve ending stinging as if she was being stabbed by a thousand needles, she slumped to a hard, wooden surface. She slowly opened her eyes, realizing she was at the same pier where they had crossed over at The Wizard's Moon. Her mouth had a metallic taste, and she felt nauseous.

Through blurred, angled vision, she saw people walking around her, giving her curious looks. She opened her mouth to ask for help, but she couldn't talk. Her entire body buzzed, making her feel as if she'd touched a live electrical wire.

A young surfer, hair bleached and nose peeling, leaned close to her, his eyes filled with concern. His hand rested on the surfboard beside him. "Hey lady, you okay?"

All she could do was move her head from side to side. Then there was a loud ringing, and darkness closed in.

She awoke to the sound of a voice over a PA system calling for Dr. Riedeman to report to emergency STAT. A curtain around her bed kept her from seeing what was going on, but from the immediate sights and sounds she knew she was in a hospital emergency room bed. Remembering the surfer, she figured he must have called an ambulance.

She still wore the white dress, but her shoes had been removed, and a white, cotton blanket covered her legs. With some effort, she managed to lift herself to one elbow and was able to reach the bedside table and the green plastic pitcher of water sitting there. She poured herself a cup and was about to bring it to her lips when a woman in white walked around the curtain.

"Hello, I'm Dr. Riedeman. So, we're awake, are we?" The woman took the water and put it back on the table then took Angela's wrist to check her pulse. Angela could feel her heart racing like she'd run a marathon, and her lips were dry.

The doctor began asking questions. Within half an hour the interrogation and exam were complete. "Well, Angela, I don't see any reason to keep you here," she said. "Your vitals have stabilized, and you have no signs of concussion or dehydration. Do you have someone you can call to come get you?"

Angela felt a lump form in her throat. She had no idea what had happened to Boaz and Jachin or if the battle had continued after she had been transported away. Even if they were alive and well, they might as well be in outer space. And her friends in Sedona were too far away for immediate help. Then she remembered Jachin's office manager, Mildred Holmes. "If I can use your phone I might be able to get ahold of someone."

The woman brought the phone to the bed, all the while eyeing Angela's dress. "Do you mind?" She fingered the sleeve. "This is the most incredible fabric. I sew, and I've never seen anything like it. What is it? A wedding dress?"

Angela thought back to the night the mysterious dress appeared. Just thinking about Jachin made her want to cry. What could she tell the woman? That the dress was made of fairy silk? And that she had experienced an enchanted evening making love to the man of her dreams in a mythical forest, but that there would never be a wedding? That she didn't even know if the man she loved more than life itself was still alive?

She cleared the lump from her throat. She had no way of knowing if Jachin and the others were safe, but she wouldn't let herself dwell on the possibility that Kadien had killed them. "The dress was...a gift. I don't know what the fabric is. And, no, it's not a wedding dress." She dialed Information.

Two hours later, Angela sat with a stunned Mildred in the woman's cozy apartment. Angela had just told her everything and now waited to see if the woman would believe her, or if she'd be driving her to the nearest funny farm.

Mildred shook her head sadly and with a deep sigh said, "It's all so fantastic. Oh, I knew there was something...unique about Jachin. But another world? And he's a wizard?" She looked as worried as Angela felt. "I hope they're okay."

Angela put her hand on the woman's, which rested on her plump knee. "Please don't repeat to anyone anything I've told you."

Mildred looked horrified. "Oh, never. You should see what's been going on around here. Someone broke into the gallery and took photos of the melted statue. The tabloids and even the respectable newspapers are already having a field day, and I have no intention of giving them more fodder. But one thing I can say about the circus is that Jachin has become infamous, and his sculptures are selling like crazy." She puffed up her chest. "I put astronomical prices on all of them. That will show the celebrity hounds."

"At least he doesn't have to hear what the media's saying about him." Angela met the woman's gaze. "I know he didn't want to leave you with all this mess. How are you handling it?"

Mildred smiled. "By refusing to answer their idiotic questions. I go to work and lock the door. I'm even getting used to the gawkers. Most of them get bored after a few minutes and leave, but we still have a handful of regulars."

"I've got to make arrangements to get home," Angela said. She looked at her dress. "And get some clothes that don't look like I'm going to a Renaissance wedding. "My wallet and all my stuff were left...well, they're gone."

"I'll take care of everything, don't you worry. I'm sure Jachin would want me to take care of you." The woman gave her an odd look.

"What?"Angela asked.

Mildred slowly smiled. "I have the feeling Jachin would want you to stay in his house while you're here. As much as I would love the company, my little apartment can barely hold me, and I'm sure you don't want to go to a hotel."

Angela didn't know if she could face the daily reminder. But she knew she couldn't stand the thought of a hotel, either. "I suppose I could stay at Jachin's, but just until I can make arrangements to go home."

Mildred frowned in concern. "Two days ago a huge pilot's strike started, so it may take a few days to get you a flight out. I suppose you could rent a car, but after all you've been through, I don't think you should make such a long trip on your own. Can you wait a few days for a flight?"

Several days had already passed since the whole adventure had begun, so Angela wasn't about to get stressed about her job or her home. Or anything here in Luteland. Life was too short. Although she'd been on spring break from her job for the past week, she was due back on Monday. She would need to call the school and arrange for a substitute teacher for the next week or so. That would give her some time to grieve and regroup.

"I'm in no hurry to get home." What did she have to go back to, anyway? Boaz was gone. And the job she had thought would give her security now seemed like a death sentence. She renewed her determination to see the world. No longer would she hide from life behind her fears.

***

After a three-day journey back to the compound, Jachin, Boaz, Lilith and Ailleann were greeted like returning heroes. All Jachin wanted was to fall into a twenty-four hour coma in a comfortable bed, and he wanted some food that wasn't cooked on a stick.

Marrion came out of the pub and raced to meet them. "Oh, my children. You have come safely home." She embraced Lilith. "My dear, I can't imagine what you went through in Kadien's fortress. Well, you're home now, and with family."

Lilith smiled. "Kadien treated me quite well, actually."

Marrion nodded knowingly. "Kadien was playing the good host, was he? All to his own means, I am sure."

Marrion shooed the crowd of villagers away with a wave of her hand as she looked sadly at Jachin. "I know about Angela. Be assured she is well. I have viewed her."

Jachin didn't respond. The darkness that he now acknowledged seemed to be wrapped around his heart, closing out all emotion, and he wanted to keep it that way.

Boaz asked, "What about Seumas? Do you know what happened to him?"

Marrion looked concerned. "Something has happened to Seumas? We knew he had returned to Sena and that he was with you, but we didn't know anything had happened to him."

Boaz explained that Jachin had had to kill Seumas in order to save the rest of the group. Jachin acknowledged that Seumas had sacrificed himself in order to force Jachin to come to terms with his dark side.

He knew he should feel sorrow for Seumas' loss, but again, the darkness kept his heart from feeling anything.

Boaz concluded her story with, "I don't think the whole Kadien-Lord-of-Darkness-Challenge-thing is over yet. He made it sound like the big event is still to come."

Marrion nodded as she led them into the pub. "Tell me about that later. First, refresh yourselves."

They all took seats along a table. Jachin noticed that the few people in the tavern now quietly got up to leave. Ailleann excused herself and, after kissing them each on the cheek, she also left.

Marrion said. "Now the real work begins. You must be trained to work together, to combine your powers."

"Tomorrow," Jachin said. "Tonight I want a clean bed and food on a plate. Lots of it."

"Ditto," Boaz said.

"And a bath?" Lilith added hopefully

Boaz moaned loudly. "And a bath!" She took The Book of Light from her backpack and set it on the table.

Maisy came to the table, expertly balancing tankards of ale. She set them down and immediately hurried off and brought back bowls of rich vegetable and lentil stew.

Later that night, as Jachin lay alone in the fresh linen sheets, he couldn't sleep. Staring at the candle flame on the bedside table, he let images of Angela torture him. He loved her. He loved her so much it hurt. But what good did the revelation do if there was nothing he could do about it?

Jachin licked his fingers and extinguished the bedside candle. The pain of the hot wick was minor to what he felt inside. He lay there looking up into the darkness, yearning for Angela and what could never be.

SIXTEEN

**Holly Tree: The ability to live and bloom
despite harsh climatic changes. To endure.**

Using the grocery bag she was holding as a shield, Angela
walked past the small group of people lingering just outside the
security gates at Jachin's beachfront home. Mildred followed close
behind, quickly unlocking the gate. They went in, ignoring the
questions and comments from the crowd.

Once on the other side of the gate, Angela breathed deeply,
trying to get rid of some of the tension. She was glad Jachin wasn't
here to see what was going on. He might appear to be aloof and
undisturbed by the clamor, but she knew he cared about what
people thought of him.

Mildred looked at her and gave a weary shake of her head.
"You thought it was bad the day all of you left. It's ten times
worse now that the melted statue was discovered. I'm sure it will
die down when they get tired of waiting for Jachin to return."

Angela had already told Marrion that even if Jachin and the
others were safe, they wouldn't be able to cross over again until
the next Wizard's Moon. By then Angela planned on being as far
away as possible. She couldn't go through the pain of seeing him.
She would ask Mildred to call her if Jachin returned, just to let
her know he was safe. From the start she knew there could never
be anything between them. When she'd first met him she'd thought
his super-star status was the obstacle between them. But his being
a royal wizard was a barrier stronger than the magical veil around
Sena.

Mildred opened the front door and handed Angela the key.
"I've written down the security code, and I'll put it on the entry
table. I'm sure you'll feel quite safe here."

Now why had she said that? She was no longer among the
wizards who could zap her with the wave of a hand, so why
wouldn't she feel safe?

As Angela walked through the door, her heart nearly stopped. Jachin was everywhere. His scent. His presence. She halted, not sure she could go any further into his home.

Mildred gave her a gentle push. "You'll be fine. I feel certain Jachin would want you here. Besides, I would feel better if I knew someone was housesitting. I can't get over here every day to water plants and air out the place."

Taking a deep breath that seemed to become trapped in her chest, Angela set the groceries on the bar and walked across the living room. Mildred began putting the supplies away.

Scenes from the day they'd left flashed through her mind. Boaz's wickedly suggestive smile from the kitchen as she fixed dinner. Jachin scowling at her from across the room. Their kiss.

Their kiss. It was a kiss that had sealed her fate and started her on the greatest adventure of her life. She remembered how she used to be so afraid of anything the slightest bit adventurous. Heck, she'd been afraid of life. But her time on Sena with Jachin allowed her a glimpse of the wonders that both their worlds had to offer. Now nothing seemed quite so intimidating or scary. But the adventure had ended as, she supposed, all great adventures eventually did.

She walked down the hallway to Jachin's office. Her face stared back at her from the table. Jachin's last sculpture. Would he ever create anything like it again? She traced the lines of the cool bronze with her fingertips. Jachin had created every line, all the time thinking of her. Had he done this out of love?

She shook off the absurd notion. They hadn't even known each other. Even now, she knew in her heart that Jachin didn't love her. How could he? She was a Lute. She smiled at the silly term she had begun using routinely. Lute. She was a Lute, a MacAlpin, and an imperfect woman who could never hope to fit in to his perfect world.

She looked down at the scar on her palm, the only evidence that the adventure really had happened. The delicate pink scar looked a little bit like a lobster...or a scorpion, reminding her of Marrion's words about the prophecy. Marrion had said that she who holds the scorpion would …. Would what? Angela couldn't remember. Evidently screw everything up.

Sena had seemed too perfect to be real. Even with the dragons, the dark wizards, and the chaos caused by the trolls, everything seemed in perfect balance.

She walked back to the living room.

"Everything seems so...normal...so real." She turned to Mildred. "I'm beginning to believe that everything that happened on Sena was a dream." She rubbed the ridge of the scar, saying in a low voice, "Maybe I'm crazy. Maybe none of it really happened."

Mildred had opened the slider, and the cool ocean breeze blew in. Angela could hear the laughter of beachgoers mingling with the crash of the surf below. She and Mildred walked out to the deck and sat down.

"What are you going to do if Jachin never comes back?" Angela asked.

"Oh, I think he'll come back if he can, if only to settle things here. I'm sure he realizes that eventually the police would conduct an investigation if he didn't come back, and I know he wouldn't want me to be caught in the middle," Mildred answered. "Until then, I have power of attorney, so I can make sure everything runs smoothly." She looked out to sea. "If there is any way on Earth to restore *The Dance*, he'll come back just to do that."

Angela had to smile. "Jachin must trust you a great deal to give you so much control over his finances."

Mildred chuckled. "Oh, I don't think it was that so much as he really didn't care about the money. He never has. If it was all gone tomorrow, he wouldn't bat an eye."

That sounded like Jachin. Angela leaned her head back to look up into the blue nothing. A bird soared so high above that she couldn't tell what kind it was. "How do I stop thinking about him?" She thought the older woman surely must have some sage advice on the subject of love.

"Why do you want to?"

"Because every time I do, I feel like my chest is ripped open and my heart is exposed."

"Maybe bringing you here was a bad idea."

Angela hurried to reassure Mildred. "No, no, I'm fine. I have to learn to live with it. I'm sure that eventually it will stop hurting." She was sure it wouldn't, but she didn't want to burden Mildred.

Mildred got up. "Well, I've got to get back to the fishbowl. I would hate to disappoint the tourists." Mildred had told Angela how she felt like a fish in an aquarium when she sat at her desk. "I'll be by tomorrow with that friend who owns the boutique I told you about. She'll bring some things for you to try on, so you won't have to wear that dress forever." She smiled. "Although if I looked like that in it, I'd never take it off." She turned to go, but then did an about face. "What size are you?"

Angela shrugged, looking down at how the white material hugged her body. "I used to be a ten, tall. But I've lost some weight. Maybe an eight? And a size eight shoe."

"I'll have her bring a little of everything, just to be sure." With that, Mildred left.

Angela leaned back and closed her eyes, feeling like a displaced fairy princess in her beautiful enchanted dress. Time. It would just take time. Surely some day she would look back on all of this without hurting. Eventually the memories would fade, and she would be free.

Pushing herself up from the chair, she went into the house, suddenly so tired she felt weighted. Halfway down the hall to the guestroom, she changed her mind and headed down the hall to where she assumed Jachin's room was. Torture, she knew, but she couldn't resist. After all, she was only human, not a wizard who could control her emotions.

When she entered what looked like the master suite, she knew at once that this was no guest room. It was Jachin's. She ran her hand over his carved dressing table as she looked around. Jachin's aura permeated the room's dark woods and uncluttered, elegant lines. For a few moments she indulged in the fantasy that he might come through the door at any moment. But then she let reality intrude. She opened the paned doors to let in the sea breeze then turned back to pad across soft carpet to the adjoining bathroom.

After showering until the water ran cold, she indulged in the luxury of using the hair dryer. Then she went back into Jachin's bedroom and crawled into his bed. She brought the pillow to her face. Although the sheets were crisp and clean, she could still smell his scent on the pillowcase. Her heart felt like it was going to break.

***

Jachin knew he was having a glimmer dream the moment he walked through the open French doors. The curtains billowed as he passed by, and someone was in his bed.

With her golden head on his pillow, and the sheet revealing the beautiful lines of her body, Angela lay sleeping. Quietly he took his clothing off and slipped into bed beside her.

He took her in his arms, gently kissing her neck and chin to awaken her. Her eyes fluttered open and she smiled, her arms going around his neck.

"Jachin, is it really you?"

"Don't talk. Just love me," Jachin said as he ran his hand down her hip to bring her against him.

She sighed with a sadness that touched his soul. But her kisses were anything but sad. They were filled with all the passion of life. Her tongue drove deep, teasing him with its silky heat. She moved back to place little bites over his lower lip. Her hands kneaded his back, her touch hungrily moving to every part of him.

Touching and kissing, he moved over her body, showing her with his lips and hands what he had no right to tell her. When he came to the tender spot on her inner thigh, he gently kissed the little clover birthmark.

"You've put a spell on me, Angel," he murmured against her thigh, his lips continuing their teasing assault as they brushed her silky skin. He felt her response as the muscle beneath his lips quivered. She moaned.

He sensed her body softening for him, readying itself for love, and his own body responded with urgent need. But he wasn't about to give up the dream so quickly. With a clenched jaw, he controlled his passion. He wanted her to come with him.

No other woman had ever made him feel the depth of emotions now racing through him. He felt loved, and he felt honored. And he wanted to give it all back a hundredfold. She loved him. He still didn't know how or why he had been blessed with the love of such a woman, but within the safety of his dream he was going to revel in it.

His fingertips ran up her hip to her waist, then over her breast. His lips followed, eliciting frustrated moans from her. Licking one nipple, he gently teased it with his teeth. Her head went back and her breath came in short gasps. His hand moved down her stomach and across the damp curls beneath, his fingers easing across silky folds.

She gasped, arching against him with need. He captured her lips with his, his tongue mimicking the movements of his fingers. She cried out with frustrated need, and he knew she was close.

Then Angela surprised him by pulling away. With a wicked smile, she pushed him to his back, the bed giving softly under his weight. She straddled his hips, and the look in her eyes was that of a practiced lover. He knew they had only been together once, and that she had been a virgin, but he knew their souls and bodies were old friends.

She guided him into her, and a thousand sensations rocked his body. Tight heat enveloped him, squeezing and stroking as she moved. She slid over his length, driving him to her deepest core, her body tensing and her breath catching with each controlled stroke.

This time it was she who demanded, "Jachin, open your eyes. Look at me." She captured his gaze, and he felt his soul being plundered. He loved her. He knew it now, but even in the dream he dared not voice it. And the knowledge felt like it had hold of his heart, squeezing it until he could hardly breathe.

Angela began to move faster, grinding her pelvis against his. Above him the curves of her beautiful body glowed with starlight. He gave himself to the passion and love he felt for her, moving with her as they crested the wave together. As Angela cried out and shuddered with release, he joined her.

Breathing heavily, Jachin brought her body to him to hold her close.

"Jachin," she said between short breaths. "I—"

Before she could finish her sentence, Jachin awoke with a start, his labored breathing echoing in his bedroom on Sena.

He leaned back, his arm over his eyes, and his body and mind crying out for his Angel.

***

Angela awoke, her throat frozen around Jachin's name. The silence in the room was broken only by a night bird's lonely cry. She kicked the rumpled covers to the foot of the bed, letting the damp breeze cool her fevered skin. The dream had been so real, even now her body felt alive with the afterglow of Jachin's lovemaking. But, instead of feeling better for having dreamed so vividly about him, she felt a renewed sense of loss. And it was raw and painful.

Sleeping in his bed had been a stupid idea. If she was ever to get Jachin out of her system, she would have to break all ties. Slowly getting up, she went to Jachin's closet to look for someuing to wear. She chose a soft tee shirt.

Hugging the material around her, she decided the best thing to do to dispel the torturous dream was to do something that would occupy her mind. She walked to Jachin's office. Once she was there she sat down at his desk and began to make a list of things she wanted to change in her life. Going to Sena and allowing herself to love Jachin had taken her to a point of no return. She could never go back to her old life.

She started the list ten times, each time crossing off what she had written. Nothing seemed right. Sure, she wanted to travel, and she wanted adventure. But nothing she wrote down sounded as exciting as it had pre-Jachin.

Turning to stare at her likeness, she said, "I just realized that I have absolutely no purpose in life. Teaching was never really me. I can't go back to it full time. Travel? Alone? I don't think so. So, Angela Catherine Dawn, what in the heck are you going to do with your life?"

She got up and walked around the statue. "Don't give me that look, I know what you're thinking. It's not an option. He doesn't love you. Even if you fooled yourself into believing Jachin did love you, you wouldn't last a week in Sena. You'd anger some wizard or other, and they would zap you into who-knows-what world. Or zap you dead. And what about children?"

Her breath caught as the possibility she had denied on Sena now came home with a force so strong she had to sit down before her suddenly wobbly legs collapsed. She grabbed hold of the desk to stop the room from spinning. Could she be pregnant?

***

The entire white wizard village was a noisy hub of preparations for the winter solstice. Jachin wasn't in the mood, so he was in his uncle's shop, sharing metalworking knowledge. He held a fine sword they had created together. Jachin knew there was no match for it. Over the past several months he had learned how to fight with a sword, so now it seemed natural to hold it in his hand and test its weight. Even though sword fighting was pretty much a thing of the past in his world, he felt right possessing one.

Lilith came into the shop. "Jachin, Marrion is ready for your last exam." She smiled. "I hope you crammed last night. You don't want to fail."

The exam she was referring to was the last of the tests of the skills they had learned during their time on Sena. It was a test of their level of skill, so not a test that could be passed or failed as Lilith's teasing had indicated. "I'm ready," he said, putting down the sword.

Together they walked toward the Family House across the crowded yard. He'd learned a lot about Lilith in the past six months, and knew she covertly used her healing powers in her work as a pediatric surgeon in the Lute world.

"What do you think happened to your practice when you just didn't show up for work one day?"

She stared into the distance and sighed. "I'm afraid to think about it. I suppose some kind of investigation must have been done. But by now, surely the authorities have given up." She flipped the long braid over her shoulder. "I love it here, but I really miss my work back home—and I do still think of it as home. Even though I know I have a mission here, I felt like I was doing something worthwhile with my life before, too. I plan to go back with the next Wizard's Moon, if only to clear up any concern caused by my disappearance. That, and I miss my friends and my adoptive family. They must be so worried."

"I told my office manager that I might be gone for a year, so I think she's probably fine. I really don't have anyone else who would worry."

He caught Lilith's sideways glance. "I'm sure Angela is worried, just like you're worried sick about her." She put her hand on his arm. "Six months until the next Wizard's Moon. Then we can go back. You can ease your mind about Angela and take care of business, and I can see my family, friends, and patients."

Little Guennie came running to meet them, hurling herself into Jachin's arms. He hugged the girl to him, nuzzling his face into her sweet neck. She squealed, pushing him away, only to tease him into doing it again.

Over the past several months he had grown to think of her as his own, and he had Angela to thank for that. Before she had opened his spirit to love, he never would have been able to take any child into his heart. Now he felt protective of all the village's children.

"I've got things to do now, Guennie," he told the child. "You can watch, but you'll have to be very quiet." It was a request he wouldn't have had to make several months ago when she hardly spoke a word. The love he'd been able to give her seemed to have made her blossom.

"Oh, I'll pretend I'm a mouse. I may squeak a bit, but I won't say a word." She giggled again. It was a sound that rang through his heart, and it was one of the few things that helped him not to think about Angela every moment of every waking hour. How was she? Had she met anyone? Was she in love? Was she happy? Had she forgotten him completely?

He hadn't had another glimmer dream since the night she had left. Had she really been in his house? In his bed? The thought that she might have brought him comfort even though he knew it couldn't be true. Still, he allowed himself the illusion of her puttering around in his beachside home and taking walks along the shore. But why would she do that, he chided himself, when she had a life to return to in Sedona?

"Jachin," Guennie said impatiently, "you're thinking about her again." She harrumphed as only a little girl could. "If you miss her so much, why don't you go see her? My teacher says it's not good to keep the sadness locked inside. She says you must do something about it. If you don't, it will turn into an ugly monster with long fangs in your stomach. She says it will eat you from the inside out." Guennie did an overly-dramatic interpretation to show him the horrors she was describing. Then she looked at him seriously. "Is that true?"

He chuckled at the teacher's use of metaphor. "She means you'll get sick if you hold all your sadness inside."

Guennie looked relieved, but then she frowned. "I don't want you to get sick. Do something."

For months Jachin had been trying to convince the counsel to lift the veils between the worlds. They were still adamant about leaving it in place. They argued that by opening the veil, they would be opening Sena to modern pollution. Jachin argued that they had a responsibility to mankind to go into the world and fight the corruption the powers of darkness were spreading. The only reason the elders didn't accuse him of heresy was that he was one of The Triad. That and the fact that Jachin's argument had a stronger ring of truth to it as each day passed. Kadien and his legions had stepped up their campaign in the Lute world, becoming more and more influential. The seers had told them about all the chaos The Dark Ones were causing.

"I can't go see Angela," he told Guennie. "You know we can't cross over until the next Wizard's Moon."

She looked down. "I know a way. Only I'm too scared to go there."

He tickled her tummy. "Oh yeah. Well, tell me where this scary place is, Miss Smarty Pants." She had quickly caught on to his slang.

She grew still in his arms and, leaning close to his ear, whispered, "The Cave."

He stopped, nodding to Lilith to go ahead. "What cave?" Angela had mentioned a cave, but when he'd asked Marrion about it, she had said she knew the ancient stories about the Cave of Rebirth, but no one knew where it was.

Jachin lowered Guennie to the ground, crouching next to her. "Guennie, this is very important. How do you know about the cave?"

"That's where my mother and father took me. Only I was afraid and ran into the forest. But they never came out. Pretty soon the night fairies came to take me home."

He had been told that Guennie's parents were dead. "I'm sorry you were afraid, Guennie. I'm sure your parents didn't mean to scare you."

She nodded solemnly. "I know. They loved me and wanted to take me with them." Her lip quivered. "But I was afraid. Teacher says our fears are our worst enemy."

He hugged her. "It's okay to be afraid, Guennie. I'm even afraid sometimes."

She giggled. "No you're not. Everyone knows you're the bravest wizard alive, and you're going to save us from the bad wizards."

"You bet I am," he said. He took her hand, and they walked to the Family House where his test was to take place.

Several people sat around the sage-scented room's perimeter. He couldn't understand why anyone would want to attend the ceremony, since this particular exercise took place inside his mind. The task given him was to try to use his powers of concentration to create a pattern within a Lute farmer's field of wheat. He had heard stories of mysterious crop circles before. Now he knew their origin. The season had limited his choice of farms to those countries with weather mild enough to grow wheat year round. The room grew quiet as Jachin walked to the front of the large common room. He said the ancient Celtic words of protection. Once the blessing was complete, he closed his eyes and focused inward to a point of light in his mind. As he held his focus, all sound gradually disappeared. Once all thought was contained within that pinpoint of light, he visualized the field. Suddenly, he was filled with a sensation of floating, and he realized he was feeling his spirit body. The sensation was new, but not unpleasant. He maintained the visualization of the field, all the while moving deeper within his source of power.

The field's image grew stronger. Yellow shafts of wheat swayed and crackled in the temperate breeze. He could smell the earth and the fresh tang of ocean in the distance. The squawking of crows broke the peaceful setting.

Jachin envisioned the precise shape of the clover-shaped mark on Angela's thigh. Then he concentrated his powers into a compact ball of energy over the field. With the snap of an imaginary finger, he released the pattern of energy toward the field. A blast instantly flattened specific areas of the wheat into the clover pattern, the edges sharp.

He blinked and reconnected with the physical world.

Marrion said, "Well done, Jachin. Interesting pattern." Jachin knew that Marrion had been along on his mental journey into the Lute world, but she didn't know why he had chosen that particular design.

She turned to the others. "Jachin has completed his tests. He is now a full wizard. He has also chosen to take his Sena name. From now on, he will be referred to as Jachin MacCuill."

They all clapped and began dispersing, coming to shake his hand on their way out.

The exercise had left him exhausted, and he would need to regain his strength before the gathering tonight. He would again bring up the issue of lifting the veil. He had an overwhelming premonition that Angela was in trouble, but no one in Sena had been able to view her or connect with her since she crossed over. That didn't mean something had happened to her, Marrion had told him, only that she had willingly shut herself off from them. All he knew was that he had to find a way to connect with her and assure himself she was safe.

If Angela had wanted to break off all ties with Sena to help her get on with her life, then he would have to accept that. The thought of her with another man caused a sharp pain in his chest and his temper to flare in jealousy. He pushed away the images of her with another man. He had no right to her, and no right to be angry if she wanted a normal life for herself. Wasn't that what he wanted for her, too? It's what he should want for her, and if he kept repeating it to himself, someday he might believe it.

"Jachin?" Marrion's voice brought him back to the present. She motioned him toward a table and chairs. The room was empty as they sat down. She looked concerned. "Jachin, I'm very proud that you have completed with great finesse every task put before you. I sensed that you gave your heart to every aspect of them."

He nodded. "Thank you. But I hear a hesitation in your voice."

She tilted her head to the side. "I also sense that you are not yet complete. You have not faced the questions you have about your birth parents and your Lute parents. A part of you is still restless and confused and in need of answers."

He shrugged, an uneasiness circling its way around his insides. "What can I do about it? They're questions without answers."

Marrion put her hand on his arm. "Meditate, and the answers will make themselves known. You, me…everyone has locked within them all knowledge, but we must find the keys to unlock our fears and prejudices in order to have access to the knowledge. I know you have anger and hurt about why you were left with Lutes. And you have feelings for your Lute parents that you haven't explored."

He didn't want to talk about his parents—birth or adopted. They were no longer issues in his life.

She went on. "You won't be whole, Jachin, until you make peace with your parents. All of your parents."

She wasn't helping. He knew he had issues with his life as a Lute—things that needed to be faced before he could join the Lute and Wizard pieces of himself together and feel whole. But, how could he do that when he didn't have all the pieces to the puzzle? He didn't know why his mother had left. Hell, he had no way of knowing who his real father was. How was he supposed accept and forgive with so many unanswered questions?

***

Nudd, Kadien's high counsel stood next to his master as The

Dark Lord looked into his scrying bowl. Lord Kadien had been watching the Lute woman for many months now, and Nudd despised the hold the woman and her unborn child had on his master.

Kadien turned to him. "I want the child while it is still within my powers to control."

Nudd knew the importance of controlling Jachin MacCuill's child. By controlling the child, he could control the father. But the look in his master's eyes was not that of a man focused on the child. Nudd could see that Lord Kadien was enraptured with the woman. This had happened once before and had threatened the dark forces. Nudd would not let it happen again.

"I will go into the Lute world and take the child the moment it is born," Nudd said.

Kadien gave a dismissive wave, and a ball of resentment began to churn in Nudd's chest.

"I have a plan that only I can carry out," Kadien said.

"May I ask what plan?" He forced himself to keep his expression neutral.

Kadien chuckled as he turned, his eyes boring into Nudd. "I know you do not always agree with my ways, but it is not for you to question my motives."

Nudd turned to look out the window and closed his mind so The Master could not read his thoughts. He knew Kadien's true intent. It was not to gain control over Jachin's child, and thus Jachin. Lord Kadien was enamored of the Lute woman, Angela. That meant she could influence him, and that was dangerous to them all.

When he was sure his thoughts were well hidden, he turned back to Kadien and said, "I feel our energies would be better spent on those who can spread our influence throughout the Lute world."

Kadien began walking in measured steps around the room, as if counting off fathoms. "Sometimes *one* controls many."

Nudd frowned at the flimsy answer, which was not really an answer at all. "I counsel you to forget the Lute woman and concentrate on the child."

Kadien came to stand before him, forcing Nudd to meet his gaze. There was the usual hardness and determination in its dark depths. But there was also something else in in his eyes—passion for the Lute woman.

Kadien said in a tone that would broach no further argument, "I must decline your advice. Tomorrow I leave for the Lute world."

Again Nudd blocked his thoughts and bowed his acceptance. But he wasn't about to let Lord Kadien jeopardize their world because of his misplaced passions. He would sooner destroy both the woman and the child than let her influence Lord Kadien at the time of the Great Prophecy.

***

As Angela hiked along Sedona's Oak Creek Canyon, she smiled, reveling in the peace and beauty around her. She stopped short when she felt her daughter kick. Then she laughed as she walked on. That morning's sonogram had shown that her baby was a girl, and ever since she'd found out, she had been daydreaming. Just three short months, and she would be able to hold her baby in her arms.

The well-traveled trail zigzagged back and forth across the water at various points, and she had to be careful not to slip and fall in as she walked from rock to rock in order to cross the creek. She'd already witnessed two hikers getting a good foot-soaking this morning. Although the creek wasn't more than two feet deep at this point, there were lots of uneven rocks just beneath the surface. If she fell, it would be easy enough to sprain her ankle, or end up with some serious bruising as well as a good soaking. But she was an experienced hiker, and there were plenty of hikers nearby if she truly needed help. Just as she thought that, her foot came down on a loose rock, and she nearly lost her balance. Righting herself and holding her distended belly with one hand, she made it the rest of the way across without incident.

She picked a large, flat, sun-drenched rock alongside the creek and sat down to rest, easing her backpack off her shoulders. Just as she was taking off her shoes and socks to cool her feet in the creek, she heard another hiker coming up the trail. A ripple of unease moved through her, but she shook off the feeling. It was a busy enough trail, and she had never been nervous before. Surely her newfound protectiveness was because she was pregnant.

Still some distance from her, the lone hiker came around the bend in the trail, and she saw it was a man. By the casual, easy manner of his stride, she knew instantly he was no threat. He was obviously wrapped up in his own meditative thoughts and enjoying the day as much as she was.

She had time to observe him. At about six-foot-four, he was muscular yet slim, and his blond hair glinted in the dappled sunlight filtering through the trees. He had a nice face, handsome and intelligent.

He looked up from across the creek and spotted her, and a shy smile curved his mouth. He nodded a brief greeting, as was the norm for encounters on the trail, and then looked down as he began to cross the creek.

Just as he got about halfway across, his foot slipped, and he fell into the creek. Angela gasped. She should have warned him about the slippery rock.

In moments he was back on his feet, sloshing out of the creek and smiling at her with a boyish grin.

"I'm very embarrassed," he said as he made dry land, his khaki shorts and tank top soaking wet. His backpack hadn't fared any better.

Angela noticed that he spoke with a slight accent, but she couldn't place it. French maybe? European for sure. "Are you okay?"

He opened his backpack. "I do not think I am hurt. But I believe my lunch is ruined." He looked up with a wry smile. "Yes, it is quite wet."

Angela was still trying to place the accent. He had to be a tourist. Although he spoke English well enough, his speech was too stilted and formal for him to have been in the States for very long.

It was as he was going through his pack that Angela noticed his knee was bleeding. "Oh," she said. "You've cut your knee."

He shrugged. "I'm afraid my bandages are also wet."

"I have a first aid kit." She reached behind her awkwardly for her backpack.

Instantly he was at her side. "Here, let me. In your condition, you don't want to strain something." He brought her backpack around to her.

"Thanks. Sit down and dry out," she said as she got the first aid kit out and handed it to him.

He sat down a comfortable distance away and began taking off his shoes and socks. "If you are sure I won't disturb you."

"No, you won't disturb me." The funny thing was, he didn't.

Over the past few months she had avoided all contact with her friends and family, wanting to be alone. But for some reason, she felt at ease with this stranger. Maybe that was the point. He didn't know anything about her.

"Are you here on vacation?" she asked, realizing she wanted to know more about this particular tourist. He had such compelling blue-gray eyes.

"Yes. I'm here on my own. I've heard so much about Sedona." He looked at her, his gaze direct and friendly. "And you? Are you visiting?"

"No, I live here." She went on to tell him more than she intended about her life, or lack thereof, in Sedona. It hit her that she must be more lonely than she had realized, if she was chatting away like this with a stranger. But, he did have the most beguiling smile and made her feel like he understood every feeling she was going through.

He responded by telling her about himself. His name was Mark, and he was from a small village in Germany. He had two sisters who were still living at home, and he wanted to see the world before he had to go back and manage his father's business.

Angela couldn't help being surprised when he looked at her for a long, quiet moment, then asked, "Would you have dinner with me tonight?"

When she looked into his eyes, it was as if she had no willpower to deny him. Not that she wanted to. She was lonely, and he was the first man in a long time to make her feel special. Maybe Mark was just what she needed to help her get over Jachin and get on with her life.

***

It had now been nearly nine months, and Jachin was no closer to convincing the elders to raise the veil between the worlds. And tonight's gathering wasn't going well. Not even Boaz or Lilith sided with Jachin as he argued his point. "From Sena we're too limited in what we can do to help. I've heard you all say that the influences of The Dark Ones are gaining a stronger and stronger foothold in the Lute world. I've been there and seen it first hand. How can we stop them if they use the dark powers to cross over at will, while we are held back by the veil?" He looked out at the crowd, each of the villagers listening with, he sensed, an open heart.

"It has been long established that we would lose our way of life if we lifted the veil," one man said. "The outside world could come in and pollute our land, our minds and our souls."

Jachin replied, "Not if we don't let them. I'm not saying we have to post signs leading people here. Only that we, as wizards, should be allowed to freely move from world to world."

His uncle Illan said, "I feel sympathetic to those of the Lute world, but I feel we need to keep our borders intact. The threat to our people and our way of life is too precious to risk."

Jachin's chest began to ache with frustration. "At what cost? What kind of people are we if we stand by and watch the darkness overtake mankind when we can help?"

Many looked away, obviously uncomfortable.

He pressed on. "I think we can protect your—*our*—way of life, while still helping the rest of mankind. You talk of the Great Prophecy, the great battle to come between light and dark forces. Is that battle supposed to take place here? I think it is already going on in the Lute world, but how can my sisters and I fulfill the prophecy you all believe in if we are held prisoners here?"

Several people began to talk among themselves, and finally the counsel agreed to put it to a vote. But as Jachin looked around, he knew he hadn't changed their minds.

At the final count, only ten people had voted in Jachin's favor. He was sure it was a victory on some level that they were allowing the vote at all and weren't shunning him. But he was still outvoted. At least Lilith and Boaz had changed their minds and had cast their votes in his favor. And he'd seen Ailleann's hand raised as well.

The meeting adjourned, and Jachin walked into the forest, sensing more than seeing his way. He needed to be alone to think.

He wasn't sure how long he had walked when he found himself on the same beach where he, Boaz and Angela had come ashore all those months ago. Just like that night, the nearly full moon turned everything to shades of blue and gray.

He sat down at the shore's edge to watch the waves and let the breeze cool his skin.

When he felt a prickling sensation on the back of his neck, he realized someone was standing just behind the line of trees. He closed his eyes and let his senses expand in an effort to determine who—or what—was there. A feeling of dark powers came to him.

As Jachin turned toward the trees, a dark wizard stepped onto the beach and stood facing Jachin. With his feet apart in a stance of challenge and his hand at his sword, the man was prepared for battle.

SEVENTEEN

Hazel Tree: You still have much to learn. Partaking of the hazelnuts of wisdom is an ongoing affair.

Angela stood talking to friends in the hall where she and Mark had just attended a jazz concert. Mark had stopped to talk to some of the many acquaintances he'd met during the month he'd been in Sedona.

"Your Mark has become quite the spiritual leader around here," Angela's friend, Betty, commented. "And that's saying something in a town filled with New Agers. It doesn't hurt that he's yummy eye candy."

"Down girl," her husband said.

Angela could tell he was only half joking.

"He's made a lot of friends," Angela agreed. "Mark loves all people, and it shows." She looked over to see him talking with a group of teens who were listening with rapt fascination. He certainly seemed comfortable with any age group. "I've never met anyone like him."

Betty gave an exaggerated sigh. "I talked to him a few days ago, and he's got my vote...whatever he's running for. Dog catcher to President."

Her husband tugged on her arm. "It's late. Let's go."

"Sure, Honey."

Angela said good night and watched as Betty reluctantly tore her eyes from Mark and left with her husband.

A larger crowd had gathered around Mark now. He hoisted himself up to the third step on the stage, continuing in a voice loud enough to resonate through the entire auditorium. "Our future will be determined by the choices we make. We cannot hope to change the world as individuals. We must become a force of one. Thinking, breathing, and acting as one. Our strength will be in numbers...but with one intent."

As Angela listened to him speak, she began to feel dizzy, and she realized she'd been standing too long. She leaned against the doorframe and concentrated on calming her breathing.

Mark was saying, "If we are joined as one with all levels of our being, the combined power of our eternal energies will be an unstoppable force with which to accomplish our goal."

What goal? Had he stated a goal? she wondered as the dizziness returned. She must have been talking to Betty when Mark had stated his goal. She had heard him talk about spiritual oneness many times, but she had never heard any particular goal.

She looked up as the room suddenly went quiet. Mark was staring at her.

Quickly he said, "I'm neglecting someone very important. Please excuse me." He hurried to her side, concern creasing his forehead.

Angela noticed the nods as the crowd began to disperse. There was a general buzz of agreement and continued conversation about what Mark had been saying.

He took her hands. "Angela, your hands are like ice."

Much to her embarrassment, Mark picked her up. Then, with a cheerful flourish, he carried her to her car. She could see warm smiles of approval from several people they passed.

Once they were at her car, Mark gently lowered her to her feet.

"Angela." He looked deeply into her eyes, and for a moment she was lost. "I am truly sorry. I did not realize you were unwell. How negligent of me to leave you alone." He ran a finger lightly down her jaw and across her chin. "We must take better care of you and your baby." His gaze deepened. "Who knows what destiny your child holds."

A frisson of uneasiness ran up her neck and across her arms. She instantly shook it off as being more a reaction to his touch than to what he had said.

Her heart began to beat faster as she realized the look in his eyes had turned to passion. The sudden intensity of it had her heart racing. His fingers trailed down her neck and across her collarbone, causing her skin to tingle beneath his touch.

She wanted to open herself to Mark, to push away the world of Sena and the man who held her heart. Closing her eyes, she tried to do just that by inwardly chanting, *Let me accept Mark, and get on with my life.*

When she opened her eyes, Mark was smiling at her. She stared into his compelling eyes, hoping they could hypnotize her into believing she might have a chance at something special with him.

But when he leaned down to kiss her, she couldn't stop herself from turning away.

His eyes momentarily darkened as if in anger, but then they regained their cheerful spark. His voice was soft, seductive, yet resigned. "Not ready, humm?"

"No. It doesn't seem right." She looked down at her belly. As silly as she knew it seemed, she couldn't bring herself to kiss one man while she was carrying another man's baby.

Mark smiled and said, "I will...how do you say it? Take it slow." His teasing smile faded as he grew serious. Glancing down at her stomach and then back into her eyes, he said, "I am determined to eventually have you both."

She chuckled. He had a funny way of stating things, and it was even cuter because his accent made him sound like Dracula.

But comparing him to Dracula wasn't fair. He was a wonderfully caring man who had just made it clear that he not only wanted her, but that he accepted her baby as part of the package. She'd only told him that the baby's father was no longer in the picture, and he'd accepted that without question. She knew enough to realize that many men wouldn't be so generous. At that moment she made a deal with herself. She would do everything in her power to make this relationship with Mark work.

Angela stood on tiptoe, and although it was awkward with her huge belly between them, she kissed him on the cheek to seal the bargain with herself.

Mark smiled into her eyes as he placed his hands on her belly, and his touch felt hot, almost electric. Her baby surprised Angela with a hard kick.

As she pulled back with a startled laugh, her breath suddenly caught in her throat. From inside her head Seumas Scot's voice whispered urgently, "Beware!" The scar on her palm began to ache.

***

Jachin stood in the sand to face the intruder. Over sound of the pounding waves at his back, he said, "State your purpose."

The man he recognized as Kadien's high counsel, Nudd,

stepped forward and bowed. "Lord Jachin."

That was the first time anyone had called him 'lord,' and he immediately wondered why the man was sucking up to him. "What do you want?"

Nudd looked a bit nervous, but he stepped closer. "I want only to tell you of ..." he glanced around, then lowered his voice. "Kadien has gone into the Lute world to destroy your woman and take the child she carries."

For a moment Jachin couldn't breathe. A child? He forced air into his lungs. This could be a trick. He might have misunderstood the man. A child?

Jachin found that he couldn't speak. His throat had closed over an enormous lump. Angela was pregnant? It couldn't be possible, could it? She'd told him it wasn't possible.

Nudd announced, "Lord Kadien wants the child as his own, and he wants the woman dead."

Through a sudden and blinding rage that he was barely able to contain, Jachin finally found his voice. "Why are you telling me this?"

Nudd looked disgusted as he said, "Lord Kadien has lost his objectivity. I want him stopped before he falls completely under the woman's spell."

Jachin was about to say that Angela wasn't a person of magic, but then, maybe she was. Hadn't she put a spell on him? Her magic might not be the same as theirs, but it was powerful nevertheless.

"What do you expect me to do about it?"

Nudd looked at him like he was nuts. "Follow them. Destroy Kadien."

"Destroy Kadien?" Jachin was beginning to understand the man's motives. Nudd wanted Kadien's throne. "Even if I wanted to do what you're asking, I can't cross into the Lute world. So how am I supposed to destroy him?"

Nudd turned away with a snort. "You are the Great White Wizard. You figure it out."

Alone again, Jachin allowed himself to sink down to the sand. Angela was going to have his baby? Could he believe Nudd?

Yes, he could, because now that Nudd had spoken the words, he knew they were true. A searing pain ripped through his chest. If Kadien was anywhere near Angela and their child, he would kill him. But how?

He got up and began running, and he didn't stop until he was at Boaz and Lilith's bedroom door. He knocked then impatiently burst in.

Both women bolted up in their beds.

"What's wrong?" Boaz gasped.

"Angela is in trouble. I'm going to the cave to cross over, but I need both of you to help me. I'll meet you at the Family House."

They both nodded, and he left them to dress.

When he reached the Family House, he closed his eyes and mentally called Guennie's name. He knew she was highly receptive to telepathy.

Within minutes the little girl had padded out onto the lawn.

He squatted down to her level. "Guennie. Are you sure you can find the cave you told me about? Even in the dark?" With the moon nearly full, it was almost as bright as day, and even the forest would be easily navigated.

She nodded, her eyes huge with wonder. "It isn't very far, but it's hidden. But I don't want to go there. I don't want to go away."

Quickly he reassured her. "No, no, Guennie. I don't want you to go into the cave. I just want you to show me the way. Boaz and Lilith will be with us, and they'll bring you back here."

The fear left her eyes. "When you cross over, will you see my parents?"

He didn't want to disappoint her. "Where I'm going is a really big place, full of more people than you can imagine. I don't even know where to look." He added, "You know I don't have very strong telepathy."

She nodded. "I know, but try, okay? I miss them."

"Of course you do, sweetie." He gave her a hug, promising himself to make every effort to locate her parents. "Now, go get on your day clothes so we can leave."

"Tonight?" Her eyes widened again. "What about the dragons?"

"We'll take care of you, don't be afraid."

She nodded and scurried off to change clothes.

A half-hour later all four of them were headed down a well-traveled path.

Guennie stopped at a huge oak. "We leave the trail here."

"You're sure?" Lilith asked.

The little girl nodded. "I'm sure. See the mark of the dragon on the tree?"

They all peered at what looked like four long gouges in the side of the tree.

Guennie said, "My mother showed them to me." Then, with a confidence beyond her years, she took hold of Jachin's hand and started into the forest.

They walked several yards before they came to a high embankment. Guennie paused, looking for something.

"What are we looking for, Sweetheart?" Lilith put her arm around the little girl.

"My mother told me they were searching for Merlin's eye."

"Ugh," Boaz said. "I hope you didn't find it."

Guennie rolled her eyes, used to Boaz's joking.

"It looks like a big crystal sticking out from the side of the hill," Guennie said.

Jachin walked along the ridge, pushing aside the ivy growing down its side. His hand hit something hard. Brushing the ivy out of the way, he saw that it was a huge quartz crystal jutting out of the rock. "Over here," he said to the others.

The clear crystal was about three feet around, and it had a large center of what looked like obsidian. The overall appearance was that of a huge, glittering eye staring out of the mountain. Jachin could feel the natural quartz's energy, but this one also had been imbued with wizard magic. Was the tale of Merlin marking the cave true?

Guennie looked at the stone and said, "Very good, Jachin!"

He held back a chuckle, not wanting her to think he was laughing at her. She just sounded too poised for a five-year-old.

Suddenly Guennie looked shaken. She stepped back. "I don't want to go in the cave."

"You don't have to go in. Is the cave entrance close by?" Jachin knelt down to put his hands on her shoulders.

She nodded, pointing just past the Merlin's Eye stone.

He patted her. "You don't have to go any closer. I'm on my own from here." He looked to Boaz and Lilith. "Go ahead and take Guennie home now."

"I'm going with you," Boaz said.

"No. If something happens to me, I want you and Lilith to

try to get to Angela. Kadien is with her, and he intends to harm both her and ...." His gut tightened. "And our unborn child."

Boaz looked shocked, but Lilith avoided his eyes.

"You knew?" He confronted Lilith.

Finally she looked up. "Ailleann told me in the strictest confidence. She knew almost from the start...you know she can sense these things. And she had medical questions about Angela's baby...you know, because of its mixed race. We talked about genetics and magic, and, well, whether or not she should tell you about the baby."

His temper flared. He had to force down the sense of betrayal. "What right did you have to keep this from me?"

She straightened and looked him right in the eye. "What good would it have done to torture yourself, when we believed you couldn't leave Sena? You told me yourself you and Angela could never be together and that you wanted her to forget about you and have a normal life in her world. Does a baby change that? We couldn't see that it would since the barriers between you still exist. Ailleann and I decided to spare you the pain and respect your wishes."

"Well, things have changed. Kadien is with her, and if my calculations are correct, Angela is due to have the baby at any time." Just saying the word "baby" was like a punch to the solar plexus. He and Angela were going to have a baby. Why hadn't he known? From the moment he'd met Angela he'd had a telepathic connection with her. But it had stopped right after the glimmer dream he'd had when Kadien had returned her to the Lute world. She must have shut her mind off from him intentionally. He didn't blame her, but that didn't stop the hurt.

"If Angela is going to have a baby, then I'm sure as hell going to be there," Boaz stated adamantly. "She needs me."

Lilith said, "I'll take Guennie back. Boaz is right. You both need to go to Angela." She looked thoughtful. "If Kadien is with Angela, he isn't forcing himself on her. I know from personal exper ?nce that it isn't his way. His most potent weapon is his charm. It's scary how easy it is to fall under his spell. He's like some kind of handsome Svengali. Even I had moments when I felt strangely drawn to him...almost as if we were...oh, I don't know...connected. It must be because we're both wizards. At that time he was the first one with whom I'd ever come into contact.

Anyway, Kadien is like a cult leader, all charisma and charm. And it's not so much what he says as the way he says it that convinces people to give over their will to him."

Jachin remembered the way Kadien had looked at Angela, and he thought Lilith was right. Nudd was wrong about Kadien wanting to kill Angela. With a sinking feeling, Jachin realized that Kadien wanted the baby *and* Angela to become his, and he'd use whatever underhanded means he could to get what he wanted.

"You're sure you'll be okay going back alone?" he asked Lilith.

"I'm sure. I, too, have learned to use my powers, remember? I'm not afraid of the night creatures."

Just then a swarm of tiny lights entered the small clearing. Guennie clapped her hands. "The night fairies!"

Jachin had wondered what had happened to the little fairy who had said she and her people would help them against Kadien. They had all disappeared right after...the night of fairy magic, when he had made love to Angela.

One of the lights fluttered around Boaz, then alighted on her shoulder. Boaz said, "They've come to help."

Jachin arched a brow. He suspected their *help* was the reason they were standing here. "I think we've had enough fairy help."

Boaz shook her head. "She just explained that the reason they tricked you was because Gaban convinced them Angela would take you away from Sena, and that the prophecy could not be fulfilled without you. Kadien would continue to gain power until he controlled all of the worlds, including Sena." Boaz blew out a sharp breath. "Man, that little weasel, Gaban! I have a major score to settle with him when this is over. First he tries to sabotage our crossing. Then he gives me the booby-trapped backpack. Then he tricks the fairies."

"Forget Gaban. I'm going, and if you're coming with me, get your butt in gear."

The group hugged, and as they said good bye, Jachin said, "Tell the others where we've gone. Just in case ...." He left the thought unspoken.

Boaz stayed close beside him as they pushed aside the overhanging vines and entered the cave. He had no idea what to expect. "You know," he said, "this could be nothing more than an ordinary cave."

But as they stood up just inside the cave entrance, he saw a huge cavern with a high ceiling. This was no ordinary cave. Every inch of the walls was covered in huge slabs and formations of clear crystal quartz. Some of the crystals were perfect prisms, their light refracting into rainbow colors.

"Jachin," Boaz whispered. "You ever hear of Merlin's Crystal Cave? Where he went to meditate?"

"Yes."

"You think this is it?"

"Beats me."

They walked a few more steps. The walls glowed, as if each crystal was lighted from inside. Heated mist rose up from various pools of different milky colors. Jachin could feel the energy radiating from the crystals, and the vibrating hum was like an electrical transformer.

"Cool," Boaz said as she looked around in wonder. "Doesn't it feel enchanted?"

"No. Damp, claustrophobic, and noisy." Jachin had never liked enclosed spaces, and although the distance between the ceiling and walls was cavernous, the humid air was like a heavy, wet blanket.

"So," Boaz said, "What are we supposed to do?"

Jachin found himself chuckling. "I'm going to send you back if you keep asking me questions. I'm not Yoda."

Boaz did a nervous imitation of Luke Skywalker's big-eared teacher, her voice high and craggy. "Follow your heart, Luke."

"My heart says get the hell out of here." He chuckled again, suddenly feeling lightheaded. He turned to Boaz. "You feeling high?"

She pushed her hair from her face, languidly twisting it into a long rope. "Yeah. So, that's how Merlin became so wise." She laughed loudly, the sound hitting the walls and breaking apart to come back as distorted echoes. Instantly, she put her fingers over her mouth.

"Come on," he said. "Let's see where this goes, and cross your fingers that it's a way to cross over."

They walked along the bubbling pools, the mist growing thicker as they went deeper into the cave. Jachin was adjusting to the closeness, just as he had when he went scuba diving. He had to remind himself that he could breathe, that he was getting oxygen, even though it felt like he was under water.

He turned to say something to Boaz, but she was gone. "Boaz!" His shout became a hundred shattered sounds, none of which sounded like her name.

They had just passed the pools and were navigating large quartz boulders when he had last seen her in the mist. He was reminded of how they'd become separated when they'd crossed the moonbeams. Were outside forces again at work?

Then Jachin heard what sounded like the murmur of a hundred voices, each with the modulated cadence of someone engaged in a lengthy discussion. He heard women and men, and even children. Some of the voices were in languages he didn't understand. Here and there he understood a few words. *Seek...accept...forgive ...learn.* The words seemed woven throughout all the conversations.

Then he heard Boaz inside his head. *Look back, Jachin. Try to see through the fog.*

Oddly enough, he wasn't sure if the voice was telling him to 'look back' to his past, or to the area immediately behind him. He turned, staring into the mist, his head beginning to ring in cadence with the cave's tuning fork hum.

An old man, strong and tall even though he had a long white beard and hair, walked out of the fog. "Welcome." He had on draping robes and walked with a long wooden staff with a crystal at one end.

"And you are?" Jachin looked behind the man to see if Boaz was close by.

"Boaz is safe. She is on the correct path. While you, Jachin, have wandered off."

The man studied him, a knowing smile curving his mouth. Jachin noticed that the man's gaze was clear, intelligent, and had a directness Jachin had seldom seen in anyone. He also noticed the eyes staring back at him were the exact burgundy-brown of his own.

Finally the man said, "You have many questions." He waved the staff around. "This is the place of answers."

"You know the answers to my questions?"

"As do you, Jachin. I am only here as a mirror. In looking at yourself, it is difficult to avoid the answers, is it not?"

This was ridiculous. He wasn't going to play a game of riddles with the man. He knew he was talking about the generational knowledge Jachin had picked up during the ceremony to recall the past. And that the man was just like the little boy, Jake—some kind of Otherworld part of Jachin. He also knew the man meant that he needed to stop avoiding the answers that had been in front of him all along. But it wasn't that simple. Some of the questions were unanswerable.

After a resigned sigh, Jachin began what he was sure would be a long questioning session with nothing coming easily. "Why were my sisters and I left with the Lutes?"

Almost before the words left his mouth, the answer came to him. Just as Seumas had said, their mother had been trying to protect them.

The man smiled as if he'd heard Jachin's thoughts.

Maybe the deeper questions wouldn't be so easy. "Why did our mother leave us with the Lutes and not in some other magic world?"

The man never moved his lips, but Jachin heard him say, "You are the bridge from your people to the Lutes. She knew you needed to live their ways in order to understand them."

"Why did she leave? We could have lived in the Lute world together."

The old man looked hard at Jachin. "You are still angry with your mother, and it is blinding you to the truth."

Pain as raw and unfiltered as that of an eight-year-old ripped through him. He had trouble speaking. "Hell, yes, I'm angry with her!" His voice was unsteady, even though he shouted. "She didn't care enough to stay with us!"

Kadien would have found you if she had stayed. The old man's voice was inside his head and echoing through the cave at the same time. *Kadien would have taken you if he had found you. Your mother had a connection with Kadien, which couldn't be broken while her spirit lived. She sacrificed herself to save her children.*

His entire body began to tremble as he said, "I don't believe you. She was a powerful wizard. She could have protected us on Sena or anywhere."

The man shook his head. "Think, Jachin. You know in your heart that she only did what she had to do. She did it with love and an unselfish spirit. She gave up what she wanted most in the world—her children—in order to protect you from Kadien. Why do you think Kadien was such a threat?"

Jachin guessed he wasn't the only one allowed to ask questions in this crazy scenario. "Kadien was a threat because he wanted to prevent us from growing up and fulfilling the prophecy."

"That is only the obvious," the man said, looking from beneath thick eyebrows.

What more could there be? What was he missing? Kadien wanted to control all of the worlds and to spread his darkness and poison throughout the heart of mankind. As far as Jachin could see, stopping The Triad was the surest way to do that. But by the look on the old man's face, he was sure he was failing this test miserably.

The man said, "What could make a powerful wizard such as Vivian afraid of Kadien? What secret gave Kadien power over her?"

The old man waved his staff. Immediately he began to change. Jachin stepped back as the man transformed into a winged dragon with red cat eyes. It writhed and hissed. *Name your greatest fear, Jachin, and you will find your answer.*

Jachin unsheathed his sword. How in hell was he supposed to figure out his greatest fear while he was about to be attacked by himself as a fire-breathing monster? Lute therapy was beginning to sound pretty good. Why couldn't they just *talk* his issues out?

The dragon lunged toward Jachin, but amazingly it kept its mouth closed.

Think, Jachin told himself. *What is your greatest fear? Your evil. Where does it come from?*

The dragon opened its huge jaws, yellow teeth glistening. Again it lunged. Jachin held his sword high, knowing this was some kind of test, but not knowing if the thing would—or could— actually kill him.

Your fears can kill, came the answer.

My fear. The evil. What is its source? He stood his ground, and the dragon's eyes glittered as they stared into his soul. *How in hell am I supposed to know its source?*

The dragon raised up, its body became rigid as it lifted off the ground and readied to dart at Jachin. Jachin knew if he didn't answer the question correctly, and soon, he was going to be attacked.

The source of his evil? What was it? His mother? His father? But who was his father?

The dragon shot forward so fast Jachin didn't have time to brace the sword. He was knocked off his feet as the beast slammed into him. Excruciating pain shot though his back, and his head began to spin. The humming in his ears grew louder as he scrambled to the side before sharp teeth could rip his flesh. Breath like rotten eggs made him gag.

Who was his father? He had to find the answer. Marrion had said he knew all the answers if he would only listen to his heart. *Who was his father? Who was evil ...*

The dragon swung around and scrambled toward Jachin, its huge jaws closing fast around Jachin's middle. As Jachin felt bones break and his heart burst, he acknowledged the man he knew was his father.

Kadien, his mind screamed as he plunged his sword into the dragon's throat.

The world went black.

***

As Angela packed her hospital bag, she reflected on how peaceful she felt when she was with Mark. He was charming, thoug..tful, and terribly romantic. Too bad her heart felt like a dead weight inside her chest. The only feelings of love she felt were for her baby. But then, many people lived long and happy lives without a man to love. She would still have her child, and a man whom she felt secure with. She never again wanted the kind of passion and emotional connection she'd had with Jachin. All she wanted was a peaceful existence with her baby.

Although for her entire life she'd insisted that, no matter what, she would only marry for love, she was beginning to change her mind. Had Mark been right when he said that raising a child on her own was selfish? She'd always believed children needed a mother *and* a father to live a normal life. And all she'd ever wanted was a normal life, right? Thoughts of living with Jachin in his magical world intruded, and she quickly pushed them away. As Mark had said, she needed to look long and hard at what her choices were, here in the real world.

She put away all thoughts about her future with or without a man. Thoughts of Jachin kept intruding, and when she began to ponder the things Mark had talked to her about, her thinking became unfocused. For now she would concentrate on the only thing that mattered, her child.

She zipped the bag and took it into the living room to set it beside the door. Her childbirth instructor had warned the class just last night that it was better to be prepared to hurry out the door just in case their labor went unexpectedly fast.

Just as she set the bag down, the doorbell rang, so she reached over to open the door.

Mark stood there with a wide smile, holding a beautiful bouquet of flowers..

"Thank you," she said as she took the flowers, all the while thinking that while she should be grateful for the gesture, she was feeling sad that in three days' time the bouquet would look...dead. She motioned him inside.

Mark saw the suitcase, and he turned serious as he looked around the small room. "Someone here? Or are you leaving?"

"Baby. Remember? Clothes for the hospital?" She pointed to the suitcase.

He smiled as he shut the door. "You're not due for another week."

She walked to the kitchen to put the flowers in water. "I just want to avoid the Keystone Cops routine I see on television so often...you know, everyone goes crazy when the woman goes in to labor, and they forget everything...including the mother."

Mark took a seat at the counter. From his weak smile, she knew he had no idea what she was talking about. Maybe in his country that type of comedy wasn't big. She said, "Anyway, the midwife said the baby could come any time now, so I thought I'd better get my hospital bag packed." She began arranging the flowers in a vase. Already they seemed to be wilting.

She looked up to see Mark staring at her with an oddly intense look. He quickly blinked it away and smiled.

"I think," he said, "that I should stay with you until the baby comes. And even after. So I can..." he hesitated a split second, "...help."

She laughed. "For heaven's sake, why? I'm perfectly fine. When I go into labor I'll call a taxi." She wasn't ready to have Mark move in, even for a short while. "As for afterwards, I have a Doula on call. She'll take care of everything ...just like my own mother would if she...could." *Or wanted to*, she added to herself. Then she brushed the selfish thought away. She was only feeling the lifelong disappointment of her mother not being there for her when she was a child.

"Why isn't your mother coming to help?" His words were a gentle accusation, but they made her defensive. "You said your parents are still alive, isn't that so?"

"My parents are archeologists. They've got commitments. And I have everything I could need. It seems silly for my mother to come half way across the world just to help out for a couple of days." Now, why was she making excuses for her parents?

He surprised her with, "I'm sure they are disappointed they cannot be here."

She breathed out the breath she'd been holding. She didn't bother telling him that she hadn't even told her parents she was expecting. Instead, she smiled at the completed flower arrangement. "So pretty."

Mark came around the counter and set the flowers aside. "Come here." He opened his arms, inviting her come to him because he'd told her he didn't want to force her to do anything. He'd said he wanted her to come to him of her own free will.

She hesitated. *You've got to get over Jachin. Shut him from your mind and open your heart to Mark.* She stepped into his arms.

***

Boaz rushed toward the awful sounds. She could have sworn she heard Jachin cry out in excruciating pain. "Jachin!" she called, but the sound was broken apart and distorted by the rock walls' humming. The mist, which had at first seemed sweet-smelling and tranquil, now became cloying.

"Jachin!" she called again, but only her own echo came back to her.

Then she rounded a corner and saw something in the path. It was Jachin, lying on his side. He was way too still.

Horrified, Boaz ran to him and knelt beside his lifeless form. She couldn't see any injuries, but neither could she see him breathing. To her astonishment she saw that his hair had turned gray at the temples.

Gently, she shook his arm, and he rolled him to his back. His lips were blue. "Jachin?"

He startled her when he suddenly gasped for breath, and his eyes flew open. His breathing was ragged, as if he had been holding his breath for a long time. Finally his breathing slowed, and he looked fearfully around the cave.

"What's wrong?" she asked as she, too, looked for whatever might have caused this to happen to him.

She watched as he frantically felt his chest and abdomen, and then brought his hand before his eyes as if searching for something. An expression of relief was followed by several deep breaths.

"God," he said, looking around again. "You didn't see a dragon? Or an old man?"

"No." She looked into his eyes, feeling relief that they were clear. She hadn't seen anyone during the time they had been separated. "Did you?"

"I was attacked." He looked at his abdomen. "And bitten. At least I thought I was."

His features settled into a hard, cold line. "I know who our father is."

What in hell was he talking about? "And just how do you know that when no one else does?"

He jerked his head to indicate the cave. "This cave is just what Angela said it was. Some kind of collective unconscious." He looked at the walls. "I think the vibrations we're hearing, somehow allow us to tap into our subconscious knowledge."

Boaz eyed him doubtfully. "And how did tapping into your subconscious knowledge tell you who our father is? And just who do you think he is?"

She took a breath, suddenly acknowledging the obvious. She held up her hand. "No, don't tell me. The Big Bad Guy."

Somehow it didn't upset her to realize Kadien was their father. She didn't feel any connection to him and knew she never would. Her Lute dad would always be the father she loved. "Jeez, talk about having a jerk for a father. I'd heard so many of my friends tell me about how rotten their dads were, but I think ours takes the biggest jerk award hands down."

Jachin frowned. "How can you joke about it? He's our father. We have his blood running through our veins."

"So? Who cares? I'm still Boaz Hamilton-MacCuill. I can

choose to be whomever I want. And I choose not to be like Kadien. I am, and will remain, a white wizard."

She looked at the pained expression on her brother's face and knew what he was thinking. "Look at me, Jachin. You are not like Kadien. The darkness is within all of us. But we have a choice as to whether or not we use it."

"But it's there. The evil is there. It will always be a threat to me...especially now that I know its source."

But, then again, maybe she was right. He looked up at her, grateful that she was always levelheaded.

At that moment, he understood that the dragon he'd just faced was a symbol of what he had been struggling with his whole life. He had the power to use the darkness or turn away from it. Hadn't that been proven when he faced Kadien at his fortress?

"You're right. I don't have to be like Kadien. I am Jachin Morgan-MacCuill." He chose to be a white wizard, and he would find a way back to Angela to face the man who was, even now, threatening her, their child, and the balance of energies in the worlds.

Boaz put her hand out. "If you're feeling okay, we need to get going. I'm getting a strong feeling that time is running out."

Jachin got up, noticing the staff next to his sword. It was the one the old man had held. He picked them both up, putting the sword into the sheath.

"Wow, cool. Where'd it come from?" Boaz asked, eyeing the staff.

Jachin chuckled as he looked at the long stick with the crystal ball tip. "Come on, I'll explain while we try to find our way out of this labyrinth."

He directed Boaz toward a small tunnel emitting a fresh, salt-scented breeze.

As they walked, crouched over to accommodate the lower ceiling, Jachin could see a strong light up ahead. The light grew brighter as they made their way along, and it was soon apparent they were nearing an opening in the cave wall.

Bright sunlight shown through a dense fog as they emerged. It reminded Jachin of his home in Laguna Beach, where just moments before the sun burned through the morning fog, the thick haze would become brilliant with refracted light.

"Do you hear that?" Boaz asked. "Waves. We must be at some

kind of shore."

They walked several yards across soft white sand toward the sound of the crashing surf. Jachin had no idea what he had expected to see, but it wasn't a beach with early morning joggers and surfers!

EIGHTEEN

**Apple Tree: A spiritual warrior who is unafraid
to face death or travel to the Otherworld.**

Marrion called a gathering of the elders as soon as Lilith told
her about Boaz and Jachin's attempt to leave Sena. Now all nine
elders, as well as Lilith, waited patiently for her to speak.

She walked to the head of the family gathering room. "We
have a situation, and immediate decisions need to be made." She
went on to tell them everything Lilith had told her about Kadien,
Angela and Jachin. She also told them that she had been in
telepathic contact with Boaz, and that she was sure Jachin and
Boaz had, indeed, crossed over through The Cave of Rebirth.

Murmurs about Merlin's cave echoed around the room.

"As I see it," she continued, "The Triad and the positive
outcome of The Great Prophecy have been put in jeopardy by
Kadien going into the Lute world and Jachin and Boaz following
him."

Illan stood up. "The prophecy does not mention where the
great confrontation is to take place. Perhaps it is supposed to take
place in the Lute world." He sat back down.

Marrion saw agreement among many of members.

Lilith stood and came to take her place next to Marrion.
Although Marrion had been acting as the clan's regent matriarch
in Vivian's absence, it was now Lilith and Boaz, as Vivian's female
descendents, who should be jointly holding the position of
reigning High White Wizard. And, although Lilith had only been
with them a short time, she had gone through the training and
memory regression and knew almost as much as any wizard in
the room. Marrion stood to the side, deferring to her niece. She
had to admit, she was glad to finally be able to hand the
responsibility over to Lilith now that her niece was ready to claim
her rank. She hoped that soon all three children would take their
rightful places among the elders.

Lilith smiled at everyone, her nature, which consisted of both
an iron will and gentleness, exuding in a rainbow aura. "I feel in

my heart that the coming of The Triad was a portent of more than the inevitable confrontation with The Darkness. I believe, just as Jachin has been trying to convince you, that our ties to the Lute world were meant as a new beginning." She smiled calmly at each of the members. "It is time to bring our powers together to remove the veil between the worlds."

Talk erupted around the room, but Lilith held her hand up for silence.

"I know that neither of our worlds is ready for complete and immediate integration," she said. "But we are ready to begin the process. It is time to take the first *cautious* steps toward restoring the balance of magic throughout the worlds. It is time to reintegrate our wisdom and knowledge into the Lute world."

One of the elders stood to be recognized.

"Yes?" Lilith said.

"What of our way of life? What will happen when our people leave and others come in? I fear the life we know will vanish."

Lilith nodded. "I believe the wizard's way of life will *change,* not vanish. Remember, I am asking for a slow change, one that will be monitored and directed to preserve the balance here as well as restore the balance there."

One of the elder women stood. "Our magic will be diluted if we mix with other races, just as it did with the MacAlpin tribe. Then they used it against us."

"One MacAlpin almost destroyed our people eleven hundred years ago." Lilith looked at Marrion and smiled before turning back to the group and saying, "And his descendent...Angela Catherine Dawn...has removed the curse by saving Jachin's life when he faced Kadien. Not all MacAlpins have given themselves over to evil. They do have traces of our blood in their veins, and I am sure many, like Angela, are kind and good."

There was more murmuring among the gathering. Marrion could see that they were trying to digest all that Lilith had told them.

Marrion stepped forward, and Lilith nodded to give her the floor. She said with a sigh, "I am convinced our lives are unfolding as they should. As far back as our Scottish Pict tribes, and even back to our Irish Tuatha de Danann roots, we mingled freely with the Lutes. Before the Lutes were corrupted by The Darkness, they looked upon us as healers and scholars. Maybe with the coming of The Triad and the confrontation with The Darkness, it is time to go among them once more, and again open them to the Universal Knowledge."

She glanced from one elder to the other, making sure all their minds were open, then went on. "Now that Kadien has crossed over, we are all sensing an increased unbalance in the Lute world. He is spreading The Darkness quickly. It is only a matter of time before he calls his legions from Sena to follow. I feel we must do all we can to help restore that balance before it is too late. We can only do that if we can cross into the Lute world."

Illan again stood. "Will we be able to lift the veil after such a long time?"

"Maybe with our combined energies, we could weaken it, but I'm not sure we could...or should...lift it completely."

"What good would there be in only weakening the veil?" Illan asked.

Lilith stepped forward and said, "With a weakened veil and all your powers, I could return to the Lute world and reunite with Jachin and Boaz. I believe we are to face The Darkness in that world, not Sena."

Another elder woman stood. "But what about Merlin's cave? Jachin and Boaz crossed over that way. Why can't you?"

Marrion shook her head. "Lilith and Guendoloena tried to find The Cave of Rebirth to show it to me, but we could not find it. It has once again concealed itself. Apparently the cave only reveals itself to certain people, such as Guinnie's parents and Jachin and Boaz." Marrion was exhausted when, far into the night, the elders finally decided to weaken the veil and help Lilith cross over. They determined, however, that they would not attempt to lift th veil entirely until they had discussed it and meditated on the matter further.

She was relieved when they also decided that Lilith should take one of Sena's residents with her, and since Ailleann had accompanied Jachin and Boaz on their quest for Lilith, she was the one they chose to go. Lilith had had the least amount of time to adjust to her wizard powers, and Marrion felt the girl needed someone with her who could help her see the traps Kadien was sure to have set for her.

"So it is settled," Marrion announced to the group. "The great gathering of power will take place tomorrow when the moon is full and our magical powers are heightened."

***

As she turned her car onto a small, unmarked road leading toward the red rock cliffs, Angela wasn't sure where Mark was directing her to go, but she was beginning to get worried. She had never been down this road before, and they were far enough away from town to be in trouble if she should go in to labor. Besides, the black storm clouds churning above the red rock formations looked like someone had angered the rain gods, and they were about to do battle.

She was driving and following Mark's directions toward what he claimed was a little known but powerful energy vortex he had heard about, and he was insisting they visit it before the baby was born.

"Mark," she said as she turned onto a dirt road at his instruction, "I've been to plenty of the vortexes, and believe me, they're not all they're cracked up to be."

She noticed a lone man walking beside the road, going in the same direction as they were headed. He didn't look up as they passed.

Mark smiled encouragingly. "Trust me. This vortex is powerful. The spots you have visited have been depleted by tourists."

She chuckled. "Depleted? Isn't that like the Pacific Ocean running out of water?"

He looked at her like he didn't understand. "I think you will come to like where we are going."

Come to like? There went his weird way of talking again. And didn't he have a sense of humor at all? So her reference to the ocean wasn't all that witty, he could have given her a courtesy chuckle. But that wasn't Mark. Come to think of it, she had never known him to show any sense of playfulness.

Without warning, her thoughts turned to Jachin, as they often did. At first she had thought him devoid of humor. But after their trek through Sena and his encounter with Jake, he had loosened up and revealed a gruff kind of silliness. Maybe it was the same with Mark. He just needed to get in touch with his inner child. Although in Mark's case she didn't know if she was willing to wait around for the change.

She glanced at him to find him studying her. Why did he

always stare at her like he had a secret?

And why in hell was she getting so grumpy all of a sudden? The nagging backache from the car ride might have something to do with it.

The uneven dirt road was bumpy and uncomfortable, and she was beginning to wonder if she, too, had lost her sense of humor. She said, "I don't think all this bumping is good for the baby. I...humpf!" She clenched her teeth and gripped the steering wheel as a pothole came from nowhere and jerked a tire to the side. She was getting more upset by the minute as her belly began to ache from tightening her muscles against the jerking of the car.

"Mark, I'm not feeling very well." She pulled to a stop beside the canyon wall.

Again he smiled, and for a moment she wanted to slap his face.

He said, "We are here. I am sure you will feel better once you stretch."

But as she got out of the car and began to adjust her tangled dress, she found that she couldn't stand up straight. Her abdominal muscles were locked in a vise grip. She stood there, holding onto the door for a few moments, trying to breathe slowly and relax her muscles.

Mark came around to stand next to her. He placed his hand on her belly. "It is time, then." It was almost as if he was talking to himself.

Time for what? Time for the baby? He couldn't know, when even she wasn't sure if her pains were cramps or contractions.

Whatever the tightness was, it was easing up and she could talk again. "I don't think we should have come. Let's go back to town. I'm not feeling right."

When she looked up at him, an easy smile curved his lips as his gaze captured hers. She felt powerless to blink or look away. She gave herself over to the feeling, and her head began to spin. Or was the world around her spinning too fast? His eyes were the darkest blue. So dark, they were almost black.

"You must trust me...Angel," Mark stated.

She stared at him in disbelief. Had he called her Angel? Only two other men had ever called her by that name. Jachin and...

"You want to love me, Angel."

She couldn't break away from his gaze. Of its own accord

her head nodded. She did want to love him. If she could love Mark, all the hurt and anguish of loving Jachin would go away.

"Say it, Angel. Say you give yourself to me of your own free will. Just say it once, and I will protect you and your baby always." His eyes bored into hers. "Say it, Angel, and you both will belong to me forever."

Angela opened her mouth, but she couldn't say the words. She wanted to, but there was a warning bell in her head. This wasn't right. Why was Mark insisting she say the words? She was getting that creepy Count Dracula feeling from him, which was ridiculous. Mark had never been anything but kind and giving. It was just that darned accent and choice of wording that made him sound Bella Lugosi-ish. Then she remembered something Marrion had said on Sena. Something about free will. A wizard could only control a person if that person willingly gave them control.

But Mark wasn't a wizard. He was just a man, albeit a charming, charismatic one. And if she couldn't open her heart to him, she would never have a normal life.

"I will love you forever," he told her.

She could tell by his expression that he meant it.

"And," he continued, "your child will be my own...as if my blood flowed through its veins."

Her abdomen began tightening again, and this time she was sure it was a contraction. She needed to get in the car and get back to town, but she couldn't seem to move away from Mark's gaze.

"Tell me," he said, "what you want most in life."

Jachin. She and Jachin raising their baby together. But she could never have that.

As the contraction eased, she said, "I want my baby to belong to a family. I want it to have a mother and father who will love it." Her throat closed up at the remembered ache of missing her own parents. "I want my child to know its parents will never leave."

Mark put his hand on the back of her neck, massaging it as his eyes continued to gaze into hers. "It is yours. If you want it. I will promise to keep you both forever."

Keep them? Forever? She had the urge to laugh, but a growing lethargy wouldn't let her. She felt giddy and lightheaded.

Angela could have sworn she heard an owl hoot in the distance, and it seemed to be talking to her. But the sound came from so far away, she was certain she was only letting her overactive imagination take hold.

She swayed, but Mark's firm hand on her shoulder steadied her.

"Say it, Angela. Say you want me to take care of you. You know you don't want to be in the world...alone."

Alone. The word repeated itself. *Alone.*

Another contraction hit, this time with a vengeance, forcing her eyes closed. Instantly the lethargy disappeared, and her head cleared. "We've...got...to get back...to...town." She tried to move, but her abdomen hurt with the effort.

But Mark gently supported her. "No, my pet. Not until you say it. I want to know the baby is mine when it is born. Then we will be sealed forever."

The contraction eased, and she opened her eyes. Mark captured her with his gaze again, his voice coaxing. "Say it, Angel. This is what you want, and you know it."

Why was she hesitating? He was right. It was what she wanted. Wasn't it?

She opened her mouth to say yes ....

***

Jachin and Boaz barely took the time to adjust to their surroundings when they realized they had emerged from the cave onto the Laguna Beach shore.

"We have to hurry," Boaz told him. "I feel an overwhelming urgency to get to Angela as quickly as possible."

They headed straight to his beach house.

Mildred was at Jachin's, watering plants when they arrived. After containing her joy at seeing them, she explained what was going on with Angela, who had kept in touch.

Jachin's heart stopped when Mildred told him that Angela was seeing a man named Mark. He didn't bother to explain to Mildred that he was certain Mark was Kadien in disguise.

Seven hours later, he and Boaz were driving through the Arizona desert toward Sedona, his mind open for any sense of Angela. The billowing, black thunderheads high above and the air's stillness told him they were driving into an impending storm.

"Jachin, slow down," Boaz said. "We don't have time to stop

for a ticket."

He eased up a bit on the accelerator. It felt good to be back among the Lutes again. Back driving a car. Back using a credit card. He now felt at ease in both worlds, and he realized it had less to do with the people who inhabited the worlds than it did with the changes that had taken place within him. Those changes had begun with Angela. He had wanted to be a better person for her, and he'd faced those parts of him which he had denied all his life because he had wanted to be a whole person in her eyes.

"Are you getting any sense of her at all?" he asked his sister.

Boaz frowned. "I'm getting some strange disturbances, but it's probably because of the electricity in the air. It's like static. I just get a sense of her, and something interferes with it. I know she's close by, though."

Jachin again opened his mind to Angela, visualizing her as she was in the forest on Sena. *Please open your mind to me, Angel. Let me in. I need to find you.*

Boaz said, "Take the next exit. It will take you into Sedona."

If Jachin hadn't been so worried about Angela, he would have enjoyed the breathtaking beauty as the red rock formations suddenly emerged when they rounded a bend. It was as if Sedona was some kind of hidden, magic valley.

"Stop!" Boaz cried out.

Jachin braked and pulled to the side of the road. "What?"

"She's close by. I can feel her. And she's afraid."

"Afraid of Kadien?"

Boaz closed her eyes to focus inward. Jachin knew it helped to enhance her powers of telepathy.

Opening her eyes, she gave a disbelieving shake of her head, "No. She's not afraid of Kadien...even though he's with her." She swallowed. "She's afraid because she's in labor." Boaz began wringing her hands. "Oh, God." She closed her eyes. "She's near a cave of some sort...close by." She put her fingertips to her temples. "Go ahead and drive, Jachin, but go slowly. I'll tell you where to turn."

***

Convincing Angela she needed to stretch her legs, Mark had walked her a short distance into the little canyon. Before she was even aware of what he was doing, she'd found herself standing in a cave.

Angela wasn't sure why she had gone with him when she'd really wanted to get back into the car and head to the nearest hospital. When she'd taken the natural childbirth classes she hadn't intended on the birth being *this* natural. She really didn't want an *a la* Flintstones birth in a cave. A midwife and a nice cozy birthing room was what she'd had in mind. With a cute little rocking chair. Doing this on her own was out of the question.

At least Mark had quit trying to get her to say she and the baby belonged to him. She'd almost said it, too, but then a contraction had hit, and she wasn't able to talk. Now all she wanted to do was go back to town.

"We've got to go, Mark. This is pretty, but I think—" She doubled over, leaning against the cave wall as another contraction put so much pressure on her inner thighs that she thought the baby might drop out at any moment. She remembered to breathe slowly, focusing on relaxing her face, her neck, her arms, her abdomen. When the contraction was over, she felt sweat beaded along her upper lip.

"We'll leave in a few more minutes," Mark said. "Look at this." He held his hands up as he turned around.

She took a deep, cleansing breath and looked around for a comfortable spot on the ground. All she saw was dirt and more dirt. She needed to get to a hospital.

The inside walls of the cave were of the same rich, red rock as the surrounding canyon. But instead of layered, crumbling stone formations like the hills outside, the cave was swirling arches which seemed to be in motion. It was as if the sediment had once been liquid and by some magic had instantly hardened as it flowed. Light from above cast an eerie but beautiful, blood-red illumination against the upper walls.

Mark said, "Do you feel the vibrations of the vortex?"

That odd humming was still in her ears, but she wasn't sure that was from the vortex or nerves. She realized she was beginning to feel better. Maybe she wasn't in labor after all. But if that was false labor, she wasn't looking forward to the real thing.

"Do you feel a renewed sense of energy and well-being?" Mark walked to her and took her hands in his.

She said, "I do feel better." She breathed deeply, instantly tasting the minerals in the cave's dust.

Mark took her shoulders in his hands and straightened her to face him. "Commit yourself to me now. I promise, you will not regret it. I will keep you safe. All you wish for will be yours."

***

"Turn down that road, Jachin." Boaz pointed to a road Jachin could barely see with the growing dusk. He made a sharp turn, accessing the road that seemed to lead to nowhere.

Over the ridges ahead, an impatient moon, enormous in the blue, peeked from behind the billowing storm clouds and gave off the brilliance of a streetlight. It was as if it couldn't wait for darkness, as though it had an urgent mission.

As they rounded a curve leading down into a little ravine, Jachin had to slam on his breaks to avoid hitting a man who was standing in the middle of the road as if he was expecting them. Luckily they barely missed him.

"Shit!" he and Boaz said in unison.

"What the hell is he doing out here in the middle of nowhere? And in the middle of the road, for gods sake," Jachin said.

"And, I might add," Boaz said, "why is he *still* standing in the middle of the road?"

They hurriedly got out of the car to see if he was okay, and Jachin cursed the delay. He felt like a ticking bomb about to go off. He had to get to Angela.

As soon as they got close to the man, Jachin *smelled* who it was. The sharp scent of kerosene made Jachin's eyes tear. Gaban was obviously in Lute disguise. "Gaban!" Boaz shouted the accusation as she held her nose.

By the amount of sweat running down the man's face, Jachin could tell Gaban was very nervous. And if Gaban was here and nervous, then that meant only one thing. His boss had to be close by.

"Get back in the car, Boaz. I'll run him down if I have to."

"No!" Fear and nervousness were evident in Gaban's voice. "I've come to warn you. You must not go any further! Kadien will kill them both if you interfere."

"Interfere with what?" Jachin bellowed. What in hell was Kadien doing out here with Angela?

Boaz started back toward the car, looking over her shoulder. "Like we would believe anything you say, you little worm."

"No, I swear," Gaban said, twisting his hands. "I know The Master will incinerate me if he finds out I've told you, but …"

He looked around fearfully. "The Dark one has taken the Lute for his lifemate and claimed the child as his own." He repeated, "He has already claimed them as his."

Jachin felt like he'd been slugged in the stomach. It had to be a lie. Angela would never go to Kadien willingly, and Kadien couldn't take her against her will. He turned and headed toward the car.

Gaban was after him in a second. "Don't you see? If Kadien takes the Lute as his lifemate...it means...it means he loves her. Love. The Dark One loves! It means she controls him. He does not control her."

Jachin only half-listened to Gaban's attempt to stall. He slammed the door and started the engine.

Gaban shouted after him, "If you let Kadien take the Lute women as his, his powers will be weakened. You will then be able to conquer him. Don't you see?"

Gaban followed them to the car, switching to a different tack. "You know all Lutes have traitorous hearts, so why bother with her? If she wants Kadien, then let her have him. What is one more Lute to you, Jachin MacCuill? You are one of The Powerful Ones. The woman has betrayed you and all of your kind."

"To hell with Kadien, and to hell with you," Jachin said as he shoved the car into drive and jammed his foot down on the accelerator. Rocks and dirt sprayed as the jeep's wheels locked into four-wheel drive and they sped off.

"That lying little weasel! Where's a match when you need one!" Boaz said. "Did he really think we would just walk away and leave Angela to that...that ...aargh!"

While Boaz's frustration was rendering her inarticulate, Jachin was too angry to respond at all. If any part of what Gaban said was true, then Angela was in more trouble than he'd thought. If she was knowingly giving herself to Kadien ....

He left the thought unfinished as something dark settled over his soul. She had no right. The baby was his.

What was he thinking? Was he actually starting to believe that manipulating little slime? Trolls were notorious for planting seeds of discontent. Jachin shook off the bad thoughts about Angela.

Angela loved him. He was sure of it. She would never willingly give herself into Kadien's hands. But if she didn't know it was Kadien...? He floored the gas pedal, oblivious to the bone-jarring jolts as the car wheels hit ruts and potholes.

Boaz said, "Just over there, Jachin. See! There's a car. Pull over!"

Jachin stopped the Jeep, jamming the gearshift into park. He grabbed his sword and the staff and got out.

The fact that the churning black clouds directly over the canyon looked like something out of a Stephen King movie didn't give Jachin the best feeling in the world.

"This way," Boaz said, running along the cavern wall.

They twisted and turned a short distance among the rocks before they came to a cave.

"They're in there." Boaz stood strait and tall, looking like a warrior ready to do battle. Jachin had no idea what kind of battle lay ahead. With Kadien, it could be physical, mental or spiritual—or a combination of all three.

The pendant around Jachin's neck came to life as he called on his powers. Together, he and Boaz cautiously moved to the cave entrance to stand and listen.

"Say it," Jachin heard a man say. He didn't like the sound of the man's voice echoing from within the cave. The command in it was seductive, hypnotic.

"Mark," Angela said, and Jachin's heart clenched. She sounded weak and detached, as if she was already under Kadien's spell. Were they too late?

Boaz started into the cave, but Angela was saying something else. Sensing what she was about to say was important, Jachin put his arm out to hold Boaz back as he listened.

"Mark," Angela said. "I...I give—."

Jachin knew then that she was about to commit herself to the man she knew as Mark. It wasn't too late!

He rushed into the cave, unsheathing his sword as he moved. He felt Boaz close behind.

"Angela! Don't say it! Don't commit yourself to him!" Jachin said as he slid to a stop across an expanse of red, swirling rock formations and stared at a blond man and a very pregnant Angela.

As his gaze moved over her extended stomach, relief flooded through him. They had made it in time. She hadn't had the baby.

The man Jachin knew was Kadien in disguise said to a bewildered Angela, "Don't listen to him. He doesn't want you.

He said it himself. Don't let him ruin our happiness. You are mine. The baby is mine. We can be a family."

Angela doubled over, sinking to one knee. She held her abdomen, and her face was squeezed tight.

Boaz shot past Jachin to go to her.

Kadien instantly morphed into his real image with all the flourish of a fairy tale wizard. His long cape billowed in a non-existent breeze, and the red eyes of the dragon on his long staff glittered maliciously. If the situation hadn't been so deadly, Jachin might have laughed at the comical, overblown drama of it all.

But Kadien proved it wasn't all for show when, with the wave of his hand, he stopped Boaz with an invisible wall. From the energy coming from it, Jachin realized it was some kind of force field.

"I can't get past this," Boaz said, glancing toward Jachin as she pushed against the barrier. It wouldn't budge. "Angela! Get up. Come to us."

Although Angela was no longer doubled over, she only looked in their direction with a glassy stare and an occasional, lethargic blink.

Jachin focused all his powers into a forming ball of white light in his chest. Then he directed the energy down his arm, using the staff as a sort of lightning rod to collect it. He pointed the staff toward the force field, willing the energy there to disperse.

With a crackle of diffused energy, the barrier dissolved. Boaz, who'd had her hand against it, nearly fell over as it gave way.

Kadien said, "Well done...*my son*." His smile taunted maliciously, as if he thought by revealing Jachin's paternity, he was dealing a deadly blow.

The evil Jachin saw in the man made him wonder all over again if his soul had the potential for such corruption.

Boaz said with a mocking smile of her own, "Well...Daddy Dearest...aren't you going to kiss your long lost daughter?"

She was poised for battle, and Jachin was pretty sure a reunion kiss wasn't what she had in mind. Jachin couldn't believe the audacity and the challenge in his sister's eyes. She certainly had guts.

Kadien's eyebrows lifted. "So, you know." His laugh was deep and hearty. "The game is ended." He gave a mocking look of disappointment, which quickly changed to one of anticipation.

"Well, perhaps not the entire game." He turned back to Angela, who stood like a zombie at his side.

Jachin wasn't even sure if Angela was aware of them. "Angel," he called softly to her with his mind as well as his voice. Although her lips never moved, he heard her call, "Jachin!"

He started toward her, but Kadien moved between them, holding his staff crossways as a barrier. "Angela and her child are already mine. There is nothing you or anyone else can do. She has freely given me her heart, which you threw away." With that, Kadien turned his back on Jachin, as Angela once again clutched her abdomen.

Boaz looked stricken and said despairingly, "We can't be too late."

"To hell with 'too late,'" Jachin said as he lunged at Kadien, knocking him off balance.

Before Kadien could steady himself, Jachin rapidly called on his powers and threw a ball of electricity at him.

The current sizzled and crackled through Kadien as he jerked with its force. Pain was etched across his face, but he did not cry out.

Then Jachin heard Angela say in a weak voice, "Stop. You will kill him."

In that moment of hesitation, Kadien made his move and grabbed hold of her. He taunted Jachin by nuzzling Angela's neck, his tongue coming out to slowly lick the length of her jaw line.

Angela suddenly snapped out of whatever trance she'd been in. She looked around, an expression of terror and disgust on her face as she realized who held her. She struggled to get away.

Kadien held her more securely, his hand grabbing her abdomen. "It is no use struggling, my Angel. You have already given me the child. Its soul is mine. My blood runs through its veins. He will be the next Dark Lord. I know you will not let the child come to me alone. It needs its mother."

Angela looked stricken and confused. "It's not true. I did no such thing." She tried to pry his fingers away from her. "I would never give you my baby."

Kadien morphed into his Lute disguise, the arms around Angela turning into those of the man she had called Mark.

In a soothing voice Kadien said in Angela's ear, "I love you, remember. Of your own free will you gave yourself to me."

She looked more confused than ever. "Mark?"

Kadien glanced at Jachin. "She has already made the bargain. She has given her word. You must know by now, Jachin, that in the world of wizards, words are magic. Once the sacred words of commitment are made, they cannot be retracted. The magic is done. She and her baby are now among The Dark Ones."

Jachin was watching for the right moment to make his move. He couldn't use his powers against Kadien while he held Angela, but he wasn't going to just stand by, either. He knew Kadien was lying. Even if he hadn't heard them speaking when he was at the cave entrance, he knew Angela would never give her soul or the soul of her baby over to darkness.

Angela had gone still, a look of pain creasing her forehead.

From beside him, Boaz said, "Breathe deep and slow, Angela. Hang in there, hon. We're going to a hospital just as soon as Gramps, there, decides to quit playing control games."

Jachin almost laughed. The angry look in Kadien's eyes when Boaz referred to him as a grandfather was priceless.

Angela moaned, her hands pressed against her stomach and her face flushing as the contraction grew stronger. A tear slid down her cheek and landed on Kadien's arm.

Kadien flinched. A dark spot on Kadien's arm indicated a bad burn. By the look of surprise and pain on Kadien's face, Jachin knew Angela's tears were acting the same way on Kadien as Jachin's had on those with evil souls. Angela's MacAlpin-wizard heritage must be the reason.

"Jachin," Boaz said, "I think she's really close. We've got to get her out of here."

"As soon as you figure out how, just let me know." He looked around. The sun had obviously set, and the only light was from the intense moonlight as the moon occasionally came from behind the clouds. Walls that had been blood red when they entered, now looked a rusty orange.

Jachin glared at Kadien. "Angela is going to have the baby. We need to get her to some place more comfortable. I'm sure," he said sarcastically, "even you don't want the baby born in a cave."

Kadien laughed. He made an arch with his hand, and a bed and a hundred candles appeared. Jachin sensed the dark powers of the magic as an evil breeze fluttered past.

"Any more requests?" Kadien asked.

Boaz said, "She'll need help. Let me come to her."

If they could convince Kadien to let go of Angela, even for a few seconds, Jachin knew he would be able to stop him.

Kadien said, "I will bring *my* baby into the world. The child will be submerged into The Spirit by *my* touch."

Jachin wrestled with the idea of physically forcing Kadien and Angela apart, but Kadien had the upper hand as he held her hostage. He knew Kadien wouldn't hesitate to use his magic, while Jachin's concern for Angela and the baby crippled him from taking any action.

Kadien loosened his hold only slightly as he moved with Angela toward the bed.

Boaz whispered to Jachin, "Well I can do something at least. A felicity spell." Under her breath she intoned the spell, which she directed toward Angela. When she was done, she said, "It will have a calming effect on her without harming the baby or her labor. She will feel slightly giddy, but still aware enough to focus on her contractions."

A look of chagrin ran across Angela's face as she looked at the bed and came to a halt. "You can't really mean I'm supposed to have this baby here? Hello? How about a little privacy?" She began to chatter as she berated Kadien. "I know you wizards just *love* to parade around in the altogether, but we Lutes...well most of us anyway, are a little more modest. You might have at least zapped up some hospital curtains or something, along with all this other—"

Her breath caught as another contraction started.

Evidently the spell was working. Although Boaz had been off the mark when she'd said *slightly* giddy.

Boaz whispered again. "He'll have to let go of her at some point, if only to reach for the baby. Do you want my help?"

"When Kadien moves away, even for a moment, you go to Angela. I'll take care of the old man."

"I was hoping you'd say that," Boaz smiled. "Just one big happy family, huh?"

Jachin was suddenly grateful to his mother for keeping them away from Kadien. But, how could she have ever let herself be taken by Kadien in the first place? He didn't have time to ponder that question right now.

A cannon-like peal of thunder rumbled through the cave. By the electric charge in the air, Jachin could tell the storm was about to break. He allowed his full powers to hum to life, borrowing even more charged energy from the air as he prepared to make his move.

***

Marrion had used her scrying bowl to locate Angela and had seen her with a man in a blood red cave. She also sensed that this was no ordinary Lute. It was a powerful wizard in disguise. And there was only one wizard who was that powerful. Kadien. Just as they had feared, Angela was with Kadien.

Now, the entire clan had gathered under a full moon to combine their energies to help Lilith and Ailleann cross over. Since they had pinpointed Angela's location, they could transport them to the exact spot.

Marrion nodded to the huge circle of wizards surrounding the two women. In unison they began to chant *Omm*, the sacred mantra to unite their souls with the Absolute.

At first the drawn out hums of the individual members were separate and indistinct, but soon they combined to become one sonorous *Omm,* which reverberated through the clearing. The air began to stir with charged energy as their personal powers joined into one great entity. Still they maintained the Omm mantra, the power growing with each intonation.

Marrion watched as Lilith and Ailleann went into a deep meditative state, readying themselves to be transported.

Then as Marrion raised her hand in a signal, they switched from the centering *Om,* to the ancient *Tuatha De Danann* word to call forth the mists. "*Froughagh"* they whispered, and the mists began to gather in the swirling wind. The full moon became obscured as the mists thickened, the world around them now existing in the dream realm.

Marrion chanted the sacred words to call upon the golden ring of energy that would transport Ailleann and Lilith. "*Fainey airhey*."

The group took up the chant, and a ring of white light surrounded the two women. The gathering held the light steady by continuing to intone, "*Fainey airhey*," even as Marrion shouted the words that would temporarily part the protective veil surrounding Sena.

Then when the power of the ring was so intense that it became blinding, she cried out, *"Etlagh ersooyl!"*

With a clap of thunder, the two women disappeared.

***

A flash of lightning lit up the cave at the same moment a boom of thunder shook the walls. The storm must be directly overhead. Jachin turned sharply to a movement at the side of the cave, only to see Ailleann and Lilith standing there.

They gave Jachin and Boaz a knowing look and walked to stand beside them. Lilith stood to his right and Boaz was on his left, while Ailleann stood beside Lilith. The pendant at his neck reflected the combined energies, and he could see the glow from theirs as well.

"Well, well," Kadien said as he changed into his wizard persona once more. "All three of my children gathered together for the great event."

Kadien straightened, but still held Angela's hand. Her contraction had ended, and she now rested on her side. When she saw Ailleann and Lilith, she waved and smiled, obviously still feeling the giddying effects of Boaz's spell.

Kadien faced them, stroking Angela's arm with his fingertips. "I have a proposition." He looked down at Angela.

"And that is?" Jachin wasn't about to agree to anything Kadien might say, but playing along might give them the chance they needed to distract Kadien. Jachin stepped forward, and his sisters closed ranks. Ailleann walked a short distance away, her gaze on Angela.

Angela suddenly looked at Jachin as if she hadn't really seen him before. "Jachin, what happened to your hair? It's gray. Don't get me wrong, you're still yummy, but, like, what happened?"

He smiled at her and was able to hold her gaze for a few precious moments. The merry light in her eyes sobered, and a look of intense sadness darkened them. But then she blinked and was once more childlike.

He had caused that look of sadness. She still didn't know he loved her. He'd been an idiot to let her go. And why? In some stupid, misguided noble gesture to save her from his world? Well, his world had followed her into hers. His sacrifice had only threatened her more.

God, she was beautiful pregnant.

Kadien interrupted his thoughts. "My proposition is this. I will release Angela and the baby...if all three of you relinquish your powers to me."

There it was. Just as Marrion had said. It was what Kadien had wanted all along. The battle beside Kadien's fortress had only been a test.

"No," Jachin said.

Kadien laughed and sat down on the bed next to Angela. He pulled her up so that she was resting against his chest. His hands began making circling motions over her rounded belly.

"Oh," Angela cried out with delight. "Did you feel the baby kick?"

Instantly, her face scrunched up in pain as another contraction began.

"Relax, Angela," Ailleann said. "It won't hurt if you relax."

Angela's eyes were closed, and she looked like she was intently focused inward. Slowly the tension lines across her face eased, and her breathing became slow and controlled. She almost looked like she was asleep, and she seemed oblivious to Kadien's touch.

But Jachin wasn't. With each stroke of Kadien's hand across Angela's abdomen, Jachin wanted to race across the room and rip his heart out.

"Leave us now," Kadien ordered. "Your decision has been made." Then he smiled, and Jachin had never seen anything so evil. "That is, unless you've changed your minds."

Jachin felt his sisters' powerful energies on either side of him.

"We've got to do something," Lilith whispered.

Jachin closed his eyes and focused on Kadien. He visualized a coiling snake of white hot energy. Then he mentally directed it into Kadien's mind.

Angela cried out in pain, and Jachin immediately withdrew the energy.

Kadien chuckled. "You see Jachin? Already Angel and I are one. She feels my pain and I hers. And I feel that our baby will soon be born." He began murmuring something in Angela's ear. She nodded slightly and relaxed her head against him.

Kadien looked at them, keeping his voice low. "I have learned much during my time with the Lutes. It is their custom to have the father of the baby act as...coach. I even went to Angela's classes with her." His laugh was malicious.

Angela was doing her deep breathing again, only now he could tell she was having trouble keeping it slow. Her cheeks were bright pink and covered with a fine sheen of perspiration. Jachin wanted with all his heart to go to her. He should be the one touching her and coaching her through this. But he had given up that right when he told her they could never be together. He pushed aside his morose thoughts and focused on Angela and Kadien.

He turned to Lilith. "The contractions are getting closer together."

Lilith nodded. "They're about a minute long and a minute apart. She's at the end of the first stage."

He gave his sister an impatient look. "Layman's terms?"

Boaz said, "It's almost show time, you lunkhead. And you would know this if you'd put aside your dumb-ass notions about you two not belonging together and found a way to cross over sooner!"

Jachin could feel his sister's pent-up energy. He said, "I know. But how about focusing on the here and now, okay?"

"Oh!" Angela shouted, her eyes wide. "My water broke."

Kadien instinctively jumped up and Jachin had the chance he needed. In a flash, he was on Kadien, knocking him to the cave's floor.

Angela screamed.

NINETEEN

Renaissance: Time of renewal, rebirth, and revival.

Jachin concentrated all of his energy on Kadien. He knew he had the power to transport short distances, and there was no better time. He focused on an area just outside the cave, then he chanted the ancient word he recalled from his regression ceremony, "*Er sooyl-jee!*"

With a feeling of being sucked through a windless tunnel, Jachin and Kadien were both transported outside. They rolled to the ground, and Jachin felt the jab of sharp rocks.

Boaz and Lilith rushed from the cave to join them. He was relieved to see that Ailleann had stayed with Angela.

Jachin came to his feet, his hand on his sword hilt. He quickly picked up the staff, which had fallen.

Kadien stood, a maniacal gleam in his eyes. "Now the children will test the father, and the winner will possess the other's powers."

Jachin spat out, "We don't want your powers. We don't want anything to do with you."

Kadien laughed, an eyebrow cocking. "Want it or not, my son, if you kill me, my powers—my *dark* powers—will be yours."

Jachin wasn't sure he believed Kadien's powers would automatically be forfeited to him if he killed him. But he did know that if he killed his father, he would lose his own soul in the process.

"So, it seems I win either way. If I die, your soul becomes mine. If you die, I take your child and lifemate as my own."

Jachin could see that Kadien saw only two resolutions to the battle. Jachin opened his own mind to his white wizard energies.

"We couldn't settle our family issues in counseling like normal people, could we?" Boaz grumbled as she stepped forward. "The ball is in our court. Jachin, Lilith, I think we finally made it to the playoffs."

They reached for each other's hands, Boaz taking Lilith's, and Lilith taking Jachin's. Jachin then held his staff toward Boaz, and when she took hold of it the circle was complete. A link of incredible power rushed through them. Their minds linked as well, and Jachin suddenly knew what his sisters experienced with their telepathic powers. Of one mind, they decided what to do.

As one they chanted the words to bring the elements of the earth to their command. A great wind began whirling, and lightning streaked erratically across the sky, turning night into day. Jachin could feel the energy through the soles of his feet as lightning struck the ground around them, and he was deafened by the resounding booms of thunder. But he could still hear his sisters through his mind. Their intent was not to kill Kadien, but to imprison him and contain his powers in a cylinder of solid crystal. To do that they needed to cull the silica from the surrounding rocks and form it into the cylinder, and every ounce of their combined powers was needed to accomplish their task.

For a moment Kadien looked uncertain. Then he slowly smiled. He raised his staff, and Jachin saw a huge dragon appear, writhing toward them like a gigantic, frenzied lizard.

Jachin ignored the beast, praying that something would distract it. At the moment it was upon them, a great owl, as big as a car, swooped down at the dragon. The reptile reared back as the owl's talons ripped the air. Then the dragon disappeared, leaving only the stench of rotten eggs and a blast of heat. The owl beat its wings once and silently flew away.

Kadien tried to break through the swirling energy field around them, but it was too powerful. His attempts to stop them with magic were deflected as if he attacked them with nothing more than balloons.

Then Kadien looked toward the cave and began to move in that direction.

Jachin's heart skipped a beat. They had to stop him before he reached Angela again. He heard Lilith's voice inside his head, *Concentrate, Jachin. We've almost got it.*

Together they refocused on the elements, and a ball of white light formed overhead. They directed it toward Kadien. Just as Kadien was about to walk through the cave opening, they lowered the ball of light over him. He roared with rage as the white light froze into one cylindrical crystal.

Jachin nodded at Boaz, and she began to chant the sleep spell that would allow Kadien to live in a state of suspended animation within the crystal.

With a startling abruptness, the lightning ceased and the wind died.

Jachin had never felt such a drain on his powers, but he knew he still had one more thing to do. They dropped hands, and he lowered his staff to the ground. A rumbling began. They all had trouble keeping their footing as the ground began to move. A great chasm opened before them, going deep into the earth.

Boaz pointed at the crystal cylinder containing Kadien, and it rose off the ground. She directed it over the chasm and let it drop.

Jachin touched the scepter to the ground once more, using the last of his energy reserves to close the abyss.

T₁ey all embraced, and Jachin could feel how much the effort to contain Kadien had depleted their magic. It would take days before any of them could attempt using their powers for anything substantial.

As they hurried back toward the cave, Boaz said, "I took the felicity spell off Angela before we left the cave. I know she would want to be fully aware when her baby came. I hope she's doing okay."

When they reached the entrance, Jachin realized there were no lights coming from within. Kadien's candles and the bed must have disappeared when they sealed him in the crystal.

"Boaz, can you manage something for light?"

She was the one who could breathe fire, and it was the only thing Jachin could think of. He didn't have enough power left to gather any elements from the ground.

She picked up a thick branch and breathed fire onto it. With their torch they cautiously entered the cave.

***

Angela nuzzled her daughter's soft, damp head as she nursed. Once Kadien and the others had left, Ailleann had made her comfortable and expertly coached her through the rest of her labor. They'd had a moment of panic when Kadien's magic bed and candles vanished.

But now, resting on Ailleann's cape and snuggling with her precious baby, Angela couldn't imagine a better birth experience. Ailleann had been the perfect midwife, and she'd used her own soft chemise to swaddle the newborn. The only thing marring her happiness was her worry over Jachin, Boaz and Lilith. What had happened? She and Ailleann had heard an incredible thunderstorm, but they couldn't tell what was going on. They were in the dark in more ways than one.

She and Ailleann looked up as a light flickered at the cave opening. Then Angela's heart soared as she saw Jachin step inside, followed by both of his sisters.

Boaz and Lilith stayed close to the entrance as Jachin slowly walked toward her. Angela was grateful when Ailleann left to join the other women.

When Jachin knelt beside her, she felt giddy with relief. "What happened to Kadien?"

"I'll explain later. Right now we need to talk about us." He was staring in wonder at the baby at her breast.

"Oh," she said, feeling a smile curve her mouth. "I guess you didn't know about the baby, did you?" Then a thought occurred to her. "You couldn't possibly think it's—"

"Stop," he said. "I know it's mine."

"She," Angela corrected, looking down at her beautiful daughter. "She's a girl. A little girl with her daddy's dark hair." The baby had fallen asleep, so Angela pressed her finger alongside her daughter's mouth to break the suction, and then covered her breast in a sudden moment of modesty.

She had just realized something. She held the baby tighter. "When are you going back to Sena?"

Jachin reached out and gently took the sleeping newborn from her arms. The little girl looked tiny and delicate in his strong hands. Angela swallowed back the lump in her throat.

"I'm not going back without my daughter," Jachin said.

Panic seized Angela, and she couldn't breathe. "You can't take my baby!"

He returned the baby to the crook of her arm, and then stretched out beside her, his head resting on his hand. He looked into her eyes, and she realized his had tears in them.

"I would never take your baby from you." He looked like he was having difficulty controlling his emotions. "Angela, can you ever forgive me for turning my back on you...on us?"

She reached out and touched the line of his jaw. "There is nothing to forgive. I told you before...no strings attached." She wanted with all her soul for there to be strings attached, but only if Jachin loved her.

He swallowed hard, and Angela realized he was as nervous as she was.

Finally, he said, "I didn't know how to love. I thought I would only hurt you. And I have hurt you." He looked around the cave. "What a hell of a place to have a baby." He looked back at her, brushing her hair off her forehead.

"Angela, I love you," he said, looking down into her eyes, and then he switched his gaze to the baby. "And I love our daughter. I promise that if you'll give me another chance I will do everything in my power to keep you both safe. We will live wherever you want—here or Sena. It doesn't matter to me as long as we're together."

She blinked back a rush of sudden tears. He loved her? Or was he saying this because he wanted his daughter? Would he leave when the euphoria wore off, and he realized she was only a Lute? A difficult, less-than-perfect Lute.

Jachin leaned down to kiss her, and her fears vanished. This was Jachin, and he was nothing if not honest. In his kiss she felt all the passion of their first kiss. But this time, she also felt a new tenderness and a connecting of souls. Could this really be happening? Could she trust that fate had finally given her the love and the family she'd always wanted?

She shut out the darkness that had hovered over her all her life and opened her heart to trust again.

Jachin cradled her against him, and they looked down at their daughter and smiled.

Just then a huge owl fluttered into the cave. It morphed into a caped wizard, and they all stared at him in wonder.

Jachin got up, unable to believe his eyes. "Seumas! You're alive."

Seumas nodded. "So it would appear. I'm not sure what happened during the battle on Sena, but I suddenly found myself back here on Lute soil."

Seumas smiled down with great satisfaction at Angela and the baby. "So, the uniting of the two worlds begins. I've been fighting for this my entire life. And the prophecy was right. She who holds the scorpion would conquer the darkness."

Jachin looked at his sisters. They didn't understand what Seumas was talking about any more than he did. Jachin said, "What do you mean?"

Seumas nodded toward Angela. "The mark on her hand. Look at it. It is shaped like a scorpion. And if it weren't for Angela, who knows what the outcome of the confrontation might have been."

He was right. Kadien had put Angela right in the middle of the battle, and Jachin had a feeling that the weakness he had seen in Kadien's eyes when he looked at Angela was real. That his feelings for her had compromised his dark powers. Goodness had truly overcome the darkness.

Boaz and Lilith drew near, as Boaz asked, "What now, Seumas? Will you go back to Sena?"

Seumas shook his head. "If it takes me the rest of my life, I will discover what happened to your mother...where she went. She couldn't have disappeared without a trace. And, I discovered something when I shapeshifted into the little dog. Dogs can follow the invisible psi trail. Your mother's is strong here in the Lute world. I plan on discovering where the trail leads."

Jachin didn't want to discourage Seumas since he sounded so determined, but he was sure Seumas would be disappointed once he found out where she had gone. It wouldn't change the fact that she was dead.

"What about all of you?" Seumas asked.

Lilith said, "Before Ailleann and I crossed over, the elders decided it's time to reopen the veil. I plan on heading up that effort."

Boaz said, "I plan to live in both worlds."

Jachin realized that that was what he wanted, too. "I belong in both worlds. And, now that Kadien is gone, we have a lot of work to do here and in Sena." He looked at Angela. "But Angela and I still have to discuss where we're going to call home."

Angela looked unsure. "What about the curse on the MacAlpins? You can't stay with a descendent of the man who forced your people into the Otherworlds to begin with. Your people put a curse on my people...on me."

Lilith smiled. "The wizards of Sena didn't put a curse on the MacAlpins. MacAlpin's traitorous act alone put the curse on his family. Wizards believe that every deed, good or bad, comes back tenfold. If we had put a curse on the MacAlpins, we would only have been cursing ourselves." She grinned as she said, "Besides, I think you've righted the wrong your ancestor did. Without you, we'd have never saved the Lute world or Sena."

"Curse or no curse, we're staying together. Just let someone on Sena try to keep us apart," Jachin said. He stroked her cheek. "You're a difficult, crazy, wonderful Lute, and you're going to become my wife." He paused. "That is...if you want to."

She smiled. "I do."

Jachin felt his heart soar. He didn't care where he lived. Now that there was every indication that the veil would be lifted, he could move freely between the worlds when needed. But, if it hadn't been lifted, it wouldn't have mattered. All that mattered was that he had his lifemate, Angel, and their daughter by his side.

EPILOGUE

Just one more thing to do before the press conference, Jachin thought to himself. *One more thing to do to make me feel whole.* In silence he walked into his gallery workroom. Angela, holding Guennie's hand, followed solemnly behind him. They had taken Guennie as their own, but had promised her they would continue to search for her parents. Next into the room came Lilith, Boaz and Mildred, who carried the six-week-old baby, Donia.

Before them sat the glob of metal that had once been his prized work of art.

He looked at his sisters. "Are you ready?"

Boaz tilted her head as she looked at the mangled statue, a frown creasing her forehead. "Sure, I'm ready."

Lilith went to stand next to the bronze, holding out both of her hands.

All three of them joined hands around the sculpture. They closed their eyes as their energies merged, and Jachin gave his sisters a mental image of what the statue should look like.

Their energy gathered, pulsing through the three of them. All sound was drowned out by the electric hum, and the energy began to swirl around the statue, using the three of them as its conduit. They focused on the image of what the statue had once been. All the elements were there, they just needed restructuring. It was a feat Jachin wasn't able to do when he had created the statue in the first place.

Slowly, they moved their clasped hands toward the metal. In his mind's eye Jachin saw *The Dance* as it had been. Boaz with her impish smile. Lilith, with a look of benevolence. And finally, Angela, who even then had looked into his soul.

With a crack of electricity, their combined energies shot into the metal. A bright light forced them to close their eyes.

When Jachin opened them, his heart calmed, and he felt a smile come to his lips.

The restored sculpture stood before them.

His sisters dropped hands and stared.

For a moment no one said anything. Mildred looked like she

was in shock, but she quickly recovered, continuing to gently bounce the baby in her arms. Lilith and Boaz stared at the statue with wonder in their eyes.

Then Angela said in awe, "You did it."

Boaz gave a loud whoop and ran to gather Angela and Lilith into her arms. "Look at us. We're beautiful!" Holding on to each other, they danced around, looking so much like *The Dance*, that Jachin was breathless. Guennie joined in the dance.

Mildred said, "Time for partying later. We've got a press conference to attend."

The women chuckled as they settled down.

"Reporters couldn't be any more intimidating than when I thought I was being cursed by the people of Sena," Angela joked.

Jachin was looking forward to facing the reporters. He wanted the chance to set things straight. He wasn't evil. He had worked the clay with his own bare hands. And just because he had a secret way of turning it into bronze, didn't mean it was evil-based. If some wanted to hold on to that idea, then that was their problem.

Once his family was seated around him at the long press table with a hundred microphones lined up before them, Jachin relaxed. He let his eyes roam around the room, smiling at familiar faces here and there. By their shocked expressions, he knew they weren't used to his new persona. Well, they would have to get used to it. This was the real Jachin Morgan-MacCuill.

Angela reached out to take his hand, and he felt a special power flow through him.

The noise in the room quieted, and he said, "Friends, I've come here today to dispel certain rumors. I'm sorry I've been out of touch for so long, but I've had," he looked at the women on each side of him and smiled at Guennie, "a kind of revelation. You see, I was adopted and only recently found my sisters. I've spent the last several months getting to know them and my birth family. I also acquired a wife, a little girl, and a baby along the way."

He laughed as he squeezed Angela's hand, and the crowd chuckled along with him. Guennie was positively beaming.

He continued, "I would like to answer your questions, so why don't we get right to it." He pointed to a reporter he knew was from the most slanderous tabloid. The very reporter who had most likely broken into the gallery to get the picture of the melted sculpture that his paper had splashed across its front page.

"Jachin Morgan," the man began with a snide smirk, "we would all like to know how your sculpture, *The Dance*, was destroyed ... melted, in fact ... without a single scorch mark to the surrounding area."

Jachin feigned surprise. "*The Dance* is in perfect condition. Why would you think it was destroyed? I saw it just an hour ago, and it's fine. You're welcome to see it as soon as we're done here, but I have to warn you, it's not for sale. As you will see, it's a family portrait."

The man stood there with his mouth open, obviously not knowing how to respond.

"Next," Jachin said as he pointed to another reporter.

After easily explaining all of the rumors, Jachin found himself being bombarded with questions about his new wife. When the tabloid reporter shouted, "Was she one of your followers? Is she part of your coven?"

"Why don't you ask Angela?" Jachin said, smiling and taking his seat.

Angela stood and faced the man. "And your name is?"

He appeared flustered by the directness of her stare, and he looked down at his notes as he answered, "Paul Richardson." If the reporter had hoped to intimidate Angela under his line of questioning, he was sadly mistaken.

"Well, Paul, to answer your question ... I guess I've been a follower of Jachin Morgan's for a long time. Before I even knew Jachin, I loved his work." She looked around the room. "As did many of you, I'm sure." She returned her gaze to the man. "But we never have, nor ever will, belong to a coven. Now, I would like to ask you a question. Why would belonging to a coven be a bad thing?"

"Why, because they worship the devil."

Angela smiled as if talking to a child. "You would do well to do a bit more research regarding covens, Wiccans ... even wizards. From what I know, they are all peaceful people who focus on the betterment of mankind." She gave the man a piercing look. "While you're maligning these harmless people, true evil walks among us, creating discord and dissension."

The rest of the press conference was lighthearted. Jachin even enjoyed posing for pictures of his new family, Boaz, Lilith,

Angela, Donia, and Guennie.

For the first time in his life, Jachin felt whole, *normal,* ... and truly happy. As he rested his hand on Guennie's head, he leaned down and gave Angela a kiss. Cameras began to click.

Jachin looked up at the reporters and smiled. "Now, if you don't mind. My wife and I have a very important date this evening."

Angela smiled and blushed. She'd just had her six-week checkup, and the doctor had given her a clean bill of health. Tonight would be the first time that she and Jachin would be together as married lifemates.

As the reporters left, Jachin whispered to her, "This time no glimmer dreams. This time no fairy magic. This time it's for real."

She turned and kissed him, letting him know that she was more than ready.